ONE BUCK NAKED DEAD DUCK . . .

A naked man ran screaming down the corridor amidst a blaze of gunfire. He'd been shot on the stairs leading down from the floor above, and hit twice more along the way. Yet he somehow made it as far as the stairs leading down to the floor below before two hundred grains of hot spinning lead caved in the back of his skull and somersaulted his flailing bare flesh all the way down to the next landing.

So there he lay, oozing blood and grinning up blankly. The somewhat older man who'd gunned him stood over him in a dusty black suit and a haze of gun smoke, clicking the hammers of two six-guns on spent brass until a firm but not unkindly voice called down. ''You've emptied both your guns into him, which may be just as well for the both of us. So why don't you drop them and tell me what this was all about. I ain't just being nosy. I'm Deputy U.S. Marshal Custis Long of the Denver District Court, and they pay me to pester folks like this.''

A *LONGARM* GIANT NOVEL

TABOR EVANS

JOVE BOOKS, NEW YORK

LONGARM AND THE UNWRITTEN LAW

A Jove Book / published by arrangement with
the author

PRINTING HISTORY
Jove edition / August 1995

ISBN: 0-515-11680-7

A JOVE BOOK®
Jove Books are published by The Berkley Publishing Group,
200 Madison Avenue, New York, New York 10016.
JOVE and the "J" design are trademarks
belonging to Jove Publications, Inc.

PRINTED IN THE UNITED STATES OF AMERICA

10 9 8 7 6 5 4 3 2 1

Chapter 1

Along about midnight a naked man ran screaming down the hotel corridor amidst a blaze of gunfire. He'd been shot on the stairs leading down from the floor above, and hit twice more along the way. Yet he somehow made it as far as the stairs leading down to the floor below before two hundred grains of hot spinning lead caved in the back of his skull and somersaulted his flailing bare flesh all the way down to the next landing.

So there he lay, oozing blood and grinning up blankly, while the somewhat older man who'd gunned him stood over him in a dusty black suit and a haze of gun smoke, clicking the hammers of two six-guns on spent brass until a firm but not unkindly voice called down. "You've emptied both your guns into him, which may be just as well for the both of us. So why don't you drop the both of *them* and tell me what this was all about. I ain't just being nosy. I'm Deputy U.S. Marshal Custis Long of the Denver District Court, and they pay me to pester folks like this."

The middle-aged killer without a live round to his name turned and smiled sheepishly up at the taller barefoot figure wearing only tobacco-tweed pants and a cross-draw gun rig. The .44-40 that normally rode its owner's left hip was staring down through the clearing gunsmoke as alertly as the steel gray eyes of the bare-chested lawman aiming it. So the older man dropped his own hardware to the rug, licked his lips, and said, "I know who you are. You'd be the one they call Longarm, and they say you can be fair as well as firm. I'd be L.J. Maxwell. I own and operate the Tumbling M, a day's ride down the South Platte."

He kicked the naked body at his feet just hard enough to rate a warning look from Longarm. "This piece of shit used to be my segundo, Sunny Jim Stanhope. He took my pay and he et my bread, and then he shagged my Edna Mae whilst I was away from our spread at the stock show!"

Longarm grimaced and said, "I take it your Edna Mae is the lady I just heard wailing like a banshee when I tore past that open doorway next to my own?"

Maxwell nodded, stared morosely down at the younger man he'd just killed, and replied, "It is. She said she was leaving me for this two-faced hound because he had a bigger dick. But I ask you, man to man, does this dead bastard's dick look unusually large to you?"

Longarm could only reply, "Not at the moment. I don't know why no spiteful woman has ever told her man that her lover's old organ-grinder was *smaller* than his."

Before Maxwell could answer, Sergeant Nolan of the Denver P.D. was at the bottom of the stairs with a brace of copper badges. Nolan and Longarm were on good terms. So the burly local lawman got out his notebook and asked, "Would this case be federal, state, or municipal, pard?"

To which Longarm was pleased to reply, "It's your misfortune and none of my own. Mister Maxwell here claims the bare-ass cadaver's one Sunny Jim Stanhope, and there's no argument about who just shot him deader than a turd in a milk bucket. Mister Maxwell alleges Stanhope was committing adultery with his lawfully married-up Edna Mae. So what'll you bet he's fixing to evoke the unwritten law?"

Sergeant Nolan stared up the stairs in dismay and declared, "It hardly seems fair that it's municipal. We just got here. *You* saw him *first,* Longarm!"

Longarm put his own gun away as he shrugged his broad

bare shoulders and replied, "I never saw him *do* it. His woman's right upstairs, if you'd like to take her statement. Gunning your wife's lover smack in the middle of Denver has to violate *some* municipal ordinance. But it don't strike me as a federal offense. So like I said, it's your case to keep and cherish and I'm catching me a chill in this cold hallway."

He turned away to remount the stairs, ignoring all the noise that seemed to be coming from the Denver P.D. and other patrons of the Viceroy Hotel. Being just a few streets over from the stockyards, the place didn't cater to a very quiet crowd, and gunshots in the night were as good as fire bells when it came to getting folks up and half dressed.

A Denver lawman passed him near the open doorway where all the shooting had started. So Longarm felt no call to go in and talk to the big fat naked gal thrashing about on the bed as she pleaded for mercy. Longarm left it to the Denver P.D. to assure her she hadn't been murdered and get a statement out of her, once she'd calmed down just a hundred percent. He gently rapped a certain way on the door of his own hired room, and another naked lady let him in. She was one hell of an improvement over Edna Mae Maxwell.

Lina Marie Logan, just in from Omaha and anxious to see all the wonders of the Mile High City, was hardly a waif, and way too pretty to be shy about the lamplight as the two of them got back in bed together. Longarm had to hang up his six-gun and slide out of his pants first. So that gave him plenty of time to explain all that noise outside to the buxom blonde who'd been on top when the gunfire had commenced.

She said she didn't care and that she'd been about to start again without him, damn it. So this time *he* got on top, hooked one of his elbows under each of her soft knee joints, and spread her smooth pale thighs wide enough to make her beg for mercy as he hit bottom every other stroke. So a good time was had by all, and then, alas, it came time to climb back down out of the stars and share a smoke while they fought to regain some firmer grasp on their gasping. As he calmed her some with a three-for-a-nickel cheroot, she became more aware of the thumpings, bumpings, and occasional outbursts of conversation all around. She snuggled closer and made as if to cover the two of them with some bedding. He said soothingly, ''The door's bolted good and I told you Nolan was a pal of mine. Every copper badge in this precinct wants to see his own name on the final report. But they won't want *us* to join their crowd. The Denver P.D. would never forgive them for sharing this manslaughter complaint with another outfit.''

She still pulled a single sheet waist high as she sighed and asked what he thought might become of that poor neglected wife, now that her lover had been shot and her husband was in for some time at hard, if not a hanging.

Longarm shrugged his bare shoulders, cuddled her closer, and told her, ''Judging by the many times I've heard this sad story in the past, she'll go back to him and he, like a fool, will buy her teary-eyed promises to turn over a new leaf. From what I just saw of what she has to offer, not too many other men are apt to give her much choice. A jolly easygoing fat gal is one thing. A jolly easygoing fat gal with a man who comes after you with a brace of Army Schofields is another thing entire!''

Lina Marie chuckled, her unbound blond hair spread across one of his shoulders and half his bare chest, and proceeded to toy with the damp hairs on Longarm's belly as she mused aloud, ''At least she might not feel so neglected. But I seem to be missing something. Didn't you just say you'd handed her jealous husband over to the local police, darling?''

Longarm nodded and explained. ''He'll spend at least the rest of the night in jail. But any stockman who can afford his own lawyer ought to be out on bail by noon.''

''But, Custis, he just *killed* an unarmed man in cold blood!'' she protested.

To which Longarm replied, with a weary sigh, ''That ain't the way his lawyer's going to present it to the grand jury. Maxwell's best bet is to remain silent whilst his lawyer paints the picture of a tormented soul, trying to save his marriage from the machinations of a false-hearted employee who'd led his poor corn-fed Edna Mae down the primrose path with buttered words and doubtless some of them French preeversions.''

Lina Marie reached a tad lower to fondle his limp love tool as she purred, "Show me what you mean by perverse, you wicked French thing!"

He laughed softly. "We got all night and there's a whole nickel's worth of tobacco left here. I wasn't offering to go down on you just yet. I was telling you how Maxwell's likely to get off, as provided by the Unwritten Law, or the principal of equity, as it reads in most law books."

She said neither term made sense to her, and added, "I thought a law had to be put down on paper and passed by some legislative body before it could be enforced."

He nodded. "That's how come they call such fuzzy legal notions unwritten. You see, the laws we have today are based on a swamping heap of earlier ones, going all the way back to Moses by way of ancient Rome. Roman laws were all writ down in Latin, which can still be read by high-priced lawyers, and they tell me Augustus Caesar and his Roman crew wrote mighty sensible and consistent for such olden times. But their punishments were a mite harsh, and since they held Miss Justice had to be blind, there was no way to let any felon off. The law was the law, and if you didn't aim to end up nailed to a cross or worse, you damned well *obeyed* the law!"

She began to stroke what was no longer quite so limp as he took a deep drag on the cheroot and said, "You didn't want to hear about equity in any case, right?"

She protested, "I'm interested in that too. Just let me work this sweet thing up again for the both of us as you tell me why I ought to care about ancient Romans being mean to people."

He smiled thinly and said, "There might be time. I want it *all* the way up, you tight little doll. The blind justice of Roman courts could lead to results so mean that even the Romans were shocked enough to write them down in Latin. That's how later law clerks, trying to work out common law for the Middle Ages, found out about things like poor old crazy ladies or bitty kids getting crucified for showing disrespect to some statue of a naked cuss sporting a fireman's helmet. The tale I find most disgusting was when they came to arrest a Roman politician for abusing his authority. There was no doubt he was guilty, and our own politics might be less corrupt if we got to hang such rascals. But under Roman law they got to execute both him and his whole family. I reckon they figured it would be tough to be a serious crook without your kinfolk knowing about it.''

She was interested enough to slow down, which hardly seemed fair, as she said, ''Well, the Pinkertons did point that out the time they lobbed that bomb through Frank and Jesse's window. But I still think it was mean to kill that half-wit boy and cripple old Mrs. Samuel.''

Longarm said, ''When the Roman lawmen came to arrest this official called Sejanus, they were stuck with the fact that Roman law forbade them to execute a virgin. So they had to rape the man's little girl in public before they could make her pay for her dear old dad's crimes against the state.''

Lina Marie gasped and said, ''That was horrid of them, and I don't care *how* blind Justice is supposed to be!''

Longarm nodded. ''Law clerks the Romans had down as dumb barbarians agreed with you on that. So they slipped in the sort of fuzzy notion of equity, which had nothing to do with equal justice but held that sometimes Miss Justice had to show some merciful common sense. Mortal folks can be driven over the line by native customs or a notion that they're obeying some older, higher law.''

She nodded in sudden understanding. ''You mean that old-time code of honor calling for a gentleman to defend his womankind and other property to the death?''

He said, ''Something like that. I told you it was fuzzy and never written down on paper. They dasn't make it lawful to gun a man for fooling with your woman, or allow you to pistol-whip every gent who implies you might be fibbing. But just the same, they reduce charges of simple assault to aggravated assault if you can prove the victim called you a son of a bitch before you swung at him. And as for killing a man you just caught in the act with your woman, how many prosecuting attorneys with a lick of sense are likely to haul a poor heartbroken wretch before a judge and jury when they know that should one juror figure the dead Casanova had it coming to him . . .''

She began to stroke his much firmer erection faster as she said, ''I see why outraged husbands seem to get away with it so often. And speaking of coming, I want to get on top again.''

He snuffed out the cheroot as she cast the bedding aside with a giggle of glee and cocked a lush thigh across him to impale her pretty self on his now fully restored virility.

It felt swell, and he was content to let her do some of the work for a change. He had a job to go to in the cold gray dawn, and at the rate they were going, he doubted he'd catch much sleep before it came time to rise and shine.

He still felt obliged to roll her over and finish in her firm but voluptuous flesh. She took it as a compliment, and said she'd evoke that Unwritten Law and scratch any other gal in town bald-headed if she ever caught her flirting with *her* long-donging darling.

Longarm had to grin as he pictured Lina Marie fighting it out bare-ass with a certain equally well-proportioned widow woman up on Capitol Hill, or another somewhat more muscular blonde down Texas way. No man with a lick of sense was going to mention marriage certificates at a time like this. So he only said, ''A body can get in trouble counting on unwritten law. There's nothing written down to say they can't punish you for busting a *real* law. It's up to the lawyers to figure out the fuzzy logic. Many an old boy, or gal, who tried to follow unwritten law wound up in real trouble from the law written down in ink!''

She wrapped her legs around his waist to keep him from rolling off as they let it soak in her some more. Not feeling up to more than that just yet, she allowed that the Unwritten Law sounded almost as mean in its own way as the draconian no-excuses laws it was meant to save poor sinners from.

Longarm moved gently in her to keep their friendship firm as he replied, ''Slick talkers or slow thinkers can ruin the intent of the law no matter how it's been written. Them Romans should have seen it was just dumb to blindfold Miss Justice and leave her armed and dangerous, whilst common sense decrees that ninety-nine times out of a hundred a body who kills another body deserves to die for it. Not as much for doing it as lest somebody else feel the same call. If folks were made to feel you couldn't kill nobody without getting hung, a heap of killings might never take place.''

She asked, ''Don't you think that poor Mister Maxwell had call to kill his wife's lover tonight?''

Longarm shrugged his bare shoulders, making her purr and wriggle back, as he said, ''Nope. They're going to let him off. For all any of us know, the dead man had it coming. But Maxwell never would have gunned him if he hadn't been brought up to feel a real man didn't have any other choice, or all that much to fear, once he'd caught a fool like the late Sunny Jim in such a ridiculous position!''

She murmured, ''This position feels just grand to *me*. What other positions do you suggest for the couple next door, dear?''

Longarm started moving faster in her as he replied in a conversational tone, ''It wasn't the physical pose Sunny Jim was in that left him no way to come out ahead. It was more like who he was posing with nude when her husband barged in on them this evening.''

She gripped him tighter with her thighs and coyly asked what he might do if some other man kicked in *their* door.

He told her, ''I'd stand a better chance than poor old Sunny Jim. For I've hung my own gun handy and it would be a fair fight, unless you fibbed about being new in town and unspoken for leastways.''

She began to grind her pelvis teasingly in time with his thrusts as she assured him she was single and casually asked why the lover caught in this same act earlier couldn't have fought back.

Longarm said, ''He could have. Had he won, he'd have been looking forward to *his* hanging along about now. The unwritten law allows the injured husband to gun his woman's lover. There's nothing writ or unwrit that allows a jasper to bust up a man's home and then put a bullet in him. I wasn't just being nosey when I asked you all them personal questions over supper at Romano's earlier. I've seen too many old boys buried young to mess with any other gent's woman!"

At the time he really thought that was all a man had to worry about as far as the Unwritten Law was concerned.

Chapter 2

The *Denver Post* and the *Rocky Mountain News* enjoyed a field day with what they described as the Sordid Love Triangle at the Viceroy Hotel. But after a couple of days on the front pages of both papers, things commenced to go about the way Longarm had expected.

Maxwell's slick Denver lawyers knew better than to enter a plea of justifiable homicide. Cockeyed Jack McCall had tried that in a Colorado court after backshooting James Butler Hickok up Dakota way, and everyone remembered the possibly unconstitutional but certainly fatal verdict. Colorado folks considered a homicide a homicide, and figured even a horse thief deserved to die by rope-dancing. So the old stockman's lawyers got the case postponed while their client had his head examined at a fancy private sanitarium down by Pike's Peak. That was the last of the case as far as any front pages went. Longarm had no idea where Maxwell's fat wife wound up. But a copper badge at the Parthenon Saloon did tell him Sunny Jim Stanhope had been buried out by the clay pits, neatly wrapped in mattress ticking, at no cost to the taxpayers and damned little to Maxwell's law firm.

By this time Longarm could see he should have asked more questions at that spaghetti joint the night he'd first wound up in bed with old Lina Marie. For while it was true she'd had no male friends out Denver way, she'd left out the part about wanting to find one in particular and settle down. It was a notion he'd run across before, womankind being less adventurous than himself. So he knew that once they got to saying they felt unfulfilled selling dry goods where they worked, or cramped for space in the furnished room that you'd found for them, it was only a matter of monthlies before you got that old ultimatum. But in this case the ploy was another gent, at work, who seemed anxious to make an honest woman of her, if only she'd forget that taller cuss with more hair who was only using and abusing her.

Longarm didn't invoke the Unwritten Law to go gunning for the son of a bitch. He just wistfully allowed there was no way he could top such a fine offer, and was sorry that he wasn't there to escort her to supper after each hard day's work, since that other gent, if he existed, seemed so set on making her feel so blamed fulfilled.

He didn't know why the pretty young widow woman he'd been planning to invite to supper instead slammed the door in his face when he showed up at her place on Capitol Hill with store-bought violets. He felt sure that whether Methuselah had really lived nine hundred years or not, he'd gone to his grave without understanding the unfair sex.

Fortunately, the head matron at the Arvada Orphan Asylum hadn't heard about him having spaghetti at Romano's with any blond hussy, and so Longarm got to work a tad later than usual the next morning with a crick in his back. He'd forgotten how athletic little Morgana could be after she hadn't been getting any for a time.

As he entered the marshal's office in the Denver Federal Building, young Henry, the clerk who played the typewriter out front, told him their boss, Marshal Billy Vail, had Attila the Hun in the back.

Longarm doubted that, but said nothing as he sat down on a bench and picked up a back-dated copy of *Godey's Lady's Book,* the marshal's wife saving her subscription periodicals for the office. Longarm had no call to sew a hem or bake a cake. But some of the pictures were interesting.

He looked up to exchange glances with Henry when they both heard loud cussing coming from Billy Vail's office. When mention was made of blowing someone's balls off, Longarm rose to his considerable height and ambled back to see who the visitor had in mind, his own .44-40 drawn but pointed down along the seam of his pants.

As he entered Billy Vail's oak-paneled inner office without knocking, he saw his stocky, bulldog-faced superior's visitor was a wiry gnome wearing a summer-weight seersucker suit with a brace of six-guns under his unbuttoned jacket. As they both turned to regard him, old Billy Vail called out from behind his cluttered desk, "Morning, Deputy Smiley! Has that slugabed Deputy Long shown up yet? Mr. Hornagy here has some serious charges he means to make to the rascal's face!"

Longarm knew how little he resembled the hatchet-faced quarter-Pawnee Deputy Smiley. So he figured his boss had to be as drunk as a lord or trying to slicker the scowling Hornagy. So he just went on aiming at the rug in the uncertain light as he calmly replied, "Long was having breakfast in that chili parlor near the corner just a few minutes ago."

This was true. As soon as you studied on it. The wild-eyed cuss in the seersucker suit and six-guns didn't take much time to study on it. He said he knew the place and was already on his way, with a set jaw and a glare of grim determination as Longarm stepped aside to let him stride through the door as tall as he was able.

Turning back to Vail with a bemused smile, Longarm asked what on earth might be going on. Vail was already up from behind his desk, and stumped over on his own short legs to snap, "Tell you along the way!" as he grabbed Longarm's left elbow to steer him out of the office and through the maze of connecting rooms and passages, adding, "That was Attila Hornagy. Don't laugh. He's one of them Bohunk coal miners from the Austro-Hungarian Empire, and they must teach history different."

Longarm mildly replied, "Henry said Attila the Hun had come to call on us. I thought he was joshing. You said the jasper wanted to bring some sort of charges against this child, Boss?"

Vail soberly replied, "I just said that to keep the conversation polite. His exact words were that he means to blow your balls off, stomp your head flat, and then kill you."

Longarm whistled softly as they came to a last side door out to the softly lit marble corridor. Vail told Longarm to let him scout ahead. So Longarm stood there trying in vain to remember that funny-looking older man with the distinctive name until Vail said, "Coast seems clear. But it won't take him long to get up to that chili parlor and back. So let's move it on out. I want you to use those janitorial stairs at the far end to slip down and out the basement entrance. He might know about your hired rooms on the far side of Cherry Creek. So you'd best go on up to my house and tell my old woman to hide you out till I get there."

They were moving in step along the otherwise deserted corridor as Vail issued these grotesque instructions. But Longarm shook his head and said, "You're not making any sense, no offense. I had the drop on that bragging banty rooster just now, and you just saw that despite all his bragging he failed to recognize me on sight. So why am I supposed to act as if he was the one and original Attila at the head of all his Huns?"

Vail popped open what might have seemed a broom closet to the visiting eye, and hauled Longarm into the grimy cement stairwell before he explained, "You can't fight him. You'd lose no matter who won. Hornagy claims that during the merry month of May, whilst he was attending a convention of the Knights of Labor, you were down in the Trinity coal camp playing slap and tickle with his young bride, name of Magda Hornagy née Kadar. She's from the same old country too. But none of that's as important as the spot it puts you in with a jealous husband out to avenge his honor as per the unwritten law!"

Longarm scowled in the gloom and growled, "There seems to be a lot of that going around this summer. I was nowhere near Trinidad in any part of of this year's greenup. Don't you remember putting me on court duty right after I came in with that prisoner in the first week of May?"

Vail grumbled, "Of course I do. I told him that, just now. That was when he raised his voice to me. He said it was natural for a man's pals to lie for him. But that his Madga had confessed to him, in Bohunk, that she'd been led down the primrose path by a slicker with a badge who'd implied they'd all wind up back in that empire they never wanted to see again if she didn't surrender her reluctant ass to him. She says you made her suck it at the point of a gun when she allowed she'd as soon be deported. I suspicion that's the part he feels most upset about."

Longarm allowed himself to be moved down the stairs, but as they descended he still said, "You mean so he says, Billy. It's established I was never anywhere near his informative Magda. Meanwhile, have you ever considered how many enemies I may have made packing this badge and my guns for you, or how convenient it might be to offer such a dramatic excuse to a grand jury, should one not make it out of town after gunning a lawman for fun and profit?"

Vail said, "Don't try to teach your granny how to suck eggs. I'll naturally send a heap of wires about two-gun Bohunks as soon as I can make sure you can't gun one another. But there's a hole in the plan you just presented. At the risk of turning your pretty head, you do enjoy a rep for winning gunfights. So one would think a man hired to gun you might not want to warn you in advance that he's out to gun you."

Longarm shook his head. "A hired gun, by definition, is a cuss who thinks he can take all comers, one way or another. His main concern, like I just said, is a good excuse to justify his actions to the folks he ain't been paid to kill. *I* found a runt in a seersucker suit called Attila amusing too. But who's to say who was bullshitting whom just now?"

Vail said he failed to follow Longarm's drift. So his tall deputy explained. "He might have just been pretending you'd fooled him with that sly introduction. You'd think a man would know who he was gunning for if he rode the D&RG northbound all the way from Trinidad to gun him. So let's say he roared in like a lion, expecting you to get him to leave like a lamb, after stating his intent to demand satisfaction."

"What for?" asked Vail with a puzzled scowl. "Seems to me a man would only make himself look more foolish if he ran all over threatening to kill someone and then . . . Oh, I *do* follow your drift!"

Longarm nodded grimly and said, "I'd be as easy to backshoot over in the Parthenon as Hickock was that time in the Number Ten. What got McCall in so much trouble then was that he just up and surprised hell out of everyone in Deadwood. Had he told all the boys in advance how old Wild Bill had been mean to him . . ."

They were at the bottom of the flight of stairs now. So Vail said, "I'll meet you later at my place up on Sherman. By then I'll have had time to wire some old pals in Trinidad and vice versa. Should our mysterious stranger turn out to be a stranger down yonder as well, I can have some of the other boys he can't possibly know pick him up, for some serious conversation. Should he really turn out to be Attila the Hungarian with a ruined marriage to avenge, we got an even more serious situation to converse about. In either case, I want you off the streets and out of sight whilst Henry and me get a better grip on things."

Longarm allowed he'd do as he was told for now. So they parted friendly and Longarm slipped out the basement entrance to the east as Vail climbed back up to his second-story office, muttering about gents who couldn't handle their fool wives.

It wasn't high noon yet, and Longarm knew he'd wind up beating rugs or splitting stove wood if he showed up at the Vail house too early on a workday. The motherly-looking but house-proud old biddy Billy Vail was married up with *knew* he worked for her man, and held that the devil found work for idle hands. She'd been like that ever since she'd found out about him and that young widow woman down the street from her.

It was too early to eat more chili, and he'd promised he'd get off the downtown streets of Denver. So he ambled on over to that rooming house he'd rustled up for old Lina Marie. He had his own key and the buxom blonde, for all her faults, would be at work until after five.

Meanwhile, he'd never gotten to read those magazines or smoke half the tobacco he'd carried up her stairs, along with the usual flowers, booze, and candy. So this unexpected afternoon off would offer the opportunity to kick off his boots and catch up on some casual smoking and reading, with nobody grabbing at his privates just as he was getting to the end of an article or the solution of a detective story. He liked those English detective stories a lot, even though those fancy English crooks seemed to use more imagination on paper than plain old American crooks did in real life.

A colored maid was dusting in the hallway as he let himself

in the unlocked front door. She looked unsettled to see him there at that hour. But he knew she knew who he was and his connection with a paid-up roomer on the top floor. So he just nodded at her and went on up to Lina Marie's garret quarters under the mansard roof.

The hall door was naturally locked. Or so it seemed. He didn't know exactly why Lina Marie had locked it until he unlocked it and stepped inside, expecting to find himself alone up yonder.

He wasn't. The buxom blonde and a total stranger who could have used more fresh air and sunshine were going at it hot and heavy on the brass bedstead against the far wall, naked as a couple jaybirds in a love nest. The jasper on top froze in mid-stroke to stare goggle-eyed as Lina Marie grinned sickly at Longarm and gasped, "Honey! I wasn't expecting you this early!"

Longarm resisted the impulse to dryly observe that seemed mighty obvious. Some kindly old philosopher had once declared, doubtless in French, that nothing a man could say as he made a last exit would be more sophisticated than simply closing the door softly after himself as he left. Gals counted coup on each cussing or slamming from a man.

But Longarm was cussing to himself as he stomped down the stairs and out of the rooming house with that colored maid staring at him.

Striding up the shady side of the street he found himself muttering aloud, "That pasty-faced and pimple-assed son of a bitch must be the boss at work she told us about. Nobody else would be screwing her so freely on company time, and damn it, that was *my* pussy he was screwing so brassy, in the very quarters I helped her find!"

He paused under a cottonwood to light a cheroot as he told himself to calm down, muttering, "Don't get your bowels in an uproar over old Lina Marie, you idjet! You were *looking* for a graceful way out of the tedious fix, remember?"

He strode on, puffing smoke like a locomotive hauling its heavy load up a nine-degree grade as he growled, "Whether I wanted old Lina Marie or not is not the point. That pale soft slug couldn't lick old Henry from the office, and there he was on top of the gal I saw *first,* as if he thought I had nothing to *say* about it!''

Longarm suddenly laughed in a more boyish tone as his common sense told him, ''Asshole! He wasn't thinking about you at all. He was just a poor mortal with a hard-on, and you know *you* laid Lina Marie the first night you treated her to spaghetti and meatballs with spiked wine!''

But as he strode east toward the somewhat cooler and clearer high ground of Capitol Hill, he found himself grumbling, ''Hold on. I asked early on if she was spoken for. She says she told that priss at work she was shacked up with *me*!''

He decided that was the part that galled him the most. The soft pale shopkeeper should have known you don't help yourself to another man's tobacco or liquor without his permission either, unless you're sure he's too big a sissy to do anything about it. So where had an infernal dry-goods pusher come up with the notion a bigger man in any better shape *wouldn't* do anything about it?

Longarm suddenly laughed in a world-weary tone as his common sense told him, ''From Lina Marie, of course. She'd have likely told him we were through before he carried her home from work early to console her. Forget the poor hard-up cuss. He never spent ten seconds thinking about you or any other man as he lusted after that brassy blonde!''

So Longarm strode on in restored good humor as he considered how everything was working out. But the unexpected ending of his half-ass love affair had given him added insight into what might be eating Attila the Hungarian. For Longarm could see that if he'd had a mite less regard for the *written* law, or a mite more regard for old Lina Marie, somebody could have been in a whole lot of trouble back there!

By the time he walked to Broadway and Colfax at the foot of the long gentle rise to the flat top of Capitol Hill, a street clock told him he'd at least burned up some time with all that nonsense. So he cut north along Broadway to where a man could part some swinging doors and see what sort of free lunch they were offering over this way.

There was no such thing as a free lunch, of course, but he still saw they'd set out some devilish eggs and pickled pig's feet, both a mite salty. So he ordered a scuttle of their draft to wash some of their free lunch down.

The nibbles weren't quite as good, but the beer was cheaper than it cost at the Parthenon Saloon near the Federal Building. Longarm had remembered that when he'd paused down the way to consider how to put off beating rugs for Mrs. Vail. He knew better than to show up really late, or walking funny, so he was nursing his beer with salty grub when a blue-uniformed Denver copper badge passed by the swinging doors of the entrance, broke stride, and came inside with a weary shake of his beaked cap, wistfully declaring, "I know I can't order another lawman, Deputy Long. But I purely wish you'd take it off my particular beat!"

Longarm smiled uncertainly and asked, "Take what off your beat, Roundsman Callahan? I was under the impression I was just in here killing time with some suds and these salty nibbles."

Callahan sighed and said, "Judge not, lest ye be judged, and I've been in a strange town with a hard-on as well. But that Bohunk gal in Trinidad was married up with a mighty wild-eyed cuss! He's been asking all over town for you. We run him in this morning as a cataclysm fixing to occur. But the desk said threats against his wife's lover don't count unless he's within pistol range."

Longarm swore softly and declared, "I wouldn't know the fool's wife from Mother Eve if I *did* wake up in bed with her! Lord knows how Hornagy ever got the notion I'd been anywhere near her!"

Callahan shrugged and replied, "That's easy. She *told* him it was you, according to him, and I don't think I want you trying to deny it on my beat to a crazy Bohunk packing two Schofield .45s! He's already been told how many professional gunslicks you've beaten to the draw. But he just don't seem to be a man you can talk sense to."

Callahan glanced out the doorway, as if expecting trouble at any time, as he added, "I don't want to tidy up after either one of you. We both know what a pain in the ass it is to write up all them reports in triplicate and then have the district attorney cuss you for sticking him with a can of worms. There's no way in hell we'd ever convict *him,* whilst charging a lawman with murder makes us all look bad!"

Longarm sighed and said, "I wish I could at least *try* for a plea of self-defense, should push really come to shove."

To which Callahan replied in a surprisingly cheerful tone, "You can't. But I'd sure hate to get stuck with the chore of arresting a man with your rep. So I sure wish you'd fight him somewheres else!"

Chapter 3

Longarm dawdled up Colfax Avenue to the statehouse, went inside and sat up in the visitors' gallery, and listened to some grouchy old birds argue about the gold-to-silver ratio until he decided he might as well go on over to the Vail house and split cordwood out back.

But even though he got there before mid-afternoon, he didn't wind up doing any of Billy Vail's chores. For the marshal was there in the flesh, dancing about on his dusty brown lawn like a Cheyenne with a vision, or a kid with worms, until Longarm got within hearing range so Billy could shout, "Where in thunder have you been? I sent Smiley and Dutch over to your quarters to gather up your Winchester and McClellan for you. I hope you've got the usual change of socks and some iron rations in your saddlebags."

As Longarm joined his shorter superior on the summer-dry stubble, he replied with an uncertain frown, "Always keep my gear handy for a sudden leap into the great unknown. But where might I be leaping in such a hurry? Did we get another tip on Frank, Jesse, or The Kid?"

Vail glanced uneasily up and down the tree-lined street atop the rise and told Longarm, "We'll talk about it inside. I had Henry type up some travel orders before I left the office just now. But I reckon I'd best fill you in a mite, and your next train out don't leave this side of four-thirty."

Longarm had left the Denver Union Depot often enough to

consult his mental timetable and decide, "That would be the UP eastbound you'd want me to catch. Who are we after in Kansas, Boss?"

As Vail led him around to the kitchen entrance Longarm was told, "You're getting off at Kansas City to cut backwards to Fort Sill, betwixt the Washita and Red River of the South."

Longarm blinked and said, "I know where Fort Sill is. But getting there by way of K.C. makes no sense. What's wrong with my catching the D&RG down to Amarillo and changing to most any eastbound for a way shorter ride?"

Vail snapped, "Trinidad. Henry was the one who pointed out there's no sensible way to get to Amarillo without passing through Trinidad, and if there's one place other than Denver I don't want you for the next few days, Trinidad, Colorado, has to be it!"

By this time they'd made it into a kitchen reeking of apple pie and Arbuckle Brand coffee. As Vail waved Longarm to a seat at their big pine table, his motherly old woman told Longarm she'd heard about the mean bully after him. From the way she said it Longarm surmised her husband had convinced her he hadn't really messed with that Magda Hornagy down Trinidad way.

Vail sat across from him and said, "Henry got off the usual wires to the law down yonder. Fortunately Denver P.D. had already wired a heap of questions about Attila Hornagy and the Trinidad law had their earlier answers handy. So they got back to us within the hour."

As his wife served their pie and coffee Vail continued. "First the bad news. Attila Hornagy seems to be who he says he is. He's the straw boss of a drilling and blasting crew at the Black Diamond Mine. They mine bituminous coal, not real diamonds of any color. He's never been locked up more than ninety days as a result of his disposition, but they report they weren't too surprised to hear he was after someone with a gun. Hornagy was brought to Penn State as a tyke by his Bohunk coal-mining kin, which is how come he talks English plain. But they seem to have reared him by a proddy Bohunk code of honor that seems to call for an eye for an eye and then some. So he's been known to wreck a saloon for serving him watered whiskey, and it appears nobody from the Austro-

Hungarian Empire will ever find a Bohunk too timid to totally kill any man who even *insults* his woman!''

Longarm washed down some pie, and was fixing to insist he'd never laid eyes on Magda Hornagy when Vail continued. ''Trinidad says Attila the Hungarian's wife is tougher to talk sense to than he is. She just got here and barely knows enough English to shop in a Bohunk neighborhood. Attila sent home for her. Reckon he thought he could trust any gal who couldn't tell what cowhands were saying to her.''

Longarm nodded absently, brightened, and said, ''Hold on, Billy! Don't that prove me innocent? I don't speak Hungarian at all. So if she don't savvy our lingo, how in blue blazes was I supposed to act up with her whilst her old man was off to that union convention?''

Vail grumbled, ''I told you earlier that you didn't have to sell *me* on where you spent the merry month of May. It's her *husband* who's after you with two Schofields.''

Vail sipped some coffee himself before he added, ''She must talk at least some English. Trinidad says an Irish neighbor woman backs up her story about some tall handsome stranger moving in with Attila's woman over a weekend and not leaving until just before all the menfolk got back from that May Day meeting. Old Magda didn't get to tell the other wives the whole story until the handsome stranger lit out. So up until then half the gals on the hillside had her down as just a brazen adulterer.''

Longarm nodded thoughtfully and pointed out, ''If other ladies in Trinidad actually laid eyes on old Magda's houseguest, it don't matter to *us* whether she made up some details after her brass cooled down or not. Why don't I just head for Trinidad instead of Fort Sill and see if old Magda's neighbor ladies think I look like that other handsome stranger?''

Vail growled, ''Because you're going to Fort Sill instead. If I thought sweet reason would work on Attila Hornagy, he'd be sitting here having apple pie with us right now whilst the three of us tried to figure out what really happened last May. I told you I told him I had you right down the hall on court duty at the very time he has you wrecking his happy home nearly two hundred miles away. He wouldn't have it. He's quit his job to track down the man who hung all them magnificent horns on him, and if you ain't the one, who in blue blazes is he supposed to shoot?''

Billy's wife refilled their cups with a weary smiles as she said, ''Men! I swear you all just get more mule-headed as you get older! I don't see how that crazy coal miner is supposed to support his young wife without a job, no matter how they work out their difficulties.''

Vail said, ''I don't either. I figure that whether they bust up or stick together, he's still going to need another job soon as he's run his fool self broke tearing all over like this. Trinidad says he cleaned out his modest bank account the day he quit at the mine. Since we ain't talking four figures to begin with, he can't keep at it more than a month at the rate he's been steaming. Worrying about where on earth your next meal or another job might be coming from has a grand way of concentrating a man's mind. So the timing of your trip over to Fort Sill and back works out about right.''

Longarm washed down the last bite of pie and leaned back in his bentwood chair to ask how come they wanted him to run over to Fort Sill in the Indian Nation.

Billy Vail leaned back in his own chair and got out one of his more expensive but far smellier smokes as he pontificated, ''Indian *Territory* since the war. If you want self-rule, like the Civilized Tribes were granted back in Jackson's day, don't ever side with the Confederacy and then brag on not surrendering for six months after Lee!''

Vail struck a match and lit his pungent cigar, ignoring the sad sigh of his wife as he continued. ''Fort Reno and Fort Sill went up west of the original Indian Nation grants in any case. Indians had no self-rule in those parts to begin with. Those western outposts were built to police far wilder nations such as Comanche, Kiowa, and Kiowa-Apache.''

Longarm had known all that. It was more important he catch the eye of the lady of the house, lest he find himself with no defense against Bill Vail's cigar. Once he did so, patting the cheroots in a breast pocket, she nodded, but headed for another part of the house with a remark about opening more windows.

Vail gazed fondly after her and remarked, ''She knew I smoked this brand the day we married up. Women and children are a lot like the Indians when it comes to counting on dreams of the future. But that gets us back to your mission to Fort Sill. The recently shot-up and calmed-down Comanche and their Kiowa allies have been moved off their old reservation in the Texas Panhandle and resettled around Fort Sill.''

''On what?'' Longarm dryly asked as he got out a cheaper but much less vile smoke. ''I know Fort Reno, to the north, better. But I've passed through Fort Sill often enough to opine such timber and game as there might have once been has been cut down and shot off a heap.''

Vail let fly a thunderhead of swirling blue smoke and replied in a philosophical tone, ''Don't never ask the Bureau of Indian Affairs for nicer hunting grounds if you mean to lift white hair and then brag about it. The trouble only got serious after that Kiowa chief came in for a government handout and gloated to Agent Tatum that he'd wiped out a wagon train.''

Longarm hung some of his own tobacco smoke between them as he thought back, nodded, and said, ''I never figured out why poor old Satanta did that. Indians I know tell me that raid was led by his rival, Mamanti.''

Vail shrugged and declared, ''Don't matter. The war that resulted was the end of both of them, and we ain't got time for ancient history. Now that everyone's agreed on Quanah Parker as the heap big chief of the Comanche and spokesman for his orphaned Kiowa children, things have commenced to get more progressive. The Comanche have actually taken to drilling in corn crops and raising pony herds instead of raiding for 'em. The Kiowa and that half-ass bunch of stray Apache they've adopted are still trying to live their old free ways. That's what you call it when you sponge off employed neighbors and the self-supporting taxpayer, the old free ways.''

Longarm asked dubiously if any of the new developments around Fort Sill had anything to do with him and his trouble with Attila Hornagy.

Vail said, ''It wouldn't have, if that fool Bohunk had kept a tighter rein on his wayward bride. But a few days back I got me this request from the B.I.A. Seems Chief Quanah Parker asked for you by name and—''

''Hold on!'' Longarm cut in. ''I barely know Quanah Parker to howdy, and I've never messed with even one of his eight wives!''

Vail got to his feet with a weary smile. "You got it ass backwards. Right now you're likely safer surrounded by Quill Indian husbands than the other kind. They asked to borrow you for a spell to help 'em smooth the rough spots of their new Indian Police out of Fort Sill. The army ain't so interested in training Indians for anything but scouting since Indian Affairs got transferred from the War to Interior Department. I was about to write back that our Justice Department has enough on its plate when that Attila jasper showed up with the avowed intent of blowing your balls off."

Vail picked up a bulky manila envelope from the sideboard and turned back to Longarm. "You'll find more about it in here, along with your travel orders and such. I had Henry type up copies of the shit from Fort Sill. Meanwhile, I sent Smiley and Dutch over to your hired quarters on the far side of the creek to fetch your Winchester, McClellan, and saddlebags packed for the field—if you know what's good for you. You'll find your stuff in the baggage room at Union Depot. Your claim check and train tickets are in this envelope."

As he handed it to Longarm he continued. "I've already told you I'm sending someone else to scout the cheating wives of Trinidad. I want you totally out of our hair at Fort Sill whilst we find out just what happened and do something about it. So what are you waiting for, a kiss good-bye?"

Longarm muttered he wasn't that sort of cuss, and so they settled for shaking hands and parting more or less friendly. Longarm was still a mite riled as he ambled back to Colfax to catch a horse-drawn streetcar. The notion of running off to join the Comanche Nation to avoid a fight with a mighty silly pest just didn't sit right, even though his common sense told him nobody important to him was fixing to call him a coward or even laugh at him. The pure fact that Attila Hornagy was probably green as hell with a gun and surely misinformed about his wife's love life made him impossible to reason with and stupid for any real gunfighter to tangle with.

The streetcar carried him the mile and a quarter to Union Depot a tad sooner and not as sweaty as if he'd legged it all the way at that pace. As he entered the cavernous depths of the sooty red brick edifice, it took a short spell for his eyes to adjust from the bright sunliight out front. So he froze in midstride and came close to going for his gun when an all-too-familiar voice near the tobacco stand let fly with, "You didn't think I'd be slick enough to head anyone off here, did you, Deputy Smiley?"

Those last two words saved Attila Hornagy from a pistol-whipping at the very least as Longarm stared thoughtfully down at the older man and paused to hear him out.

Hornagy nodded at the envelope in Longarm's left hand. "Some last-minute instructions from Marshal Vail, eh? I guess all of you had me down as just another dumb greenhorn. But I'll have everyone know that whether I was born in the Carpathians or not, I graduated from the eighth grade in Penn State!"

Longarm cautiously said, "Anyone can see you're as smart as your average cuss, Mister Hornagy."

The mining man with the wayward wife said, "Damned right. I found out where Longarm lived, and got there just in time to learn that you and another deputy had just left with his traveling gear, Deputy Smiley. I knew he'd be leaving town from here or that Overland Stage from in front of the Tremont House. So I came here first, telling them over at yonder baggage window that I was a pal of Deputy Long's, and what do you think I just found out?"

Longarm managed not to grin as he soberly replied, "It's a sin to tell a lie, and they shouldn't have given out such privileged information. But I've worked that dodge and they usually do."

Hornagy looked so smug it would have been cruel to tell him he was full of it. So Longarm didn't as the older man crowed, "They told me he means to catch that train to Kansas City in an hour or so. So guess who'll be here to see him off, the home-wrecking son of a bitch!"

Longarm sighed and said, "Bragging right out that you mean to gun another man could be taken as criminal intent, Mister Hornagy."

The avowed assassin replied with a sly grin, "Who said *exactly* what I'm going to do when I catch up with the man who made my poor little Magda *bus* him against her will? Go ahead and arrest me, if you think you can hold a man with simple justice on his side. Your Denver Police arrested me earlier, and had to let me go.''

Longarm was about to ask if *bus* was the Bohunk for what he surmised it had to be. But then they were joined by a Spanish-speaking streetwalker called Consuela, who sidled up to Longarm and said right out, ''*Buentardes, El Brazo Largo. ¿A 'onde va?*''

So it was safe to assume Attila Hornagy spoke no Spanish. For the soiled dove's words would have translated as, ''Afternoon, Longarm. Where you headed?''

Before she could say anything worse in English, Longarm had her by one elbow and they were rushing for the platform doors as if they had a train to catch.

The young whore laughed and gasped, ''*Madre de Dios,* you must really need some! But that's what we're here for and I'll try anything that doesn't hurt too much!''

He got her out of Hornagy's sight as he tersely told her in his own version of Spanish that he was working under an assumed name and didn't want that suspect in the seersucker suit back yonder to know just who he might really be.

Consuela laughed incredulously and replied, ''*Pero El Brazo Largo,* everyone inside the depot knows who you are!''

She'd made a good point, and damn it, that southbound Billy Vail had advised against was already pulling out a platform over!

So Longarm was running, a lot, as the southbound D&RG cleared the end of its boarding area, picking up speed. He skimmed his envelope through the space ahead of him, and dove headfirst for a grab at the brass rail of the last car's observation deck. A strong small hand grabbed the wrist of his as it was slipping, and he was grateful as hell as he hooked a booted ankle over the same rail. Then the brunette in blue who'd risen from her wicker seat just in time helped him roll aboard, even as she chided, ''Didn't anyone ever tell you that's a very dangerous way to board a train?''

To which Longarm could only reply, ''Not half as dangerous as my staying where I was might have been, ma'am.''

She allowed her handle was Cora Brewster as he bought her some sarsaparilla soda inside the club car. It seemed the least a gent could do, and she didn't seem to mind when he ordered a schooner of needled beer for himself. They took a corner table near the rear windows, and after that things sort of went to hell in a hack.

She was getting off at Trinidad, for openers, which inspired him to introduce himself as Deputy Gus Crawford. When she remarked they had another such Crawford writing for the *Denver Post,* he said he'd noticed that and made a mental note she was sharp as well as pretty. Then she said that she and her husband had started the first dairy herd down Trinidad way.

Billy Vail had warned him not to even pass through Trinidad, and he figured he could use some practice at behaving himself around a pretty lady with a firm grip and those trim hips a gal got from a heap of horseback riding. So he never even asked if she minded him smoking. He'd been meaning to cut down in any case, and that helped him, some. It was easier to keep his thoughts about her clean as he sat there dying for a smoke.

The conductor finally came back to their end of the train. Cora naturally had her ticket handy. Longarm started to explain how he'd boarded at the last minute without having had the time to pay at the depot. But the conductor said, "Don't give it a thought, Longarm. It won't break this line to carry you free as far as Trinidad, and as a matter of fact, it feels much safer having *you* aboard as we pass Castle Rock."

The intelligent brunette waited until the conductor had punched her ticket and headed back the other way before she asked him with a puzzled frown why that conductor had just called him Longarm.

Before Longarm could reluctantly confess the truth, she added in a knowing tone, "You don't look anything like that notorious Longarm, Mister Crawford."

It was Longarm's turn to sound puzzled as he replied, "Do tell? I didn't know you'd *met* the notorious cuss they keep writing fibs about in the *Post* and *Rocky Mountain News.*"

She said, "I was never introduced to him when he passed through our town last May—leaving quite a wake, I might add. I only had him pointed out to me a time or two as he passed by, each time with still another immigrant girl. You'd never know it from those stories about him in the newspapers, but Colorado's answer to Wild Bill would seem to be some sort of foreigner."

He asked who'd ever told her a thing like that.

She replied without hesitation, "Nobody had to tell me. I heard him speaking Hungarian to a pretty little greenhorn from Bohunk Hill as I was standing in the open doorway of a notions shop across from the Papist church in Trinidad. Hungarians are Papists, like most of the Irish mining folk. They call Hungarian something else, it sounds like Mad Gear. But once you've heard folks talking it you know it has to be Hungarian. It sounds nothing like the Spanish, High Dutch, or Welsh you hear in coal-mining country."

He said he'd take her word for some cuss talking Bohunk in the merry month of May to the pretty immigrant gals of Trinidad. Then, choosing his words carefully, he said, "That conductor just now seemed to fancy I was this Longarm jasper. So ain't it likely there could be some resemblence betwixt me and this cuss we're talking about?"

Cora Brewster turned on her club car stool to peer across their small round table more intently as Longarm fought to keep a poker face. The intelligent and apparently sharp-eyed brunette took her time and sounded convinced as she flatly stated, "No resemblance at all. You're both tall and sort of rangy. At the risk of turning your head, you're both good-looking and you both wear guns and mustaches of heavy caliber. After that you look nothing like one another. I don't see how that conductor could have taken you for that nasty Longarm."

The real Longarm replied, "He must need new specs. Did this tall drink of water down Trinidad way say right out he was Deputy U.S. Marshal Custis Long, or might it have been someone else's decision, Miss Cora?"

She started to say something without thinking, caught herself, and gained even more respect from Longarm when she decided, "As a matter of fact, the first townswoman who pointed him out to me gave an outlandish Hungarian-sounding name I don't recall. She was a shop girl from somewhere in the Austro-Hungarian Empire as well. But you'd have to ask *her* if you wanted to know exactly where. She said he was a notorious womanizer and a big bully who took advantage of his fellow greenhorns, knowing his way around the American West better.''

Longarm smiled thinly and said, ''That sure sounds like the West-by-God-Virginia rascal I keep reading about in the *Denver Post*. But how did his fellow Bohunks uncover his true identity if he started out as one of their own badmen?''

She sipped more soda through her love-grass straw as if to allow herself time to choose her words before she confided, ''It all came out in the Hornagy scandal. Trinidad's not half as big as Denver, so a scandal as juicy as that one gets told and retold until everyone has every detail whether they wanted them or not.''

Longarm sighed and said, ''I know this young widow woman back in Denver who'd agree with you on back-fence sass in any size town. I swear that if you drop a jar of olives on Lincoln Street, it'll grow to a wagon load of watermelons by the time the gossip gets all the way to Sherman, a block up the slope. So ain't it possible to mistake one tall cuss with a mustache with another?''

Cora Brewster sipped more soda and demurely decided, ''I've never confessed adultery to a husband after midnight. So I can only try to imagine the scene inside the Hornagy cabin when she told him she'd been seduced by a blackmailer who'd threatened to have the two of them deported. I remember how surprised we were at the notions shop to hear it had been an American government official instead of the immigrant bully we'd thought we'd noticed pestering the immigrant girls of Bohunk Hill while their men were down in the mines or out of town to those anarchist meeting immigrants go in for.''

Longarm frowned thoughtfully out the grimy glass at the passing grassy swells. ''Hold on,'' he said. ''I'm missing something. Just who come down off the slopes of Bohunk Hill to tell the rest of the world Attila Hornagy had caught his woman with the one and original Deputy U.S. Marshal Custis Long, ma'am?''

She shook her pretty head and replied, ''Nobody. Had the poor man actually found an intruder under his roof, dressed as suspiciously as in his shirtsleeves with his vest unbuttoned, the code of any gentleman, foreign or domestic, would have called for the spilling of blood on the spot!"

Longarm soberly said, "I know how that fool code's supposed to work, ma'am. I told you I was a lawman. Is it safe to say Hornagy beat his wife and announced his even grimmer intentions about a famous American lover after she *told* him that was who he was after?"

Cora Brewster demurely replied, "I told you I wasn't there. But I suppose she must have, since her husband never actually caught her with anyone!"

Longarm took a deeper pull on his beer than he'd meant to as he mulled one gal's suspicions about another over and over in his own head. Then he said, "There's no better way it works. Hornagy was out of town a spell on union business. When he came back he must have heard his woman and some other pretty Bohunk gals had been seen carrying on with a handsome stranger. It was you, not me, who allowed everyone but at least one jealous husband was pretty. A gal trying to cover up for a handsome Bohunk boyfriend might grab at an American name off a newspaper she'd just wrapped the garbage in. It might be as tough for a Bohunk to come up with an American name on short notice as it would be for a scared American to recall some Bohunks are called Attila!"

He scowled down into his beer stein and added, "There was a front page or more covering some court proceedings last May too. So how do you like a false-hearted woman betraying her husband with another man, and then betraying a federal deputy she'd never laid eyes on to her husband's vengeance, by naming him as the one to be struck down on the field of honor?"

Cora Brewster wrinkled her pert nose. "If what you say could be true, Magda Hornagy carried casual adultery on to premeditated murder! The only question left would be just whom she had in mind. They say this Longarm is fast on the draw and quick on the trigger, while poor little Attila Hornagy is at best a handy man with a star drill and dynamite!"

Before Longarm could get into the unwritten law and the edge it gave even a mediocre fighting man, the Trinidad gal added, "I heard a lot of the Hungarian folks down our way have tried to persuade poor Mister Hornagy to forget it. They seem to feel there's no shame to accepting things in their new land as they just have to be. They've told both the husband and wife it was more like a natural disaster than an affair of honor. They feel it's hopeless to resist the iron whim of any government official, and they've warned Attila Hornagy the Americans will surely hang him if he kills such a famous American lawman, even though he'd be in the right with simple justice on his side!''

Longarm didn't answer right off. There was more than one way to shovel any stall, and he didn't want to pile on any more lies he might want to take back in a hurry. He knew he'd doubtless be able to convince this bright young Trinidad gal he couldn't be the jasper she'd had pointed out as himself earlier. She'd just told him he looked nothing like the man she'd been told was Longarm. She knew lots of other Trinidad gals. Including more than one who'd be as willing to depose in writing that they'd seen yet another handsome stranger messing with those sassy Bohunk gals while their menfolk hadn't been looking.

But Billy Vail had issued direct orders forbidding him to go anywhere near Trinidad. Meanwhile, it was going to take them at least another four hours to get there at this speed, Lord willing and no trestles were down. So Longarm let her rattle on about treacherous young wives stuck with musty old men as he sipped away the rest of his beer and asked her if she'd like some sandwiches to go with her next soda.

She hesitated, then calmly replied, ''It's been hours since last I ate back in Denver, and I fear we'll be pulling into Trinidad past my usual supper-time. But I think we'd better go Dutch treat, Deputy Crawford. It wouldn't be right for me to lead a strange man on, and it's not as if I can't afford some ham on rye. I forgot to tell you I was just up to Denver on business, and we made out right handy on some yellow cheese we've started to make at our dairy.''

Longarm felt no call to press it. The pretty gal's husband or a hand who worked for them figured to be waiting for her when they both had to get off at Trinidad. He wasn't looking forward to the overly hearty handshakes and cautious smiles such occasions seemed to call for. But when a man had to change trains he had to change trains, and at least it would be old Cora, not himself, who got to explain how innocent it had all been, for as many times as it took to sink in.

He caught the eye of a colored club car attendant, and once they were fixed to order he made sure they'd be getting separate tabs.

Cora Brewster had been serious about that ham and rye. She made Longarm feel a mite prissy by ordering a scuttle of beer to wash it down.

He allowed he'd have his next beer by the scuttle instead of the far smaller schooner, seeing it saved trips back and forth from the bar, and ordered Swiss and salami on pumpernickel.

He could tell she'd been raised almost as country as himself, and as a rule country folks got right down to business with their grub so they could get on with any chores that needed tending. But as Longarm and Cora found themselves with nothing better to do than talk as they chugged on south with the foothills of the Front Range to their right and the rolling swells of the High Plains going from tawny to golden in the late afternoon sunlight, they just nibbled, sipped, and speculated about that tearful Bohunk gal confessing she'd been untrue with a lawman called Longarm when her husband hadn't really caught her in the act with anyone.

Meanwhile, back in Denver, the somewhat confused streetwalker called Consuela meant no harm to El Brazo Largo, known to be more friendly to her own people than many of his kind. It was loyalty to her own social class as well as La Raza that inspired Consuela's hiss of warning as she spied two Mexican street urchins stalking a little old gringo in a seersucker suit, over by the baggage windows of the crowded Union Depot.

The bigger boy, who usually held the mark from behind as his wiry compadre grabbed for his watch chain and wallet, drifted over to the slightly older whore, a violet-scented cigarette rolled in black paper dangling from his pouty lip as he quietly observed, "We know he wears a gunbelt under his jacket. For to use a gun on anyone one must be able to get at it, no?"

Consuela warned, "He looks like a harmless *viejo* to me as well, Hernando. Just the same, if I were you, I'd choose someone safer for to go after. That one is *muy peligrosa, muchacho mio*."

The young thug shot a more thoughtful glance across the waiting room, turned back to Consuela, and demanded, "That old gringo? You can't be serious! Little Pancho here could take him in a fair fight if he did not have those guns and nobody else interfered! What do they call this big bad gringo we are supposed to be afraid of, eh?"

Consuela said, "I do not know. I have never seen him around here before. But he has been here long enough for one who reads the ways of men on the street to suspect he is stalking someone with the guns he wears partly concealed. You have heard, of course, of El Brazo Largo?"

Hernando nodded thoughtfully and said, "The one his own people call Longarm? I know him on sight. They say he's *muy toro*. What about him?"

Consuela said, "That one just ran El Brazo Largo out of town! I saw it happen less than an hour ago. They were talking—in a tense way, I could see. Then suddenly, the smaller one said something and El Brazo Largo grabbed me by one arm and dragged me out to the loading platforms, begging me not to tell anyone who he really was!"

Hernando whistled as he gazed across the hazy waiting room with a lot more respect, marveling, "Hey, they say El Brazo Largo faced down both Thompson Brothers in Texas! You say he asked you not to tell that older man who he was?"

She answered, "*Sí.* Then I told him there were a lot of people around this depot who knew who he was, and the next thing I knew he was running for the next train out!"

Hernando gasped, "*Madre de Dios,* we owe you for warning us! The *hombre malo* who could run Longarm out of town is nobody Pancho and me wish for to dance with!"

That would have been the end of it if Hernando hadn't spotted a hard-faced Anglo that Consuela wouldn't have wanted to speak to a few minutes later. The rangy hardcase, dressed like a cowhand on his way to a funeral, was as mean as he looked. So naturally Hernando and Pancho admired him. But as they approached, the black-clad rider leaning against a sooty brick wall scowled at them and said, "Beat it, you greaser faggots. I'm down here at the depot to meet somebody. I don't want no nickel cocksucker!"

Hernando persisted with, "I can't fix you up with no cocksucker. I don't know your sister. *Pero, quien sabe?* Maybe I got something much better for you. What if I could point out the hombre who just ran the famous Longarm out of town? The *hombre malo* who took such a *pistolero* would be famous as Wild Bill, no?''

Blacky Foyle, the terror of many a West Denver saloon, raised a a thoughtful brow and replied, ''I ain't sure I'm ready to be famous as Wild Bill, albeit they do say he has a fine fence around his gravesite up Deadwood way. The man who'd go up agin a man Longarm was afraid of would have to take such affairs more serious than a sunny child like me. But why don't you point this dangerous jasper out to me, and mayhaps I won't call you a cocksucker no more, Hernando.''

Chapter 4

Trinidad, Colorado, had sprouted from where the original Santa Fe Trail had crossed the Purgatoire by way of a handy ford. Later, by the time they'd shortened the freight wagon route by way of the Cimarron Cutoff, they'd found soft coal seams in the foothills to the west and given Trinidad a better reason for being there. The steel rails laid west to replace the old wagon ruts were more interested in firebox coal and boiler water than the shorter but more barren cutoff. So now the seat of Las Animas County enjoyed its own trade with the outside world in coal, cows, and farm truck.

By the time their train was passing the outlying spreads of the prosperous transportation hub, Longarm and Cora Brewster had moved on back to the observation platform again and he'd learned more about the butter and egg business of Trinidad than he'd ever thought he'd need to know.

But there were worse ways to while away the hours aboard a train than jawing with a pretty lady, and the malicious gossip involving him and a Trinidad gal he'd never met made a heap of otherwise tedious facts about the transfer point seem far more interesting.

As the sun sank ever lower and the spreads off to either side got smaller and more closely spaced, Cora was rambling on about how much more even an immigrant coal miner's family spent on fresh eggs and dairy products next to, say, your average single cowhand. Longarm had been getting paid as a single cowhand when he'd decided he'd rather sign on as a junior deputy six or eight years back. So he politely repressed a yawn and said, "I've got a pretty good picture of domestic doings up on Bohunk Hill, Miss Cora. What I really need a married woman's advice on is that mighty odd but apparently voluntary confession by Magda Hornagy. Setting aside who in thunder she'd been sparking whilst her husband was out of town, why would she tell him all she'd done, in dirty detail, with any other man by any other name?"

Cora wrinkled her pert nose and replied, "I wasn't there. But I imagine a woman would confess to added details if her husband beat them out of her, or if she really wanted to rub it in. I could answer more surely if I knew whether they were still together or not."

Longarm stared soberly at the lamplit window in a cozy soddy they were passing as he mused aloud, "I don't know. Attila Hornagy never brought her up to Denver with him. Maybe she's waiting for him down the line with a candle lit in the window for him. Maybe she run off with that other cuss. The one she said was . . . somebody else."

Cora agreed a cheating wife or more had been known to lie to save a lover. But after that she pointed out, "That swaggering lothario I only saw in passing, but more than once, didn't strike me as the sort of man who'd treat a girl to a ride to the next town, let alone more than a few nights' food and lodging. If she was dumb enough to run off with him, she'd have been home with her tail between her legs by the time her husband returned from that union gathering."

Longarm stared back up the receding tracks, noting you could no longer make out the point they came together on the horizon in this tricky twilight. He said, "Maybe she did. I sure wish I had time to nose about on Bohunk Hill and find out exactly where she is and exactly what she has to say about this mysterious cuss her husband has down as a federal deputy. But the night train I'll be riding east won't give me a full half hour in Trinidad."

She said, "I could find out anything you could, seeing I live just on the edge of town and know most of the tradeswomen. Why don't you give me a list of questions to ask? Then I could post them to your Denver office and you'd find them waiting for you there when you got back from your mission to Fort Sill."

Then she spoiled it all by adding, "You never did get around to telling me why they're sending you to Fort Sill, Deputy Crawford."

He muttered. "Just delivering some instructions."

Knowing that any nosey lady trying to write to a Deputy Crawford in care of Fort Sill would eventually have her letter returned unopened, he said, "They're sending some others from my home office down to nose about the scene of whatever transpired. I'm more interested in the other man than a wayward wife who'll either be at home or somewhere else. There's no telling which way he went after he turned the head of old Attila's wife. But he must have left town, or that jealous Bohunk wouldn't be searching high and low for him in Denver."

Cora must have spotted a familiar landmark in the passing softly lit scenery. For she bent forward to pick up the carpetbag she'd had resting on the decking near her high-button shoes as she asked how Longarm knew that other Longarm hadn't just been hiding out in some other part of Denver.

It was a good question. Longarm replied, "I just said he could be most anywhere. Tall drinks of water who look like Americans of the Western persuasion ain't all that rare. But him being some sort of furriner might make it easier to pick him out of a crowd."

She said they were almost there, and rose to her feet with her modest baggage as she added, "A lot of hardcase wanderers of our West seem to be foreign born. I mean, aside from the Canadian Masterson brothers, we have the Italian Renos, the Alteri boys, and the much nicer but probably more dangerous Charlie Siringo. Then there's Johnny Ringo, born a German Jew as Rhinegold, and isn't that fast-drawing Chris Madsen supposed to be a Swede?"

By this time Longarm had risen to take her carpetbag from her as he replied with a bemused smile, "Deputy Madsen's from Denmark, ma'am. But you were right about his famous quick draw. Where did a boss milkmaid, no offense, learn so much about our current crop of Western gunslicks?"

She said collecting newspaper accounts of wilder Western

folks had been her husband's hobby, and that he'd often said someday a lot of folks would likely pay good money for the true facts behind all those wild tales. She said she'd helped her husband keep that scrapbook up to date, and that she still sometimes leafed through it, thinking back to when she'd pasted something in.

Longarm said, "This jasper sparking the Bohunk gals of Trinidad spoke neither Eye-talian, Yiddish, nor Danish to the immigrant gals he was pestering. So that narrows it down a heap."

Then something else she'd just said sank in and he demanded with a puzzled look, "Did you say your man *used* to keep up with such hombres, meaning he ain't around to do so anymore? It's no beeswax of mine, but that ain't a black dress you have on this evening, Miss Cora."

The train was slowing to a stop as the sun was setting. So it was hard to read her eyes as she quietly replied, "I put my widow's weeds away two years ago. Jim was killed over a year before that. A Jersey bull Jim was trying to medicate tossed him and then trampled what was left of him."

Longarm didn't answer. It might have sounded smug to observe that the milking breeds were thrice as dangerous as any beef critter. As the train braked to a steamy stop, they saw their observation platform was just even with the north end of the plank loading platform. Longarm gripped his own envelope with the same arm holding her carpetbag, and opened the side gate of the platform with his free hand. They both knew he wasn't supposed to do that. So maybe that was why she was grinning like an apple-swiping kid as he helped her off their train. He asked if she'd have anyone picking her up, and if she did, where.

She said she'd left her trotter and shay at the livery across the way, and quietly added, "I could drive you over to Bohunk Hill and introduce you to some of the more respectable miners' wives, if you have the time."

He asked how far from the center of town they were talking about. When she said about halfway to the coal seams up the river a few miles, he sighed and said he didn't.

When he added the eastbound he meant to transfer to would be pulling out within half an hour, she softly replied, "There will always be another train on that same track, and I'd be proud to put you up for the night out at our place later."

He was so tempted it hurt. But he somehow managed to decline her tempting offer, and so they shook hands and parted friendly on the walk out front. As he turned back inside Longarm grumbled, "Next time Billy Vail accuses me of placing pleasure before duty, I'll have a wistful answer for him indeed. But of course, nobody would ever believe I just spoiled such a lovely evening for all concerned without anyone holding a gun to my head!"

Chapter 5

Old Billy Vail had known what he was picking when he'd picked Fort Sill as an out-of-the-way place to send a rider. It was after midnight when Longarm had to get off the one train and board another running closer to due east along the Saint Lou line. He had enough time between trains to send a wire to his home office at night rates. So he did, knowing Billy Vail was still going to have a fit, but that as soon as he calmed down to take a breath, he'd see the deputy who'd disregarded his orders to avoid Trinidad had made it on to Amarillo without incident and would have made it to Fort Sill, his own way, by the time Western Union got around to delivering a night letter.

Only the fancier varnish express trains passing through the Texas Panhandle sported those new Pullman dining cars, and no such on-board facilities would be open after midnight in any case. But Mister Fred Harvey, Lord love him, had opened one of his round-the-clock depot restaurants at Amarillo. So after Longarm had sent his night letter, he saw he had just enough time for a hasty but warm and rib-sticking late-night snack.

He sat at the counter, along with the few others grabbing a bite at that hour. The fellow traveler to his left was a trim-waisted gal in a tan whipcord travel duster and big veiled summer boater. It was tougher to judge a woman's age under a travel-dusted veil. But she had a handsome profile for a gal of any age. The Harvey gal who came to take orders down at their end was more certainly around eighteen.

She was pleasantly plain, with her chestnut hair pulled up in a neat bun and the white linen apron over her coffee-brown uniform as starched as if she'd been on the day shift.

Longarm naturally waited till the lady to his left ordered herself a Spanish omelet with a mug of hot chocolate. Longarm asked for chili con carne with black coffee. You didn't have to say you wanted your black coffee strong at a Harvey. He knew they made their chili right too. The Harvey gal was back in no time with everything piping hot.

Too hot, Longarm feared, if he was supposed to catch that other train at the top of the hour. He mushed more oyster crackers into his chili than he'd really wanted. He resisted the temptation to pour coffee into the saucer and blow on it, knowing how country the gal seated next to him might consider that.

As he was stirring like hell and she was pouring extra cream from the counter into her hot chocolate, a somewhat more country boy under a dove-gray Texas hat took the last seat at their end of the counter, to the left of the gal in the tan duster. It was none of Longarm's business until the rustic asked the lady if she'd like him to saucer and blow her hot chocolate.

The lady naturally didn't answer. Longarm put away some warm grub and washed it down with scalding java before the pest asked her how come she was so stuck up. The lady had already paid for her order on delivery, that being the Harvey way in a world where folks had a heap of trains to catch. So she only had to rise from the counter, pick up her overnight bag, and head for the door without even looking at the fool kid.

Longarm still didn't care. But then the pest jumped up to follow after her, asking if she needed help with her bag. It wasn't until he made a grab for it, causing the lady to trip and almost fall, that Longarm swung off his own stool to his considerable height and firmly announced, "That's enough, cowboy. You've rode past flirty into scary, and I want you to leave that lady be."

The Harvey gal behind him moaned, "Oh, Lordy!" and went to get someone bigger from the kitchen as the lout in the big hat kept clinging to the traveling gal's baggage, growling, "If I was you I'd be down on my knees in my sissy suit, praying for my life right now. For they call me Pronto, and the name is well deserved. You see what I'm packing in this tie-down holster, hero?"

Longarm regarded the other man's six-gun with detachment as he quietly replied, "Looks like a single-action John Adams. I've always admired well-preserved antiques."

Then he nodded at the lady in the tan travel duster and added, "You just go on and catch your train, ma'am. Ain't nothing but some schoolyard bluster likely to take place around here. Let go her bag, cowboy. I mean it."

The well-armed cuss let go of the overnight bag, but not as if it was because he'd been asked to. He dropped into a gunfighter's crouch as the lady lugged her baggage for the door. She was unable to keep from asking in a jeering tone, "Do you boys stage this scene for all the girls, or just the ones from out of town?"

Then she was sweeping out the doorway, nose in the air, and only Longarm laughed. The would-be Texas badman who still seemed willing to fight over her asked uncertainly, "What's she jawing about? Are we supposed to be up to something I never knew we were up to?"

Longarm nodded and said. "Yep. She thought we took turns insulting gals in railroad depots so's we could take turns rescuing 'em. I can see how that *might* be a good way to meet women, once you study on it."

The younger and obviously less-experienced cuss scowled at Longarm and insisted, "Hold on! I never agreed to let you rescue her from me. I don't even know you. I thought I was out to rescue her from *you*!"

Longarm shrugged and said, "Either way, she's gone and I got my own train to catch. So it's been nice talking to you, but like I said . . ."

"What about our showdown?" the depot desperado asked in a plaintive tone.

Longarm said, "I'm sure you could find plenty of other young gents willing to shoot it out with you at this hour for no good reason. But the only quarrel betwixt us just dismissed us both as a pair of unskilled country boys, if we ever had a quarrel to begin with. Fighting over a woman is sort of dumb. Fighting over a woman who doesn't like you is just plain stupid."

Longarm didn't wait to hear any counterargument. The depot loiterer wasn't crouched as tensely now, and while Longarm kept an eye on everyone as he circled for that same doorway, he was really more worried about the older-looking cuss who'd come from the kitchen in a cook's apron carrying a foot of carving knife.

Nobody drew or threw as he got out of range in the steamy light of the big depot. He'd only polished off a third of his chili and maybe half his coffee. But sure enough, his Saint Lou night train was fixing to pull out as he hurried along Track Number Four in the tricky light. Way down the platform, he saw that pretty but sort of snotty gal in the tan duster boarding one of the Pullman sleeping cars and staring his way, as if worried he was fixing to lope after her all the way to Saint Lou. He had no call to go on down and assure her he'd be getting off in the wee small hours. So he never did. He boarded a coach car carrying no more than that bulky manila envelope, and took a seat under an oil lamp to catch up on all those onionskins Henry had typed up for him not a full twelve hours earlier. Time sure could drag when you weren't having any fun.

As his train pulled out of the depot the Harvey night manager, who'd been watching through a door crack, came out from the back and said, "That was close. I thought we had your word you'd start no more trouble if we let you have free coffee, Pronto."

The kid with a hat and gun a mite big for him returned to the counter with a smirk, saying, "I wasn't looking for trouble. I was courting a lady fair when that jasper in the sissy suit horned in."

The night manager said, "That was no jasper in a sissy suit, you romantic young cuss. He's passed this way before. So I'm sure it was that deputy marshal they call Longarm!"

Pronto grinned and said, "I backed him down, no matter who he thought he was. Polly here heard him say he didn't want to fight me and saw him go around me!"

The Harvey girl just looked confused. The manager said,

"I saw it all from the kitchen too. You're lucky to be alive, Pronto. Had he been anxious as some to run up his score, you'd have never stood a chance. For they say Longarm's taken on some of the fastest guns in both the East and West, and won easy!"

Pronto sneered, "Don't care what anyone says about him. All I know is that I made him *crawfish*! Wait till I tell all the boys I backed down the famous Longarm in the flesh! Mayhaps then I'll get me some *respect* around Amarillo!"

The cook headed back for his kitchen with a snort of disgust. The night manager sighed and said, "I wish you wouldn't brag too loud, Pronto. We try to run a decent place here, and gunfire can play hob with a customer's appetite!"

While they were talking, a brakeman off a night freight came in to take a seat at the far end of the counter. Pronto had that effect on the regulars around the Amarillo depot. The burly brakeman was a decent tipper who never got too fresh. So Polly moved quickly up the counter to serve him.

The newcomer naturally asked the Harvey gal what the argument at the far end might be about. Polly told him, "Pronto's filled with himself just now because he thinks he backed down the famous lawman Longarm. You know how Pronto likes to glare at smoother-shaven gents. His victim was as likely a whiskey drummer as a famous gunfighter."

The brakeman frowned thoughtfully and muttered "Longarm, you say it might have been? That's funny. Someone on that night rattler crew from the north was just jawing about some little squirt in seersucker chasing that same Longarm out of the Denver depot at a dead run!"

Polly looked unconcerned as she replied, "We all have to grow up sometime. What if the famous Longarm has just gotten tired of silly showdowns?"

The brakeman flatly stated, "Then he's as good as dead. Once a man has established a rep as a gunfighter, he can't afford to lose his nerve."

Polly said, "The customer Pronto just had words with didn't seem all that terrified. He just walked away from a silly fight with a silly kid, if you want to know what it looked like to me."

The brakeman shook his head and explained, "Nobody's

likely to ask what it looked like to *you,* Miss Polly. Your point's well taken that a serious gunfighter may take pity on an occasional squirt. But should word get about that a man of Longarm's rep backed down within the same twenty-four hours from not one but *two* untested nobodies . . . well, do I have to go on?''

He did, because Polly said she didn't understand what on earth he was talking about. So the brakeman said, ''They all seem to lose that edge it takes after they've been through enough gunfights. That's all greener gunfighters, who still feel immortal, have to hear. The most famous but far from the only example would be Wild Bill Hickok up in Deadwood. He'd taken to drinking more and practicing with his pistols less, and Cockeyed Jack McCall wasn't the only one who'd noticed. So if McCall hadn't gunned Wild Bill in the Number Ten Saloon, it would have been some other gun waddy in some other saloon.'' He paused. ''I reckon I'll have ham and eggs,'' he said casually.

Chapter 6

Longarm had been studying his railroad timetables, and so he'd seen that if he rode on down the line to Cruces, he'd be better than forty miles further from Fort Sill and there wouldn't be a northbound for the next two days.

On the other hand, a body getting off at Spanish Flats in the chill before dawn might hire a livery mount and make it on up to Fort Sill by the time that weekly combination serving the Indian Territory ever left Cruces.

So as the moon still hung high, Longarm got off at Spanish Flats, due south of Fort Sill, thankful to be packing so little baggage for a change. Since he hadn't been planning on getting off there before he'd consulted his timetable after midnight, Longarm felt no call to worry about the few other passengers getting off at the same stop in the tricky light. He could still taste his midnight snack back in Amarillo, and he knew he'd sleep lighter if he quit while he was ahead. He knew they'd expect him to pay in advance at that hotel across the way whether he arrived with his usual McClellan and saddlebags or just this fool envelope. So he did, and in no time at all he was sound asleep in his small but tidy hired room.

It felt as if he'd slept less than an hour, but the sun was up outside as somebody commenced to pound on his locked door with a heap of authority and what sounded like a pistol barrel.

Longarm rolled out of bed in his underdrawers and grabbed for the .44-40 slung from a handy bedpost as he rose and called out, "I hear you, damn it. Who is it and what do you want?"

The pounding was replaced by; "Clovis Mason of the Texas Rangers, and we've had a complaint about you, stranger. Where did you get off signing the register downstairs as a federal deputy, by the way?"

Longarm held his own weapon politely pointed at the floor as he cracked the door, nodded at the badge on the other gent's freshly laundered white shirt, and opened wider, saying, "I signed in under my right name because that's who I am and I have nothing to hide. I am Deputy U.S. Marshal Custis Long, and I'm bound for the Indian Agency up at Fort Sill on government beeswax. I've barely talked to a soul here in Spanish Flats, and you say someone's made a complaint about that?"

The Ranger, somewhat shorter and stouter than Longarm, stepped in to regard the half-naked hotel guest dubiously and replied, "A lady says you've been following her all the way from Amarillo after you conspired with another gent to try and move in on her. I hope you have some identification before we go on with this bullshit?"

Longarm hung on to his own pistol as he moved over to fish his wallet from the duds he'd draped over a chair. The Ranger hadn't drawn his own .45-30—rangers were like that—but he'd been eyeing Longarm through narrowed lids until he spied the federal badge and identification. As his poker face got more human he said, "I'll be switched with snakes if I don't buy you're being the one and original Longarm! But why in thunder did that newspaper gal just come over to our company to charge you with mashing and menacing her all through the night?"

Longarm put his wallet and gun away and got out a couple of his cheroots and some waterproof Mexican matches as he calmly replied, "I didn't know I was. I recall her accusing me of some diabolical plot when I told a cowboy to leave her alone back in Amarillo a few hours ago. I did see her boarding the same eastbound later. If she got off here in Spanish Flats, I can see why a pretty gal who thinks she's even prettier might think I followed her all this way to gaze upon her beauty some more. But you'd think she'd give a man half a chance to get fresh with her before she pressed charges. You say she claims to be a newspaperwoman?''

Mason said, ''Our captain made her prove it. Her own identification shows she's a Miss Godiva Weaver, writing for the *New England Sentinel.* I can't say I've ever heard of it.''

Longarm handed the Ranger a smoke and struck a light for the both of them as he wearily replied, ''I have. It's one of them exposé weeklies that accuses our teetotaler first lady, Lemonade Lucy Hayes, of being a secret drinker. It's no wonder a female reporting for the rag suspects me of lusting after her fair white body.''

He got his own cheroot going and asked, ''Did she say what she was doing out our way, aside from being stalked by drooling maniacs?''

The Ranger took a drag on his own cheroot and replied with a thin smile, ''Says she was headed home with one scoop when she got a tip on another up to the Kiowa Comanche Reserve. That's what you call a latrine rumor, a scoop. When we told her we'd heard of no Indian trouble up yonder, she handed us the usual shit about big bad palefaces screwing the buffalo and shooting the women of poor old Mister Lo, the Poor Indian.''

Longarm put on his shirt as he made a wry face and said, ''I told you I'd read her rag. Lord knows there are rascals on both sides a just Lord would fry in Hell forever, but that *New England Sentinel* only knows about bad palefaces. That's doubtless why they said those three women the Ute rode off with from the White River Agency a spell back were either treated with the utmost respect or, failing that, deserved to be raped by one and all.''

Mason said, ''You don't have to instruct *this* child. I've fought Mister Lo. But fair is fair and we haven't had any trouble with the rascals since old Quanah Parker saw the light, remembered he was half white, and brung his bands in to eat more regular off the taxpaying Taibo. That's what they call us, Taibo.''

Longarm sat on the bed to haul on his pants as he resisted the temptation to explain the distinctions between the Comanche words for white folks. He didn't savvy more than a few dozen words of the Uto-Aztec dialect the Comanche spoke himself. So he neither knew nor cared exactly why they called you Saltu if they were willing to parley with you and Taibo if they were out to lift your hair. He'd never figured out exactly why a Paddy got so upset if you called him a Mick, come to study on it.

Mason didn't know anything more about the news tip inspiring a mighty suspicious newspaper gal to leap off a train out West and accuse Longarm of attempted rape. The Ranger had smoked enough of the cheroot to excuse himself by saying he had to get on back and report why he hadn't arrested or shot anybody that morning. As he let himself out, Longarm reached for his own stovepipes, saying, "Hold on. I got me at least two days on the open range to Fort Sill and as you can see, I ain't even dressed right for that much riding. Where would I go if I want blue denim, a Winchester, and a couple of ponies with the gear and grub to get me there and back?"

Mason asked if he was buying or hiring. When Longarm allowed he meant to just hire the riding stock and their harness, along with a Texas roper and packsaddle, the Ranger suggested a general store down the street to the north, with a livery that wouldn't cheat him directly across the way. So Longarm rose, they shook on it, and the Ranger left him to his own devices.

Longarm strapped on his six-gun and went down the hall in his shirtsleeves to take a good leak and wash the sleep gum from his eyes. He needed a shave, but his soap and razor were still up in that Denver baggage room, if he was lucky. So he let that go for now, went back to his room to put on the rest of his outfit, and went downstairs for a late breakfast.

As he consumed it in the back booth of a nearly deserted chili joint, he read Henry's typed-up onionskins casually a third time. Then he dropped them in a trash barrel out front as he was leaving. There'd been nothing all that secretive or hard to remember, and it was getting tedious to tote that dumb manila envelope all over.

He found the livery Clovis Mason had suggested, and evoked the Ranger's name to see if they'd treat him as a customer who might know which end of a pony the shit fell out of.

The old weatherbeaten geezer who led him out back to the

corral acted sensibly enough until they'd agreed on a couple of aging but still servicable cow ponies, a paint and a bay, both mares, and got down to brass tacks about money.

The old hostler wanted four bits a day for the hire of both the mares and the riding and packing gear Longarm would need to get him up to Fort Sill and back. That sounded reasonable. So did the old-timer's asking for a deposit against the loss of anything he hired out. But Longarm didn't think he was reasonable when he asked for a deposit of the full market price, and then some, for, say, two fine cutting horses and a spanking-new roping saddle silver-mounted.

Longarm snorted in disgust and said, "I was only aiming to ride them old plugs a week or so. Nobody said nothing about my proposing either should take my name and bear my children. I'll deposit, say, a hundred in cash for the whole shebang, and that's only on account I doubt I'll have to forfeit any of it."

The hostler naturally protested that the bridles and saddles alone would cost better than a hundred dollars to replace, and so it went until they'd settled on a deposit both found outrageous and Longarm was free to walk the two mares across to that general store, with the stock saddle cinched atop the paint and the bay stuck, for now, with packing.

He went inside to discover that, sure enough, they sold almost anything a man or beast might require out on the open range in the late summer months.

He bought some vulcanized water bags and a sack of oats for the ponies, knowing there'd be plenty of sun-cured but fairly nourishing grama to graze along the way.

He bought extra smokes and a few days' worth of canned grub for himself. It hurt to spring for a new Winchester when he knew he had an almost new one strapped to his McClellan in that baggage room up Denver way. So he bought a couple of boxes of Remington .44-40 that fit his revolver as well, and let the saddle gun go for the time being. He bought some new denim jeans, along with a razor, soap, and such. His hickory shirt and tweed vest would get him by after sundown this far south in summertime. But he figured he'd better pick up a vulcanized poncho along with the minimal bedding he might need for a night or so in the middle of nowhere much.

Once he and the shop clerk had loaded all his purchases aboard the two horses, Longarm led them on up the street until, as he'd hoped, he spied a pawnshop.

He was coming out of it a few minutes later with an older but well-kept Winchester Yellowboy, the original model with its receiver cast brass instead of machined steel. Most Indians and some cowboys still favored the Yellowboy over newer models because its rustproof receiver made up for its loading a tad slower in a setting where a gun might be tougher to strip, clean, and oil very often. The Yellowboy, like the Henry all Winchesters were based on, would shoot as fast as any other saddle gun when fast shooting was called for.

Longarm was lashing the antique weapon to his hired saddle by its stock-ring when a familiar figure in a tan travel duster and veiled hat paused on the nearby walk and declared in a self-possessed tone that she believed she owed him an apology.

Longarm finished what he'd been doing, ticked the brim of his hat to the lady, and told her he was pleased to see she'd been talking to Ranger Mason, but that no apology was called for.

As he joined her in the shade on the walk, he decided her hair was a dark shade of honey under that veil and that her eyes were hazel. He said, "I can see how it must have looked to a lady on her own late at night, Miss Weaver."

She smiled under her veil and replied, "I see I wasn't the only one talking to Ranger Mason this morning. I really do feel foolish, and grateful, now that I know you really did save me from the pest back in Amarillo. Ranger Mason tells me you're on government business, bound for the Kiowa Comanche Reservation just to the north."

Longarm nodded, since it wasn't a secret mission, but explained, "I ain't sure you could say it was *just* to the north, ma'am. I know the reserve of which we speak starts officially at the Red River, a fairly easy ride from here. But whilst the Red River forms a south boundary to the lands set aside for all those Indian nations, the ones I'm out to visit will be way closer to Fort Sill, a good forty miles or a hard day in the saddle north of the river."

She said, "That's what everyone keeps telling me. I have

to see old Chief Quanah of the Kiowa Comanche. Will you take me with you?''

Longarm laughed incredulously. It wouldn't have been polite to ask a reporter for a pesky paper why anyone with a lick of sense might want to. He just said, ''Quanah ain't much older than me. Folks take him for older because he's sort of weatherbeaten and he started so young it seems he's been whooping it up for ages. He ain't the chief of the Kiowa or even all the Comanche. He led the Kwahadi or one division of the Comanche Army during the Buffalo War. He seems to speak for more of them now because he's half white and speaks good English.''

She said she'd heard as much, and had a lot of questions to ask the big chief. So he gently told her, ''He might not be up at Fort Sill right now, Miss Weaver. I just read some B.I.A. dispatches. They say Quanah's on a sort of inspection trip of the older nations that were sort of civilized somewhat sooner. It reminds me of those trips Peter the Great took to other parts of Europe when he set out to civilize Russia.''

She started to say something about wanting to talk to some other Indian chiefs in that case. He started to tell her it was out of the question for her to come along. But then she headed him off with. ''I have to find out if there's any truth to those rumors of corruption in the newly organized tribal police. I haven't been able to get a line on whether the ringleaders are white or red or whether there's nothing to it at all.''

He said, ''Well, seeing you're bound and determined, and seeing we both seem interested in the Indian Police, we'd best see about hiring some riding stock for you, Miss Weaver.''

She said she already had her own horse and saddle awaiting her pleasure at her own hotel. So he told her to go fetch them while he went back to that general store for a few more trail supplies.

So she did, and they were riding north for the Red River of the South within the hour, which was between nine and ten A.M. Longarm was too polite to comment on her sitting her hired roan sidesaddle. Folks rode best the way they'd first been taught, and if she sat a mite forward, as Eastern folks were prone to, it wasn't as if he expected her to circle any stampedes between hither and yon. Lord willing and the creeks didn't rise, they'd make Fort Sill in a hard day's ride, and her livery nag would bear up better with her modest weight carried so.

He saw she'd lashed her own bedding across her saddlebags. She doubtless hadn't been told it was best to wrap the blankets inside a waterproof canvas ground-cloth. Folks who insisted on calling the Western grasslands the Great American Desert seemed to think rain never happened out this way.

He had to ask if she knew how to use the Spencer repeater she'd slung from the off side of her girlish saddle. She said her father had let her practice on tin cans back East when she was little. He shrugged and refrained from pointing out a .51-caliber Spencer was hardly meant for a kid's backyard plunking. He doubted they'd have any call to shoot at anything between here and the river, and once they were on the Kiowa Comanche hunting ground beyond, shooting was reserved for hunters of the Indian persuasion.

As they followed the dirt wagon trace north across over-grazed and unfenced range, even a gal from back East could see a considerable herd of beef had eased in from their right to avoid the town but make for the same river crossing up ahead. He didn't tell her how he figured the trail drive was only an hour or so ahead. She could read how suddenly cowshit dried as the sun rose high.

He found it more interesting that some outfit was still driving beef north this far east. As settlement spread westward, so the cattle trails kept shifting. All but the most westerly counties of Kansas had been closed to cattle drives by now, and most cows were following that new Ogallala Trail further west these days.

Godiva Weaver broke into his train of thought by asking him out of the blue if he could answer a question about cowboys that nobody else had been able to. He said he'd try.

She said, "I know everyone seems to feel you Westerners ride at least twice as good as the Queen's Household Guard, but it seems to me you all ride with your stirrups too long and seated too far back for your poor mount's comfort."

Longarm smiled thinly and said, "I hope you told the others you talked to you were a reporting gal. I've seen some riders act mean because someone asked them their right name."

He stared up the trail to see that there did seem a haze of dust on the northern horizon as he continued. "I've never ridden with Queen Victoria's outfit. I know professional jockeys get more speed out of a racehorse by leaning their weight forward on a flat straight course. For just like a human being carrying a pack on his back, a horse can run a tad easier with the weight across his shoulders."

She said that was what she'd meant.

He said, "There's more to riding a pony than tearing sudden and straight, Miss Weaver. To begin with, you want to stay in the saddle. That's way easier if you're balanced over the critter's center of gravity when it spins to the left or right, sometimes without your permission. Cowhands ain't the only ones who ride back a ways with a boot planted firm down either side. Cavalry troopers, polo players, and others inclined to ride more zigzaggy than some tend to sit their mounts in the same unfashionable way. It's true your mount would no doubt like to carry your weight further forward. But you see, a man who makes his living riding a horse ain't as likely to fret more about horses than his own neck."

She sniffed and said, "I've seen the way you all treat cattle out this way as well."

He wrinkled his nose and found himself saying, "I don't have to treat cows one way or another, ma'am. Now that I've a better-paying job I only *eat* them, the same as you and all your kith and kin. Next to a slaughterhouse crew, your average cowhand could be said to pet and pamper the cows he's paid to tend to. Have you ever tried to befriend a free-ranging beef critter, Miss Weaver?"

When she laughed despite herself and confessed the thought had never occurred to her, Longarm said, "Don't. Mex bull-fighters just plain refuse to face a Texas longhorn in the ring, even for extra prize money. When and if we catch up with that herd out ahead of us, don't dismount for any reason within at least a couple of furlongs. They seem to feel anyone they catch afoot was designed for them to gore and trample. I don't know what you've seen cowhands *doing* to such delicate critters, Miss Weaver. Some old boys will rope and throw an already cut and branded yearling just to prove it can be done. On the other hand, cows kill folks a lot just for practice. So I reckon it evens out. You said something before about the Indian Police up ahead acting ornery too. No offense, but to tell it true, I'm more concerned about lawmen abusing their authority than a fool cowhand abusing livestock."

They could see the river ahead of them now, with the dust from that trail herd hanging mustard yellow just above the far shore, as she said, "I told you back in town I had to get Chief Quanah's version before I decided who's behind it all. Our informant only told me big money has been changing hands, with somebody being paid a lot to look the other way. I'm sure we'll find out that the tribal leaders are innocent dupes of some crooked white men, of course."

Longarm rose in his stirrups to stare thoughtfully up the trail ahead and say, "I can't tell why from here, but that herd out in front of us seems to be milling in place on the far bank of that regular crossing. It's been dry a spell and the water ought to be low enough up the river a ways. Do you know for a fact that white men have been leading some Indians astray, or might you share the opinion of so many that Mister Lo is simpleminded as well as poor?"

As she followed him off the beaten path at an angle, Godiva Weaver protested, "My paper and I have always shown the greatest sympathy for the poor Indians, Deputy Long. We know the poor Comanche only wanted to lead peaceful lives in communion with the natural world, until selfish white men drove them to acts of desperation."

Longarm snorted in disgust and said, "That may be sympathy, but it sure ain't much respect. The Comanche up ahead learned to ride a generation ahead of most other Horse Indians by watching the early Spanish do so, helping themselves to some horses, and teaching themselves to ride better. In no time at all they were the terror of the Staked Plains, and pound for pound they've killed off more of the rest of us, red or white, than all the other Horse Indians combined. They'd be mighty hurt to be dismissed as posey-picking poets back in the days they still recall as their Shining Times."

He made for the silvery surface of the Red River, more clearly visible through the streamside cottonwood and willows now, as the newspaper gal said, "Everyone knows they were great warriors if forced to fight."

To which Longarm could only reply with a laugh, "Nobody ever had to force a Comanche, a Kiowa, an Arapaho, or South Cheyenne to fight down this way. All the plains nations, and the Comanche in particular, gloried in blood, slaughter, and horse thievery. I know they were more in the right than usual when they rose up against the buffalo hunters a few summers ago. The Indians had been cut down enough by cannon fire to go along with Washington on West Texas hunting grounds no bigger than a state or so back East. So those greedy hunters should have left them and what was left of the south herd alone. But the Indians could have saved themselves a heap of casualties in the end if they'd dealt with the trespassers less gruesomely."

He waved his free hand expansively to the north and added, "So that's why we've set up Indian Police wherever the Indians are halfways willing to enforce the B.I.A. regulations more constitutionally. It costs way less salary and resentment to swear in tribal members as uniformed federal lawmen than it might to post white military police at every agency. I've been asked to see just how well they've done so up around Fort Sill. You were saying they ain't been doing it so well?"

She nodded primly and replied, "We were tipped off to brazen bribe demands by the Comanche Police. Apparently they can be paid to look the other way no matter what a white crook wants to do on Indian land, if the price is right. Or contrariwise, they might arrest you for singing improperly, just to shake you down!"

They were closer to the river now. Longarm pointed at the water just ahead and observed, "The river runs too deep for our fording yonder. Let's ease upstream a ways. Indian Police don't have authority to arrest white men. They can prevent a felony in progress and turn white crooks over to the nearest white lawman. Otherwise, their orders are to report non-tribal evildoers to their agent or somebody like me."

She suggested, "Maybe the whites they intercept on or about their reservation don't know that. Anyone with a badge and a gun can stick out his chest and bluff, whether he has the legal authority to act that way or not, right?"

Longarm spied a stretch of water that seemed to be simmering to a boil a furlong upstream and said, "That stretch looks no more than stirrup deep. But let me go first anyways. Poorly trained or greedy lawmen of all complexions have been known to abuse their authority. Bluffing a paid-up Texican white man out of a bribe might not be as easy for an Indian. But like the old church song says, farther along we'll know more about it."

He led the way cautiously down the crumbling bank. The paint he was riding entered the water gingerly, but didn't put up half the fuss the bay did until he'd dragged it into the shallow water a ways.

Godiva Weaver's roan was either better-natured or else it was smart enough to see the two ponies ahead of it weren't drowning. So they were all soon across the medium-wide and mighty shallow Red River of the South in no time.

As they rode up through the timber along the far bank, Godiva asked how far ahead the Kiowa Comanche reserve was, and when he told her they were on it, she allowed she'd expected a fence or at least some signs posted.

Longarm said, "A lot of folks seem to. An Indian reserve ain't a prison camp, no matter how some Indians act. It's a tract of land set aside by the government for said Indians to live on, undisturbed and not disturbing nobody. It's usually the smaller reserves you'll find posted like private property. Everybody knows Texas is supposed to start just south of the Red River, and like I said, most Indians served by the Fort Sill agency would want to camp closer."

She asked, "Then what are those wigwams doing down that way?"

Longarm reined and stood up to stare soberly eastward along the riverside tree line. He could see all those cows still milling amid billows of trail dust, and atop a slight rise beyond the trail, there was surely a ring of the conical tents the Eastern gal had just misnamed.

He said, "That's a tipi ring, Miss Weaver. A wigwam is the same thing made out of bark and mentioned by someone speaking Algonquin. Tipi seems to be a Sioux-Hokan word for lodge or dwelling, but all the plains nations who live in 'em seem to use tipi or something close. The question before the house ain't what they are but what they might be doing yonder. You just heard me say why I'd hardly expect a Kiowa or Comanche camp this far south."

He unfastened his recently purchased and fully loaded Yellowboy and heeled his mount into a thoughtful walk as he mused aloud, "The trail hands in charge of that herd seem perplexed too, seeing they don't seem able to move their cows past them Indians."

As she gingerly followed, Godiva hauled her own saddle gun up to brace it across her upraised right thigh as she asked if this was really any of their business.

Longarm soberly replied, "Ain't none of *your* beeswax, ma'am. I'm paid to be sort of nosey. So why don't you rein in here and leave it all to me?"

She said she was paid to be nosey too. But at least she hung back a couple of lengths as Longarm handed her the lead line of the pack pony and forged ahead.

He hadn't forged far when he made out about twenty riders, nine in literally half-ass blue uniforms with their bare tawny legs exposed, and eleven white men dressed more cow-camp. The bunch of them seemed to be arguing about something between a drawn-up chuck wagon and the tipi ring dominating the trail ahead from its rise. Far less formally dressed Indians were watching from up yonder. As Longarm rode in, he got out his badge and pinned it to the front of his vest.

As he'd hoped, that seemed to keep either side from shooting at him. As he got within easy shouting range, the gray-bearded trail boss seated on a buckskin pointed at a sort of haughty Indian Police rider and wailed, "Praise the Lord the B.I.A. sent you to talk sense to these savages, Marshal! This fool Comanche thinks we have to pay him a dollar-a-head trail toll, and I got better than nine hundred head here!"

As Longarm joined them, the sergeant in charge of the long-haired but cavalry-hatted Indians looked downright surly until Longarm said, "Quanah Parker and the combined tribal councils have set the price at a dollar for passage with grazing, and two bits an acre a season for just grazing. Lots of big cattle spreads charge more, and they have full permission from the Bureau of Indian Affairs. So I'm sorry as hell, but that's just the way it seems to be."

The Indian sergeant beamed and said, "I know who you are. We were told you were coming to talk to us about our blue shirts. I am Tuka Wa Pombi. I did not see why we needed a Taibo to tell us anything. But my heart soars to see they have not sent us a fool."

The grizzled trail boss protested, "The two of you are surely talking foolish about this herd me and the boys are supposed to deliver up Fort Sill! I ain't packing anything like nine hundred dollars, and even if I was I wouldn't owe it to no blamed Comanche! The Comanche or at least their blamed agency already *owns* all these cows! They've been bought and paid for off our Running X spread in Baylor County, for purely Indian consumption, and whoever heard of the jasper *delivering* the goods having to pay a blamed delivery fee?"

By this time Godiva Weaver had reined in just a few paces away, looking as if she expected to be introduced to everybody. Longarm could only hope she'd understand his apparent rudeness. The trail boss nodded and ticked his hat brim to the lady. None of the Indians seemed to see anyone there. He knew they weren't trying to be hard-ass. Like most warrior breeds, Comanche weren't supposed to start up with a stranger's woman unless they were fixing to offer plenty of ponies, a good fight, or both for her. Allowing you'd noticed a woman but didn't mean to bid on her was an easy way to get into a fight whether her man had wanted to trade her or not. The notion a stranger would sit still for another man just sort of looking was a deadly insult to all concerned.

Longarm turned to Tuka Wa Pombi and asked if he knew what an I.O.U. was. The Indian said he did but made Longarm explain it twice lest he miss any of the details. Once he'd grasped that the Taibos were ready to part with some of their paper medicine that could somehow be turned into solid silver, he agreed an I.O.U. was better than an all day standoff.

The Running X trail boss insisted, "I ain't good for any nine hundred dollars worth of credit! I don't make that much in a year, and if I did I wouldn't be able to save it all, the way prices has riz since the war."

Longarm said, "Make it out in the name of the original owner of this beef and oblige him to settle up with the new owner, Chief Quanah Parker of the Comanche Nation. Then let the two of them work it out."

The trail boss started to object, blinked, went poker-faced, and then got out a tally pad and a pencil stub as he said, "I follow your drift."

So a few minutes later the chuck wagon crew was leading out to the north, followed by the wranglers herding the remuda of spare ponies. Then, a ways back, came the *madrina* or judas cow, trained to lead the way and naturally followed by the herd, six or eight critters abreast, with the flank and drag riders yipping softly but constantly to keep them moving.

Longarm and the newspaper gal watched a spell, and then Longarm suggested they circle wide and head on up the trail ahead and alone. Godiva had no call to argue. She'd already heard cows moved between eight to sixteen miles a day, and she knew she could get further than twenty miles a day on foot in dry weather and good shoes.

Longarm set a somewhat faster pace, trotting their ponies a few furlongs, walking them about a mile, and letting them water, graze, and rest a good twenty minutes every time the trail crossed a wet draw. There were more of those than usual this far east. Despite all the belly-aching on the part of Mister Lo and the opposition newspapers, the rolling grasslands and timbered watercourses the government had reserved for this patchwork quilt of Indian nations was far from the sterile desert some held it to be. When Godiva commented on some late-blooming wildflowers along the trail, Longarm said, "The grass grows taller and thicker than out where the buffalo roam much more numerously even in these trying times. After all that blood and war paint wasted a few summers back to save the south herd, and despite all the Kiowa or Comanche dreams of a last big reservation jump, there ain't enough buffalo left to support that many Indians."

He stared off to the east across the miles of open range as he added, almost to himself, "Funny how fast the buffalo thinned out. Back home in West-by-God-Virginia the elders told tales of buffalo running wild through the woods and even smashing down log cabins on occasion. The Eastern herds were gone well before my time, of course. But you could still hunt buffalo along the banks of the Mississippi just after the war."

She laughed in a superior way and declared, "There's no mystery as to who's hunted the buffalo almost to extinction in the few years since the invention of the repeating rifle! The supply of buffalo robes and bone meal might have lasted indefinitely if white men hadn't been so selfish! Why didn't they just buy them from Indians?''

Longarm got out a fresh cheroot and, seeing she didn't smoke, lit up before he muttered, ''I used to see things that clear and simple. Poets reporting Indians never killed more buffalo than they needed never hunted buffalo with Indians. A pack of contesting riders running a buffalo herd downed every buffalo they could and, wherever possible, ran the whole herd off a cliff. Then they held one swamping supper and stuffed themselves with grease running down their chins till they all got sick. But more than half the meat still spoiled, even after the dogs had eaten a heap. I've heard all those sad stories of white hide skinners leaving buffalo carcasses scattered across the prairies to rot. They're true. A man making as much off one buffalo hide as them cowhands back yonder make after two days in the saddle ain't inclined to conserve wild game.''

He blew smoke out his nostrils and continued. ''Professional hide hunters seldom used repeating rifles, by the way. The tools of their trade were the single-shot Big Fifty with a telescope sight.''

The Eastern girl grimaced and said, ''I stand corrected. The game hogs shot off all those buffalo one at a time. What about the rights of the Indians to their traditional game?''

Longarm shrugged and said, ''Nobody back East had any use for a buffalo hide skinned the traditional Horse Indian way. They sat the dead critter up on its belly, like a big old hound by the fire, and skinned it by cutting along the backbone. They either didn't know how or didn't want to preserve the fur for a lap robe. They held that a rawhide skin, preserved their greasier way with brains and tallow, should have the softer belly skin in the center. For all I know they were right. But no white folks back East would pay any three dollars and fifty cents for such a hide. They wanted 'em dried flat, untreated, with the thickest back fur down the middle. After that, it depends on who you ask about the Horse Indian's traditions.''

He reined in and stood in the stirrups to stare back the way they'd just come as he continued. "What the Indians call their Shining Times was one of those golden boom times, like the beaver trade or the New England whaling industry before Drake's oil wells back in Penn State. Mister Lo got the horse and fanned out across these plains as a wondrous new species *after* the white man and the horse got to these shores and multiplied some. They figure 1700 as the earliest date you'd have noticed any substantial numbers of Indians on horseback, and the buffalo were already in trouble. They were butchering 'em fast as they knew how before they *had* the horse, let alone the guns they admire just as much as we do."

She insisted, "There are still far more white men and they have killed far more buffalo."

He nodded soberly and said, "That's the way things work. If it was the other way, or if just Mister Lo and his horse and gun had been left to shoot the buffalo off, he'd have managed. Or it would have *looked* as if he'd managed. A spell back I was riding herd on these ancient bone professors up around the headwaters of the Green River. They told me these swamping giant lizards called dinosaurs had roamed out this way long before either us or any buffalo. And yet there they all lay, dead for a coon's age. So what do you reckon wiped *them* out?"

Godiva laughed incredulously and demanded, "How should I know? Some ancient species of animals have simply gone extinct. Everybody knows that."

Longarm settled back in his saddle as he replied, "I know mankind has been trying to wipe out the coyote, the rat, and even the bitty housefly for as long as anyone remembers. So there must be more to this extinguishing business than meets the eye. The coyote and more'n one breed of deer have been holding up swell under the same hunting pressure. So it might be something *else* we've been doing. Both red and white old-timers have told me the buffalo used to migrate like geese, north or south from the Canadian Peace River to the Rio Grande, as the grazing got better or worse. But now there's a north herd and a south herd, both dwindling, staying north or south of the Union Pacific's main line east and west. Must make it tough for a buffalo momma to raise her calf when it gets too cold, or too dry, on what still looks like a sea of grass to us.''

Then he casually handed her the pack pony's lead and told her, ''I'd like you to ride ahead for a spell. The trail ahead is plain as day. So you can't lead us too far astray.''

She took the lead from him, but naturally asked how come. He told her, ''May not be nothing, but I'd best bring up the rear with this old Yellowboy for now. Can't tell whether it's a kid from that tipi ring, an innocent traveler on the same trail, or something worse. But he, she, or it is raising just enough dust to make out from here, and every time we change pace, that dust does the same.''

Godiva gasped, ''Good Lord, you think we're being followed?''

To which Longarm could only reply, ''That's about the size of it.''

Chapter 7

The old sod house seemed to be melting like chocolate under the afternoon sun as it stood knee-deep in tawny grass atop a rise to the west of the trail. Before Godiva could ask, Longarm swung the bay he was now riding around her and softly called out, "Stay here whilst I scout it. If I'm riding into anything, drop that lead and ride back to those Texas trail herders fast."

Then he moved on up the grassy slope to within easy pistol range of the apparently deserted soddy, covering its gaping doorway and unglazed window spaces with his Yellowboy. He reined in and dismounted near a rusted-out but handy seed-spreader moldering in the weeds and grass of many a summer. He tethered the bay mare to the rusty draw-bar and moved in zigzag on foot to dive through a window space instead of the doorway, roll upright on the grass growing in the roofless interior, and allow at a glance he had the one-room ten-by-twenty-foot interior to himself.

He went back outside the easier way and waved Godiva and the other two ponies in as he strode down to retrieve that bay. By the time he had, the newspaper gal had joined him. So he said, "There's nobody here but us chickens yet. We'd better hole up inside them bullet-proof walls until we see just who might be following us."

That made sense to her. As they got all three ponies inside the hollow shell, Godiva asked if he had any idea what it was doing there.

He'd had time to think about that. So he told her, "Any telltale trim or hardware was carried off by salvagers a spell back. These sod walls don't look halfways old enough for Spanish times. Without roof eaves to call their own, the only thing shedding the winter wet would be that thatch of dandelions and such topside. Indians pitch their tipi rings atop rises such as this one when the weather's hot and even a south breeze is better than nothing. But they camp down in timbered draws out of the wind in wintertime. Those Indians who live in houses nowadays usually pick a southeast slope, halfways down. The only folks who'd have perched a prairie home smack atop a rise like this would be white folks who had plenty of winter fuel to burn."

As he was watering the three ponies in one far corner, Godiva said she'd understood all the land around for miles to be an Indian reservation.

Longarm explained, "That's likely why the folks who squatted or homesteaded here moved on. We're well west of the original Indian Nation. This government-owned land was ceded to the Comanche and such after Quanah Parker brought 'em in and surrendered in the bitter spring of 1875. He and his raggedy little army of Comanche, Kiowa, Arapaho, and South Cheyenne had scared the army almost as much as the army had scared them with field artillery at Palo Duro Canyon. So once the cold and hungry but still armed and dangerous Indians had agreed to behave their fool selves betwixt the Washita and the Red River, the government would have cleared anyone else out."

Standing closer to the doorway, with her Spencer repeater held at port arms, Godiva quietly said, "Deputy Long, there seem to be some Indians coming."

Longarm made sure the three ponies were securely tethered as well as unsaddled, with plenty of watery oats in their nose bags, before he moved over to join her, thoughtfully levering a round into the chamber of his own saddle gun.

The quartet of Quill Indians sitting their ponies across the trail were bare-chested and had feathers and paint along with their braided hair and rawhide war shields. All but one had his legs encased in dark-fringed leggings. Longarm told the worried white girl beside him, "Kiowa. Black Leggings Society. That's something like the Lakota Dog Soldiers you may have heard tell of."

She hadn't. Lots of folks who gushed over noble savages didn't seem to know much about them. He said, "Suffice it to say the Black Leggings boys take whatever they may be up to sort of seriously. I'd like you to move across to a back window and let me know if you see anyone moving in on us from the far side. We'll know in a minute whether the ones already exposing their position mean to parley or charge across that trail at us. They're likely still trying to decide."

He was pleased to see how briskly she took up her position at one of the two rear windows, with her trim tailored duster and veiled hat somehow adding to her almost military bearing. But as she propped her elbow in an angle of the dry sod to train her old Spencer across the draw behind the abandoned homestead, she asked him in a puzzled tone, "Aren't the Kiowa supposed to be settled peacefully on this big reservation? Why on earth would they want to charge anybody?"

He held his Yellowboy more politely, muzzle down, as he stood exposed in the doorway, saying, "You just heard me tell you they looked undecided, ma'am. More than half the Indian trouble you've ever heard of was the result of one blamed side or the other making some thoughtless move the other side misunderstood. Them old boys across the way may be as confounded by the sight of us as we are by the odd way they're acting. This *is* the Kiowa Comanche Reserve, after all, and they may just be wondering what us Saltu are doing on it."

Then he smiled thinly and added, "At least, I *hope* they have us down as nothing worse than Saltu. See anybody out back?"

She replied, facing the other way, Lord love her, "Not a soul for at least a quarter of a mile, with no timber on the next ridge over. How long are we supposed to just stand here like this?"

Longarm answered, "As long as they seem to have us pent up in here with the odds on our side. They can see we're behind stout cover with repeating rifles. Whether they were there or not, they'll have heard of a place called Adobe Walls, an old trading post over to the Texas Panhandle, where charging white guns firing at you from cover turned out to be a bad move. Twice.''

She said, ''I read about those fights at Adobe Walls. In the first one Kit Carson and those army troppers had some cannon with them. In the second fight for Adobe Walls, the place was being held by a big party of professional hunters armed with scope-sighted rifles!''

Longarm said, ''Same deal. The Indians outnumbered them way more than we're outnumbered, unless we haven't seen all them Black Leggings yet. There's no way four riders could make it down off yonder rise and as far as this doorway with me lobbing sixteen rifle rounds and five from my pistol at 'em.''

She showed how keen a reporter she was by demanding, ''Don't you carry six bullets in that six-shooter, Deputy Long?''

He replied, ''Not if you value your own toes, ma'am. It's best to grab for a double-action aimed down along your own leg with the hammer riding on an empty chamber. I got a double-shot derringer in my vest pocket, by the way. Would you like to borrow it till we see how this turns out?''

She said, ''I don't see why. I've seven shots in this rifle.''

Then she *did* see why, and soberly added, ''I guess a hand pistol would be surer at the end. Is it true the best way is to suck on the barrel like a lollipop and just pull the trigger?''

He said, ''I wouldn't know. I've never committed suicide yet.'' Then he got out his derringer, unhooked it from his watch chain, and tossed it in the grass near the hem of her travel duster as he added, ''Don't blow your brains out just yet, ma'am. Seeing the boys across the way seem stuck for ideas, I'd best try to commence the parley. I have to lay this old Winchester aside to talk with both hands. So keep a sharp watch out back.''

She didn't turn, but had to ask, ''Talk with both *hands*?''

He leaned the Yellowboy against the inside sods as he explained. ''Sign talk. Hardly anyone speaks Kiowa. It ain't close to any other Horse Indian dialect. So it was the Kiowa themselves who invented the now universal sign lingo of the plains.''

He stepped just outside the doorway, raising his right hand

with trigger and middle finger pointed at the sky to signal friendly notions. Then he pivoted his upraised palm to say he had a question, pointed at them, and made the sign for calling before he cupped a hand to his ear, adding up to, "Question, you are called? I want to hear." Which was about as tight as sign lingo worked.

Behind him, Godiva Weaver called, "What's going on out there?"

To which he could only reply, "Nothing. They're staring smack at me but they don't seem to want to answer."

She suggested, "Maybe they're not Kiowa after all."

He shrugged and said, "Wouldn't matter if they was Arapaho, Caddo, or Shoshoni. All of 'em use the same sign lingo no matter how they talk. That's why sign lingo was invented to begin with. Think of how a nod, a head shake, or a stuck-out tongue meant the same things by different names to an Anglo, a Mex, or a Dutchman. Then lard on a mess of other such signals until . . . Kee-rist!"

Then he threw himself backward through the doorway as a rifle spanged in the distance to send a buffalo round humming like an enraged lead hornet through the space he'd just occupied.

Longarm rolled sideways to grab for his propped up Yellowboy as, behind him, Godiva Weaver cut loose a lot with that Spencer.

He didn't ask what she was firing at. He warned her not to waste any as he popped up in the corner of a front window space to prop his own rifle over the soggy sod sill.

He found no targets for his overloaded Yellowboy. The far side of the trail had been hastily vacated by the sons of bitches who'd replied so rudely to his request for a parley.

He moved over to the newspaper gal's position, saying, "Change places with me. You've only got two rounds in that Spencer now. So see if you can reload as you guard the empty slope."

Then he saw what she'd been aiming at out back, and whistled in sheer admiration as he made out the three bodies scattered in the tall dry grass. He didn't see anybody moving out yonder now. He still trained his own rifle on the view to the west as he told her flatly, "Three stopped with five rounds is what I'd call downright swell marksmanship, Miss Weaver. Where in thunder did you learn to shoot so fine?''

She answered simply, "I grew up on an army post. My father was stationed at Fort Marion after the Seminole had calmed down. It was awfully hot for most sports. So we spent a lot of time on the rifle range.''

Longarm watched the scattered brown forms out back as he slowly concluded, "You surely must have. You either killed the three of 'em totally or scared 'em so bad they're afraid to draw breath now. Were they charging mounted or afoot?''

She demurely replied, "On horseback, of course. There were five of them. I'd have gotten them all if they'd been coming slower!''

He said he believed her, and asked how they were doing out front. She said, "Not a sign of life. They must have thought their main body could move in past a mere girl as they kept you distracted from that other side. But I guess they've learned their lesson, and I'll just bet that's the last we'll ever see of them!''

He said, "Don't bet next month's salary or your favorite hat on that, Miss Weaver. They're still out there. The leader who got 'em in this mess would never be able to show his face at a dance if he just cut and run. They have to stick around until dark, if only to see if they can recover their dead.''

He started to say something else. But he figured she had more than enough to worry about. So he held the thought.

It didn't work. A gal paid by a newspaper to think on her own two feet had gotten good at it. In a desperately casual tone she asked, "Is it true Plains Indians never attack at night, Deputy Long?''

To which he could only reply, "Never is an overconfident word, and my friends call me Custis, Miss Weaver.''

She said, "In that case you'd better call me Godiva. For anyone can see you're the only friend I have for miles right now! What if we made a break for it just after dusk? I don't see how just the two of us could defend this hollow shell against an all-out attack in total darkness, do you?''

Longarm said, "Nope. But it's barely high noon, and that leaves us nigh eight hours to figure something out.''

She brightened and said, "You mean you do see a way out

for us, other than a running gunfight against odds or digging in to be dug out like cornered clams?''

He chuckled at the droll picture and replied, ''Nope. I only said I had around eight hours to study on it. I agree with you on the only two choices we seem to have, Miss Godiva.''

Chapter 8

By late afternoon the interior of their roofless shell was an oven, and Godiva had removed her travel duster to reveal a sweat-stained frock of brown paisley cotton. She'd set her veiled hat aside as well, but left her hair pinned up to let her neck sweat all it wanted. Longarm had been right about her hair being a dark shade of honey, and if she looked a mite more mature without that veil, she was still on the brighter side of thirty. Some kindly old philosopher had once remarked, doubtless in French, that a woman was ripest just before she commenced to wrinkle.

He didn't see what good that was likely to do either of them as he stood at a window space in his shirtsleeves, sweating like a pig as he soberly stared through the shimmering heat waves at nothing much.

They'd long since told one another the stories of their lives, and he was starting to feel testy every time she asked him if he'd come up with any answers yet.

When it came, like most good answers, the answer was childishly simple. They heard a distant mouth organ wailing a plaintive tune about pretty quadroons, and Godiva gasped, "Good heavens, you don't think that's some Kiowa playing like that, do you?"

Longarm drew his six-gun and fired all five shots in the wheel at the cloudless sky above. So her ears were still ringing as he explained, "Time, tide, and trail herds wait for no man.

But at least that Running X outfit won't ride into any ambush."

Godiva clapped her hands and said she'd forgotten about that trail drive they'd forged on ahead from. Longarm went on reloading as he replied, "I hadn't. But I never expected them to make such good time."

The mouth organ music had faded away. Longarm climbed up on a sod sill to stick his head over the top of the south wall. Sure enough, he could just make out the gray canvas top of that chuck wagon against a settling haze of trail dust. So he called down to Godiva, "They've paused to consider their options about half a mile back along the trail."

He dropped down beside her to add, "No sense offering my head up yonder for target practice, now that I have everybody placed."

She glanced at the three sweaty but saddle-free ponies across the one grassy room as she asked whether he thought they ought to try running a blue streak for those nice Texican cowboys.

Longarm shook his head and replied, "Just said I didn't want to present them with tempting targets. I don't know about the younger riders with him, but that trail boss is an old-timer who knows he's on Kiowa Comanche range. Having heard way more shots than any jackrabbit hunter would let fly, he'll likely bunch his cows in that cottonwood we passed through just before we spied this soddy. Then he'll have his best riders scout ahead until *they* spot this soddy. By that time those Indians will have made up their minds whether they want to stand and fight or slip away discreetly. Don't ask me which choice is more likely. Next to Kiowa, Comanche and even South Cheyenne can be paragons of sweet reason. That buffalo war that got so many Comanche killed was started by Kiowa taking the bit in their teeth and challenging the whole U.S. Army to a stand-up fight on open prairie."

Godiva started to say she'd heard the poor Indians had been provoked into that suicidal uprising of the early 1870s by nasty white men. But recent events had given her a new perspective on at least *some* Indians. So she held the thought for now.

A million years went by. Then, through the rising heat shimmers, Longarm spied a Texan on foot with his own saddle gun at port atop that same rise the Black Leggings riders had been on earlier. So he let fly a cattle call and stepped out in the open, waving his hat until the cowhand spotted him and waved back.

Nobody ever figured out how those three dead bodies out back had managed to vanish in broad daylight. But by the time they had it all scouted safe around the soddy, the only Indian sign for miles seemed to be one feather and a whole lot of horse apples. The trail boss had to agree with Longarm that sometimes birds just flying over had been known to drop a feather that signified nothing much.

By now the sun was getting low, and old Harry Carver, as the trail boss introduced himself more formally, decided the timbered banks of Cache Creek, just to the east, were as handy a night campsite as he was likely to find. So Longarm and Godiva saddled their ponies and rode there with Carver and the four riders he'd chosen to scout ahead with.

That chuck wagon had crawfished down off the skyline along with the cows, of course. They'd wound up in the brushy draw that ran north and south in line with the drier trail. By this time the cook and his helper had rustled up a supper of sourdough bisquits, mesquite-smoked ham, and black-eyed peas.

Everyone had time to tend their riding stock first, and to her credit and despite her prissy sidesaddle, Godiva Weaver knew how to settle her mount in for the night, although she borrowed some oats from Longarm to do so. She said she hadn't been planning on the way to Fort Sill being so far.

Longarm didn't tell her you always had to figure on an easy ride stretching out some. For he could see she'd already learned that.

As the sun went down and the crickets started chirping in the trees and brush all around, they were seated side by side on an old fallen log, eating from tin plates and sipping coffee from clay mugs while, somewhere in the gathering dusk, that plaintive mouth organ began to moan about Aura Lee. Longarm nodded at the tailgate of the chuck wagon across the clearing and observed, "They're about to serve the last of the coffee, Miss Godiva. I'd be proud to fetch you another mug, if you'd like."

She shook her hatless head and replied, "I'm afraid I'll be too wound up to sleep tonight as it is. So much has happened all in one day, and I'm just now starting to relax. You *did* say it was safe to relax now, didn't you? It's so peaceful down here with all this company, and I've always loved this twilight time of the day."

Longarm glanced up at the gloaming sky through the cottonwood branches and replied, "Everybody seems to. This English traveling man who'd spent time in East India told me one time the Hindu folks call this time of day the Hour of Cow Dust, and I had to agree that sounds sort of poetical too, albeit I don't see why it ought to."

She nodded and said, "I do, now that all those longhorns have settled down amid the trees after a long hot day on the trail. The dust has just about settled now. But you can still smell just a hint of it as the cool shades of evening creep in all around us. Where am I supposed to sleep tonight, by the way?"

Longarm smiled thinly and said, "In those blankets lashed to your saddle, of course. I'd invite you to climb into my bedroll if I wanted my face slapped. Harry Carver ain't asked, but I'll have to offer to stand my own turn as night picket. Finish your grub and we'll see about finding some soft ground upslope to spread out our bedding."

She didn't argue, although she seemed a tad uneasy a few minutes later as Longarm indicated a shallow hollow between two trees as her best bet to get a sort of rugged night's rest. He noted her dubious look and said, "Forget anything you might have heard about piles of leaves. Dry leaves are dusty, don't really pad a hip bone worth mention, and they can keep you awake all night as they rustle every time you twitch. A couple of thicknesses of wool over bare dirt work way better."

She asked about the still-green leaves above that were ripe for easy plucking. He shook his head and told her, "Not as much padding as you'd think. Also, they draw bugs and stain your bedding. Half the trick of sleeping on the ground is sleeping on one side or the other with your knees drawn up. It's only where you grind a bone against the firm mattress that you wind up sore."

She dimpled and replied, "Thank you for not implying I

was just a trifle mature across the hips. Where will *you* be reclining, on one side or the other, all this time?''

His own bedroll still across the arm that cradled his Yellowboy, Longarm pointed with his chin at another clear space a few paces off and said, ''I was figuring on unrolling her yonder, past that clump of rabbit bush, unless you're worried it's too close for your own comfort, Miss Godiva.''

She shook her head and softly replied, ''It's a little *far*, as a matter of fact, should anything go boomp in the night around here. Isn't it funny how glades that appear so pretty in the glow of sunset can look sort of ominous after dark?''

He said, ''The almanac says we'll get at least a half-moon later tonight. I'd best spread my own bedding before I go see when Harry wants me to stand guard.''

It only took him a few seconds to unroll his own bedding at an angle on the wooded slope. But once he had, Godiva was already down atop her own blankets, moving her trim but soft-looking hips in an experimental way as she decided, ''I see what you meant about bones.''

Longarm just strode off down the slope, wishing women wouldn't do that. He'd met that well-read and so-called sophisticated type of spinster gal before. You'd think independent single women who'd learned to talk like that suffragette leader Virginia Woodhull would know better than to talk bolder than they really meant to be around men. Miss Virginia Woodhull was always raving and ranting about the way men hurt women's feelings, as if men didn't have feelings themselves.

He found the trail boss jawing with some others around the small night fire near the chuck wagon. Carver seemed to think it was swell of a deputy marshal to bear his own share, like a dollar-a-day rider. When Longarm pointed out that he and Miss Weaver had been coffeed and beaned after their rescue from wild Indians, Carver allowed he could stand the first watch—along with three others, of course. So that was the way he spent the next four hours with his Yellowboy as the darkness fell and kept on falling. Neither the stars nor that moon the almanac had promised showed at all that night. For an overcast moved in from the west as the sun went down, and just kept coming, till the night air was downright clammy and Longarm was starting to worry about getting soaked to the skin before he could get to that vulcanized poncho atop his bedding.

But there was neither thunder nor enough back-wind to matter when, around a quarter to midnight, a gentle rain commenced to patter all around as he ghosted through the trees along his quarter of the far-flung picket. Carver had suggested, and they'd all agreed, it made the most sense for the dismounted picket guards to circle wider than the night riders holding the herd down in the draw. Any Indians out to lift stock, or hair, would be more inclined to creep in on the sounds of the mounted hand further down the slopes, whether they knew what he was making all that noise about or not.

Young Waco, the kid who played that mouth organ, had been replaced by a tenor of the Mexican persuasion who kept singing to the cows about a *cielito lindo,* or pretty little patch of sky, despite the way the real sky was acting.

The cows didn't care. You sang softly to a herd at night to keep them from spooking at more sinister night noises. It was only on a vaudeville stage, or maybe in town on a Saturday night, that anyone ever sang those whooping and hollering Wild West songs, lest they see the last of their herd stampeding over the far horizon.

The rain had soaked Longarm's shoulders downright uncomfortably by the time someone called his name and he was relieved by a cowhand smart enough to start out with a rain slicker. So he was peeling out of his wet shirt and vest as he moved downslope to his bedding with a rude remark about the weather. He tossed his wet hat atop the rainproof poncho, but hung on to his wet duds as he proceeded to slide into his roll.

Then he said, "What the blue blazes?" as Godiva Weaver gasped, "Oh, it's you. You startled me!"

Longarm said, "That makes two of us," as he slid on in beside her, noting how warm and damp it all felt at the same time. It was his bedding the two of them were under. So he felt no call to ask her permission.

She said, her breath warm on his wet face, "When it started to rain, I remembered you were smart enough to bring along a rainproof bedroll. I've stuffed both my own blankets and my silly self in here, and it still feels just a bit too firm under my poor tailbone, thank you very much."

Longarm could only mutter, "I noticed it was mighty warm in here. A mite crowded too. The only way the two of us are going to fit comfortably will call for you to let me stretch this one arm under you so's you can rest your head in the hollow of my shoulder."

She cooperated in the contortions it took to settle them, his peeled-off wet duds, and his shooting irons into a more or less comfortable position as the wind and rain picked up.

He said he was sure glad he'd made it back just in time to save himself from the cold shower he deserved.

Snuggled against him with the edge of the poncho pulled over both their heads, Godiva shyly confided, "Maybe we could both use a cold shower right now. I don't mean to pry, but where did you ever get all these muscles I can feel now that you've shed your clothes above the waist?"

Longarm shrugged the bare shoulder her head was resting on and replied, "Pure misfortune, I reckon. I'd have never worked half as hard growing up if I'd been born into wealth instead of a hardscrabble patch of West-by-God-Virginia. Had I wound up alone in here, I'd have slid these damp jeans off my muscular hind end as well."

She laughed girlishly and demurely said, "Well, don't let *me* stop you, you big damp silly."

He considered her words before he soberly replied, "Unless you mean that sort of naughty, this is pushing past flirty into cruelty to animals, Miss Godiva."

She answered simply, "I'm never cruel to animals I'm fond of, Custis. What's the matter? I know I'm almost thirty, and I told you how that mean thing broke off our engagement. But he said it was because I wouldn't quit my job at the *Sentinel,* not because he found me disgusting in bed!"

So Longarm had to prove he didn't find her disgusting by kicking off his boots and jeans, moving her thin cotton frock up above her trim waist, and just rolling his own naked body between her welcoming thighs.

He didn't ask her how come she'd removed all her underthings to crawl into a male traveling companion's bedding. But she confessed she'd been gushing for him since before sundown as she finished the chore of shucking her frock over her head while he proceeded to put it to her.

It was a good thing she was as wet as she'd said inside. For she was tight as a girl in her teens despite her mature curves, and when Longarm tried to hold most of his weight off her, in consideration of the packed earth under her friendly tailbone, Godiva bounced her soft rump even friendlier and told him not to hold back, but to crush her, crush her, crush her. Gals who read a lot tended to talk like that when they were screwing.

After she'd been crushed enough to come more than once, Godiva wanted to get on top. So he let her, and didn't object when such a frisky little thing said it was awfully stuffy under all that vulcanized canvas and threw the poncho down to straddle him bare-ass in the gentle rain. For it felt swell to lie there, kissing both her cool nipples in turn as the rain ran off them while, below the waist, the two of them felt warm and wet as hasty pudding.

By the time Godiva bounced herself to climax and collapsed atop him, her bare back had gooseflesh and he had to roll her over on her back, haul up the covers, and warm her up some more. Then he rummaged around near the bottom of the bedroll till he found a dry feedsack he'd packed away as a towel, hardly expecting to use it for such delightful drying.

He figured they'd just doze and cuddle with the rain gently tapping on their vulcanized cover. But Godiva seemed to be crying as she rested her damp head on his bare shoulder.

Longarm didn't ask why. No man who'd slept with more than one woman in his life would be dumb enough to do that. So just as he expected, Godiva finally volunteered that she just didn't understand what had just gotten into her.

He said, "Aw, come on, I ain't built *that* unusual, honey."

She giggled through her tears and replied, "Yes, you are. But I've no complaints about that. I'm just so ashamed of practically begging for it. Whatever must you think of me, Custis?"

He patted her bare shoulder and said, "That you wanted some almost as badly as I did? What just happened was natural as falling off a bronco. I'd be more concerned for the both of us if we'd just fallen asleep like babes in the wood, assuming said babes were way the hell younger than either of us."

She sighed and said, "It's true I'm a more experienced woman than I like to admit. I guess you could tell there's been more than one man in my unusual life."

He said, "Why, no, I figured you learned to screw so fine from reading romantic books. Have you read that new novel by Mister Zola about that frisky French gal Nana? I'll bet you hundreds of young gals are trying out those wild positions Nana and her frisky female roommate got into in that one chapter right this very minute!"

He chuckled and added, "Gives a man a hard-on just to picture those two pretty frustrated things trying to screw one another without a pecker to their name!"

Godiva reached down between them to gently take the matter in hand as she sniffed and said, "At least *we* don't have that problem. I'm not sure I want to be compared to Emile Zola's fallen women of the Paris underworld."

As she started to jack it up for him, she added, "I'll have you know I don't do this with every man I meet!"

"Nor I with every gal," Longarm primly replied as he found himself rising to the occasion. Then he moved his own free hand down her smooth belly to part her damp pubic hair with skilled fingers as he murmured in a more serious tone, "Don't give away all the magic by telling me all your secrets. You don't really want to know who taught me to strum your old banjo like this, do you?"

She sobbed, "Jesus, that feels good! Just keep that up until I'm almost there, and finish me off with this lovely thing I have in my own hand! I promise, I won't say a word about anyone else!"

Chapter 9

So a good time was had by the both of them, all the way up to Fort Sill. A good time at night anyway. Days on the trail with a herd of cows could get tedious.

It could have been worse. The Running X had contracted to be paid by the head, half in advance and half on delivery. So Harry Carver was only worried about getting them up the trail alive. With Quill Indians still skulking out yonder, for all they knew, that made for a faster pace than most market herds were driven. But less than a dozen drovers could only get cows to move so fast, and so the one day's hard ride on horseback stretched out to almost another seventy-two hours on the trail, meaning two more nights bedded down to one side after dark. Godiva could really get acrobatic on a clear cool prairie night with no covers in the way and nobody but Longarm to watch her wriggle and jiggle.

He wriggled and jiggled a heap himself, of course, but by the third night he was tempted to ask her to quit showing off and just enjoy it with him. For, not unlike that Nana gal in Mister Zola's sassy novel, she seemed to be working harder to pleasure him than to please herself, and while he was getting it all free and had no call to compare her with the hookers in that book, he recalled with some discomfort how they only relaxed and let themselves go all the way with old pals they felt more comfortable with.

He tried to make her feel more comfortable with him. During the sunlit hours on the trail he let her ride along beside him as he rode flank for old Harry Carver, and despite riding sidesaddle, the newspaper gal and erstwhile army brat got to where she could head off a straying yearling pretty fairly. When complimented, she sniffed and said it was no great wonder they called gents who did this as a full-time occupation cow*boys*. Longarm was too polite to start a stampede and show her how a top hand was occasionally called upon to earn his forty a month and beans.

It was after dark, with her duds off, when Godiva reverted from high-toned Eastern gal to dirty past the line of duty. Longarm had to draw the line their last night on the trail together when she sucked it hard again for him.

He demurred, "We're bedded down on a grassy rise with that water down in the creek too crowded for a midnight dip, honey."

She insisted, "I don't care. I've never had anyone built like you in me before, and I want to say you came again and again."

She said, "Let me get on my hands and knees, like a puppy dog, while you ravage me!"

So he did.

But when they finally rode into Fort Sill late the next day, he could sense a certain coolness in her manner, even before she broke free of the outfit to gallop on alone toward the cluster of frame barracks and outbuildings clustered around a flagstaff in the distance.

Longarm didn't chase after her. Aside from knowing how dumb a man looked chasing skirts at full gallop, he knew Harry Carver and his Running X riders could use all the help they could get right now. For like cowboys, although for different reasons, cows tended to get excited in the vicinity of any settlement. So you had to work harder to keep a herd together as you drove them on in.

But just as the cows were really commencing to act up, as was only to be expected, a dozen-odd riders came down the trail to head them off. As they rode closer, most of 'em seemed to be Indians or breeds, dressed like fringy cowhands. But their straw boss was a white civilian working for the B.I.A.

As he reined in by Harry Carver he explained they weren't supposed to drive the fool herd into the Fort Sill Parade, but downwind, to some corrals Chief Quanah had just flung up for the stock.

When Harry pointed out how he understood the beef to be meant for Kiowa consumption as well, the B.I.A. rider nodded but said, "It sure is. But try getting a damned Kiowa to feed himself like any grown child. Chief Quanah has his Comanche meeting us halfway. He ain't but half Indian, you know. His momma was a white gal, carried off and raped by hostiles whilst on her way to California with a wagon train."

This was not true. But Longarm only cut in to introduce himself and ask where Chief Quanah might be at the moment.

When the B.I.A. man suggested Quanah Parker might be visiting with his white uncle, Judge Isaac Parker, at Fort Smith, over beyond the Cherokee Nation, Longarm knew he didn't know. As any lawman had to keep in mind, witnesses who didn't know all the facts tended to fill in the blanks with guesswork.

Instead of saying this to a man who worked at Quanah Parker's own agency, Longarm asked the way to that agency. The B.I.A. man explained their main base was up in Anadarko, with a liaison post at Fort Sill and then substations further out in all directions on the sprawling Kiowa Comanche Reserve. So Longarm allowed he'd start at the fort, seeing how the army would want a report on that shootout in any case.

He shook hands with Harry Carver, rode back to pick up his hired paint and packsaddle, and rode on as the Running X riders drifted the herd around to where they wanted it.

Like Fort Cobb to the northwest or Fort Reno due north, Fort Sill had been built more as a small town for lots of soldiers than what Eastern folks pictured when they thought of a frontier outpost. Laid out in haste to enforce the treaty of Medicine Lodge with field artillery and the Tenth (Colored) Cavalry, Fort Sill had been neatly built on a dead-flat stretch of prairie where the grass grew stirrup-deep as well as emerald green well into summer.

This, as any plainsman, red or white, could have told you, was because the big grassy flat was a seasonal marsh, with the parade a boot sucking quagmire in wet weather.

A rare engineering officer of color, with the unlikely name of Henry Flipper, Second Lieutenant, U.S.A. Army, had salvaged the impractical site with ingenious drainage works, including the famous channel now called "Flipper's Impossible Ditch" because an optical illusion made it seem as if water was running uphill after a heavy rain.

These moatlike ditches, along with enough fencing to keep man or beast from falling in, made up such perimeter defenses as they thought such a big garrison, backed by cannon and Gatling guns, was likely to need against sane Indians. Most of the really *crazy* Kiowa and Comanche had gone under in that last big buffalo war.

Longarm rode through the official "Hog Farms," the tolerated shantytown you usually found outside such an outpost's gates. A sleepy white trooper posted by the gate to give directions, it being an open post, waved Longarm on to the nearby guardhouse, where he could report in to the Officer of the Day. The cheerful young O.D. said the Tenth Cav had just left for the border to stalk Apache, and that neither he nor any of the other recent replacements from the East had heard a thing about Longarm's mission. He had a clerk take down Longarm's account of that brush with apparent hostiles and said that they'd file it, but that he suspected some young bucks had just been drinking.

The O.D. said they'd take care of Longarm's riding stock, and ordered one of his enlisted men to show their guest to the hostel set up for such surprises. It was across the dusty parade, between the sutler's store and officers' mess. The enlisted clerk inside showed Longarm to a tidy spartan room, handed him the key, and said they were already serving supper. So Longarm tossed his saddlebags and rifle on the bed, dug out his razor and a cake of naptha soap, and then got to work at civilizing himself.

It wasn't true they had running water in every guest room, but they did have indoor plumbing, with separate facilities for ladies and gents, out in the hall. So Longarm treated himself to a warm tub bath and shaved his jaws cleaner than he'd been able to manage along the trail, even in mixed company.

Then he put on a fresh shirt and that somewhat rumpled but far more prissy tweed suit, with a shoestring tie. He had to tell the desk clerk who he was when next he appeared in the lobby.

They had no hotel dining room because civilian guests were such rare events. The clerk explained tidy white civilians got to grub at the officers' mess next door, and that he'd best get cracking if he expected his mashed potatoes warm.

He thanked the enlisted man for the suggestion and got right over to the officers' mess. An orderly by the door took his name down, and said the meal would cost him eighteen cents.

Longarm payed without arguing. He knew that despite the way some raw recruits bitched about rank and privilege in the army of a fool republic, the officers paid for their finer food and fancier beer hall out of their own pockets. So eighteen cents was a bargain for the fine steak, mashed spuds, choke-cherry pie, and extra coffee he wound up with.

He asked an orderly how come he seemed to be eating alone at such an early hour. He was told everyone had headed up the line to the officers' *club,* another proposition entirely.

Every officer arriving on a post was assigned to a place in the officers' mess and had his meals docked from his pay. But their club amounted to a private lodge. There was a noncommissioned officers' club on most big posts as well. Nobody had to join up and pay dues at either, if he didn't give a shit about promotion in this man's army. Lower-ranking enlisted men and thrifty sergeants got to drink non-alcohol beer or soft cider at the sutler's store. Commissioned officers got hell or worse for hanging out there with their troopers.

Longarm glanced into the sutler's as he passed the saloon-like swinging doors. He spotted some visitors dressed cowboy or Indian at the tables inside. But none of the Rocking X riders had made it in from wherever they'd gone with those cows.

Longarm found the officers' club at the far end of the line, set on a corner angle to catch such summer breezes from the south as the fickle weather out this way allowed. As he mounted the steps to the wrap-around veranda he heard music. It sounded like a banjo, fiddle, and pennywhistle doing an Irish jig through Georgia. But when he got inside, the big dance floor was bare. The Irish-sounding trio in U.S. Army blue was jigging away in a far corner. Officers in dress blues and ladies in frilly summer dresses were seated at tables along the walls or clustered around the punch bowl and toy sandwich tray on a trestle table closer to the front. Longarm caught a couple of haughty looks as he handed his hat to a trooper by the door and approached the refreshment stand. Some of the gals looked surprised to see him too. But none of them managed to stare as snottily as your average second lieutenant. The army of a democratic republic made up for its low pay and slow promotions by allowing its officers to act like little tin gods, fooling with one another's goddesses as often as possible.

Before any shavetail could ask him who he thought he was, Longarm spotted Godiva Weaver holding court at another table in the company of a saturnine civilian in a fringed white elkskin jacket, a florid gray-haired officer with the silver eagles of a bird colonel on his epaulets, and a once-pretty redhead who'd gone to fat and didn't seem too happy about the attention the younger beauty seemed to accept as her due.

Godiva didn't greet Longarm as if he was the lover she'd begged to cornhole her the other night. But she looked as if butter wouldn't have melted in her mouth as she introduced Longarm all around.

The lean civilian was a liaison man from the main B.I.A. agency a day's ride to the north. His name was Fred Ryan. The colonel and his lady were the Howards of Ohio. Longarm was too polite to ask what had become of Colonel Ranald Mackenzie, who'd won the buffalo war, or Brigadier Ben Grierson, who'd accepted the Indians' surrender here at Fort Sill and had to feed them. Colonel Howard pointed to the one empty chair at the table and told Longarm to sit a spell, adding, "We're waiting for the cool shades of evening before we risk any polkas in wool pants. Miss Weaver here just told us about you nailing those Kiowa down near the Red River."

The B.I.A. man said, "I'm not surprised this is the first we've heard of it. Had they lifted your hair, they'd have never been able to keep from bragging about it, and we do have some few informants among both nations. I reckon the inspired leader who led them into such a dumb fix doesn't want to talk about his spirit dreams now."

Longarm said, "I reckon not. I understand the Comanche beat that old medicine man with whips after Adobe Walls, and would have killed him if Quanah hadn't stopped them. The medicine man's vision had assured him that nobody in that big party of professional hunters could hit the broad side of a barn with a Big Fifty scope-sighted out to a mile. Might you know a Comanche police sergeant called Tuka Wa Pombi, by the way?"

Fred Ryan frowned thoughtfully and replied, "Can't say I do. The breed who keeps the roll for Quanah's new police force over at their sub-agency would be the one for you to talk to."

When Longarm asked where he might find Chief Quanah himself, he lost a bit of respect for those fancy fringes and Comanche beadwork, even though it was Godiva who gushed, "You were right about Chief Quanah touring the other agencies to see how the more established tribal governments work, Custis. Mister Ryan here thinks the best place to head him off would be Fort Smith, just the other side of the Cherokee Nation. He has a great-uncle holding court there."

Longarm cocked a brow at Ryan and demanded, "Quanah Parker has a great-uncle working at the Fort Smith federal courthouse?"

Ryan nodded confidently and asked, "Who did you think old Judge Isaac Parker was, his great-aunt? It's a well-known fact that after the Texas Rangers rescued Quanah's white mother from the Indians, her uncle, Isaac Parker of Texas, took her in despite her shame."

Longarm laughed incredulously and said, "I've seen that in print too. But it's a fine example of what we in the outlaw-hunting profession call leaping to conclusions from disconnected evidence. I can't say whether Cynthia Ann Parker had an uncle named Isaac or not. But Judge Isaac Parker of the Fort Smith federal court is only in his early forties as we speak, and comes from Missouri, not Texas. So it don't add up as soon as you put all the figures down."

He resisted the impulse to reach for a smoke in the already damp and stuffy surroundings as he added, "I ain't as certain as the Texas Rangers that they rescued anybody, speaking of leaping to conclusions. Would anyone here care for a glass of punch? I don't know about you all, but them cool shades of evening had better get cracking."

Both gals at the table agreed they could go for some refreshing. But when he rose to go fetch three glasses, the colonel's lady, the plump Elvira Howard as she was called, got up to come along, saying he'd have trouble managing three glasses and that she'd been looking for an excuse to stretch her poor limbs.

Longarm didn't care. They walked over to the refreshment stand, and he ignored the toy sandwiches since he'd just had supper. But as he'd hoped, the ruby-red punch smelled of rum. For while enlisted men were forbidden hard liquor on post by the Hayes Administration, rank had its privileges and rum punch was one of them.

As he filled a glass and handed it to Elvira, she declared, for no good reason Longarm could see, "If I were kidnapped by Indians I'd kill myself before I'd let myself be ravaged and be forced to bear halfbreed babies like that white-trash Cynthia Ann Parker!"

He filled two more glasses as he quietly observed, "The Parkers of North Texas were considered quality, Miss Elvira. They owned land and didn't owe back taxes. As for letting herself be ravaged, that ain't exactly the way Miss Cynthia Ann might have seen it. She'd been captured as a little girl and adopted by a Comanche lady who liked children. She'd spent eight or nine years growing up amongst 'em, and it was only after she'd been initiated as a full-grown Comanche woman that the distinguished war chief Peta Nocona courted her fair and proper, playing his nose flute at her and reciting all the wondrous coups he counted. It sounds like bragging to us, but Horse Indians seldom lie about their deeds or riches."

He put the ladle back in the punch bowl and picked up both glasses as he added, "Cynthia Ann could have said no. But I reckon she figured Peta Nocona was a good catch, considering. He married up with her as honorably as an Indian knows how, and by all accounts he never treated her mean. The couple had two sons, Quanah had a younger brother they usually call Pecos or Puma because his real name would be improper to say in mixed white company. Back around '60, just as the War Between the States was starting, the Rangers raided the Comanche for a change, and took back Cynthia Ann and a baby daughter called Topsannah. Her white kinfolks were happier about all this than she was. In less than five years little Topsannah had died, and the lonesome white captive who'd spent a quarter of a century as an Indian died soon after. Some say on purpose, whilst others say she just pined away.''

As they headed back to the table Elvira quietly declared, ''At least she had *some* fun out of life before time's cruel teeth caught up with her! I can't see myself *marrying* even a handsome Indian, but I guess a Comanche camp would be more diverting than . . . My God, why can't the entertainment committee come up with something *new* once in a while!''

Longarm didn't have to answer. They were already within earshot of the table. Longarm handed Godiva her punch and he and Elivira both sat down. As they did so they saw the conversation had drifted back to that shootout at the abandoned ruins. Ryan seemed to hold that his Kiowa had doubtless been out to make some point. He agreed they were harder to figure than the more progressive Comanche, but to his credit as an Indian agent, he held few Indians ever attacked for no reason at all.

Colonel Howard, who sounded as if he'd been at some rum without the fruit juice and such, snorted, ''Oh, no? What about that ornery old Kiowa devil called Satan? He was the one who stirred up all the troubles starting in '70, wasn't he?''

Ryan gained more ground in Longarm's eyes by gently pointing out, ''Big Satanta and crazy old Satank might have translated their names as White Bear and Sitting Bear. Neither one invited those white buffalo hunters to collect hides on hunting grounds ceded to the Indians in the Medicine Lodge Treaty of '67.''

But Longarm knew old broken treaties were as tedious to hash over as whether Adam or Eve had sinned the most. So he sipped some punch, finding it strong enough but way too sweet, and opined, ''I've been ambushed on my way to an assigned chore before. I don't mean to boast, or imply Miss Godiva here ain't prettier than me, but somebody here at Fort Sill sent for me to smooth out some wrinkles in your Kiowa Comanche Police and—''

''We don't *have* any Kiowa on the force,'' Ryan said quickly. ''Under Quanah, the Comanche have drilled in corn and agreed to give beef instead of buffalo a try. But we haven't been able to recruit many Kiowa. They sneer and call other nations woman-hearted if they meet the bureau halfway. Then they cry like babies and demand government supplies because they won't give farming a chance and, big as it is, this reservation simply isn't big enough to feed substantial numbers on hunting and gathering alone!''

Longarm nodded soberly and replied, ''I just said that. I've been on other reserves where holdouts begged for increased allotments and complained the Great Father was trying to murder them because their agent wanted to vaccinate their kids and teach them how to read and write. The old-timers ain't just stupid. They're afraid they'll lose their hold on their tribesfolk if they don't keep control of the older medicine, the traditional chants, and where the next meal might be coming from.''

Ryan nodded and said, ''Quanah and the other Comanche leaders have managed to hold on to their authority and still get their kids vaccinated against the pox. Quanah's improved his own English, learned to read and write, and they say some of his white relations down Texas way have started to brag on him.''

Godiva Weaver said, ''I can't wait to meet him now that I know he's neither as old nor as stern as he looks in those published tintypes.''

Then she caught Longarm's amused expression and quickly added with flushed cheeks, ''To interview for my paper, I mean. Maybe he can tell us why those Kiowa attacked us.''

Longarm shrugged and said, ''I thought I'd go ask the Kiowa at their own agency tomorrow.''

Ryan laughed incredulously and said, ''You won't even get them to speak English to you, even though a lot of them know how!''

Colonel Howard looked confused and declared, ''You can't ride out to the Kiowa alone after they just tried to kill you. We can give you a cavalry escort, if you really think you can get anything out of the treacherous devils!''

Longarm shook his head politely and replied, ''Thanks all the same, Colonel, but it's been my experience you get even less out of sullen Indians when you make 'em feel proddy. We all know the elders are either in control of their young men or they ain't. If any Kiowa who's at all high on the totem pole gave orders to have me stopped before I got here, he'll know I got here. Sometimes silence can be golden when a lawman knows how to question a suspect.''

He took a sip of punch and added, ''Any old-timer who's *lost* control of his young men might be way more willing to complain about it. Didn't General Sherman and Agent Haworth get a Kiowa chief to bear witness against Satanta and that medicine man, Mamanti, at the end of the buffalo war?''

Ryan nodded soberly and said, ''The chief was Kicking Bird, and he pointed out two dozen heap-bad Injuns to save the rest of his band at the end. Then Mamanti cast heap-big medicine, likely arsenic, and Kicking Bird kicked the bucket. The Kiowa are one of the few Horse Indian nations who go in for political assassination.''

Colonel Howard muttered, ''Mean as hell. Sorry, ladies. Nobody can hold a candle to Comanche when it comes to blood and slaughter. They were a bigger nation, ranged further out from the mountains, and got into fights with Texicans first. So they perforce soon learned to fight more scientifically than anyone but, possibly, Cheyenne. Cheyenne got to digging trenches and reloading their own spent cartridges in the end. But before he saw the light, Quanah Parker led his boys as cleverly as if he'd gone to West Point. The Kiowa never progressed past dirty. Quick, sneaky raids and, as Mister Ryan just said, resorting to poison like red versions of the Borgias!''

By this time it didn't feel any cooler, but it had gotten darker outside. So Elvira Howard interrupted the discussion of Indian warfare to gently but firmly tell her husband, ''If the dancing is ever to get under way this evening, don't you think the colonel and his lady had better take the floor?''

Colonel Howard didn't argue, but from the way he lurched to his own feet as his plump wife rose, he was one of those gents who held his rum better while sitting down.

As the older couple moved out on the empty dance floor, Ryan said something to Godiva Weaver, and the next thing Longarm knew he was seated at the table alone. But he didn't care. Like most men, the tall deputy mostly danced as an excuse to grab on to a gal for the first time. He found it perfectly logical that few men really liked to dance with ladies they'd already slept with or never meant to. As the dance floor filled with swirling couples, he figured any gal left over along the walls would be somebody's wife, somebody's daughter, or mighty ugly. So, having finished the sickly punch and wanting a smoke, he got up and headed out to the downwind veranda.

Nobody else seemed to care, and it was cooler and more peaceful out there in the semi-darkness as he smoked a cheroot and that louder dance music played in one ear while, off in the distance, someone was playing "Cotton-Eyed Joe" on a mouth organ. It sounded like that Running X rider who'd been serenading them along the trail north out of Texas. Harry Carver and his boys were likely sipping non-alcohol beer or soft cider down at the sutler's. Although as in the case of the rum punch inside, hard liquor could always find its way onto a post no matter what Lemonade Lucy Hayes got her husband, the President, to say.

Longarm blew a thoughtful smoke ring as he pondered that notion. He knew how the Reed-Starr bunch over by Fort Smith ran stolen stock and moonshine in and out of the Cherokee Nation. But that shabby clan of trash whites and Cherokee breeds didn't act like Quill Indians, and went out of their way to be nice to the Indian Police.

On the other hand, if Quanah Parker's Comanche Police were less willing to be bought off, and someone was worried about an experienced white lawman teaching them more than they already knew . . . That worked, up to a point. The point where things got tough to picture was where, in any direction, a Black Legging rider sporting feathers and paint loaded up on rotgut. Anyone running substantial amounts of liquor would be running it in for the troops. There were close to a thousand soldiers out here, all drawing at least thirteen dollars a month, and while Indians like to drink at least as much, they wouldn't have as much money to spend on such forbidden pleasures.

Longarm blew another smoke ring and muttered, "Then what edge would anyone acting sullen in buckskin have over a friendly Indian, mayhaps with a job on the post, when it came to peddling moonshine to the thirsty peacetime army?"

He became aware the dance music had stopped inside when some others came out on the veranda, not to join him but to cool off. He saw Godiva and old Ryan, speaking of buckskins, but they were down a ways and he had no call to pester them. Old Ryan was acting mighty attentive, and he'd likely told the newspaper gal already that he'd have his own quarters close at hand, doubtless more luxurious than a spartan room at that guest hostel.

Godiva must have told the B.I.A. man she wanted some of that swell rum punch. For she was suddenly alone as Ryan ducked inside again.

Longarm stayed where he was, and sure enough, the newspaper gal moved down along the railing to join him, saying, "Fred Ryan has just offered to wrangle me a seat on the B.I.A. mail ambulance bound for Fort Smith tomorrow morning."

Longarm nodded and replied, "You told me down in Spanish Flats you were out to interview Quanah Parker. I reckon it's possible for you to catch up with him in Fort Smith. He'd got to be out there in *some* direction. Meanwhile he's expected back *here* some time or the other."

She sighed and said, "Fred told me you'd probably say something like that. I naturally didn't tell him about . . . our getting sort of silly on the trail. But he seemed to take it for granted that I was sort of . . . under your influence."

"You no doubt straightened him out on that," said Longarm with a thin smile. It had been a statement rather than a question, but the honey blonde sighed and said, "It's not as if we'd made a lot of promises, Custis. We all say silly things when we're . . . excited. But we never agreed our . . . friendly feelings meant anything permanent, did we?"

Longarm saw Fred Ryan down the veranda, looking confused with a glass of punch in each hand. He told Godiva, "Your ride to Fort Smith is looking for you. Do us both a favor and move it on down to meet him, honey. I follow your drift, and you have to be an elderly English fop to carry off those sophisticated scenes you womenfolk seem to get more out of."

She started to say something else. Then she laughed, like a mean little kid, and turned away without another word.

As he watched her flounce down the veranda to get her rum punch, and Lord only knows what else before the night was over, Longarm had to laugh at himself. For while one part of him was just as glad it had ended so carefree, another part of him couldn't help feeling a mite used and abused, the way a lot of gals had felt, no doubt, when the shoe had been on the other foot.

As Longarm turned the other way, he spied the plump Elvira Howard just down the veranda rail, fanning herself fit to bust. As their eyes met he just nodded in passing. It would have been rude to ask a lady how much of that conversation she'd grasped. There wasn't a speck of doubt she'd been listening.

Making his way around to the main entrance, Longarm went back in just long enough to get his hat. For as the dancers swirled inside the poorly ventilated club, the mingled smells of sweaty army blue wool and cloying perfume would have been a bitch if he'd anybody of his own to dance with.

He knew any gal he started up with in the shantytown just off the post was as likely to get him in trouble as some officer's wife or daughter at the fool dance he'd just left. So he decided it might not kill him, just this once, to get on back to his hired room and turn in early alone, the way they kept telling him he ought to.

Chapter 10

Neither non-alcoholic beer nor soft cider was any more tempting than rum punch. But that familiar mouth organ slowed Longarm down as he might have passed the sutler's.

Glancing through the swinging doors, he saw Harry Carver and some other Running X riders, mixed in with about as many troopers, quietly admiring the kid who was playing "La Palmona" now by the cold stove in the center of the combined shop and canteen.

He went inside to join them, partly because it was still a bit short of his usual bedtime, but mostly because Billy Vail paid him to be nosey and everyone passing by an army post usually spent more than a few words of gossip at the sutler's.

Nodding to Harry and the others he knew, Longarm strode on to the rear counter and asked the old geezer behind it for a fistful of his usual smokes and some waterproof matches, if they had them.

The sutler was able to fill both orders and still give him change for his silver cartwheel. It would have been rude to ask right out if they sold anything harder than the soft drinks approved by Miss Lemonade Lucy. He figured he'd just order a beer, bitch about the way it tasted, and see what happened.

He suspected it might not work when, pouring a tin cup of the suds that was not yet fermented and hence still sweet, the sutler asked him if he was by any chance that famous federal lawman everyone had been talking about earlier.

Shooting a morose glance at the riders who'd likely been gossiping about him, Longarm allowed he was Deputy U.S. Marshal Custis Long.

The beer tasted sort of tangy, as if there might have been a hint of alcohol somewhere among the suds, as the sutler nodded and said, "Just as well young Quirt McQueen and some soldiers blue went on out to Shanty Town for some real liquor, I reckon. I know the kid's all talk, but sometimes he don't know when to stop and—"

"The little shit said he was after you, Longarm!" Harry Carver shouted as he rose to join them. "I told him you might be by to say adios. That's doubtless what inspired him to tear-ass off across the parade to scare folks in Shanty Town."

Longarm frowned uncertainly as he sipped sweet suds and ran the handle through his brains in vain. When he said he had no memory of any feud with anyone called Quirt McQueen, the sutler explained, "He rides shotgun messenger aboard the mail ambulance as it runs from the Anadarko Agency to Fort Smith by way of here. He would have it known he killed a man in Dodge, whether anyone remembers him in Dodge or not."

Longarm cocked a brow and softly remarked, "Dodge ain't all that far from Anadarko now that you mention it."

The sutler snorted, "That's what I meant. Quirt's staying here overnight, to ride on with the B.I.A. dispatches along with the mail in the morning. Somebody told them about that Indian trouble you-all had down to the south. Quirt said you'd likely thrown down on innocent Kiowa because he knew for a fact you were a four-flushing show-off."

Harry Carver nodded and said, "He told us you'd bullied him and made him lick spit over in Dodge one time because he'd been a lot younger and everyone had told him you did wonders and ate cucumbers."

Longarm put the rest of the insipid non-alcohol beer aside as he insisted, "I don't know anyone called Quirt McQueen or, hell, Quirt anything that makes a lick of sense."

He lit one of his new cheroots to get rid of the sweet taste, and then he stated firmly, "It's not my habit to make anyone lick spit for no good reason. You say this sworn enemy I can't seem to recall is spending the night here at Fort Sill?"

The sutler nodded, and made Longarm feel better by explaining the two-man ambulance crew would be bedding down across the way at the B.I.A. installation, assuming young Quirt didn't get lucky in Shanty Town. He made a wry face and added, "All but a few of the higher-priced whores on the far side of Flipper's Ditch were servicing the Tenth Cav until just a few weeks ago. But Quirt's a breed and he likely thinks any white gal is a step up from his sisters."

Longarm dryly observed, "I take it you are neither an admirer nor afraid of this Quirt McQueen, Mister . . . ?"

"Vernon, Ed Vernon, and you take it right." The sutler replied as he reached under the counter, adding, "I can't abide big-mouth gun waddies who never shoot off anything but their mouths! If I've told that kid once I've told him a dozen times not to make war talk around here if he's only looking for innocent merriment!"

He brought up a bottle of thick brown glass and quietly began to fill three shot glasses as he grumbled on. "I've seen dumb bragging matches shift from bluff to bloodshed in the wink of an eye, and a couple of times stray rounds came perilously close to these tired old eyes. The last time Quirt got into one of his swaggering snits, I thought we were going to have us a dead breed and a couple of hung darkies on this post. It was all I could do to talk a couple of Tenth Cav into overlooking the babbling of a bratty kid. Fortunately, they liked grown-up liquor too."

Longarm gingerly tasted the amber liquor he'd been offered and had no doubt in his mind as he gravely pronounced, "Maryland rye. The real stuff. No moonshiner born of mortal woman ever sold you anything as fine as this, Ed."

The sutler smiled innocently and replied, "I never said any such cuss ever did. Do I look like the sort of fool who'd serve moonshine on a military reservation to a federal lawman? You'll note I've only *served* you gents, from my own private stock. I'd have to call any man who said I'd *sold* him hard liquor a liar."

Harry Carver looked puzzled and allowed he failed to see all that much difference, since Miss Lemonade Lucy had declared Fort Sill a dry post.

It was Longarm who explained. "She did and it is. The

administrative order signed by her husband forbids the trafficking in or possession of strong drink by the surrounding Indians or the troops posted here to make 'em behave. Neither commissioned officers nor us way less disciplined civilians are required by federal law to follow the stern Articles of War nor tedious Army Rules and Regulations to the letter."

One of the closer cavalry troopers, possessed of a keen nose, got up to drift over, grinning, as he quietly asked, "Do I smell the aroma of rye whiskey coming from this corner, Mr. Vernon?"

The bottle had already vanished. But Ed Vernon made no attempt to hide or polish off his own glass as he gravely replied, "If you did it was your misfortune and none of our own, Trooper Baily. We can serve you our beer or we can serve you soft cider. It was your own grand notion to sign up for a hitch, not mine.

The cavalryman told Vernon to do something that didn't even sound like fun, and went back to hear some more mouth-organ music. Ed Vernon chuckled and said, "It's the few native-born Americans we have the most trouble with. Most of the new recruits are German or Irish greenhorns who never read the U.S. Constitution or heard that a trail hand starting out can make twice as much as any soldier blue and drink like a grown man whilst he's at it."

Longarm didn't care. He told the sutler in a friendly but firm way, "I'm paid to ask questions, and so I'm asking you politely where you get this rye whiskey and how much you keep on hand here."

Vernon smiled easily and replied, "I have no secrets from my dear old Uncle Sam. I just told you I ain't been selling, and I only keep enough for my ownself and my pals. As to where it comes from, I send back East for it and have my hired help pick it up with other wares at the railroad freight dock at Atoka, about a hundred and sixty miles to the east and about as close as the Missouri, Kansas, and Texas Line ever gets to this dusty swamp."

Longarm half closed his eyes to draw maps in his mind as he sipped the fine whiskey. He had no call to ask why Vernon sent away for such private stock. He nodded thoughtfully and said, "That railroad stop at Atoka would be in Chocktaw country on the far side of the Chickasaw reserve. What happens when your whiskey comes to a reservation line?''

Vernon looked blank, then replied, ''It crosses it. Ain't no exact lines drawn across the the buffalo grass betwixt here and Atoka. You just ride or drive 'till you're on or off any fool reserve. How come you ask? Ain't no way to get lost on an established wagon trace.''

Longarm waved his empty shot glass at the trail boss beside him as he explained. ''Harry and his cows got stopped by your Indian Police at the reservation line to the south the other day. They said they'd been told to collect a toll on such wealth on the hoof. Yet you say a man can drive in from the east with a wagonload of valuables and those blue shirt riders don't say boo?''

Vernon shrugged and replied in an easy tone, ''You have to meet up with riders before you can say what they might have to say. I can't recall me or my boys meeting up with any of them Indian Police on the trail save to say howdy. They ain't allowed to pester white folks.''

Longarm knew that, strictly speaking, this was not true. But he didn't want to get into the complicated federal regulations giving the Indian Police limited authority on their own range. So as he stood there thinking hard, Ed Vernon got out that bottle some more to pour three more drinks as he said a mite uncertainly, ''Quanah Parker has never tried to impose no import duty on the goods I sell to his own as well as these troops—at a fair price and modest profit. If ever a fool Indian *did* try to shake me down extra for the fees I already pay the government for my sutler's license, this child and all his goodies for sale would be long gone!''

Longarm said, ''I'm sure the Army and the Indians already know that, Ed.''

Vernon said, ''I can tell you there's no Comanche police patrols along the western reservation line. That's Kiowa country, and not even Quanah can make Kiowa toe the line. They say it all goes back to when some Kiowa followed a younger and wilder Quanah up to Adobe Walls, along with some Arapaho and South Cheyenne. They say the experience made a Christian out of Quanah and disillusioned the Kiowa considerable. As the leader of the largest contingent, Quanah got to lay out the plan of attack, with the help of his private medicine man. But to make up for that he let the Kiowa under White Bear and Lone Wolf lead the charge, anxious to count coup."

Longarm cut in. "We all know what happens when seven hundred riders charge across wide-open short grass dotted with prairie-dog holes at professional riflemen with telescope sights. If we could move it on up to the here and now, you're saying those police patrols are a sometime thing, with at least the one we rode into way closer to an open shakedown than I'd allow if I was running things."

Harry Carver shrugged and pointed out, "You told me when we first met that they'd sent you to straighten out an Indian police force. I don't see what's so mysterious about 'em needing guidance, old son."

Longarm grimaced and put a hand over his empty shot glass to decline a third shot as he said, "I'd best ask them about that in the morning then. Maybe they know something about those wild and woolly Kiowa we brushed with as well. Meanwhile, I reckon I'd best just sleep on it. So I'm calling it a night if it's all the same with you gents."

Vernon simply bade him good night. But Harry Carver followed him out on the plank walk to say, "Me and my boys will be riding back to Texas tomorrow. So it's been nice meeting up with you if we don't meet for breakfast. What are you aiming to do about that kid who says he has it in for you, pard?"

Longarm said, "Nothing, the same as he figures to do about me for all his war talk. I must have missed a recent dime novel by Ned Buntline. For I met up with another such asshole in Amarillo not too many nights ago."

The grizzled train boss spat out into the darkness and opined, "There seems to be a lot of that going around since the papers first began to rank gunfighters as if they were competing athletes. Is it supposed to score higher if you beat a lawman to the draw instead of just another mean drunk?"

Longarm smiled thinly and replied, "War talk about a sober paid-up lawman is not only impressive but safer than, say, starting up with a morose cuss such as Clay Allison or Johnny Ringo. Either one would be delighted to blow you away and claim self-defense. But pests I keep bumping into seem to have boned up on what that High Dutch philosopher Nietzsche describes as the tyranny of the weak. That's the way women, servants, and hardcases with a yellow streak get to sound off against gents they don't really want a fair fight with. A snotty schoolboy's safer sticking his tongue out at the teacher than the schoolyard bully. An armed and dangerous drunk in Dodge is safer challenging a sober lawman than another mean drunk. Neither that kid acting big in Amarillo a few nights ago nor this Quirt McQueen here on a dry army post really expected a grown man to slap leather on 'em just for acting like fool kids!"

Harry Carver thought, shrugged, and decided, "You must be right. I'd doubtless pistol-whup either one of the little shits if they was to talk like that about *me*!"

Longarm didn't want to go into all the bother it was after you got into a gunfight and won. He yawned on purpose and allowed he had to get a few winks before he rode over to the main Comanche agency in the morning. So they shook on it and parted friendly.

Longarm strode into the guest hostel to find nobody at the key desk. He didn't care whether the orderly had ducked out to take a crap or lit out for the night. He had his own key in a side pocket of his frock coat. So he just went on up to the top floor.

He found the hall dark, with the wall lamps trimmed or never lit that evening. As he groped his way along the doorways in the gloom, he decided someone had deliberately doused the lights. For someone was sure carrying on behind more than one door, and the place had been nearly empty when he'd arrived around sundown. He was paid to be nosey and would have been curious in any case. So he prowled about before he made for his own door. Moving quietly and listening sharp, he could tell almost every guest room seemed to be occupied, if not by a sudden influx of guests, then by couples who'd beaten him down here from that officers' club dance. He heard what sounded like male and female gaspings, male and male gaspings, and at leat one set of female and female gaspings. It was small wonder someone had paid that desk clerk, or simply ordered him, to take the rest of the evening off!

When he got to his own room, he felt annoyed at himself for having taken that desk clerk for granted. Longarm had long made a habit, in strange hotels, of rigging a match stem in the crack of a locked door to warn him if it had been unlocked in his absence. But earlier that evening, anxious to make it to supper and unaware of that war talk about him on a damned old army post, for Pete's sake, Longarm had simply locked up and gone on about his business.

There was nothing he could do now but draw his .44-40 before, feeling like an old maid peering under her fool bed, he unlocked the damned door with his free hand and stepped into the darkness to slide swiftly along the wall as he kicked the door shut after himself.

He'd have shot the figure reclining across the room for sure if she hadn't giggled girlishly and whispered, "Where on earth have you been all this time? I was about to start without you, you slowpoke!"

Longarm laughed weakly with relief and whispered back, "Don't ever scare me like that again, honey. I figured you were gone and lost forever, like My Darling Clementine."

She started to ask who Clementine was, then giggled some more as she heard the distinctive sounds of a man undressing in the dark as fast as he knew how. As he hung his six-gun handy near the head of the bed, she started to explain why she was there instead of in her own quarters. But Longarm hushed her with, "Don't spoil the magic by excusing the feelings of a healthy young gal. I'll allow I felt a mite confused up the line at the dance tonight. But if you don't confuse me no more right now, we'll worry about the cold gray dawn when it gets here, agreed?"

She whispered, "Ooh, I was hoping you'd see it my way, you animal!"

So Longarm got rid of the last of his duds, and slid under the bed covers to find she was stark naked as well. He threw the fool covers down, lest they overheat, as he took her smooth nude body in his arms and hugged her tight for a welcome-home kiss.

Then, even though he went on kissing her, being only human, Longarm stiffened in surprise as it came to him that, whoever she might be, she couldn't be Godiva Weaver of the *New England Sentinel*!

The only other obvious suspect didn't work either. For the naked gal in his arms was neither as willowy as Godiva nor as short and plump as the colonel's lady. She was a gal of average height with a firm but junoesque figure. One suspected she hourglassed even better with a corset on. From the way she grabbed for his old organ-grinder with a skilled and friendly touch, one doubted she could have been one of the younger wallflowers looking so neglected at the dance earlier. That meant, no matter how you sliced it, he was in bed with some officer's lady and already stiff as a damned poker, with her cocking one long leg across him and crooning, "Ooh, is all this I have in my hand for little old me?"

It sure seemed to be as Longarm, seeing he was damned if he did and damned if he didn't, allowed her to impale her warm wet self on his raging erection, moaning, "Oh, yesss! You're everything they said you were and, praise the Lord, I knew I'd get to do it at least once with a real man before I died!"

There was only one way a gent could respond to such a flattering lady. But when he rolled her on her back and spread her long legs with an elbow hooked under either of her knees, she sobbed, "Oh, not too deep! Give a girl a chance to get used to all this! I've only been married to a mortal human long enough to sense I was missing something, and to be frank, the few times I've done this with someone else, I've been bitterly disappointed!"

Longarm had to move faster in her to keep from going soft as he growled, "I thought I asked you not to spoil the magic. I don't want to share this moment with other men. But since you brought it up, I can't help feeling curious about this *they* you were jawing with about my physical endowments. I don't recall disclosing them to any of you Fort Sill ladies."

She wrapped her long legs around his waist and purred, "That's where you're wrong, you naughty tomcat. When Elvira Howard came in to tell us you'd broken up with that newspaper woman, a certain member of our little group who used to be somebody else in Denver volunteered how sweet you were when she told you she'd gotten the chance to marry a certain cavalry john.''

Longarm thought back and silently nodded as that meshed with what had once been a henna-rinsed barmaid who'd doubtless changed some in the past few summers. Since *this* one dismissed a lieutenant as a john, it was safe to assume her man was at least a captain.

That was all he needed, after being sent all this way to avoid a showdown with a coal miner over a wife he'd never trifled with. He told himself this was as far as he wanted to go with any fool captain's wife, but then they were coming and, try as one might, it was tough to keep from saying stupid things and making empty promises while you pounded the rolicking rump of the most beautiful gal in the universe against the rosy clouds of heaven with a host of angels singing dirty to the both of you. He realized he'd been humming in time with their humping when she began to croon in his ear, to the same frisky tune:

> Oh, some folk'l say he is a knave,
> Some folk say he can't behave,
> He screwed a virgin to her grave,
> With that old organ-grinder!

Then she pleaded for him to screw her to death because she was coming some more, and so he did his best until, as all good things must, it ended for now in a great gasping shudder of painful pleasure and they just floated down from the stars like thistledown, too satisfied to say anything until, still soaking in her, he asked her if she smoked.

She murmured, ''I dip snuff too. But I don't want you to strike a match, darling. I've been thinking about what you said about magic.''

He kissed her soft throat and gently protested, ''That's not fair. You tracked me down to commit premeditated fornication knowing all my secrets, and I don't know your name or even what you look like!''

She kissed him back and moved her hips languidly as she murmured, ''Just think of me as the your fairy godmother, you good little boy. I'm not sure I'm ready to tell you who I really used to be. I'm afraid you may have just turned me into somebody else.''

He said he didn't follow her drift.

She hugged him tighter with her crossed legs and softly told him she wasn't certain what she meant either. Then, before he could ask or she could explain further, some other gal was screaming fit to bust and all hell seemed to be busting loose out in the hall!

Longarm rolled from between her bare legs to land on his bare feet between the bedstead and one window. As he peered out into a mess of swirling gloom his mysterious visitor hissed, ''Come back here and don't get into it! It sounds as if they're fighting over some other army wife, and it's not as if anyone will be looking for *this* one, darling!''

But Longarm was already hauling on his pants as he told her, ''I wouldn't bet any eating money on that. I'm a peace officer, and at least a dozen others are disturbing the peace considerably right outside that hardwood door!''

As if to prove his point, something at least as large and solid as a human head thunked against the far side of the door, followed by an anguished moan of, ''Take it easy, for Gawd's sake! You know I can't hit back, you crazy old goat! And I haven't done a thing a lot of your other junior officers haven't done, damn it!''

Then the brawl rolled down the hall in a serious of loud thuds as Longarm shucked into his shirt, pinned his badge to the front of it, and strapped on his six-gun, muttering, ''Bolt the door after me and don't open up to another soul, hear?''

She started to protest as, somewhere in the night, a voice rang out, ''Corporal of the Guard! Post Number Nine and all is not well by a long shot!''

Knowing the military police were surely on the way, the half-dressed federal deputy stepped out in the hall to spy other guests gaping at nothing much. The action had apparently spilled down the stairs while he was getting up.

He moved down the stairs in his bare feet, his .44-40 undrawn on his left hip as he eased in on all those loud voices ahead. A voice of authority had just assured one and all that it was in full charge. But a sardonic Irish brogue replied, ''Faith, and begging the major's pardon, me darling general orders say that after Guard Mount and until I've been relieved as Corporal of the Guard, I'm to be after taking orders from the Sergeant of the Guard, the Officer of the Day, and nobody else, with the possible exception of the Regimental C.O. I forgot to ask about that. But sure and since you can't be any of the officers just described, I'll be placing you under arrest, sir."

By this time Longarm had moved down far enough to take in the sad scene. A muscular stark-naked man reclined on his rump in a far corner, covered with bruises and bleeding from the nose and mouth as a half-dressed fellow officer tried to help him with a damp kerchief.

The obvious Corporal of the Guard and two other enlisted members of his interior guard had a little old gray-haired and fully dressed major against the lobby desk. He seemed twice as mad and three times as confused as a gamecock caught by one leg in a rat trap. When the Irish noncom spotted Longarm and his badge, he nodded and told him, "The O.D. told us you'd checked in here and ordered us to keep an eye on you. So who might *you* have slept with after that dance, and what's the story about you and that darling Quirt McQueen?"

Longarm laughed lightly and replied, "I can promise you that shotgun messenger never walked *this* child home from any dance. I take it these other gentlemen were fighting over somebody else just now?"

The corporal shrugged and said, "I ordered one of me boyos to sneak her out the back and escort her home for now. It will be up to the colonel to decide whether she and the major here still *have* a home on this post."

The elderly field-grade officer protested, "See here! I was the one who was wronged by that smooth-talking Casanova I had every right to shoot down like a dog!"

Whirling on the younger man still bleeding in that corner, the outraged major half sobbed, "You know you deserve to die, don't you, Chalmers! My Meg and me had been married for nearly fifteen years, and you spoiled it all for a few moments of lust, you two-faced hound!"

The battered lover looked up and snorted impatiently, "Aw, shove a sock in it, you old fool! Your precious Meg has been giving it away since the two of you hit this post, if not before, and I only did my duty by taking pity on an aging beauty who was begging for some!"

The poor old major tried to go for his jeering junior officer. But the others stopped him and Longarm, seeing his own services weren't needed, eased back up the stairs, muttering to himself about beauties of any age who got poor weak-willed men in trouble. Then he felt a whole lot worse about them as he saw that room clerk and a couple of the interior guardsmen had lit up the hall to fling open each and every damned door along the damned hall!

Pasting a self-assured smile across his own face, Longarm strode to join them, trying in vain to come up with a damned good story in a damned short time as, sure enough, the fool clerk was opening the door he'd told that fairy godmother to bolt on the inside!

But as he joined them, the clerk just nodded at him and explained, "The Corporal of the Guard said to check every room, Deputy Long."

Longarm gravely allowed that he understood. His fairy godmother like all the others, had obviously slipped into her duds and down the back way with a skill born of some practice.

As he bade the enlisted men good night and shut the door after them, he couldn't help feeling a mite tense about his fairy godmother's married name.

For that damned unwritten law could be a bitch when a man *knew* who might be gunning for him. He was going to feel dumb as hell if he'd come all this way to avoid one jealous husband, only to be totally surprised by some outraged total stranger!

Chapter 11

After a breakfast of bacon and flapjacks with butter and sorghum molasses, Longarm went across to the stables to see about getting to that Comanche Agency. The livery ponies he'd hired in Spanish Flats had been ridden some since then. So he asked the remount sergeant to lend him a cavalry mount that could use the exercise. The sergeant showed him a big gray gelding they kept as a spare for their mounted band. Cavalry bandsmen always rode grays, and doubled in battle as litter bearers. Nobody had ever explained the part about gray mounts to Longarm's satisfaction.

When he got his hired stock saddle from the tack room and cinched it up, he could see the critter stood close to sixteen hands high and had the barrel chest of a serious traveler. They told him the brute was called Gray Skies. Longarm didn't know why until he'd mounted up, fortunately inside the paddock, and suddenly found out what all those soldiers blue had been grinning about.

But he stayed on, cheating some by hanging on to the horn and locking his denim-clad calves against the gelding's big shoulders in a way few could have managed in cavalry stirrups with more natural legs. So after he'd settled down to sullen crow-hops, Longarm tore off his Stetson to whip Gray Skies across the eyes with it, yelling, "Powder River and let her buck! You call this big fat puppy dog a *horse*?"

So, seeing the joke was on him, Gray Skies decided to be

a sport about it, and they rode off across Flipper's Ditch as pals, or at a more sedate trot leastways.

They'd told him the Indian village he was looking for was better than a half hour ride. So he didn't slow down to take in the shantytown between. There seemed to be fewer Indians and more colored folks than you usually saw around Western military posts. The Tenth Cavalry was likely expected back once the current Apache scare wound down. It was none of his beeswax how any army men spent their free time. It hadn't even been his own notion to help that army wife enjoy herself the night before, blast her devious ways and wasn't it a shame they'd had to quit so early.

He hadn't ridden far across the prairie out the far side of the ragged-ass settlement before he heard a whip crack behind him and turned in the saddle to spy that B.I.A. ambulance, or light-sprung cross between a surrey and a covered wagon, following him down the ruts at a good clip.

Not wanting to be taken as a kid who raced with wagons, Longarm reined off the trail and sat his big gray on a slight rise to watch them tear on for Fort Smith. As they got closer he saw they had the canvas cover rolled halfway up on its hoops to let him see the passengers seated between the load in back and the jehu and shotgun messenger up front. They were going like hell and bouncing pretty good behind the full six-mule team. Neither Godiva Weaver nor the pouty kid up front with that Greener Ten-Gauge seemed to notice him as they passed. But the buckskin-clad Fred Ryan waved. So Longarm waved back.

He rode on through the settling dust of their passage, trying to compare the gyrating pussies of two different gals in his mind, even as he wondered why that seemed so tough. He'd long since noticed how easy it was to recall the ones who'd got away, or the very few who'd been really bad in bed. But it seemed to be the great lays a man got mixed up in his fool head. Sometimes he wondered if that might not be the reason some few gals just lay there like a side of beef. They just wanted to be remembered.

The grass all around had grown higher than one saw around Denver by the time it dried out and went dormant but still nourishing in the midsummer sun. For they were just east of the old Chisholm Trail and hence on what the grass professors called the mid-grass prairies. They meant the almost-perfect zone for growing winter wheat or beef, with neither too little nor too much rain. He could only imagine how the buffalo might have roamed before they'd been shot off this far east. He could see how the Indians had felt when they'd all wound up on the shorter grass of the Texas Panhandle and the hide shooters had still kept at it.

The Indians suspected, and Longarm knew, some of what passed for a heap of yahoo butchery had been deliberate government policy. Or at least the policy of General Phil Sheridan's pals in Congress. The old war hero and Indian fighter had only been half joshing when he'd told Congress they ought to issue a medal showing a buffalo hunter on one side and a surrendering Indian on the other.

Longarm couldn't help feeling sorry for both the buffalo and the Indians. But having done his share of scouting, he had to admit life on the High Plains could be more healthy when you didn't see as many of either coming over the skyline at you.

He topped a gentle rise to spy a dozen head of those longhorns he'd accompanied north from the Red River. A couple of Indian kids dressed like feathery cowhands were drifting them down the grassy draw as if to move them further from the traveled trace and yet another sudden surprise. Cows on unfamiliar range could spook and go tearing off a day's ride when somebody snapped his fingers at them the wrong way.

Longarm waved casually to the distant Comanche, and they waved back in as relaxed a manner. But it was too early to tell whether the B.I.A. and Quanah Parker were going to turn the most dangerous horsemen on the High Plains into peaceable stockmen or farmers.

In the meantime, the way they'd been acting seemed a welcome change from the way Comanche *could* act if they put their minds to it. They said that in his wilder days Quanah had adopted a colored deserter, a bugler from the Tenth Cav, who'd taught the Comanche Warrior Lodge what all the bugle calls meant the soldiers were fixing to do next. On occasion the runaway bugle boy had confounded the hell out of army columns by tooting contrary orders at them.

Longarm spied a white church steeple ahead. He let Gray Skies trot faster, assuming the big gray had been out this way before and knew there was shade and water in the offing. Horses were neither smarter nor dumber than cows. They saw their world different. The way Comanche, or at least Quanah Parker, seemed to grasp the good and bad points of the Saltu path.

As he rode on toward the cluster of frame structures, white-washed in the middle but with unpainted siding further out, Longarm reflected on other nations who spoke related dialects and tended to think of themselves as simply Ho, or Real People. As he did so he decided Quanah deserved some credit for speeding things along, but there was something about the bandy-legged and big-headed breed that made them quicker to catch on to new inventions than some others, red or white.

Those professors who studied ancient Indians all agreed the Uto-Aztec-speaking variety had originated as ragged-ass digger tribes in the Great Basin between the Rockies and the High Sierras. A mess of Desert Paiute still lived that way, if one wanted to call a steady diet of pine nuts and jackrabbit living.

Yet close kinsmen wandering south into the Pueblo country had seen the advantages of apartment houses and farming at a glance, and turned themselves overnight into Pueblos just as advanced as, say, the Zuni or Tanoan. They called themselves Hopi, and were easy to get along with as long as you didn't start anything.

Other poor raggedy bastards speaking the same lingo had gone on down to Mexico to turn into the highly civilized but mighty cruel Aztec as soon as they'd gotten the Toltec to show them how you *really* built a pueblo.

Some held there was a mean streak in all the related Ho nations. But Longarm wasn't so sure. He'd found Hopi decent enough and Papago downright gentle, for folks who'd licked the Chiricahua more than once. So it was up for grabs whether the recent terrors of the Texas plains were going to take one fork in the trail or another.

It was those morose Kiowa he was most concerned about at the moment. So he heeled Gray Skies into a lope and tore into the Comanche agency to the delight of a heap of kids and dogs. The shaggy yellow dogs had long since learned not to actually bite as they snarled and snapped around a big gray's hooves. Gray Skies knew they were only funning as well. Longarm had never decided whether Indian kids missed by accident or on purpose as they tried to assassinate a visiting white man with bird arrows and horse apples. But he knew they seldom hit you. So he just kept riding for the flagpole in the center of things, and sure enough, a sign informed him the two-story frame house across from the church and school house was where he wanted to get started.

As he reined in, an older and skinnier white man came out on the porch while a middle-aged Indian lady in a print house dress shyly watched from the doorway.

As Longarm dismounted, the Indian agent barked something in the Comanche dialect and a kid who'd been winding up to throw a horse apple ran over, grinning, to take charge of Gray Skies for their distinguished guest. Longarm hung on to the Yellowboy saddle gun, having been a kid once himself.

As he joined the older couple on the porch, the agent said to call him Conway. He explained he already knew who Longarm was because the mail ambulance had just passed through and Fred Ryan had told them to expect him. He added, "Fred said you and a newspaper lady with him had brushed with Black Legging Kiowa. Makes no sense, but come on in and we'll talk about it."

He hadn't introduced the Indian woman. As they entered the combined front parlor and reception room, she seemed to be tearing out the back door, as if she was shy as hell or going somewhere else.

Longarm didn't comment. He knew some called gents like Conway "squaw men," while others considered them only practical. He'd just come from a government installation where white men stuck way out in Indian country were trying to get white women to go along with the unusual conditions.

Conway waved him to a seat on a hardwood bench designed not to stain too easily, and got a bottle from a filing cabinet as Longarm brought him up to date as tersely as he knew how. Conway poured two tumblers of clear corn liquor, and handed one to Longarm as he perched his own lean rump on a three-legged stool, saying, "I just sent for Sergeant Tikano. He'd know better than me about them reservation police. Quanah left his own boys in command whilst he's gone.''

Longarm sipped gingerly at the moonshine, and asked the agent just where the chief might be, doing what.

Conway shrugged and replied, ''Try getting a straight answer out of a poker-faced breed who braids his hair and figures long division in his head. He *said* he was riding off across the headwaters of Wildhorse Creek to see about leasing some grazing rights to some kissing cousins on his mamma's side. I don't recall him ever telling his half-assed police to collect any passage or grazing fees for him.''

This turned out to be the simple truth when they were joined a few minutes later by a blue-uniformed Indian who'd have been a giant, if his arms and legs had been proportioned like those of a white man. A lot of Comanche seemed to be built that way. But Sergeant Tikano overdid it a mite with his barrel chest and big moon face.

Conway didn't pour the Indian a drink. Tikano simply went over to that filing cabinet and helped himself. Federal regulations forbade a white man to serve hard liquor to a ward of the government. But no lawman, red or white, was supposed to take a glass out of an Indian's fool hand.

Conway repeated what Longarm had said, in a rapid-fire mixture of English and Comanche, as the big Indian sat down on the bench next to their visitor. The sergeant took a solid swig, grimaced, and declared in no uncertain terms, ''No Kwahadi Comanche would call himself a sheep of any color. I think he was trying to have fun with you. A Kwahadi who spoke your Saltu tongue that well would have heard what your people mean by a black sheep.''

Longarm nodded and said, ''Makes sense. Might one of your police officers by any name be authorized to collect tribal fees for the rest of you?''

The Indian flatly answered, ''*Ka!* Quanah takes the money from Saltu he does business with and puts it in a Texas bank to have litters. I don't know how this *puha* is sung, but it works well and Quanah buys good things with some of the money while the rest keeps breeding for us in that big iron box!''

Conway cut in. ''We've looked into Quanah's business dealings, and it sure beats all how sharp as well as honest that wily breed has got since last he lifted hair! He sort of plays both ends against the middle, now that he's been accepted by quality folk of both his momma and pappa's complexions."

Longarm didn't want to get into how some Hopi had taken to oil lamps and buckboards without giving up their blue corn or Katchina religious notions. So he said, "Be that as it may, I can see why your chief sent for me if nobody can say where a particular police patrol is supposed to be, or who'd be leading it! You got a whole heap of range to police, Sergeant Tikano. Don't you have, say, a wall chart divided into numbered beats for your boys to ride?"

The Indian and his agent exchanged puzzled looks. Longarm nodded and said, "I'm commencing to see what I'm doing here. Might you at least have a table of organization?"

When that didn't work he tried, "A list of riders signed up to draw government wages as nominal peace officers?"

It was the agent who brightened and said, "Oh, sure, I'm the one who pays them extra on allotment day. We have us a force of about two dozen so far."

Longarm frowned and observed, "That's hardly enough to patrol a reserve bigger than some eastern states!"

Tikano shrugged in resignation and explained, "We haven't been able to get many to join. The others laugh and refuse to obey when they see a Real Person dressed as a Saltu. Quanah says we are not to beat anyone just for laughing at us. We can only use force if we see them doing a really bad thing, but of course, nobody does anything bad when one of us is around."

He sipped more corn and continued. "In our Shining Times our old ones made laws. But they were not the laws the Great Father expects us to follow today. When young men were appointed to make everyone obey the rules that had to be obeyed, they were not the same lawmen every day. One group would be appointed to keep order during the hunts for Kutsu, I mean the Buffalo, while others would keep order in camp during the New Women dances. Nobody made others behave long enough to make a lot of people cross with him, and as I said, our old laws were not the new laws. In our Shining Times it was very important that a hunter who had hunted well would share his meat with others. Whether he slept with one woman, two women, or another man was between him and Taiowa, the one you Saltu call Holy Ghost. Our new police force would have more respect if we were allowed to take away the ponies of a man who refused to help a neighbor, instead of locking up the neighbor when he helped himself!''

Longarm finished his drink, silently declined another, and got out three smokes as he quietly said, ''Nobody's asked me to write a Comanche civil or criminal code, praise the Lord. I'd best wait until Quanah returns before I set out to overhaul your whole setup. What can you tell me about them Black Leggings Kiowa, and how do you cotton to the notion of them working in cahoots with at least one dishonest Comanche patrol leader? That mysterious bunch wearing paint only hit us after I'd identified myself to old Tuka Wa Pombi and told him I'd soon be having this very conversation with you gents.''

Sergeant Tikano didn't like it at all. He said, ''There are other Kiowa closer, but the elder who keeps the *puha* bundles of their Black Leggings would be old Necomi, camped this time of the year a half day's ride to the northwest in the Wichita Hills. I'll send a rider over to see what he has to say for himself. But I don't think he will want to tell us much, whether he knows anything or not.''

But Longarm said, ''I'd as soon ride over for a word with him my ownself, seeing the Kiowa seem to resent you and your own riders and, no offense, I've been questioning witnesses longer.''

The white agent protested, ''Necomi won't tell you shit! He hates us white folks to a man, and lies to other Indians when the truth is in his favor!''

Longarm smiled thinly and replied, ''That's what I meant about my being more experienced. Most of the suspects I question hate my guts and lie like rugs. But when you know how to deal the right questions to a poker-faced liar, it's surprising what you can get him to tell you.''

Sergeant Tikano snorted impatiently. ''The two of your are buzzing in my ear like flies above a pile of shit. Necomi doesn't speak a word of Saltu. Do you speak Kiowa, Great Saltu Lawman?''

Longarm grinned sheepishly and replied, ''I talk sign well enough to get by.''

The Indian said, ''Hear me, if you ride alone into Necomi's

tipi ring you will want to keep both hands free to slap leather at all times. Agent Jed speaks straight about Necomi. He looks down upon anyone who is not a Black Legging Warrior and saves up his hate, as the red ant saves up grasshopper legs, for *you* people! I don't think you want to ride over there right after putting three Black Leggings on the ground!''

Longarm got to his feet with a grimace to hand out the cheroots as he explained, ''If I only had to do what I wanted to do, I'd be overpaid for pursuing wine, women, and song. In the meanwhile I see no way to ask Quanah Parker what he wants me to do with his police force until he gets back, and by that time, I ought to be able to make it to the Wichita Hills and back, so . . .''

''If you ride in alone they will kill you and say you were never there,'' Sergeant Tikano told him with a scowl. Then he brightened and decided, ''I don't think even Necomi would kill a woman of Quanah's own band, and you will need someone with you who can speak for you in Kiowa!''

Longarm struck a match to light up the three of them before it went out—that was considered good luck in cow camps—and asked, ''A Kiowa lady belonging to your Comanche band?''

The Indian nodded and offered to explain along the way. Jed Conway blinked and demanded, ''Hold on. You don't mean little Matty Gordon, do you?''

The Indian just shrugged, asked who else they had to translate for Longarm, and led the tall deputy outside, pointing past the church and schoolhouse while explaining, ''Yaduka Gordon is a halfbreed like our Quanah. He married a Kiowa woman called Aho when we used to feast with them after the fall hunts. They have a daughter he calls Matty because he speaks no Kiowa. Her Kiowa mother named her something as tongue-twisting as Matawnkiha because Kiowa talk funny. I think it means something like Growing Daughter in her mother's tongue. But it means nothing in our own.''

They started walking as the Indian went on. ''Growing up among Ho, the girl naturally speaks both her father and mother's tongues, along with your own. Quanah has made all our children go to the B.I.A. school so that none of you Saltu will be able to laugh at them or take any advantage of them in times to come."

Longarm nodded soberly and said, "Jeb Conway just allowed your chief was smart. Whatever happened to that colored army deserter he had blowing bugle calls for you all over by the Palo Duro that time?"

The erstwhile hostile shrugged and said, "I never saw him after the blue sleeves found our last good hideout. No Saltu were supposed to know about that secret canyon in the Texas Panhandle. Our Tonkawa enemies told your Star Chief Sherman where we hid among the berry trees in the depths of that big well-watered canyon."

Longarm was almost sorry he'd asked as the Indian went on. "They marched against us from every direction, with repeating rifles and breech-loading field guns. There was Star Chief Miles from Fort Dodge. Three Fingers Mackenzie marched up from Fort Concho with many soldiers. Many. Yellow Leaf Chief Price came at us out of New Mexico. Eagle Chiefs Davidson and Buell marched whole regiments at us out of Fort Sill and Fort Richardson. And you ask me what happened to *one man*?"

He pointed at an unpainted but neatly kept cabin and said, "That is where we are going. Hear me, those blue sleeves swarmed over us like red ants over a dead rabbit. They burned our lodges and destroyed all our winter food. They rounded up most of our ponies and then they shot them, shot them, until even the buzzards were too sick of dead meat to eat any more. Wherever we tried to make a stand they threw canister and exploding shells into us. Those of us who lived were the ones who ran away. Hear me, I admit this. We ran like rabbits run from Old Coyote, for the same reasons. It was Quanah who led us from the death trap of Palo Duro and made us feel like men again because he rode into Fort Sill ahead of us and told the blue sleeves we would fight on forever if they didn't treat us right!"

That wasn't the way Longarm had heard it. But he didn't argue the point. It was just as likely the newspaper accounts of a discouraged and starving Comanche chief, pleading for his life and something to eat as they held him and his kin in the Fort Sill guardhouse for a spell, were a slight exaggeration as well. For either way, Quanah had gotten better terms for his followers, and himself, than many another hostile had managed in as tight a spot.

The harder row to hoe was going to be getting both sides to stick to them. Even the older kids had to have awful memories of blood and slaughter followed by sheer starvation on the run. Then there were all those white folks with bitter memories of Comanche war whoops and mutilated kith and kin.

Sergeant Tikano broke in on his thoughts by calling out to the house as they crossed the swept dirt yard. An older gal in red Mother Hubbard, who might have been leaner and prettier sometime back, popped out the front door like a big old cuckoo-clock bird to fuss at them in their own chirpy lingo. The Indian lawman replied in English, "I think we should all speak Saltu, Umbea Aho. This is a friend of Quanah's. We call him Saltu Ka Saltu in our own tongue and Longarm in his own. We know your man is with Quanah to help him sell grazing rights. For some reason older purebloods make our old enemies scowl. We've come to talk to you about your daughter, Matty. Longarm has to ask old Necomi questions, and we thought Matty could help because she speaks Kiowa as well as Saltu."

The motherly Aho gasped, "My Matawnkiha is only sixteen summers grown! She has been initiated into the Real Women's Lodge, but she has never lain with a man and Necomi's summer camp is far, very far. How can you expect a mother to send her only daughter off with this big Saltu? I don't care how you or Quanah feel about him. My Matawnkiha is too young for him!"

As if to prove her point, they were joined in the dirt yard by a petite belle of any harvest dance, and as soon as she giggled up at him, Longarm had to concede her mother had a point.

Matawnkiha or Matty Gordon looked more like a lovely twelve-year-old than the sixteen years she doubtless bragged upon. Her mixture of races made her look a tad more Border Mexican than Quill Indian. She had her shiny black hair bound with red ribbon and flung over one bare shoulder. The rest of her petite body was covered, sort of, by thin white flour sacking, stitched together as a shin-length summer shift and cinched around her tiny waist by a beadwork belt. Longarm knew that the beadwork was Kiowa because it tried for a floral design on that dark background. Comanche beadwork was almost always angular and abstract, to a stranger's eyes, against a white background.

But the kid's moccasins were traditional Comanche, too big for her tiny feet, with a bundle of buckskin thongs sprouting from the heels where a white rider might wear spurs.

Longarm knew she wasn't a Comanche raider out to blur his own trail by dragging thongs across his footprints. So it was safe to assume the little gal had her daddy's old slippers on.

Matawnkiha had obviously heard part of the conversation before coming out to join it. You could hear the pleading tone in her voice as she spoke to her mother in what had to be Kiowa. Longarm could pick up on a few words of the far-flung Uto-Aztec dialects such as Comanche, Shoshoni, or Ute. But it was small wonder the Kiowa had invented the sign lingo of the plains nations. Some said it was related to one of the several Pueblo dialects. But otherwise Kiowa seemed to be orphans.

Whether to be polite or just avoid cussing in Kiowa, the outraged Aho Gordon wailed in English, "Hear me! I never raised you to be just another play for the Taibo! Is that what you want? Is that why your father and I ate lean cow meat so you could go to that school and learn to read and write?"

Longarm started to assure the lady he wasn't a damned cradle-snatcher. But little Matawnkiha showed she'd been paying attention in class by bursting out in Kiowa some more, in a way that made her worried mother's jaw drop, even as you could see some of her resolve fading. Longarm quietly asked Sergeant Tikano what was going on. The Indian muttered, "How should I know? I told you why you'd need someone like her to get through to old Necomi. Why do you Saltu think all of us speak one tongue grunting like pigs?"

The younger Indian girl kicked off her dad's floppy moccasins and scampered off across the yard barefooted as her mother turned to them and said, "She has gone to see if the agency school teacher, Minerva Cranston, wants to ride with you."

Longarm frowned uncertainly and asked, "You have an agency schoolmarm who speaks Kiowa, ma'am?"

The erstwhile Kiowa woman snorted, "Of course not. She is Saltu. But my daughter and the other young people say she is very strict when school is open during the cooler moons. She will not allow the young men to pinch the girls or pull their hair, even when they laugh about it. So I don't think Minerva Cranston would let you screw Matawnkiha when the three of you made camp so far from me. I think we should go inside and have some coffee and fresh pastry now. My husband's father was a Saltu trader, and I only feel cross with Saltu who want to screw my daughter. Now that I don't think you can, I don't want to stab either one of you anymore."

She proved her good intent by taking them inside, seating them both as a deal table near her kitchen range, and serving huge mugs of coffee and big servings of what seemed to be pies stuffed with blackberries imbedded in beef hash. Sergeant Tikano was watching to see what Longarm would do about that. But Longarm had been invited inside by Horse Indians before, and decided their home cooking was best described as *unusual* instead of downright awful.

Her coffee was good. Longarm liked his coffee black. So that got around the common Indian notion that white flour was better than cream and sugar in their coffee. For *that* was *really* an acquired taste.

By the time they'd polished off the greasy pie and second cups of coffee the daughter of the house was back with a taller, far thinner, and far more severe-looking white gal. She didn't seem to find Longarm all that delightful either.

Minerva Cranston wore her mouse-colored hair in a bun. Her pale face was not really ugly but sort of plain. The wire-rimmed specs she had on sort of hid her best feature, a pair of intelligent-looking gray eyes. Longarm figured she'd been fixing to go riding. She'd put on a practical split skirt of suede leather and a hickory work shirt a size too big to tell a man what sort of tits she might have.

Her Spanish hat hung down her back on a braided thong around her slender throat. Her Justin boots were cut sort of Border Mexican as well. That didn't mean she couldn't be fresh from the East. Thanks to Ned Buntline's dime novels, everybody knew, or thought they knew, the way folks were supposed to dress out this way.

He figured she was close to his own age, and he knew *he'd* been all over. So instead of asking her where she came from as they shook hands, he asked how come she wanted to go visit those Quill Kiowa. He felt he had to warn both ladies of the possible danger, pointing out he was only out to question the Kiowa about hostile Kiowa because he'd run into some.

He felt no call to mention other ladies once he'd told them more than one Black Legging had gone down.

Little Matawnkiha was already behind a curtain, changing into her own riding duds, as Minerva Cranston went into a dry dissertation on the book she was writing about Indians.

Longarm didn't care. He didn't cotton to the notion of riding into a possibly hostile camp with one female to worry about, let alone two! But since it seemed the only way he might get a thing out of the leader of the Black Leggings Lodge, all he could do was ask Sergeant Tikano about the infernal riding stock this loco expedition was going to require.

Chapter 12

Ouachita, Washita, and Wichita were just different spellings for a nation that wasn't there anymore. Early white travelers had met up with them as tattood hoe farmers growing corn, beans, squash, and such on prairie bottomlands from the Arkansas River to the Red. Then less-settled wanderers had learned to chase buffalo, and everybody else, on horseback. So the surviving Wichita had run off to join their much more warlike Pawnee cousins up Nebraska way, where they'd become the Pawnee Picts, leaving a heap of handy place names for rivers, towns, and such where they'd lived much earlier.

The Wichita Mountains northwest of Fort Sill would have only been hardwood-timbered rises if they hadn't been surrounded by so much flatter prairie. But they offered summer shade and winter windbreaks at a fair distance from the well-meaning Kiowa agents up around Akota, and so Longarm wasn't surprised to see tipi smoke rising against the golden western sky as he, the two gals, and five ponies topped another grassy rise after one tedious afternoon in the saddle.

Little Matty, as both whites had taken to calling her, had turned out more childlike and bossy than expected. Minerva Cranston spoke no Kiowa, nor more than a few basic words of Comanche-Ho. So Longarm was able to follow the nasty comments and snide suggestions Matty was offering as the two of them rode a few lengths behind him. He could tell the prim-faced schoolmarm didn't want to be teased like that. So he refrained from telling either just how safe they were from a full-grown man, for Pete's sake.

As they got within a tough rifle shot of the ring of tipis on a rise, an old maniac in a crow feather cloak with his face painted red and black came tearing toward them on foot, followed by a mess of kids and dogs, to shake a turtle-shell rattle at them and sound off like a jackrabbit caught in a bobwire fence.

Matty heeled her pony up beside Longarm's army gray and calmly told him, "That's Pawkigoopy. He's telling us we'll all be struck down by his medicine and eaten by owls if we don't turn back."

She shouted at the crazy old coot in Kiowa, and as if some puppet master had quit jerking his strings, Pawkigoopy stopped shaking his rattle at them and asked in a conversational tone what his daughter wanted and why she was riding with enemies.

It took Matty a few minutes to explain all that to Longarm and Minerva Cranston, of course. First she told the medicine man what all of them were doing there, and then she told her white companions what he'd said after he'd said to follow him on in.

They did. The dogs snarled mean as hell and the kids said mean things as they approached the tipi ring, but nobody shot or threw a thing at them. That was how sore this particular band seemed to be.

Artists who sketched Indian villages for Currier & Ives or Street & Smith tended to picture them the way white folks might have pitched a circle of tents, with all the entryways facing inward around that big central bonfire. But that wasn't the way most Indians set things up when it was up to *them.*

To begin with, unless they were holding a ceremony or torturing captives, they had no call to put all that fuel and effort into any central fire at all. You wanted a thrifty fire of your own inside your tipi when it was cold, or just outside it when you were cooking a meal in warm weather.

Then you wanted your entryway facing east to catch the dawn sunlight and screen the interior from the hot afternoon sun, no matter where you'd pitched your tipi poles in the defensive circle. As they rode in he saw some of the Kiowa had lifted the south-facing rims of their tipi covers clear of the grass to suck in air at ground level and exhaust heat out the top, between the smoke.

There were eighteen such lodges in the ring, with the one at the twelve o'clock position to the north a tad bigger and painted in black and yellow tiger stipes on its southern half. As the medicine man told them to rein in, Longarm saw the northern half of the big tipi was covered with coup signs, or what might have passed for that Egyptian picture writing. He'd already known from those horizontal stripes that something or somebody with a heap of medicine would be waiting for them inside.

They dismounted. Some kids in their teens came over to take charge of all five ponies, saddle or pack. Then an imposing figure in a full war bonnet and Hudson Bay blanket came out of the tiger-striped tipi to stare at them as if he was rehearsing for a career in front of cigar stores. It wasn't true that only blue eyes could stare cold as ice. The small sloe eyes staring out of that dried-apple face at Longarm looked as friendly as a hangman fixing to pull the lever.

Matty said that was Necomi, and started to introduce them to one another in Kiowa. But then the old chief snorted in disgust, and his English was just fine when he said, "Hear me, I am Necomi. I count coup for every eagle feather in this bonnet, and I will not have my words spoken to any damn enemy by any woman! Not even an *old* one like this other I find too skinny to screw!"

Longarm said, "Watch your mouth, Chief. These ladies are with *me* and mayhaps *I* count some coup as well."

Necomi stared long and hard before he said, "I know who you are. They told us you were coming, Longarm. Are you threatening me here in my own camp?"

Longarm calmly replied, "Ain't sure. Are you threatening me?"

The old Kiowa almost smiled. He managed not to, and said, "They told me you were crazy. Come inside while I decide whether I want to smoke with you or let the army and our agents wonder forever what could have happened to the three of you."

He ducked inside. Longarm shrugged and started to follow

the hospitable son of a bitch as, behind him, he heard Matty warn the schoolmarm, "No! That is a warrior society lodge and we are women!"

As the Kiowa kid had sounded mighty demanding, Longarm decided the two gals would be all right for now.

Inside, the air was murky with tobacco smoke, and while some of the last rays of sunset were shining through the rain-resistant, oil-soaked, and painted hides all around, it took him a few moments to make out the other old gents seated solemnly around the inward-slanting walls of their fair-sized meeting hall. Since it was high summer, they hadn't hung the usual hide curtain that made for a more vertical backdrop while it kept the drafts at bay. Thanks to all the smoke, they could use even more drafts about now.

Necomi indicated a seat for their guest on one corner of a big red blanket. As he took his own seat across from Longarm and out a piece from the others in the council circle, Necomi said, "If you have come to hear what is wrong with this agency, you have come to the right place. We are so angry we are weeping tears of blood, and if they don't start treating us better they will feel their own blood running down the sides of their heads! Hear me, I am Necomi. Two times I fought your people at Adobe Walls. Both times under our own great war chief, Satanta. Hear me, Quanah Parker was only a child when we fought Eagle Chief Carson and his big brass guns at Adobe Walls. If we let Quanah lead the second time, against those buffalo thieves, it was only because he brought the most warriors and that crazy medicine man who said nobody could hit us on open prairie with those telescope sights!"

Longarm was aware some of the others were whispering translations as he dryly observed, "They've brought out longer-ranging express rifles since. I ain't here to hear sad tales about lost battles. The defeated vets of the Army of Virginia will be proud to tell you how close they came to winning in many a trail-town saloon. But meanwhile, some more ambitious gents who once fought in butternut gray have gone on to become cattle barons, mining magnates, railroad builders, and such. When a man's licked fair and square, he can get back on his two feet and go on, or he can lay there whimpering for as long as he cares to, and nobody else will *give* a damn."

Necomi shook his head, an alarming sight with all those feathers aflutter, and protested, "We know about the war between the blue and gray sleeves. We thought it would be a good time to take to the warpath. We did not know Eagle Chief Carson would have Ute scouts and those big brass guns. We were not able to make peace the way the gray sleeves did when they could fight no more. They had been beaten by their own kind of people. All they had to do was stop fighting and go on living the same way they had always lived."

Longarm chuckled softly and warned, "Don't ever say that in Old Dixie. Nobody ever gets to go on living the way they always lived. The world keeps changing and, like that Na-déné spirit Changing Woman warns us all, the only folks that never have to change at all are the dead. Kit Carson used his field artillery on the Na-déné we call Navajo too. They never got the honorable terms Quanah Parker got for *his* allies. They were marched to Fort Sumner and taught to plant peach trees. Some of them learned to read and write whilst they were at it. After a few years and a lot of letters, the Eagle Chief Sherman and the Great Father in Washington allowed them to have their old hunting grounds back as their reserve, provided they gave up some of their old ways, such as raiding the Pueblo or Mexicans when they were low on supplies."

By now the sunset outside was shining through the greased hides as red as fresh blood. The Indians all around looked sort of spooky as Necomi protested, "Hear me! We agreed not to raid anybody after the B.I.A. said they would give us plenty of supplies to make up for the poor hunting on this reservation. But they never give us all that we need. Never! When our women have served up all they issued us and we ask for more, they say there is no more and we should not eat all they give us so soon!"

Longarm nodded soberly and said, "I've had that same argument when I came back for seconds with an empty mess kit. Gents who dole out government grub are like that, even when they ain't stealing any. I was trying to get to the point about the Navajo. Thanks to having all that time on their hands, the men have learned to hammer silver coins into conchos, rings, and such that sell for as much as those nice saddle blankets their womenfolk weave. They sell such goods for more money or swap 'em at their trading posts for nicer rations and play-pretties than the tax-collecting government is ever going to give any former friend or foe."

He let that sink in before he added, "Cochise led even wilder Na-déné in his day, and yet he died prosperous in bed, after he settled for terms he could live with and then sold firewood by the wagon load to the white-eyed settlers and silver miners in those parts."

"Cochise is dead. His son, Nana, rides with Victorio along the warrior's path tonight!" snapped the unrepentant Kiowa leader.

Longarm muttered, "Bullshit. There've been *two* Bronco Apache by the name of Nana so far. Neither one could claim Cochise as his sire. The elder son and heir of Cochise was named Taza. He was just as smart and tried to carry on the same way until he died of pneumonia on a visit to Washington. He was buried with full honors in the Congressional Cemetery. You and those lazy newspaper reporters who grab easy answers out of thin air must have found Nana easier to recall than Taza, being there's a sassy French novel called Nana on the stands right now. Cochise did have a younger boy called Naiche, but not Nana, and it's true he seems more sullen. If he's riding with Victorio tonight, he'll doubtless wind up dead as well. Did you gents know Quanah Parker just bought a whole herd of beef, without having to beg an extra dime off the B.I.A.?"

He let that sink in before he added in a desperately casual tone, "I reckon he means to share some of it with his Kiowa brothers, seeing he's such a big sissy. I'll tell him you all could use some extra grub over this way, once them two gals and I get back over yonder."

He couldn't tell whether it had worked or not. In the ruby red gloom the old chief grumbled, "You did not come all this way to tell us we should be good children of the Great Father. We knew about that herd Quanah said he would send for. Of course he intends to share with us. I only said he was not as important as you and your people seem to think he is. I never said he was not a Real Person!"

Another old Kiowa, almost invisible against the dark north wall of the big tipi, forgot his manners as he impatiently snapped in fair English, "Tell us why you came here, Longarm. Tell us what you want from us."

Longarm nodded soberly and told them. They listened mutely, and he couldn't read any expressions on their shadowy faces as he brought them all up to date on that brush with those other Kiowa. Once he had, he added, "I didn't count coup on the three we put on the ground. But I got a good look at them before their friends carried their bodies away. Their faces were painted half red, their beadwork was red or green with lighter flower designs. Their chests were bare, streaked with red, and their leggings were black leggings."

There was a low rumble of anxious-sounding Kiowa. Then Necomi held up a hand for silence and said, "Hear me, Longarm. If you are speaking with a forked tongue, we shall be very cross with you! If somebody is raiding along the Cache Creek Trail, pretending to be members of our warrior lodge, we shall be very cross with *them*! The Kiowa nation is not on the warpath yet. So none of our young men have permission to ride out against your people."

The talkative elder to the north chimed in. "Young men can get a lot of their own people killed that way. Everyone knows how crazy that Cheyenne crooked lancer Woquini was to kill that rancher and his wife and daughters without telling his own people! They had no idea why the blue sleeves had come, and many stood like corn stalks until the blue sleeves cut them down at Sand Creek!"

Necomi silenced him with a stern look and told Longarm, "None of our young men could have attacked you at those sod ruins. You say you killed three of them. Where are their women, with ashes in their hair and gashes in their cheeks, if what you say is so?"

Longarm calmly replied, "My heart soars to learn nobody here as a ward of my government has women keening for him. But what if they haven't heard yet? What if a leader who got three followers killed was too ashamed to come back and tell anyone what a foolish thing he had done?"

Necomi shook all those feathers again and insisted, "That would be a very shameful way to behave. After Satanta and Quanah both had their horses shot out from under them, and many more had been killed or wounded, they agreed, like men are supposed to, they had been foolish to rely on Isatai's medicine chant. So it was time to break off the bad fight. Nobody initiated as a Kaitsenko, a fighting Kiowa, would do a thing like that!"

His old pard chimed in. "Even if he did, we would have heard about three missing members of *any* lodge! You say you killed not one but three, more than two days ago. Who has been sleeping with their wives all this time, the ones who led them to their deaths for no good reason?"

Longarm shrugged and said, "I keep telling folks how easy it can be to grab for easy answers. Didn't you gents just confound the sons of Cochise with a spicy French book and some other Na-déné entirely?"

That set off a real consultation. When it died down Necomi told him, "Nobody is supposed to wear black leggings and shoot at anyone unless we say he can. We have heard what you have to say. We don't see how your words could be true!"

Longarm smiled thinly and replied, "I reckon you'd have had to have been there. Ain't it possible this one chapter of the Black Leggings Lodge might lose track of no more than a dozen kids out for a lark on such a big reserve? I mean, who's to say they couldn't have been Comanche or some of them Kiowa-Apache who came along from the Texas plains with the rest of you all?"

Necomi snapped, "*We* are to say! We and only we who sit in council here in this Do-giagya-guat, copied to the last medicine mark from that one that was burned in the wars with you people. The Comanche fought beside us many times. The Kiowa-Apache fought as our brave younger brothers and we honor them, even though they talk funny. But hear me. We don't initiate every Kiowa warrior as a Black Legging, and it would be easier for a Kiowa *girl* to join than it would be for a very great man of any *other* nation!"

Longarm nodded and said, "I'll take your word for that. The fact remains that the bunch we tangled with were painted and dressed as a bunch of your Black Legging boys."

Necomi said, "You keep saying this. We are going to find out why. You will be taken to your women now and given something to eat. If you try to leave before we say you can, all three of you will die. I have spoken."

A couple of lesser Kiowa stood up as if to lead him somewhere. Longarm said, "Hold on. How are we supposed to find out anything if I don't have any say in it?"

One of the Indians bent to lay a firm but gentle hand on Longarm's shoulder as their chief said, "I told you I had spoken. You are very rude. Even a fool who knows nothing of our ways should see how simple it is to just count noses. Everyone who wears black leggings will be easy to account for, or at least three of them won't be. If we are missing three members we will know you could be telling the truth. If we are not, we will know you are lying, and none of us invited you to come here with a forked tongue!"

Longarm got to his feet, lest somebody haul him up by the scruff, but insisted, "Try her this way. Say somebody out to raise Ned but wanting to shift the blame, just got decked out as a Black Leggings war party."

Necomi didn't answer. But one of those herding him for the tipi's only doorway murmured in English. Longarm recognized the high-pitched voice as it insisted, "He doesn't want to talk to you anymore, Longarm. Come with us. You are only making Necomi and some of the others cross with your silly suggestions!"

As they got outside where the gloaming light was much better, Longarm could make out the middle-aged Indians better. The one who tended to speak out of turn said, "I am called Hawzitah. I can read. But I don't believe much of what you people put in your books. We are taking you to your women. You can't have your ponies or repeating rifle yet. Is that a double-action revolver?"

The other, less talkative Kiowa shooed some kids away as they came over to make faces at Longarm. He told Hawzitah he'd guessed right about the .44-40 riding on his hip, hoping they might not search him and find his double derringer. The older Indians didn't seem worried about a white man with five in the wheel well inside an Indian camp. Hawzitah pointed at a plainer fifteen-skin tipi rising pale against the purple eastern sky and said, "In there. The door is on the other side, of course. Is it true Red Cloud has allowed his young men to join the Indian Police up at his reserve?"

Longarm nodded and said, "Old Mahpiua Luta, as you say

Red Cloud in his lingo, is fixing to die rich in bed, like Cochise. He made his point and got the best terms he could. Then he stayed the hell out of it when Crazy Horse and Sitting Bull demanded a rematch back in '76. So now he's got a cozy cabin instead of a drafty tipi, come the starving moons and wolf winds, and like Quanah, he's been pulling in extra money by leasing grazing rights to neighboring stock outfits.''

Hawzitah muttered, ''I would like to have more money to spend on good things, and when there is no need to move camp a lot, a cabin does seem a better place to spend the hungry moons. But why do Red Cloud and Quanah think they need Indian Police? What's the matter with the way we've always kept order among ourselves?''

Longarm said, ''You ain't living the way you've always lived. You used to be able to keep order in camp and guard the women and ponies with a handful of men left behind while the rest of you rode oft to kill buffalo, Wichita, and such. None of you had much more than that to lose as you lived the way that High Dutch writer, Karl Marx, keeps telling us all to live.''

As they circled out around the tipi, he noted the pony line about a furlong out against the darkening hills, and continued. ''You just said your ownself how you'd like to buy good things at the trading post. Police work gets more complicated when folks leave things worth stealing behind locked doors. Also, you all have a stake in the value of your land.''

The older Indian snorted, ''You call these empty plains and wooded hills without many deer *land*? Hear me, in Palo Duro Canyon, over by the Shining Mountains, buffalo, deer, even elk grazed among the soapberry trees while our ponies grew fat on grass that stayed green all summer!''

Longarm smiled thinly and said, ''You should have seen Dixie before the war, or the emerald fields of Erin before the potato blight. But if we can stick to what you have here, Quanah's getting a dollar a head off trail herds passing through and leasing grazing rights at six cents an acre a month. You're right about it being bleaker here than over in that Indian Eden. But one cow needs at least five acres to graze, so add it up.''

As the Indian tried to, Longarm said, ''No offense, but as both Quanah and Red Cloud must have noticed, Texas trail hands are more likely to take a man in uniform for a peace officer than a raiding hostile. After that, having regular police gets around the problem of a mixed bag of folks on a big reserve who may not know every bare-chested cuss who yells at them by name.''

He lifted the entrance flap as he quietly added, ''The Cherokee, Chickasa, Choctaw, and such have had Indian Police and private property for a good while now.''

He didn't listen as the older man behind him muttered darkly about Cherokee not being Real People anymore. He was more interested in the two frightened faces staring at him in the dim interior of the guest, or perhaps confinement, tipi.

A smudgy little cow-chip fire was burning on the sand in the center. Old buffalo robes and some cleaner-looking blankets had been spread around the circle of twenty-two poles. There was no sign of their own bedding, saddles, or that damned old saddle gun. As he hunkered down across from the small breed and pallid schoolmarm, Matawnkiha said, ''We're hungry.''

Longarm told her their hosts, or captors, had said something about feeding them, and added, ''It seems we're stuck here for at least the night. They may have been trying to scare me into making a break for it. I told 'em I'd told the Comanche Police we were headed over this way. I don't reckon they'd want to hurt any of us close to home.''

Minerva Cranston said, ''I'm afraid I'm going to be sick. I don't mind the smell of tallow, and linseed oil's not so bad, but mix them together and . . . Never mind. Why do you think they're behaving toward us in such a confusing way, Custis?''

Longarm sniffed uncertainly. ''Got to cut down on my smoking. Now that you mention it, I do suspicion somebody wiped some of that army issue tent dubbing over these old greased hides. Reckon buffalo tallow is tougher to come by these days.''

She insisted, ''You haven't answered my question, Custis.''

He shrugged and replied, ''Don't have a good answer. I keep telling folks how dumb it can be to guess at easy answers when you just don't know. They might be behaving so confused because we've confused them. They might be trying to figure how they want to cover up something they know all about.''

He asked the ladies if they cared if he smoked. When neither told him not to, and Matty said she wanted one, he handed her a cheroot, lit his own as well, and brought them up to date on his conversation with the elders of the Black Leggings Lodge.

When he'd finished, Matty said she was still hungry. Then she said something that sounded dirty in Kiowa as she stared past Longarm at the round entryway behind him.

Longarm turned to see a grinning kid of eight or nine peeking in at them. The kid said something in Kiowa that made Matty laugh in spite of herself. She explained, ''I asked the fresh thing what he wanted, and he asked when are we going to take off all our duds and get dirty. He says he's never watched folks like you and Miss Minerva do it.''

The schoolmarm sighed and said, ''I used to admire the way Indians disciplined their children without corporal punishment. After some time among them I'm not so sure.''

Matty wound up to tell the little shit what a shit she thought he was. But Longarm had a better idea. He fished out some pocket change as he told Matty what he wanted her to ask of the unsupervised brat. She did, but after he'd tossed the kid a nickel and he'd scampered off in the gathering dusk, she told him he'd just seen the last of both the kid and his money.

Then she added, ''They told us before you got here that Necomi had said to feed us. It's after dark and my mother's people are used to early suppers. Do you think some big pig has helped himself to meals meant for us?''

Minerva sighed. ''That tallow's kept the linseed oil dubbing from drying out all the way. I don't think you're supposed to put linseed oil on leather to begin with. I don't care if they ever feed us. Do you think someone would shoot me if I went outside to throw up?''

Longarm got out another cheroot, lit it from the tip of the one he was smoking, and when she silently refused it, threw it on the cow-chip fire between them to stink the place differently, saying, ''A nose that delicate must be a heavy cross to bear, Miss Minerva. I said I could make out that army dubbing once you brought it up, and I agree it don't smell like roses, but there's worse smells than that in this imperfect world. How did you ever get by back East in a city running on horsepower and cooking with soft coal?''

She sighed and replied, ''Why did you think I applied for this job out West? You're so right about it being a cross to bear. Like a lot of myopic souls, I seem to have developed my sense of smell beyond a comfortable level. How I wish things were the other way, with my eyes this keen and my nose not so delicate.''

He didn't have any call to mention that eagle-eyed gal he'd met in Montana who spotted cracks in every ceiling, spots on every rug, and called a man a liar when he swore he'd shaved that same day. He asked Matty what she knew about the old rascals holding up their supper so long.

The little Kiowa breed only knew the bunch over this way by rep. She said Necomi was considered a true-heart, in a stubborn old-time way. She'd heard old Hawzitah didn't count all the coup he was said to be entitled to. She said his fellow Kiowa considered him an odd cuss in other ways. He was always asking questions, curious as a young kid about what everyone was up to, even the blue sleeves over at the fort. When the black blue sleeves had been there, he'd asked them all sorts of questions about what it felt like to live like a Saltu without being a real Saltu. Maggy said she didn't see why anyone would want to ask such stupid questions, and that even the black blue sleeves had laughed and called Hawzitah the Kiowa Professor.

She said the medicine man, Pawkigoopy, acted crazy and had some of her elders scared of him. She couldn't say why. Nodding at her white teacher across from Longarm, she said, ''I don't think I would like to be saved and dunked in water. But Umbea Mary seems to be a friendier spirit than Piamumpitz, who eats little children when they play outside at night!''

Longarm said he didn't think it was too late for that kid to be out fooling around, and asked her to tell them more about the spooky medicine man.

She said, ''I don't live over this way. All I know is what I hear when some of her old friends come to visit my Kiowa mamma. I've heard them say it's not a good idea to ask Pawkigoopy to chant over you or your children when bad spirits get into them. They say he asks for presents afterwards, or for the younger mothers of sick babies to sleep with him. They say the men would beat him for behaving that way if they were not so afraid of his *tu-puha.*''

Minerva had been trying to learn the Comanche dialect since she'd been teaching their kids, and so she moved her lips in thoughtful silence and then murmured aloud, ''Black medicine? Would that be anything like black magic?''

Longarm nodded and said, ''Different nations call it *puha, wakan, matu,* and so on, but we translate it as medicine because that's about as close as we can get to a sort of mishmash of cure-all and luck on demand. Decent Indians ain't supposed to use it to hurt instead of help. But I reckon a warrior with strong medicine guiding his arrows could be said to be hexing the poor cuss he's aiming at. Comanche and other Ho speakers such as Hopi or Shoshoni hate what we'd call witchcraft and can't abide it in a medicine man. But these Kiowa have a rep for admiring a good malediction chanted in unison. So I reckon you might call a spiteful cuss like Pawkigoopy as much a sorcerer as a medicine man.''

That kid suddenly popped through the entry with the saddlebags Matty had said Longarm wanted. As Longarm handed over a couple of quarters, quantity being more impressive than face value, Matty asked him about that saddle gun. The kid said he'd only found their riding and packsaddles in a nearby tipi. He didn't know who had the Winchester Yellowboy right now. He said he hadn't tried to locate a big gray gelding because the night watch along the pony line whipped at kids and dogs with knotted thongs.

As the half-naked kid hunkered nearby to watch with interest, Longarm got out some canned provisions and began to open them with his pocket knife, explaining, ''I brought along canned beans and tomato preserves because you can eat 'em warm or cold.''

He opened an extra can of the sweetish tomato preserves so the helpful Kiowa kid could have some as well. A man just never knew when he might need a pal in such uncertain surroundings.

They consumed the beans, followed by the grease-cutting preserves, by handing the cans around and just slurping good.

Minerva said the lingering whiffs of linseed oil and stale greasy tallow didn't make her stomach churn as much now that she'd put something in it.

The Kiowa kid said his name was Pito, and asked if he could have the empty tin cans. Longarm said he could, even though Matty warned him he was being taken. Pito lit out, richer by fifty-five cents and some raw material for stamped conchos, with his already dirty face smeared with tomato preserves.

He hadn't been gone long when a couple of shy, or scared-looking, Kiowa gals came in with an iron pot and some trading post china bowls. As they dished out generous helpings of a sort of cracked corn and venison stew, Maggy told Longarm and Minerva the Kiowa gals apologized for such a late supper. They said they'd had to start from scratch. Minerva murmured, "The poor things probably didn't eat that well themselves this evening. It smells delicious. I didn't know Plains Indians cooked with garlic."

Longarm had never heard they did. He raised the bowl he'd been served to his nose, sniffed hard, and quietly warned in English not to dig in just yet.

He waited until the two women had backed out before he grabbed the bowl from Matty's greedy young hands and snapped, "Spit that out, in the fire, so's there won't be any on view later."

The kid did as she was told but demanded, as her spat-out stew sizzled really strong fumes of what seemed to be garlic flavoring, what on earth was he fussing about.

The white gal across from Longarm said, "It smells delicious."

Longarm said, "It's supposed to. But that ain't garlic your keen sniffer picked out of the stronger flavorings, Miss Minerva. Kiowa use garlic about as often as Eye-talians cook with buffalo berries. But they do sell flypaper at most trading posts, and the arsenic you can boil out of the stick-em does smell more like garlic than anything any *honest* Kiowa cook would be stirring in!"

The two gals stared thunderstruck at one another. Then Minerva gasped, "We have to make a run for it before they come back and find us alive! How long do you think we have, Custis?''

Longarm began to dig a hole in the sand with his pocket knife as he said, ''Indefinitely. I doubt the one who's out to poison us will be anywhere near come morning. He, she, or it will be down at the far end of camp, waiting to hear from the others.''

He saw they both looked scared as hell. So as he began to pour poisoned stew into the hole he soothed, ''Don't you ladies see the bright side yet? If the elders wanted us dead they'd just have us taken out a ways and shot. So I'm betting someone who failed to get his own way at that council decided to murder us on his own.''

Matty asked, ''What if you're betting wrong?''

To which he could only reply in a conversational tone, ''Oh, in that case we're as good as dead. I can't leave without the two of you, and I'll be switched with snakes if I can see a way for the three of us to slip out of camp and get far enough to matter.''

Matty said, ''Hear me, I have played *nanipka* with both Comanche and Kiowa and I have seldom been caught!''

Minerva murmured wistfully, ''She means hide-and-go-seek.''

Longarm said, ''I know what she means, and seldom ain't enough when you're playing with bigger boys for keeps.''

Matty insisted she could sneak really swell.

Minerva took a deep breath, sat up straighter, and told Longarm, ''The two of you could probably make it without me. There's no sense in all three of us dying and . . . since I'm done for anyway . . .''

Longarm snorted, ''Aw, stop carrying on like a gut-shot swan and pay more attention when someone's talking sense to you. When I allowed I could be wrong about that bet, I wasn't saying it wasn't worth our blowing on the dice. There's a better than fifty-fifty chance if we sit tight. We're almost certain to be tracked down and killed if we try to make Fort Sill or anywhere else on foot.''

Minerva Cranston still looked pale as a ghost as she tried

to smile and managed, "Oh, in that case maybe we'd better just sit tight."

So that was what they tried their best to do.

It wasn't easy.

Chapter 13

The Old Farmer's Almanac said summer nights averaged ten hours from dusk to dawn at that latitude. It only felt like a few thousand years when a body could neither sleep nor read in bed. They had no beds, and about a hundred years into the night that fire had died out and it was black as a bitch in there.

Both gals had somehow wound up snuggled against Longarm on either side as he reclined with his back propped high enough on his piled-up baggage for him to face the fainter black oval of the one entrance, gun in hand as he rested his weary wrist in his own crotch. On his right little Matty was softly blowing bubbles as she somehow managed to doze on and off. Minerva's straw-blond head rested lighter against his left shoulder until her occasional stifled sobs inspired him to wrap a soothing left arm around her trembling torso and point out that the longer the night dragged on the better their chances got. He said, "If the majority was in favor of killing us, they'd have made a play for it by now."

Her teeth chattered on her when she first tried to answer. Then she got them under control again and murmured, "I'm not this terrified of the Indians who *don't* want to kill us. I can't help thinking how easy it would be for the ones who spiked our supper with arsenic! Do you think they think we're alive or dead in here by now?"

To which he could only reply, "Don't know. So I can't say. We get a lot of crooks who can't resist coming back for a peek at the scene of their crime. But the smarter ones know better. I'm betting on old Pawkigoopy as the author of our woes. Kiowa medicine men are said to use more scientific curses than your average rattle-shaker. If it's him, he's likely been at such sneaky stuff long enough to stay clear and sit tight till somebody else finds his professed enemies laid out stiff by his visions. It's all right for a medicine man to have grim visions. Sitting Bull told everyone he'd had a vision of soldiers all covered with blood. But he never said he'd used poison or even chants on Custer and the Seventh Cav. They admire a prophet, but wizards make 'em proddy."

She didn't answer for a moment. She was probably considering what he'd just said, a rare trait in even a halfways pretty young gal. He knew he'd judged her right when she said, "It would be even more foolish for our secret enemy to fire bullets through these thin hide walls, wouldn't it?"

He patted her far shoulder and said, "Mighty foolish. He'd have no way to aim at anyone in particular, whilst for all he knew, he'd be giving his fool self away by attacking folks he'd already killed."

She asked, "Then why do you have that six-shooter in your lap?"

He chuckled and replied, "Ain't in my lap. Got the muzzle resting on the blanket under me. I meant what I said just now about nobody with a lick of sense creeping in on us tonight. I got my gun out for two simple reasons. I have the gun to work with, and this cruel world is afflicted with murderous fools."

She timidly asked how often he ran into them. He told her they were reasonably rare, but that his job required him to brush with more than his share. When she asked him to elaborate, he didn't want to brag on some of his wilder cases, but settled for explaining how he'd wound up over this way to begin with.

She sounded dubious as she asked him if he was sure he'd never even met that wayward wife of Attila Hornagy.

He sighed and said, "That's what makes my situation so awkward. Nine out of ten folks, just hearing his wild accusations, tend to wonder if there ain't at least a spark to go with all that smoke. I can say I've never laid eyes on Magda

Hornagy until I'm blue in the face and no judge or jury will ever find that jealous maniac guilty if ever he manages to get the drop on me.''

Minerva proved she was smart enough to teach school by whistling silently and saying, ''But if *you* killed *him*, even if he drew first, everyone would say you were a home-wrecking killer!''

Longarm sighed and said, ''My boss wants me to lie low over here in the Indian Territory whilst he tries to find out who Hornagy can really thank for his lack of domestic bliss.''

They both laughed as the same thought hit them at the same time. Matty stirred in her sleep and asked what was so funny. Longarm told her softly to go back to sleep as Minerva murmured, ''This sure seems a fine way to lie low. How on earth does that child manage to sleep so soundly at a time like this?''

Longarm said, ''She's likely tired. Her mother said she was sort of young and carefree. That's how we got you into this, I regret to say. As things turned out, I could have got in this much trouble with no help from either of you ladies.''

Minerva sighed in weary agreement and murmured, ''It sounded like such a lark when they asked me to chaperone the two of you, as if any of us are ever going to get the chance to be naughty again!''

He started to point out there'd be plenty of time to act as naughty as she cared to in times to come. Then he couldn't help wondering if she was trying to come. It would have been rude to ask a lady why she was moving and rustling like that in the dark. She must have been able to tell from his awkward silence what he suspected she was up to. For she suddenly stopped, sighed, and murmured, ''I must be going crazy. My Aunt Ida said the little girl across the way went crazy because she couldn't leave herself alone until the right man came along.''

Longarm thought it might sound cruel to agree with a lady who was already confounded enough. He quietly said, ''There seems to be something about feeling hurt or scared that makes folks sort of, well . . . fidgety. Wounded soldiers are always proposing to their nurses, and there's some argument as to whether hanged men stiffen up so silly before or after they hit the end of the rope.''

She softly asked, ''Are you saying all this has made you feel more amorous than usual, Custis?''

He chuckled and said, ''I always feel more amorous than usual. But I got to cover that doorway, no offense.''

She stiffened and demanded, ''Did you think for one moment I was suggesting anything improper, good sir? I was only asking a question, not extending an invitation!''

He tried to say he hadn't meant to sound dirty. But she'd already rolled away in the darkness to flop down on some piled buffalo robes, and after a suspenseful silence he could hear her breathing harder in time with the softer sounds of what seemed like a frisky puppy thumping its tail by the back door to be let out.

He was mighty tempted to just roll over and help her scratch what ailed her, but he didn't see how he could let little Matty's head fall that far without waking her.

That conjured up a really silly scene in Longarm's head. But he managed not to laugh out loud as he considered how the sassy little gal Minerva had come along to chaperone was really chaperoning her elders without half trying, or really knowing what was going on.

As he heard Minerva moaning in the darkness, ''Custis, please!'' he softly murmured, ''You'll be sorry you ever said that once we get out of this fix alive. But no offense, this is about the last time or place I'd ever risk getting caught with my pants down!''

Chapter 14

Longarm hadn't been trying to doze off, but he saw he must have when he awoke with a start to see daylight in the entryway across from them and heard all sorts of commotion outside.

He eased Matty's drowsy head from his lap, and rolled over to holster his gun and stab the tipi cover with his knife. When he put an eye to the puncture he saw ponies swirling in a haze of dust in the center of the tipi ring. Minerva sat up on her pile of buffalo robes to ask what all the fuss was about.

Longarm replied, "Ain't certain. They've run all their riding stock inside the ring for safekeeping and never mind the mess. Some kids from another band might be out to have some fun. On the other hand they might really be worried about something."

A figure appeared in the entryway to call out in bad English that the man, not the women, was wanted at the Do-giagya-guat. So Longarm tossed the pocket knife near her, saying, "Open some more cans and don't eat or drink anything else before I get back, hear?"

Matty sat up, rubbing her eyes, to ask what they were supposed to do if he never came back. Longarm didn't offer any suggestions as he rolled to his feet and ducked outside. It would have sounded hard to point out it wouldn't really be his problem.

He followed his Kiowa guide through the swirling confusion, noting he didn't seem to be under guard as the Indians worked to get set for something ominous.

He found old Necomi and the other Kiowa elders out front of that big painted tipi, along with five younger Indians dressed much the same with different beadwork. When he heard everybody talking in English he caught on. The visitors had to be Kiowa-Apache, allied or adopted and hence half-ass Kiowa who spoke another lingo entirely. He knew Na-déné, spoken by the so-called Apache, Navajo, and such, was as tough for either a white man or Indian as Arabic or Turkish might be for your average cowhand. You could ask a Comanche or a Lakota what a buffalo was, and while one would say *tatanka* and the other called it *kutsu*, they agreed to call the critter *something*. But Na-déné speakers would ask you whether you meant a buffalo off a ways or in plain sight, grazing, running, or hell, shitting.

Kiowa could only powwow with their little brothers in English or Sign, and Sign being slower, the meeting that morning was being conducted in the hated tongue of the blue sleeves.

Necomi told the head Kiowa-Apache, a scar-faced runt called Eskiminzin, to tell the damned government rider his sad story. So the runty Kiowa-Apache did. He said his own band ranged west of the Wichitas, as close to the reservation line as they could manage without making the Great Father angry. He said they'd been raided more than once by riders who'd sure as hell looked like Kiowa Black Leggings.

Necomi sighed and told Longarm, "Maybe you did not lie about the riders you fought with over by Cache Creek. But somebody is lying about being members of our lodge and we are very cross, very!"

Eskiminzin said, "My Kiowa uncle is not as cross as the women we left back along Elk Creek, throwing dust in the air and calling us cowards because we let the Comanche Police bring our ponies back for us without killing any two-hearted Kiowa raiders! Listen to me, all of you, there must be blood for blood, and one of our pony guards was stabbed in the back by those Black Leggings!"

The outraged Necomi roared, "No Black Legging rider owes any blood to anybody! We just told this other twittering magpie from the Great Father that our lodge has done nothing,

nothing, to be blamed for all these silly fights! Hear me, when and if we *do* put on our paint and follow the warpath again, we will not be stopped by a few shots or less than a thousand enemies!''

Longarm didn't wait for the runty Eskiminzin to tell the older man he was full of shit. In a more soothing tone he asked about those Comanche Police. He pointed out, ''Elk Creek ain't all that close to the Comanche range southeast of Fort Sill, is it?''

The Kiowa-Apache grumbled, ''We never invited Quanah's white-eyed Comanche in blue sleeves to patrol along Elk Creek. They told us they had to patrol all the reservation lines because nobody else was willing to join them. Maybe we were not so cross the second time they rode by, right after those Black Leggings killed that boy and drove off two hundred of our best ponies!''

Longarm nodded soberly and said, ''Chores such as that were what Quanah and the B.I.A. had in mind when they commenced to organize such forces for this big reserve. I don't think any of your Kiowa brothers from the real Black Leggings Lodge ran that stock off on you. I think Necomi here was right about some big fibbers pretending to be a bunch more feared and respected than your average band of horse thieves.''

Necomi gasped, ''Riders who were never initiated into our lodge in the leggings and paint of members? Who would do such a terrible thing? Who would *dare*? Tanapah, the great bright eye in the sky, would tell all the other spirits, and *then* where would they be? Everyone knows it is wrong to use another person's *puha*, or even to paint one's pony in the same way, without offering him a present and getting his permission!''

Eskiminzin nodded gravely and volunteered, ''This is true among my people too. I paid the first very rich Aravaipa *ranchero* for the use of this prosperous and powerful name. It would have been bad medicine if I had just stolen the name like a chicken!''

Longarm nodded and said, ''I understand about your old ways. Sort of. Maybe these raiders pretending to be honorable Kiowa have forgotten the old ways. Tell me about those Comanche Police recovering your run-off stock without having to gun any of the rascals.''

The Kiowa-Apache shrugged and said, ''None of us were there. The blue sleeves said that they only had to track the stolen ponies a day and a night. They said they found them in a draw at dawn. The men who'd run them off were not there. So the Comanche only had to round them up and herd them back to us. Their sergeant said he did not think the stinking Kiowa wanted to fight Comanche. So they ran away in the dark.''

Necomi gasped, ''That was a bad thing to say! Hear me! Any rabbit-killing Comanche who thinks even a Kiowa girl-child is *afraid* of him had better stop dreaming and wake up!''

Longarm shook his head and said, ''Don't get your bowels in such an uproar, Chief. There used to be some troublemakers called Romans on the far side of the Great Bitter Water. They liked to get the rest of us white folks to fighting amongst ourselves by spreading just such an easy mess of fibs. Then they'd move in and stick us with spears. They called their game divide and conquer.''

Eskiminzin asked innocently, ''You mean the way your Eagle Chief Carson got the Utes to fight our western cousins for him over in the Canyon de Chelly?''

Longarm laughed sheepishly and said, ''It worked, didn't it? What I'm saying about these mysterious raiders is that anyone can slip on a pair of black leggings. And they've been acting more like plain and simple outlaws than any warrior society I know of. I got a good look at three of them, dead, over by Cache Creek. So I'd be mighty surprised to discover they were a gang of Minnesota Swedes. But how do you boys feel about them being Mexican bandits, dressed up in Kiowa duds to confound the law, both red and white?''

Eskiminzin shook his head and said, ''They were heard shouting back and forth. Nobody could tell what they were saying, but it did not sound at all like Spanish. Many of our people speak enough Spanish to deal with Mexican . . . ah, horse traders.''

Longarm dryly observed, ''That likely accounts for all this sudden interest in horseflesh and the reservation borders. I'll ask directly, with a better chance of getting a straight answer, when I catch up with those Comanche Police. Did they say which post they were working out of, Eskiminzin?"

The runty Kiowa-Apache looked blank. Longarm nodded and muttered, "Never mind. Some damned body is supposed to keep files on everything, and recovering two hundred head of *goats* would rate a commendation. I don't suppose you could give me that patrol leader's name?"

Eskiminzin soberly replied, "I could not even give you *my* name, if you mean my *real* name, given to me in a vision by White Painted Woman. But the Comanche who brought back our ponies said we could call him Black Sheep, in your tongue, after we told him his Comanche words meant nothing, nothing to a real person."

Longarm cocked a brow and marveled, "That Tuka Wa Pombi sure gets around! A few days ago he was trying to collect passage fees off a Texican trail boss, and when I asked about that at their nearest field headquarters, none of the Comanche Police I spoke to had ever heard of a comrade by such a name."

Eskiminzin shrugged and said, "There are many reasons, many, for a man to give different names at different times. He may be trying to avoid an evil *chindi*, or the husband of some wicked woman he met when he was full of *tiswin* and forgot you are not supposed to do that with another man's woman."

Longarm smiled thinly and declared, "That last notion sounds way more reasonable than ducking evil spirits. There can't be all that big a police force. So sooner or later we're bound to meet up and I can just ask him. Did they say where they were headed next?"

The Kiowa-Apache nodded gravely and replied, "They said they had to take the money to Chief Quanah."

Longarm frowned thoughtfully and asked what money they might be talking about.

The runty Kiowa-Apache explained, "The money they need to buy more blue sleeves and guns. They said if our young men would not join the Indian Police, then the least we could do would be to pay our fair share. Meeting in council, our elders agreed. They had brought back our ponies. They had done a good job of tracking after our own young men had lost the trail where slickrock runs down into Elk Creek. We were surprised that Comanche could do this.''

Necomi scowled and said, ''So am I. Our little Kiowa-Apache brothers range closer than the rest of us to their old hunting grounds between these hills and the Washita bottomlands. Would you say I was crazy if I wondered about liars dressing up as both Black Leggings and Indian Police?''

Longarm shook his head and replied, ''I would say great minds are inclined to run in the same channels. No Indian Police led by anyone by any name are authorized to collect money in the name of Quanah Parker. The Bureau of Indian Affairs, run with government money by Little Big Eyes or Interior Secretary Schurz, pays and equips all the Indian Police on all the reserves. Chief Quanah's business dealings are matters of civil law, backed up as such by federal or local courts, depending on what the problem might be.''

Necomi was first to get the picture. He said, ''This Black Sheep was not supposed to ask those drivers for money. He was not supposed to ask our little Kiowa-Apache brothers for money. He is . . . what?''

''A crook,'' said Longarm flatly. ''There's this more pallid outfit over near New Orleans called the Black *Hand* instead of Sheep. There's no natural law saying an Indian with a droll sense of humor and an eye for easy money couldn't read the *Police Gazette* and see how the Black Hand flimflams other folks less inclined than average to send for the regular law.''

He saw none of the Indians gaping at him knew what he was talking about, even if they spoke English. So he simplified the protection swindle of the notorious Black Hand, and even a Horse Indian could see how once a bunch of friendly-acting toughs could pretend to protect a neighborhood from meaner-acting members of the same gang.

Eskiminzin gasped, ''It would be easy, easy to track stolen ponies over slickrock and through running water if you knew just where some secret friends had left them for you!''

Necomi said, ''That is why there was no fight. Those riders acting as if they were Kiowa Black Leggings never really wanted all those ponies! Where could they have sold them on this crowded reserve? I think it was all a trick to make you pay good money for your own ponies!''

Longarm nodded. But before he could answer, Necomi cut

in. "Then what are these forked tongues when they are not pretending to be other people? Are they wicked Kiowa or evil Comanche?"

It was a good question. Longarm said it was too early to say, and asked if he and the ladies were free to go ask. Necomi said they had never been prisoners and that he'd have his young men cut out and saddle their ponies for them. They'd just agreed a cuss with a forked tongue was no good. So Longarm turned and strode through sunlit dust and dark Kiowa curses to rejoin the two gals. Along the way he met up with old Pawkigoopy, shaking his rattle and chanting while the others did all the work to secure their camp. When the medicine man saw Longarm bearing down on him alive and well, he looked as if he'd been fed something awful himself. Longarm just grinned wolfishly and hauled out a couple of cheroots, asking the goggle-eyed Indian if he'd like a heap strong smoke.

Pawkigoopy ran away, calling on his spirit pals for help against what had to be Longarm's heap stronger medicine.

Longarm lit one cheroot and put the other away as he circled out of the tipi ring to rejoin the gals from the east. He was glad their particular tipi faced away from the swirling confusion inside the tipi ring. Since every tipi faced the same way, the folks on the other side of the circle were stuck with the settling dust and fly-blown horseshit whether they were under attack or not.

As he ducked inside he asked if either gal had tasted anything but their own supplies. Matty said a Kiowa gal had offered them some coffee, but they'd poured it on the cold ashes when nobody had been looking.

Longarm said, "Good thinking. We're fixing to ride out any minute, so let's pull ourselves together in here."

Minerva Cranston commenced to pin her hair back atop her skull as she murmured, not meeting Longarm's eye, "I suppose I owe you an explanation for the way I carried on last night."

He shook his head and said, "Save it for the next sewing bee. Right now the inner thoughts of a teasing schoolmarm are the least of my worries."

He scooped up his saddlebags and told them to join him

outside as pronto as possible. Then he ducked out of the tipi to see that things had simmered down a bit, with most everybody and his or her belongings forted up inside the circle of thin-skinned but mysterious hide shelters.

Unless you had the element of surprise riding with you, it could be injurious to one's health to blindly charge a tipi ring. For some would be empty, while others might be hornet's nests of dug-in riflemen. Horse Indians fought differently, but that wasn't to say they fought stupidly, or didn't learn new tricks along the way. Dull Knife's band had given the army a scare, despite the hopeless odds, when troopers inspecting the Cheyenne's last encampment near White River found more than one deep pit inside a tipi with its cover rolled up a few inches all around to offer a ground-level field of fire.

Dull Knife had only given in because he was low on food, blankets, and ammunition, as well as smart. Army pals had told Longarm some of the more recent hostiles had learned to reload their brass cartridges with home-brew black powder and fashion fresh slugs from hammered telegraph wire. They used mushed-up match heads for cartridge caps. The War Department had wanted to forbid the sale of kitchen matches at Indian trading posts, until cooler heads had pointed out how many Indians who didn't know that trick would surely get matches from the settlers all around them, even as they pondered why the army found this so important.

A brace of Kiowa kids came around the bend on foot, leading Gray Skies and the other four ponies. So Longarm yelled for the two tardy gals to get their tardy rumps out there, and once they had, he soon had the three of them riding east at an easy lope.

He reined in on a rise a quarter mile out and made sure nobody was right on their tail. Then he told his two female companions to stick tight and follow his lead.

They did as he whirled Gray Skies and plunged down the far slope, to where the pony trail crossed a barely wet and braided sandy rill along the bottom of the draw. He warned them not to cut any corners with their own hooves as he headed Gray Skies upstream in the fetlock-deep but patiently running water. Matty seemed to follow his drift, but Minerva called forward, "Where are we going, Custis? I thought we were headed back to Quanah's agency over *that* way!"

Longarm called back, "Let's hope everyone else thinks we are too. We'd never make it that far across open prairie with anyone serious on our trail. So we'd best head up into the woody Wichitas and see if we can't make Fort Sill the long way round instead."

Matty whooped, "I like to shop at Fort Sill. They have ribbons of different colors than our Indian trader sells, and red licorice whips and ladies' fashion magazines. Why don't they sell fashion magazines at our trading post, Custis? Don't they want us to be fashionable?"

He figured she might be on to something, but he said he just didn't know. As they rode up the streamlet, chokecherry and box elder pressed in more densely from either side. So by the time they came to where the water sprang from the sandy head of the draw, they were out of sight of the trail they'd forsaken. Longarm led the way around some bow-wood, or Osage orange, and through some cottonwoods to ride up as steep a slope as they could manage, hoping nobody would scout for any sign where nobody with a lick of sense would force his mount to go.

When they cut a more sensible deer trail cutting northeast at a gentler angle, Longarm decided to follow it. If anyone was slick enough to figure where they might be headed, they wanted their mounts in shape for a running gunfight down the slope. Longarm studied on that as he led the way single file. He had his Winchester Yellowboy again to back his six-gun and derringer. Matty had insisted on packing a nickel-plated Harrington & Richardson .32-18 in a saddlebag as if she might be fixing to start off a pony race on demand. Minerva hadn't brought any firearms at all. When asked, she'd allowed nobody had ever shown her how to fire a gun. So that was another way she'd turned out different from that newspaper gal, Godiva Weaver, cuss the two of them combined.

They had to rest and water their ponies more than once, working up through the scrubby timber or high chaparral, depending on what was rooted where on the rocky slopes. Longarm was paying attention to the sky, knowing how easy it was to get turned around in hills that hadn't read the same large-scale map. So it was little Matty, staring back the way they'd come, who called out, "Down in those blackjack oaks, past that outcrop we passed half an hour ago!"

Longarm stared long and hard before he made out brownish movement way down yonder. He nodded but said, "Anyone following this trail could have as innocent a reason. But why don't we give them a chance to prove they ain't dogging us in particular?"

They didn't know what he meant, so he led them a good way along the apparent natural trail along the crest of a side ridge that only groped its way to a wooded knoll that overlooked the real trail from two furlongs north and forty feet higher. As they neared the sort of island in the sky, he reined in and dismounted, telling them to do the same as he explained, "The winds up here have tangled those blackjacks, and better yet, there's an undertangle of hellish bow-wood, if only we can get these ponies through it."

They could, but it wasn't easy, even with little Matty helping. Being a Horse Indian raised in bow-wood country, she knew how to deal with the ornery natural bobwire.

Back East, where they called it Osage orange, bow-wood growing in a park like some floral pet could stand on one trunk about the size and shape of a crab apple, although thorny as a rosebush and bearing a sort of mock orange hard as wood. But out here where it had to fight a more ferocious climate for its life, the results were wilder. Bow-wood branches coppiced, meaning you got two or three new thorny sprouts wherever you busted off or simply peeled some bark off a wind-whipped limb. The Indians had cut stouter branches to make a heap of short tough bows of the springy wood before they'd switched to more lethal firearms. Early settlers had planted and trimmed bow-wood into buffalo-proof hedgerows before both the buffalo and slower-growing fencing had given way to bobwire. Up here on the knoll the wickedly thorned and wind-pruned greenery had taken the time to grow. So with Matty holding some branches back, and him cutting a few more, they soon had themselves and their ponies forted up inside what the surprised Minerva described as a natural bower.

That was what she said you called a shaded clearing roofed over or walled by tough sunlit branches, a bower.

Longarm tethered the ponies as deep in the little glade as he could get them, and told the otherwise less useful Minerva to pick some bow-wood leaves for them while he and Matty scouted the far sides of the knoll. No warm-blooded critter would eat oak leaves, but bow-wood grew those thorns to protect its juicy leaves.

Gingerly parting the sticker-brush to the north with Matty and her small revolver in tow, Longarm saw that approach was steeper but brushier. So he told Matty, "If those other riders are on their own business, they'll pass on by. If they're after us, and figure out where we are, they'll circle afoot to creep up this slope through all that tanglewood."

He cradled the Winchester Yellowboy in one arm as he drew his Colt .44-40 and handed it to her, saying, "It's an insult to shoot a grown man with a .32-Short. But take both pistols over to the far side and keep an eye on that trail whilst I guard our back entrance. I don't want no needless gunplay. I'd rather have 'em *guess* where we might be. Do you know how to twitter like a horned lark?"

The breed kid proved she could by doing so. But then she told him she didn't think any horned larks would be this far off their usual prairie range.

Longarm nodded and said, "That's why I chose such a signal. It's *possible* to hear grassland birds up here amid all this tanglewood, but unlikely enough to make for a handy code whistle. Horn-lark me once if you see those other riders doing anything. Whistle twice if they seem to be searching for us. Three whistles will mean they're getting warm. Now *git*! I don't know how much time we have to get set for whatever."

Matty nodded and scampered off through the dappled shade, a gun in each hand. Longarm took off his jacket and hung it on a thorny bow-wood branch, along with his hat. Then he got down on his belly to lizard through the sticker-brush with the Yellowboy cradled in his elbows until he had a clear field of fire down the far-from-clear northern slopes.

Putting himself in the boots or moccasins of someone trying to work his way *up* through all that tanglewood, he decided on the three best ways to creep. That wasn't saying some son of a bitch with a different view of this knoll couldn't plan an entirely different approach. But a man with fifteen rounds in an antiquated repeater had to start with *some* damned plan.

He levered a round into the hitherto empty chamber, and slid another round into the magazine, making that sixteen rounds to work with. He could only hope that would be enough.

He'd just told himself not to be such an old fuss when Minerva Cranston spotted his boot heels sticking out the other side of his thorny green tunnel and gasped, "Oh, there you are. Custis, I feel so helpless and I'm so scared! What's going on out there?"

He could only reply, "Nothing. As the morning warms up you don't hear half as much skittering. There's a red-tail circling off to the northeast above another wooded rise. That's about the size of it. Not even an interesting cloud to ponder, as far as the eye can see."

She got down on her hands and knees to crawl forward through the brush, catching her thinly clad rump in a thorn and bitching about it.

Longarm laughed, not unkindly, and observed, "That was the first thing they warned us about when I was a young and foolish recruit. Green troops always seem to know enough to keep their heads down. So a soldier's first wound, if it ain't fatal, is likely to be undignified. Lay flat in the dirt and sort of slither your hips as you walk on your elbows. Why do you want to move this deep in the brush to begin with?"

She worked her way up his left flank as she panted, "I told you. I'm scared skinny and you have that gun. And, as I tried to tell you earlier, there's a reason, if not an excuse, for the silly way I tend to behave when I'm upset. Don't you want to know why I was so . . . forward last night in that tipi?"

He didn't, but as he'd learned aboard many a stagecoach or steamboat, there was no stopping a woman once she'd decided to tell you the story of her life, and what the hell, that fool hawk wasn't up yonder to admire now.

Minerva said she'd been about Matty's age, feeling just as put upon, when she'd run off from her strict upbringing with a handsome drifter called Ace. She said she hadn't known he was a gambling man with a drinking problem until they wound up stranded in a fleabag hotel over in Dodge.

Reflecting that the childish Matty *might* be dumb enough to fall for a saddle tramp called Ace, Longarm gently asked how come he'd gotten the impression she'd first come west as an employee of the B.I.A.

Minerva answered simply, "I left a few things off my civil service application. How does a spinster qualify herself as a schoolteacher by declaring she finally left a depraved brute after he'd offered a night in bed with her as table stakes in Laredo?"

Longarm calmly asked who'd won.

She laughed bitterly and said, "I didn't wait to find out. The older and probably wiser gambler Ace propositioned wanted to hear I approved of the wager, as he put it, before he bet hard cash."

Her voice dropped almost to a whisper as she continued, half to herself. "They called him Baltimore, and I guess I never got to thank him properly. After I got hysterical, and they'd carried Ace across the street to the infirmary, Baltimore led me firmly but gently to the boat landing and put me on a riverboat bound for Brownsville. He gave me some money and told me he'd take care of everything there in Laredo. I guess he did. I never tried to find out. I knew Ace had only been pistol-whipped, and I was afraid that if he ever got me back in his power there might not *be* a Baltimore the next time."

Longarm nodded soberly and said, "I've heard similar tales from parlor-house gals who weren't so lucky. If I live to be a hundred I will never understand how nice gals from gentle homes manage to pass up all the nice young neighborhood gents in favor of some weak-chinned self-styled roughneck calling himself Ace, Duke, or Frenchy. I reckon a total stranger who needs a bath is more exciting than the boy next door, eh?"

Minerva sighed and said, "Ace smelled of larkspur lotion and put on a fresh shirt every day when we were in the money. There were times we were too broke for that. The gambling life means steak with champagne some nights, with beer and beans more often."

"Sounds mighty glamorous," Longarm muttered dryly.

Minerva said, "I liked it best when we were broke. That was when Ace seemed to pay the most attention to me. When we were in the money he stayed up half the night and came to bed too tired to . . . you know.''

Longarm muttered, ''I told you I'd heard the same story many, many times. A bum with nothing better to do is naturally going to spend way more time playing slap and tickle with his gal than a gent with a job to go to. Why are you telling me all this, Miss Minerva? You got away from the useless rascal just in time, didn't you?''

She answered simply, ''No. Not all the way. There have naturally been other men since. Some of them fine men. What you'd describe as the boy next door. I haven't been able to feel anything for any of them. I think it's because I feel so . . . safe with them. I know you don't have any idea of what I'm talking about, but . . .''

''Aw, I ain't that ignorant,'' Longarm told her. ''I check out books from the Denver Public Library when I'm low on pocket change near payday. I've read about them Vienna alienist doctors who worry about what folks are really thinking when they talk sort of *loco en la cabeza.* You're confounded about feeling hot around menfolk because a poor excuse for a man broke you in bass-akwards!''

She protested, ''Custis, Ace and I never went in for anything all that perverse. We just made sweet love a lot when things seemed to be going bad for us. I remember this time in Cheyenne when Ace and I were waiting for a wired money order and couldn't show ourselves outside our hotel room for three whole days and nights.''

''I said I followed your drift,'' Longarm told her, trying to ignore the way his privates had started to throb against the soil under him.

She said, ''You're so understanding. I felt so silly this morning. But last night, alone in the dark with no other man to turn to as those memories of other tense nights came back unbidden . . .''

Longarm grimaced and groaned, ''I know you're feeling tense again. So am I. But it ain't the same. Your Ace might have been enough of a baby to grope for a nipple when he should have been working on a way out of a tight spot. But we ain't holed up in some rooming house to avoid our creditors, Miss Minerva.''

She gasped, ''What a horrid way to talk to a lady!''

So he said, "*Act* like a lady, or at least a grown woman, and I'll be proud to kiss your hand, or any other part of you, once we make it to Fort Sill alive."

He couldn't resist adding, "Fortunately, they have locks on the bedroom doors at the army guest hostel. So I won't be able to get at you once you're feeling less inspired."

She told him he was a brute. He said, "Never mind what I am and go see why Matty's tweeting like a horned lark getting eaten alive by red ants!"

Minerva gasped, "Dear Lord! Is that who all that chirping over to the east is coming from?"

Longarm said, "Never mind. I see them now. Just like I thought they might, they've circled through the brush below. Matty never fooled 'em with her lark whistles. We'll soon see whether they expected me to be covering this side with a Winchester!"

Chapter 15

A long time crept by and the sun just kept rising in a sultry blue sky. Nothing else seemed to be happening. From time to time some shrubbery down the slope would sway as if a ripple of breeze was moving in the still summer air. Longarm was almost certain the rascals who'd surrounded them just out of rifle range were flashing rare glimpses of brown skin instead of blue shirt as they moved from one patch of deeper cover to another.

Longarm and Matty had the nervous Minerva dashing back and forth with messages from time to time. Although neither had all that much to report. Matty's story was that she'd barely spotted a distant party of what looked to be Kiowa, riding single-file, when they'd all reined in to dismount, lead their ponies off the trail, and commence to sneak all about.

When Longarm sent a message asking Matty which side they'd dismounted from, she didn't remember. Minerva asked what difference it made, and Longarm could only say, "None most likely. Even Indian Police would be inclined to mount or dismount Horse Indian style, from the off side."

"Off side?" asked the mighty green schoolmarm.

Longarm said, "That's the right-hand side of a pony. You mount it from the near or left side if you're a white rider. Being contrary or mayhaps self-taught, most Horse Nations get on and off the opposite way. It don't matter all that much.

I'm fixing to be surprised as all get-out if these fake Black Legging Kiowa turn out to be Irishmen.''

Prone beside him under the bow-wood, Minerva asked how he knew they were fake, adding that she couldn't see anybody down yonder.

Longarm replied, ''That's about all I'm halfway sure about. Chief Necomi, Hawzitah, and those other elders run the *real* Black Leggings Lodge. Had they wanted any of us hurt by their outfit, they had us in their power last night. So why would the leaders of the real warrior lodge turn us loose with arms and trail supplies this morning if they meant us any harm?''

She pointed out, ''Somebody in that band tried to poison us last night, didn't they?''

He nodded, but said, ''That makes the Kiowa leaders look even more innocent. Like I said, they *had* us had they meant to really make us vanish from this earth, as Necomi suggested they might. He was only trying to scare the truth out of me about that earlier brush with those mystery riders. When the Kiowa-Apache backed my story we got to be pals again. I suspect that medicine man, Pawkigoopy, might have at least a part in all this confusion. On the other hand, he could just be a mean old Kiowa medicine man. None of them could have been all that happy about our whipping them and turning a once-proud nation into wards of the government. So it's possible Pawkigoopy or some other malcontent was just trying to murder us on his or her own!''

Minerva said he'd never know how cheerful that notion made her.

She asked how else those Indians down the slope could have known which way they'd gone unless someone in Necomi's band had told them.

Longarm said, ''They tracked us. They tracked us good. Nobody could have told them we'd be cutting this way through these hills because I never *told* nobody.''

He stared down through the shimmering silence thoughtfully as he added, ''They must really want us bad. I sure wish I knew why.''

Minerva stared pensively down at the dusty green tanglewood and wondered aloud whether anyone was still there.

Longarm flatly stated, "They're there. Like us, they're trying to decide their next move. Playing chess for keeps is tough enough when you've some notion what the other player might be thinking."

Minerva asked Longarm if *he* had any moves in mind.

Longarm glanced up at the cobalt-blue sky before he replied, "I ain't so sure about the only one I've come up with. If we yell for help it's likely to inspire an all-out attack before help could get here. I figure, just as they must figure, a daylight charge up steep slopes could cost 'em. Henceways, if we just sit tight up here, they ain't as likely to move in before sundown."

Minerva gulped but said, "I read somewhere that Indians seldom attack after dark."

Longarm grimaced and asked, "How often do you *want* 'em to? Captain Walker of the Texas Rangers recorded one time that Comanche hate to charge on horseback in total darkness, for reasons anyone ought to be able to see. Then some Eastern writer turned sensible cavalry tactics into Heap Big Medicine. Likely the same authority on Indians as the one who decided they prayed to a Great Spirit who presided over a half-baked Christian heaven called the Happy Hunting Ground."

The schoolmarm, who prided herself on her own study of Indian lore, demanded, "Well, don't they?"

Longarm said, "Sure they do, if they're Christian converts. A heap of 'em are, more than once, with Anglo-Protestant missionaries holding the mistaken notion they've saved the souls of pagans already taught a heap of tales from the Good Book by earlier Spanish or French church workers."

A blackjack oak trembled as if caressed by a mountain breeze. So Longarm muttered, "They're tethering their own ponies as if they mean to stay a spell. I wish I could at least guess their nation. Different Indians do use somewhat different tactics and—"

"Over there! By those big yellow flowers!" gasped Minerva, even as Longarm fired into the clump of sunflowers.

They heard somebody yip like a kicked pup. Then Longarm had pushed the schoolmarm one way and rolled the other as a fusillade of rifle balls shredded leaves where they'd just been.

Longarm fired thrice at the dirty cotton bolls of gunsmoke giving away positions down the slope, rolling over once each time he gave them some to shoot at. Then, figuring any marksman worth his salt had to guess he'd keep rolling the same way, he rolled back through his own shot-up positions, watching in vain for another target of opportunity until he found himself back in conversational range with the bewildered schoolmarm. He smiled reassuringly at her and told her to go tell Matty what had happened, see what Matty had to say, and get back to him.

She moaned, "Oh, Custis, I'm so scared, and so excited between my thighs that I fear I'm about to climax!"

He said, "It'll feel just as good on the run. Get moving! This is a goddamn gunfight, not a time to start screwing, girl!"

She blushed beet red and jumped up to run off through the dappled shade as, down near those sunflowers, he heard someone shouting something. It could have been "*agua,*" which was Mexican for water. A cuss stretched out on a dusty slope with two hundred grains of .44-40 lead in him would doubtless want some. But an *Indian* asking another Indian for a drink of water in Spanish?

Longarm was backing out of the natural bow-wood hedgerow as Minerva rejoined him, flopping to her knees in the dust beside him with her straw-colored hair half undone. She gasped, "Matty said nobody seemed to be moving in from her side! Oh, Custis, I'm so hot!"

He had to laugh, although not unkindly, as he handed her his pocket derringer and placed her awkward thumb on the break lever, pressing it as they broke open the simple mechanism together. She protested she didn't know anything about guns. He just extracted the two live rounds, thumbed them back in place, and twisted the tiny brass weapon in shape to fire both as he dug out some spare rounds for her.

He said, "They don't know how much you might or might not know about guns. They won't know what you're firing, at whom, if you just blaze away and roll somewhere else every time you spot any motion.''

She sobbed, ''You're crazy. I couldn't hit the side of a barn if I was standing inside it! You can't run off and leave me to defend this side!''

He said, ''I ain't going far, and I'll be back like a shot as soon as I hear you fire one round. I just heard one of 'em call for water in Spanish. Lord only knows what Mex outlaws could be up to this far north. But they might not know any more than you about Kiowa, Comanche, and such, no offense.''

He saw she was just kneeling there. So he set his Winchester to one side and placed a gentle hand on each of her trembling shoulders with the intent of steering her back through that bow-wood screen.

She seemed to misread his intent. It sure felt silly to wrestle with a kissy schoolmarm as she tried to haul him down atop her with a derringer in one hand and fistful of ammunition in the other. But he was bigger and stronger, as well as more worried about their lives beyond the next five minutes. So he finally had her posted belly-down and aimed the right way.

This left him free to scoop up his Yellowboy and move over to the grounded saddles near their tethered mounts in the deeper shade.

Opening a packsaddle, Longarm broke out a kindling hatchet and a ground tarp before he got to work on some lower oak branches. He found some dry duff sprinkled with acorns, and even a few dry twigs. But he broke open a couple of .44-40 rounds to sprinkle eighty grains of gunpowder on his tinder before he piled the green lengths of oak wood atop it. He thumbed a match head aflame to light his small pile of piss-poor firewood. Then he ran over to where Matawnkiha Gordon was holding the fort with a pistol in each small tawny fist. When he asked Matty how she was doing, the Kiowa, Comanche, and Scotch-Irish gal said things had been quiet as a graveyard on her side, and asked him what all that shooting had been about on his side.

He brought her up to date in a few terse phrases, and asked, ''Seeing you speak both Kiowa and Comanche, no offense, do you recall any word in either lingo that sounds like *agua*, the Spanish for water?''

Matty thought, then shook her head and said, ''*Uka* means to eat in what you people call Comanche.''

Longarm shook his head and said, ''My ears ain't *that* far off, and even if they were, a man lying wounded on a dusty slope would surely want some water to drink before he demanded a ham sandwich.''

Matty said she didn't see why Mexicans would want to dress up like Kiowa Black Leggings and carry on so oddly. Longarm told her he was still working on it, and ran back to see how his smudgy fire was doing.

It was smoldering a lot, with much more dense gray smoke than visible flames. He nodded in satisfaction, set the Winchester aside again, and used the ground tarp to send up a series of smoky dots and dashes. Then he scooped up his saddle gun and rejoined Minerva, just in time.

Those two shots he'd heard on his way to her side had been fired blind, with the beginner's luck and natural aim of a gal shooting at a frightening target with both eyes shut.

She'd hit the half-naked cuss in the thigh, and he was still crawling back down an open stretch when Longarm called out, ''*Como no, cabron! Alte o te voy a mandar pa'l carajo!*''

The swarthy bare-chested cuss in black leggings kept going, so Longarm shot him in the ass and he didn't move in any direction once he'd finished flopping down the slope a good ways.

Longarm got himself and Minerva well clear of his own gunsmoke as he muttered, ''I told him I'd send him on to Hell if he didn't stay put. Matty agrees with me that one of them was calling for water in Spanish before. So that fool we both shot should have known what I was saying.''

Minerva moaned, ''I'm about to come! Won't you even stick a finger in there for me, Custis?''

To which he could only reply, ''Not just now. The next few minutes should tell the tale. I just sent up a pillar of smoke they ought to be able to see from Fort Sill. So those sneaks just down the way must have a much better view of it. Indian or Mex, they ought to be able to figure out why. So now they're making up their minds whether they want to charge like Pickett or ride for their lives. They know they don't have until nightfall now. I figure it won't take a full hour for my old pal, Colonel Howard, to order out a patrol once somebody points out our mysterious smoke signals. It might move him faster if you'd like to toss on more leaves and flip-flop that tarp from time to time."

Minerva grimaced and declared, "I've been taking notes on Indian customs. But I don't even know Morse code, Custis."

Longarm said, "Just try for any old dots and dashes. The cavalry are more likely to ride over and see who's sending 'em up than they are to worry about decoding it!"

She didn't seem to be moving. He insisted, "Give it a try. A patrol from Fort Sill would be hard pressed to make it here in less than four hours if we got 'em started right now!"

She moaned that wouldn't be soon enough, and started to back out of the sticker-brush. He told her to hang on to that derringer and just let fly a blind shot from time to time in the two directions neither he nor Matty could cover. She got to her feet, bawling like a baby but heading for that smudge fire. So Longarm concentrated on the slope he hoped they'd choose to charge.

If the cavalry came at all, they'd be moving in from the southeast not much later than noon. He knew that down below they knew they had to shit or get off the pot a lot sooner. You didn't want a cavalry column less than two hours behind you as you lit out, even when you'd won. Admirers of either cowboys or Indians might not know it, but the well-shod and oat-fed cavalry stock selected by the Army Remount Service tended to outlast and overtake more casually cared-for ponies.

Staring down through the shimmering sunlight, Longarm tried to put himself in the other side's fix. It might have been easier if he'd had a better line on who in the hell they might be.

He composed some nasty Mexican insults with care, knowing how tough it was to cuss in Mexican. English enjoyed the luxury of words that were dirty all by themselves. You had to be more poetic in Spanish. Son of a bitch lost its sting translated into *"hijo de perra,"* because you had to settle for a plain old female hound. *"Cabron,"* meaning goat, was a meaner thing to call a Mexican because a goat, like a betrayed husband, wore big but nearly harmless horns.

Recalling what some border raiders had once tried on him and a mess of Ranger pals, Longarm cupped a palm over his mouth to blur just where he might be calling from as he bawled, *"Ay, que mariposas, es probable que son sesenta y nueve!"*

Somebody pegged a shot where they thought he might be. He couldn't say whether the one behind that outcrop was annoyed at the suggestion he was a butterfly sucking off a pal, or whether he'd just sounded off longer than he should have.

He yelled, *"Tu madre!"* which was usually good for a flying bottle in any well-run cantina, and sure enough, that same hothead behind that same outcrop let fly another round.

Longarm didn't return the fire. His hidden target was over four hundred yards out. He was hoping they could see how easy it would be for him to nail anyone at fifty as they struggled up the last barren yards of that steep dusty slope.

So what was holding them from just riding on? If they knew who was up here, they knew one man and two gals weren't packing a treasure worth dying for.

Longarm grumbled, "You sneaky sons of bitches think we know something about you that we don't. But what could that be? You know that by now I've reported my suspicions about fake Black Leggings to real Black Leggings. I've asked everyone who'll listen about Indian Police acting suspicious as hell. So what's left? What could I be missing?"

He spotted movement nobody but an experienced deer hunter on the prod might have spotted. Somebody was sidewinding through some knee-high mountain campion. Longarm considered what that gal had said about the quality of mercy in that play about Venice. On the other hand, Miss Portia had never had to stop so many bastards with one old saddle gun. So he fired, and damned if the jasper rolling down the slope from that clump of brush wasn't clad in dusty blue from head to toe. Longarm chortled, "Hot damn if I ain't smart! It's just like I was only suggesting, back in that Kiowa camp! Those fake Indian Police are in cahoots with fake Indians!"

He yelled, *"Bolla de idiotas! No me jodas!"*

So then it got very noisy, with shot-up twigs and chewed-up oak leaves raining down on him as he grinned down at the billowing gun-smoke and muttered, "I asked you not to screw with me, you idiots!"

Then the guns fell silent, and a long time crept by as the sun rose ever higher and he tried to determine whether they were moving in or moving out.

Minerva rejoined him on her hands and knees to gasp, "Matty sent me. She says a lot of riders are moving along the slopes from the southwest. She says she can tell they're busting through the chaparral on horseback because of all the dust. Those cavalry troops from Fort Sill haven't had time to get here yet, have they?"

To which he could only reply grim-lipped, "Not hardly. Stay here with that derringer. Fire it a heap if anyone shows his fool face to the north. I doubt anyone will. But you never know for certain."

As he crawfished back under the blackjacks, Minerva protested, "I couldn't repel a charge with this toy if I knew how to use it! Where do you think you're going, Custis?"

He grunted, "Where I expect more action, of course." Then he got to his feet, Yellowboy at port, and added, "They knew right off it was a lot steeper on this side. By now they must have noticed how we've been covering it."

He moved off through the trees as he grumbled, "What'll you bet they'll try the gentler slope from the trail, if and when they go for broke!"

He kicked more greenery on the smudge fire in passing, and then he was kneeling by Matawnkiha Gordon to say, "We're swapping places. Go cover the tougher-looking backyard whilst I watch this front way in with a tougher gun."

Unlike her white teacher, little Matty had been raised on tales of blood and slaughter. So she merely said, "I think they're bunching on this side too. There's no dust downslope now. But I keep spotting moving branches, and there's no wind at all right now!"

Then she was fading back through the dappled shade, and

Longarm had slid into her place behind a fallen log. She'd chosen a swell position. She'd gone a night and then some without a bath as well. But the female odor lingering in the crushed grass didn't disgust a man worth mention. The kid's Kiowa mamma had known what she'd been about when she'd insisted on a chaperone.

He had to laugh. He knew Matty's momma would laugh too if she ever found out who'd been chaperoning whom on this expedition.

His new position offered a whole new set of tactical considerations. There wasn't much cover between this wooded knoll and the trail about a furlong south, with fair cover growing right up to the far side and the open slope they'd have to cross no steeper than that streetcar line up Denver's Capitol Hill. He figured he could drop eight or ten if they rushed him in a bunch. He didn't know what he'd do if they charged across the trail spread out in greater numbers.

He glanced up at the sky. He didn't need to dig out his watch to see no cavalry patrol could have made it far enough to matter as yet.

Longarm asked a carpenter ant crawling along the log, "Do you reckon we're just spooking ourselves? Those fakes have to know they ain't got all day to hit and run. So what if they've just run?"

He figured Comanche would have charged by this time. In their day they'd been admired for fighting just as bravely, or dumbly, as Texas Rangers. Most other Indians considered a fallen hero a dead fool. There was no shame in calling off a "bad fight" because the idea was to make the enemy die bravely, not to get your fool self killed.

Counting those others Godiva Weaver had nailed the other day, the gang had taken mighty heavy losses for the nervous moments they'd been able to manage for him so far. He asked that ant how come the rascals had kept coming back for more. The ant didn't seem to know. Longarm insisted, "It has to be a better reason than my guns and boots. Some leader with a personal hard-on has to be ordering them to lift my hair in particular!"

He warned himself he was thinking in circles. Not wanting

to give away his position with tobacco smoke, he plucked a stem of grass to chew as he softly sang:

> Farther along, we'll know more about it.
> Farther along, we'll understand why.
> Cheer up, my brother, walk in the sunshine.
> We'll understand this, all by and by.

Then he spotted riders coming along that trail from the southwest. There sure were a heap of them. All wearing feathers, paint, and those black buckskin leggings as they sat their ponies tall, as if they didn't have a worry in this world.

Longarm wasn't sure they did. He had sixteen rounds in his saddle gun, the gals had his other guns, and there had to be at least fifty of the befeathered riders headed his way!

Then he recognized a familiar war bonnet. It was the only thing about old Necomi that hadn't been daubed with red, black, and yellow paint. And that had to be good old Hawzitah riding beside the chief, in spite of the way he'd whitewashed his head and shoulders. So Longarm half rose to shout, "Look out, Necomi! We're surrounded up this way and you boys are riding into an ambush!"

That inspired a Kiowa reply that sounded like puppy dogs getting their tails docked in a meat grinder. As half his followers dropped off the trail to beat through the brush and cuss it just awful, the more dignified Necomi rode closer to shout, "Which side was sending up those smoke signals? We could not read them. But when we see smoke above our own hills we wish to know why!"

Longarm called back that he'd been trying to signal Fort Sill. The older Kiowa shouted, "We can talk about it later. My scouts say some of those fork-tongues wearing black leggings just rode off to the northeast, and I wish to talk to them before they die!"

Longarm broked cover to signal danger with his free hand as he cautioned, "Call your young men back! I just told you I sent for the U.S. Cav! What would *you* do if you were a green trooper and you saw Kiowa in feathers and paint coming your way at full gallop?"

Necomi was smart enough to picture that. He swore mightily and rode closer, protesting, "This is not sensible! We could catch them if we really tried. But they will be far, very far, by the time the blue sleeves get here!"

As they closed to within conversational distance, Longarm nodded and said, "I know. If your young men were dressed as Indian Police, those mysterious rascals would never get away. But they're not. So now all we can do is wait here and explain all this confusion to the infernal army!"

Chapter 16

The morose Necomi didn't wait an hour for the hated cavalry. He headed for home with most of his followers. But the more progressive or more curious Hawzitah thought his two dozen painted warriors ought to practice their scouting. So they did. Longarm had to take their word when they reported no bodies after a thorough search out at least a mile in all directions. The knoll he'd chosen for a stand was surrounded by tangle-wood-choked draws, timbered north slopes, and high chaparral most everywhere else. But once real Kiowa came back with signs as small as torn-off feathers, blood-spattered grass stems, and one brass uniform button, Longarm had to concede they'd have hardly overlooked a full-grown corpse out yonder.

He was stoking the smudge fire atop the knoll with fresh green branches, with the two gals hunkered nearby, when old Hawzitah came through the blackjacks again to report, "They were riding shod ponies. Many shod ponies that dropped blue sleeve sign. Those who paint themselves do not feed their ponies oat seeds for the birds to peck at. I think all of them, whether in blue sleeves or paint, were riding police ponies. By the time those other blue sleeves get here they will have made it east to the post road to Anadarko. Nobody will be able to pick out their sign from the other hoofprints on such a well-traveled trail, even if they forget to change their clothes!"

Longarm grimaced, stared thoughtfully down at the brass

button in his left hand, and said, "I'm afraid you're right. This button tells me the ones in uniform may not be wearing government issue. The B.I.A. salvages cast-off army blue for the Indian Police. But some dress more spiffy. Agent Clum, over to the San Carlos Reserve, managed to get local settlers to outfit his Apache Police in spanking new blue tunics with their own pewter badges a spell back. I'll ask the Comanche Police sergeant I know whether this button looks like one he'd want his own boys to polish."

Minerva Cranston had been listening with interest. So she chimed in. "What good would that do you either way, Custis? We've all agreed those mysterious uniformed riders don't seem to be Comanche. There are no *other* Indian Police on this particular reserve. So it's obvious they begged, borrowed, or stole those uniforms somewhere else!"

Longarm shook his head and said, "They might have *bought* 'em. You can buy such livery, from a maid's uniform to an officer's full kit, in any fair-sized city, east or west. Indians acting on their own would be more likely to just steal new duds, no offense, Hawzitah."

The old whitewashed Kiowa smiled and replied, "A fighting man takes what a fighting man needs. I count coup on all the good things I have stolen from your kind. But I think I see what you mean. Those forked tongues have cheated many people of much money. They may not have the courage to just kill Indian Police and strip them. They may just buy those blue uniforms and black Spanish hats they were wearing when our younger brothers bought their own ponies back from them."

Longarm suggested, "Their leader might not have cottoned to all that much attention from the *real* Indian Police. As it's commencing to shape up, the gang's been taking advantage of how thin *everyone's* spread out, with less than five thousand folks, red and white, hither and yon across an area the size of, say, Connecticut."

Hawzitah asked what a Connecticut was, adding that it sounded like a Cheyenne word.

Longarm said, "I think it means something like a long river in the Algonquin lingo, which your Cheyenne pals speak. All it means to us is the name of a state back East about the size of this reserve. As long as we're discussing such matters, are you *certain* you've never heard anyone who paints himself call anything an *agua*? I took it for a wounded Mex requesting some water. But you're the expert on local vocabularies, Chief.''

Hawzitah shook his whitewashed head and said, ''Not Kiowa, Comanche, or Kiowa-Apache. Not Arapaho. Not Cheyenne. I can't speak of Wichita. We killed all the Wichita that didn't run away. We never had many powwows with the tattood root grubbers!''

Longarm thought about this. It made no sense to go about it in such a sneaky way if you were a left-over Wichita trying to reclaim the old homestead. But the mysterious riders hadn't made a whole lot of sense no matter *what* they thought they were up to, and the younger so-called Pawnee Picts had stopped tattooing themselves of late. He'd hold the thought until he had the chance to ask some Caddo speaker whether *they* had an Indian word that sounded like the Spanish word for water.

He told Hawzitah, ''I got a reason for asking a religious question. Might you know any Horse Nation that buries its dead in the ground instead of leaving them up in the sky?''

The traditional Kiowa made a wry face and said, ''The agents tell us we should bury our dead, as if they were food scraps we wanted the worms instead of the winds to dispose of. Some of our people who died in the guardhouse at Fort Sill or the B.I.A. hospital in Anadarko *have* been buried your disgusting way. I have told my sons that should ever you people treat me that way, they must dig me up in the dark of the moon and leave me high on a windy rise, up in the sky, to let clean winds blow me away.''

The old Kiowa made a wry face and asked, ''Why are we talking about my sky burial? When a man has seen more than sixty summers he is not greatly cheered by such talk!''

Longarm said, ''Wasn't talking about *your* healthy body, pard. Talking about at least a half-dozen dead strangers nobody's seen hide nor hair of since. Don't it seem to you a body buried in an unmarked grave under thick sod would attract less notice than a traditional cuss spread out on a four-poster eight or ten feet off the ground?''

Hawzitah shrugged and said he couldn't answer for crazy two-hearts.

A younger Kiowa with his face painted solid yellow and the rest of him covered with red polka dots came through the trees to shout something at old Hawzitah.

The whitewashed leader told Longarm, "My young men had spotted dust, a lot of dust, on the prairie flats to the southeast. It is coming this way, lined up with this smoke you keep playing with. I think it must be that column from Fort Sill. Don't you?"

Longarm nodded and said, "Them other riders must be long gone with no intention of investigating this smoke. They knew what I was up to before you boys run them off."

He glanced down at the two gals and added, "We could save us all a heap of wasted time if we saddled up and rode on down to meet 'em."

Minerva protested, "What if those fake Indian Police are hiding in the bushes between us?"

Longarm started to dismiss this as a stupid question. Then he muttered, "Out of the mouthes of babes, when you're dealing with the great unknown. Could you and your young men escort us down off these timbered slopes, Chief?"

Hawzitah thought, nodded, and said, "It would be grand if we met those forked-tongued Wichita or Mexicans in our own hills! But your words about blue sleeves and war paint sounded wise. I think we will just ride with you as far as the open prairie between here and all those blue sleeves!"

So that was how they worked it. Longarm piled a last armful of green oak branches on his smoky fire before he helped the two gals get the four ponies ready to go. No Horse Indian was about to help anyone else with his or her own ponies. Then, mounted on Gray Skies, Longarm led the way directly on down through the high chaparral of the sunbaked southern slopes toward what surely seemed the rising dust of a fair-sized cavalry column.

Along the way, he got in a few more words for the real Indian Police, explaining once more to Hawzitah how his own young men could track down and count coup on sneaks such as the ones they'd just brushed with. He told the older man how those Apache Police had won medals, big shiny ones, for saving the life of their agent, John Clum, in a fight with renegades. He told the Kiowa leader how the great Lakota war chief, Red Cloud, had encouraged young men to join the so-called Sioux Tribal Police. He said, "Cochise met us halfway and died prosperous in bed. Red Cloud and Quanah Parker have both been making honest money on the side, without cutting their hair or joining the Women's Christian Temperence Movement."

Hawzitah answered dubiously, "I have heard all this. Maybe it is true. I will think about it."

Then he said, "Today I am painted for fighting in the old way. So I think this is about as far as my young men and I should ride with you!"

Longarm felt no call to argue against common sense. So they split up amid some cottonwoods where a draw fanned out across the rolling prairie, and Longarm led just the two gals toward that mustard haze of trail dust betwixt them and Fort Sill.

They saved the platoon led by a callow second john at least an hour and change by meeting them miles short of the hills. The patrol leader answered to Second Lieutenant Standish, and he naturally wanted to ride on and see if they could cut the trail of those fake Indian Police. He allowed the army had been getting reports about the rascals from all over. It usually took folks a day or so to figure out they'd been taken, after they'd paid off peace officers who were said to be paid by the B.I.A.

Longarm shook his head and pointed out, "Kiowa who know this range better, no offense, assure me the rascals have made it over to the post road by now. They could just as easily be headed for Fort Sill as Anadarko by now. So why don't we all just see if we can make the fort by supper-time? I promised to bring these ladies back, and by now the little one's momma ought to be having a fit!"

Standish, to his credit, thought before he asked, "Wouldn't it be awfully stupid to ride into an army post in fake uniforms after a firefight with a federal lawman?"

Longarm nodded but said, "Be even dumber to ride that way to the B.I.A.'s main agency at Anadarko. A white soldier might be slower to spy a fake resident of this reserve than a rider for the real Indian Police.''

Standish nodded grudgingly, but said, ''If I was one of those crooks I think I'd put on my cowboy outfit!''

Longarm smiled thinly and said, ''I suspicion they dress more like Indians just traipsing about. Down where Cache Creek runs into the Red River they seem to have had some of the outfit in uniform, with at least a dozen more pretending to be quill dependents in a nearby tipi ring. Thinking back, with my eyes half-shut as I try to picture that setup, I ain't dead *certain* that what I took for women and kids had to really *be* women and kids. What do you call them Lakota boys who dress up and even walk like *weyas*? That's what Lakota call their women, by the way. Don't never call a Lakota *weya* a squaw.''

Standish promised he wouldn't and said, ''I've heard of those Sioux fairies. I find Indians sort of confusing. You think *that* could be what we're up against down this way?''

Longarm chuckled dryly and said, ''My point is that it's easy for anyone to look like anything at a distance. It wasn't long after I talked sense to what I took for Indian Police that what I *took* for Kiowa in feathers and paint tried to keep me and a newspaper gal from going on to ask possibly embarrassing questions.''

He rode on a bit further with his eyes shut all the way. Then he opened them with a nod and said, ''That tipi circle down by the Red River wasn't set up traditionally. It was set up the way you or me might set up a tipi ring, with all the doorways facing one another as if they were seated around a table.''

Standish squinted into the distance as if he too was picturing an imaginary Indian camp. ''Looked about right to me,'' he decided.

Longarm said, ''Me too, just passing by. Both of us are white men, not Horse Indians housewives. I'm commencing to doubt the bunch I met to the south were real Horse Indians. Such riders, even if they left their womenfolk behind, would be inclined to pitch a traditional camp, with every tipi open to the sunrise, not some Currier and Ives notion of an Indian village green!''

As they rode on the young officer, new to both the army and the West, but not to pictures of Indian camps, observed,

"We have more than a few tents pitched downright sloppy along Flipper's Ditch around the fort, Deputy Long. Now that you've brought it up, I can't recall just which way any doorway might be pointed."

Longarm made a wry face and said, "I was talking about *traditional* Indians. Dispirited drunks and broken old men pimping for their wives and daughters might pitch a tipi upside down for all it matters."

Standish nodded, then asked, "Who's to say that's not the sort of reservation trash you've run up against then?"

Longarm said, "Me. They've come after me in particular more than once. They've come at me too brave, or desperate to be beggars or even pimps. After that, we know they swindled some Kiowa pretty slick, and tried to slicker that Running X outfit out of serious money. That sass who calls himself Black Sheep had me half convinced he was a real lawman, and you may have noticed the real badge I showed you back there where we first met."

Standish shot a thoughtful glance at the late afternoon sky. "In sum we have a band of clever desperados out here somewhere," he said. "I sure hope we can make Fort Sill before that storm blows in from the south!"

Longarm stared up at the darkening sky until he spotted silently flickering lightning deep in the badly bruised clouds. "We're a good three hours from the fort and less than an hour from that gullywasher headed our way," he said, "I know I ain't in command of this column. But if I was I'd circle the ponies and pitch me some of those swell army pup tents you all ought to be packing!"

Standish said, "Don't be ridiculous! We're only six or eight miles from the fort. We could make it in less than an hour and a half if we loped our mounts a good part of the time!"

"Through a gullywasher?" Longarm marveled. "They give no prizes for killing your ponies and catching pneumonia out our way. If I was in command I'd camp on high ground and let the gathering storm blow over before I rode on."

Standish let a little steel creep into his voice as he quietly replied, "You're not in command, Deputy Long. My orders from Colonel Howard were to investigate those distant smoke signals and report back to him as soon as I knew what they might mean. You've been kind enough to save us part of the trip. But meanwhile my commanding officer is waiting, probably with everyone on the post braced for an Indian raid. So I'll not waste a whole night out here in the dark just to keep from getting wet!''

He must have meant it. He raised his free arm and waved his men foreward, calling out, ''In column of twos, slow gallop, *ho*!''

Longarm sidestepped Gray Skies, and waved down Minerva and the young breed gal leading the pack brute as the soldiers blue lit out at a lope as if anxious to meet up with that storm from the south.

Matawnkiha Gordon said, ''I know. It's going to be raining fire and salt by the time we can hope to make camp!''

But the kid was good and so, with Longarm's experienced help, they had a canvas half-shelter facing a good fire with its back to the rain as the afternoon sky turned twilight dark and proceeded to sweep the rolling short grass all around with silvery sheets of summer rain.

They'd tethered the four ponies to some rabbit brush on the downwind side of their rise. They'd piled their saddles at either end of their flapping lean-to. That kept some of the swirling wet drafts at bay. They'd spread their bedding on the grass before it had managed to get wet. So they enjoyed a cold but reasonably dry supper as they huddled side by side in the gathering dusk with the storm showing no signs of letting up.

Minerva asked if they thought those soldiers had made it to the fort by this time. Longarm said he doubted it, and Matty said it would serve them right if they all drowned. Eating pork and beans from a can, she declared, ''You Saltu are always in such a hurry to go nowhere. The three of us are as warm and dry as anyone can hope to be when Waigon spreads his wings. That gold bar chief was stupid. Stupid!''

As Longarm chuckled in agreement Minerva whispered, ''Waigon?''

He said, ''Thunderbird. I thought you were taking down a heap of Comanche, Miss Minerva.''

She sighed and said, ''I keep hearing new words. Didn't you say you were a Christian, Matty?''

The little breed shrugged and said, ''When they are giving

presents at the agency Sunday school I am. At times like these, when I have to look out for myself, I remember your Jesus Ghost didn't know how to fight when they came to kill him. He let himself be killed without a struggle, as if he was not a man of *puha*! When I asked the missionary about this, he said I was too savage to understand what the Jesus Ghost was doing for me. Maybe he is right. Nothing the Jesus Ghost ever did for me would keep me dry and feed me fine beans if I was out here on my hands and knees, praying like a Saltu girl!"

Longarm put a warning hand on Minerva's knee to keep the white gal from arguing religion with a pagan breed in the middle of such a storm.

The rain seemed to be easing off as the wind, if anything, blew harder. It got dark as hell, save for the ruby glow of their wind-fanned night fire. When Minerva suggested they build the fire back up, Longarm sadly asked, "With what? Those sage brush roots and cow chips we started with were *dry* when I first put a match to 'em. As of right now there's nothing flammable for miles that ain't wet as a mad hen."

He patted her knee in the dark again. "We'll be warm enough under our bedding, and it ain't as if we ain't had a long hard day. So what say we all turn in with the extra tarp over us?"

Minerva took his wrist in both hands to move his hand down the inside of her thigh, under her damp summer dress, as she allowed his words made a lot of sense.

He started to ask her what in thunder she thought she was doing. But he knew little Matty could hear every word, and it was all too clear what she was doing once he discovered, with the back of his hand, she was wearing no underdrawers between those smooth and almost clammy bare thighs.

He murmured, "I didn't know you were feeling scared again, Miss Minerva. I'd be lying if I denied you're making me feel . . . just about as nervous. But can't it wait until all three of us make it on to Fort Sill and that swell hostel I told you about?"

She began to rub his bare knuckles along the warm crease in her fuzzy lap as she half murmured, half moaned, "I thought we were all bedding down for the night out here, Custis."

On the other side of him, Matty yawned and declared, "You two do as you like. I'm tired. I've eaten. I want to go to sleep now. I have spoken!"

Suiting actions to her words, the little breed raised her end of the casually spread bedding and proceeded to get under some of it. Longarm didn't ask how much of her own duds she was shucking as she tossed at least some yards of damp cotton atop the tarp beside him.

He just got to his hands and knees so Minerva could get under at her end. Then he wriggled in between the two of them, having removed no more than his hat, boots, and gun rig. As he snuggled down he felt Matty's bare back with one hand, and didn't explore further down her arched spine. To the other side of him, Minerva lay naked as a jay, facing him, and he didn't have to depend on accidental brushes with either hand. Minerva had his right hand gripped in both hers as she hauled it back down to her fuzzy moist groin and whispered, "As I was saying before you interrupted me, you shy boy . . ."

"Minerva, for Pete's sake!" he protested, not wanting to say anything less delicate.

The passionate schoolmarm seemed to follow his drift. For she was casual and innocent as she quietly asked, "Are you still awake, Matty?"

The young girl muttered, "Go away. I was plucking sweet grass to weave a *yattah* for my *umbea*, and you brought me back from the dream country. Talk to Custis if you can't sleep."

Minerva did. She whispered, "She's too sleepy to pay attention, even if the wind wasn't flapping that canvas over us. Won't you even *finger* me, for land's sake?"

It seemed the best way to quiet her down. But even as he started to strum her old banjo with lust-slicked fingers, he murmured, "It can't be later than six or eight. So it ain't as if this was all that desperate a situation, ma'am."

She began to move her compact hips as if she was being laid as she moaned, "Speak for yourself. This is all so deliciously *sordid*, and for all we know, those Indians could be creeping up on us this very minute! I want to come again before I die, and doesn't this remind you of that night we did it in that Pullman berth with those Hard-Shell Baptists sleeping just across the aisle from us, Ace?''

Longarm had a better notion what was eating her now. He'd met other gals who seemed to get a dirty thrill out of taking chances at being caught in the act. There'd been that older gal back home in West-by-God-Virginia who'd never let him have any in her hayloft unless her sister was milking the cow down below.

The sister had been more sensible about doing it out in the woods a mile from their dear old dad and his Greener Ten-Gauge. But then there'd been that French gal touring with Miss Sarah Bernhardt who'd confided she just loved to suck dick in a theatre box, with the show going on and the orchestra droning passionate sounds.

He knew he ought to be ashamed of his fool self as she proceeded to unbutton his fly while she snuggled her naked body closer. But of course he never was. Her naked body felt more tempting in the dark than it looked inside a summer-weight outfit in sunlight. So he kissed her back when she pressed her parted lips to his and hauled out his rock-hard organ-grinder. For he was made of mortal clay and when you got down to brass tacks, what in thunder was a sixteen-year-old kid going to do to them if she figured out what they were doing to each other?

As if she'd read his mind, without taking her lips from his, or missing a stroke as she pulled his pecker, Minerva begged him to put it in her, adding, ''It feels so romantic out here on the wet windswept prairie with the children fast asleep!''

He fingered her faster to encourage what she was doing to him, but he still felt awkward about the other gal under the covers with them, and so he whispered, ''Wait till we get to that hostel at Fort Sill and I'll romance the hell out of you across a brass bedstead with the lamp lit and the mirror tilted our way!''

To which she demurely replied, ''What kind of a girl do you take me for? I could never go up to a man's rented room like some woman of the town!''

He said, ''I figured we'd hire separate rooms and act sort of sly, seeing you find that exciting. But how about your own place or, hell, your schoolhouse back at your agency? That sounds sort of risky to my way of thinking.''

She sniffed and stopped stroking, just hanging on, as she told him, "It would only be distasteful. The door bolts on the inside and none of my Indian pupils would dare attempt to break in. And there's no soft place to lie down, and the whole place smells of chalk dust and unwashed children and their greasy lunch bags."

He sure wanted her to move that soft hand on his hard shaft some more. He tried slowing down with his own fingers. She called him a mean and began to stroke him some more even as she pleaded, "Can't we finish right, darling?"

When he didn't answer, she murmured louder, "Matty? How are you coming with that basket for your momma?"

When there was no answer, Longarm reflected that the wind-flapped canvas and moaning prairie all around was making at least as much noise as discreet screwing. So he moaned himself and rolled atop her with his duds on, at first.

Then his naked shaft was in her to the hilt, and she was peeling his duds off for him with her hands as she moved those schoolmarish hips in a way that might have made her a rich woman in Leadville or Virginia City. The best part was that they didn't bounce the solid prairie under little Matty the way they'd have surely bounced any bedsprings they were sharing with her. Longarm didn't ask why Minerva tossed the top tarp aside as she wrapped her slender but surprisingly strong legs around his waist and softly begged him to thrust harder and faster. He knew full well how his bare ass would have whipped the covers back and forth across that sleeping kid's skinny naked hips. And thinking about the dark tawny Matty's younger and likely even tighter little twat, just inches away from the one he was in, inspired him to start hitting bottom with every stroke as Minerva gasped, "My Lord, you're not at all like Ace after all, and to tell the truth you may be curing my warped hankerings for that tinhorn brute!"

Longarm allowed he was about cured of some heartless gals who'd used and abused *him* more recently. Then they came hard, and she agreed a shared cheroot might save both their lives.

It was tricky to light up, even with a wax Mexican match. For the wind eddied in under their flapping canvas shelter. But the match cast enough light to tell Longarm he'd been right about that other gal's skinny bare ass.

As if she sensed the light, or perhaps because of the chill in the air, Matty covered her bare butt with her blanket as she muttered some sleepy Kiowa curse words without turning over to face them.

Longarm hastily shook the match out, aware of how much of them the kid would have seen as he lit that cheroot. Then he and Minerva were snuggled under the tarp, naked limbs entwined, as they shared the one smoke. He wondered what other unmaidenly vices she indulged in, but he never asked. Billy Vail hadn't sent him all this way to investigate an almost pretty schoolmarm's morals.

But being a woman, Matilda naturally wanted to hear more about those other gals who'd been this mean to him. He figured that went with Professor Darwin's notions. He'd read how Mormons, Turks, and other such harem keepers were only carrying on traditions far older than, say, Queen Victoria. Menfolk, like apefolk, wolves, elk, and such, were inclined to hog all the females they could, fighting off any other males that might come courting.

But womenfolk, descended from many a great-granny who'd been part of some caveman's herd, were more inclined to size up the competition with a view to outscrewing them. So Longarm knew the horny schoolmarm wouldn't get sore if he told her the truth about that fickle newspaper gal or the mysterious stranger who'd taken cruel advantage of his weak nature the other night at Fort Sill.

Minerva laughed sort of dirty, and said she'd wondered why he'd seemed so anxious to lure her to that army hostel. She agreed it had doubtless been some army wife with a hankering for novelty. When he said he was worried about her damned army husband finding out, Minerva said she doubted many wives were in the habit of confessing such side trips to their menfolk.

He had to tell her the whole dumb tale of Attila the Hungarian and the confession of his Magda before he could ask her opinion, as a woman, on *that* mess.

Minerva agreed it made little sense from a male or female position. After a thoughtful drag on their shared cheroot she said, "The only thing I can think of is that she was trying to protect her real lover. Didn't you say he'd been heard to speak Hungarian to her?"

Longarm replied, "I never said it. Neighbor gals who know way more about the lingo say this rascal claiming to be me was some sort of greenhorn from their old country."

Minerva passed the smoke back to him as she pointed out, "He might not have told anyone he was anybody. When her husband heard she'd been billing and cooing with a tall dark stranger, it was Magda herself, a greenhorn bride who barely speaks English, who told her man an American lawman had done them both dirty, remember?"

Longarm did. He said, "It's already been suggested there was this article about me in the papers about the time old Magda would have had to come up with some answers in a hurry. I'm glad you think that was what she might have been doing too. My boss has other deputies looking into it, and since all roads seem to lead to the same reasons, that's likely where they'll wind up. They'll get the real story out of the lying sass, and I'll be able to turn this other stuff over to the army and real Indian Police. Lord knows they ought to be just as good as tracking flimflam artists across their own range."

She took the cheroot from his lips and flicked it far out into the windy darkness as she cooed, "You don't have to leave just now, do you?"

So a grand time was had by all, or at least two out of three of them, and they even got some sleep, once the storm had blown itself over and it got too quiet to get dirty under the covers with little Matty snoring away.

They got up, ate a cold breakfast, and were on their way again as the sun rose off to the east in a cloudless windswept sky.

That shavetail's complaint that they'd been almost there when the storm hit had been well taken. They'd ridden less than an hour when they topped a rise to make out the fluttering flag and higher rooftops of Fort Sill to the south.

Seeing the Comanche sub-agency lay east-northeast of the actual fort, although within the sprawling limits of the military reservation, Longarm led the gals that way until they spotted the steeple of that church Quanah Parker and his band attended when they weren't beating drums for other *puha*. Somebody must have spotted them riding in, for old Aho Gordon came tearing out on foot to meet them, wailing at her daughter in Kiowa and saying awful things about Longarm in English until Matty calmed her down in their own lingo.

The dumpy Indian gal stopped cussing Longarm, and switched to cussing those lying two-hearts who'd endangered her only child and cost her two sleepless nights. She told Longarm she was sorry she'd called him a baby-raper, now that she'd been told he'd behaved so properly to both of his companions, and added she'd heard rumors of riders dressed as Kiowa who failed to respond to the hand signals all Horse Indians were familiar with.

As Matty helped her mother aboard her own pony to ride pillion into the agency with them, Longarm said, half to himself, "Paid-up Scotch-Irish outlaws have been known to gussy up like Indians, and a breed or Mex would look even more convincing to anyone but a real Quill Indian. We've established no Black Leggings Kiowa are wearing paint with permission of their lodge leaders. I'm pretty sure those tipis I took for Comanche down by the Red River were circled wrong for traditional Horse Indians. I know one I winged was calling out in Spanish, unless it was one of his pals calling *for* him. In either case, no Indian on this reserve would have reason to call for water in Spanish, whilst few Mexicans would be likely to be fluent in the sign lingo of these plains."

Minerva said, "Didn't you tell me that when you and that other girl tried to signal peaceful intent from that sod house they pegged a shot at you, Curtis?"

He smiled thinly and replied, "Didn't know you were really that interested. But the more I study on it, the more it looks as if those fake Black Leggings ain't real residents of this here reserve!"

They rode on into the settlement, to be greeted by yapping dogs, laughing kids, and Police Sergeant Tikano, who said he'd already heard some of it from a rider from Fort Sill.

The three ladies seemed headed for the Gordon cabin to sip tea or something. Longarm and his two ponies wound up out front of the police station, a frame structure cut to the same pattern as a B.I.A. schoolhouse. As Tikano was ordering one of his uniformed policemen to take the ponies around back and tend to them, the older white agent, Conway, came over from his larger house to join them. Longarm waited until they were inside, where the moon-faced Comanche sergeant seemed to keep his *own* moonshine on file, before he got out the brass button his Kiowa pals had found on the mountain for him.

Tikano handed him a tumbler of moonshine as he took the button in his other hand, held it up to the light, and decided, ''Ahee, it looks like it came from one of our uniforms. When we started to organize, the army gave us ragged old tunics and the B.I.A. gave us straw hats. The kind Saltu farmers wear. Quanah said we looked like scarecrows. He sent away to Saint Louis for real uniforms and felt hats like the soldiers wear. That is why this button has crossed *poggamoggons* instead of U.S. on it.''

Longarm took a polite sip of firewater and said, ''I thought they were supposed to be war clubs. So what we're talking about would be fake Indian Police in real uniforms that were lost, strayed, or stolen?''

Conway allowed that made sense to him too. But the Indian scowled and declared, ''We are missing no uniforms. None. We have less than a hundred Indian Police, counting the noncommissioned officers. All of them are Comanche, so far. All of them are known to me as Hou-Huam with true hearts. Hear me, each man has been issued one uniform. One. None of them are missing. None of them have reported the loss of the fine uniforms Quanah bought them. Even if one, or even two of our men got drunk and were ashamed to report such stupidity, didn't you say there were *many* of these forked-tongued *koshares* wearing big blue falsehoods?''

Longarm nodded thoughtfully and said, ''That's about the size of it. But a tailor who'd sell uniforms to Quanah would sell the same sort of uniforms to most anyone else. You wouldn't know the name of that outfit in Saint Lou, would you?''

The Indian and his agent exchanged glances. Conway shook his head and said, ''Quanah never asked my permission. I had nothing to do with the whole shebang. As I understand it, Quanah got permission to start his own police from the main office, up at Anadarko. They have a telegraph line to the outside world at Anadarko. We don't. Have to depend on the army line out of Fort Sill in a real emergency. Fortunately we don't have many, betwixt the cavalry and Quanah's new police force looking out for us."

Longarm nodded absently, and turned back to Sergeant Tikano to ask, "Did you say no Comanche held higher rank than noncom? Who does that leave as the commissioned officers in your outfit?"

The Indian looked sincerely puzzled as he polished off the last of his own drink and said, "Nobody. I mean, there's no Saltu dressed up as an Indian Police Officer. We take our orders from Quanah. Maybe he takes orders from army officers, or our boss agent up at Anadarko."

Longarm cocked a brow at Conway, who said, "Makes sense to me. I know I don't order even Sergeant Tikano here direct. Whenever we have trouble here, Tikano and his boys seem able to get on top of it without my help. I have *asked* them to arrest troublemakers who sass me on allotment day. But I reckon you'd have to ask at Anadarko if anyone other than Quanah rides herd."

Longarm insisted, "Some B.I.A. official has to approve their payroll. Quanah can't be hiring and firing out of his own pocket, can he?"

Conway shook his head and replied, "I just now said somebody up to Anadarko has to have the final say. You might ask Fred Ryan, if he's made it back to Fort Sill yet. Fred's in closer contact with headquarters thanks to that army telegraph line. That's how come Fred's our liaison man at Sill. He gets to relay heaps of messages back and forth. He'd likely know the address of that tailor in Saint Lou. For I doubt Quanah would have ridden all the way up to Anadarko to wire out for uniforms when he could have done so from Fred Ryan's office."

Longarm figured Fred Ryan was likely still in Fort Smith that morning, but said he knew how to use a telegraph key, if push came to shove and the Signal Corps would patch him through to a line off the reservation. So seeing nobody at the sub-agency could shed more light on the subject, he said he had to get on over to the army post.

He tried calling on Minerva to say his proper good-byes.

But she seemed too busy over by the school to chat with him. So he just rode on out with a clear conscience, seeing he didn't seem able to terrify her by the safe sane light of a sunny morning.

Chapter 17

Longarm walked his tired ponies most of the modest way over to Fort Sill. He'd ridden them harder earlier, and it was that awkward time of the morning when folks were either too busy or too sleep-gurnmed to chew the fat with you. That summer gullywasher would have wiped away any sign that even greenhorns might have left, and the one man who might be able to clear away a heap of cobwebs, Quanah Parker, was nowhere to be found just yet.

Crossing the post road, Longarm read by the rain-paved mud how a whole mess of riders and at least six wheeled vehicles had just that morning headed north. Any signs young Standish and his patrol had left riding in through that storm were naturally long gone. Longarm decided it stood to reason that Colonel Howard had sent out other patrols in more strength, once Standish had reported in. But unless they'd been wired further news about those fake riders, it seemed to Longarm the wrong way to go about it. The so-called Indian Wars had always been a tad distinguished for useless wear and tear on the U.S. Army. A heap of Mister Lo's diabolical cunning was nothing more than the facts of life on the High Plains. There were a lot of directions to ride on a sea of grass twice the size of the Baltic. Columns crossing it in the open, bold as big-ass birds, were invisible below the horizon to a scout on horseback less than ten miles away.

Longarm rode through the seemingly deserted shantytown

outside the east gate of the cavalry post. He knew the whores, pimps, and gamblers were there. Night owls with no profit to be made this side of the army flag coming down again had no call to be out on their muddy streets at this hour. He passed a seemingly random grove of canvas tipis. He smiled to himself as he noted that despite the casual way they'd been put up by the side of the wagon trace, all four covered entrances faced due east.

Mexicans playing Kiowa wouldn't have been brought up in any sort of Indian shelter facing any direction. Longarm knew that despite the obvious Indian ancestry of many a Mexican, Spanish notions of orderly living had produced a sort of Papist Pueblo culture, with the faith and superstitions of the Spanish peasant plastered over the tortillas and red peppers contributed by Aztec, Chihuahua, and such. Mestizo or even pure Indio Mexicans started out with the same 'dobe bricks as, say, a Zuni from New Mexico, but after that they had all their front doors facing the street, no matter where the sun might rise in the morning.

He nodded at the sentry lounging by the gate and rode on through, muttering, "Nobody in that gang ever pitched a tipi around real Horse Indians. They'd have only had to do it once before the kids laughed at them and called them total assholes. If *I* knew better, from just my own friendly visits, it's a safe bet those rascals learned about the Indian Police and Black Leggings Lodge from Ned Buntline's Buffalo Bill Magazine!"

As he crossed the churned-up muddy parade Longarm warned himself not to chase moonbeams further than they might be shining. That one slicker calling his fool self Sergeant Black Sheep hadn't had a Mexican accent and he'd seemed at ease with police routine, whether he'd ever been sworn in as a lawman or not.

Longarm asked Gray Skies, "How do you feel about an American crook of Mex descent who spent some time on a small-town force or, hell, did some time in jail!"

When his mount failed to answer, Longarm insisted, "Anyone serving more than thirty days on a vagrancy conviction would pick up the way real copper badges walk and talk. That one could even be a breed. Only the one who called for water in Spanish has to have been a Mex for certain."

By this time they'd made it to the stables, where a remount noncom he'd talked to earlier was coming out the open end to greet them. The soldier's Class B uniform for the day showed he only supervised the mucking out of the stalls inside. So Longarm didn't offer him any reins as he dismounted, saying, "Good ponies you boys loaned me. I noticed a whole shit-house of riders just left from here a short while ago."

The two-striper nodded and replied, "You noticed right, and the old man was sort of pissed that you hadn't made it back yet. Him and the First Battalion just rode out to track down them painted Kiowa."

Longarm sighed and said, "Aw, shit, I'd best switch this saddle and bridle to that bay I rode in on and see if I can catch up with Colonel Howard before he hurts somebody, or vice versa! They took the post road north, right?"

The man they'd left behind nodded and said, "Headed up Anadarko way. Somebody said something about them wild Indians crossing the post road or following it one way or the other. They never came this way. The agency guns around Anadarko are forted up and ready for the red rascals, of course. The army and the B.I.A. have been burning up the wires, trying to figure which way the rascals went."

Longarm started to lead the two jaded ponies inside as the remount man tagged along, volunteering, "That Colorado pal of yours is with the column driving a buckboard."

Longarm handed the reins to another remount man dressed in faded blue fatigues as he asked with a puzzled frown, "Pal of mine, you say?"

The noncom said, "A Mr. Horny-something. Said he'd driven all the way up from Spanish Flats looking for you."

Longarm knew it was useless to hope. But he still made sure they were talking about Attila Hornagy, from Trinidad, Colorado, before he decided, "I might not ride after that column just yet. Got to send me some telegrams first. Where might I find your signal officer at this hour pard?"

The army regular looked awkward and suggested, "You might find the liaison office less busy, Deputy Long. They got their own telegraph setup, and with Agent Ryan over by Fort Smith, his breed clerk can't have all that much to do."

Longarm didn't ask whose wife the signal officer might be

with as so much of the outfit rode off to glory. But that reminded him of the other night and so, seeing the enlisted men always knew, he asked what the colonel had decided about those two officers who'd been fighting in the hall at the hostel.

The remount man grinned lewdly and said, "Long gone. Colonel Howard rides with fairly easygoing reins, but he won't put up with downright stupid. Both officers were transferred out the next morning, one to Fort Douglas in Mormon Country and the other down to Fort Apache. We all felt the sassy wife on her way to Fort Apache got off lucky, once she'd been caught with the regimental Romeo."

Longarm nodded and agreed it seemed rough on the innocent wife of that Romeo.

The remount man nodded, but said, "That's how come he was only sent to Fort Douglas, despite his wayward dong. The colonel's lady, Miss Elvira, said they had to consider the innocent victim of the untidy triangle. Fort Douglas ain't much worse than here for the wives, and her horny husband deserves the slow rate of promotion over yonder in the Great Basin."

Longarm didn't ask how they'd learned this much tending to the regimental riding stock. He knew senior-grade officers rated lots of household help, and he hadn't even had to serve breakfast to the older couple himself to learn old Elvira tended to call the shots about social matters on or about this post.

He agreed she seemed an understanding old gal, and left the two army ponies in the care of the army as he ducked out and circled the parade the less muddy way until he came to Fred Ryan's liaison office near the Headquarters and Headquarters building. He'd never figured out why the army felt you ought to say "Headquarters" twice. But he didn't really care.

Finding the door of the B.I.A.'s more modest doghouse unlocked, he went inside, where a baby-faced breed wearing a white shirt and shoestring tie looked up from a desk behind the counter and primly told him the boss wouldn't be back until later in the week, if then.

Longarm nodded and said, "I know Fred Ryan rode the mail ambulance east. We waved to one another in passing. I'd be Deputy U.S. Marshal Custis Long, and I'm sure old Fred would be proud to let me use your telegraph key, seeing the army signal officer seems away on serious business as well.''

The young breed rose warily to come over by the counter as he confessed to being Hino-Usdi Rogers of the Cherokee persuasion. When Longarm bluntly asked him what a Cherokee might be doing here in Kiowa-Comanche country, Rogers looked embarrassed and explained how Ryan had brought him along to a newer post after hiring him and training him at the Tahlequah Agency in the Cherokee Nation. Longarm didn't care. Ryan had obviously been with the B.I.A. longer than the Kiowa or Comanche had been with this agency.

Rogers opened a flap at one end of the counter, but warned Longarm, even as the far taller deputy stepped through it, that he wasn't half as fast with a telegraph key as the Signal Corps crew next door.

Longarm said, ''I can send and receive Morse pretty good. Used to tap into enemy wires during the war. I hope you've some connection with the Western Union grid so's we can get off wires to Denver and such?''

The Cherokee breed ran fingers through his thick black hair and looked as if he'd been caught with them in a cookie jar as he told their visitor he wasn't sure. He said his boss, Fred Ryan, usually made the long-distance connections and let him do the more routine sending and receiving.

By this time he'd shown Longarm to a table in the rear where a telegraph key and some writing material waited under a shelf of wet-cell batteries. Before he sat down, Longarm casually asked if Rogers or the army had wired those orders for police uniforms from Saint Lou.

The breed kid brightened and said, ''Oh, that was us. It was exciting to chat by wire with big-city folk. Agent Ryan patched us through to the Western Union office in Saint Louis, and then handed the task over to me. You see, he makes the important decisions while I keep the files in order, do the routine typing, and—''

''We got a young gent called Henry clerking our Denver office the same way,'' Longarm said. ''You told me Ryan broke you in a spell back at the Cherokee Agency. Now I'd best contact the central Kiowa Comanche agency at Anadarko and see if they can shed any light on Colonel Howard's campaign plans.''

They couldn't. No army messages were on the line at the moment, and it only took a few minutes for someone at the B.I.A. in Anadarko to hear their own key clicking and ask who in thunder wanted what.

It seemed nobody in Anadarko knew why Colonel Howard was headed their way in battalion strength. Longarm started to send something dumb about Attila Hornagy. But he never did. With any luck the fool immigrant would never think to ask questions about telegraph messages, and even if he did, it was going to take him yet another full day to get back here, giving him at least two on the trail if everyone pushed hard.

Anadarko lay a tad farther away than the thirty miles a cavalry column averaged in a day's ride. Even if Howard got there well before sundown and Hornagy heard right off, there was no way he'd be able to drive a jaded team directly back alone, at night, even if the army would let him. Longarm knew they wouldn't even let a lone civilian drive by day before they had a tighter grip on this current Indian scare. Colonel Howard never would have led that big a force out chasing after a few dozen at the most if he hadn't been taking the situation seriously.

Once he'd figured how much time he had to work with, Longarm made a few penciled notes to compose the longer message he had to send his Denver office.

Before he could, Hino-Usdi Rogers shyly marveled, "You surely send and receive good! You've a faster fist than Agent Ryan, and I can't keep up with him half the time!"

Longarm got out a brace of smokes as he explained, "The trick is not to think in dots and dashes. It takes a spell to think and then send dit-dit-dah-dit for the letter F. If you remember it sort of sounds like 'Get a haircut!' and move the key in time with the words, you've sent your letter F already."

The breed kid laughed, and asked if there were any other silly ways to bring Morse to mind. Longarm offered a couple that were sort of dirty, if effective. The young breed blushed like a gal, and declared he'd never forget the letter V sounded like "Stick it in deep!"

He blushed so girlishly and refused the offered smoke so primly that Longarm shot a thoughtful look at his thin white shirtfront. But although he'd met up with gals getting by in a man's world that way in the past, Hino-Usdi had no tits worth mentioning.

Lighting his own smoke, Longarm patched himself through to the main line, and after some argument with a Western Union section manager who didn't recognize his fist and required some bragging, Longarm got through to their Denver office and had them take down a long wire at day rates, collect, to be delivered to his home office.

He brought Billy Vail up to date on his situation so far, using as few words as possible but still spending many a nickel. Then he pointed out that Quanah Parker seemed to be off the reservation on other business, and that Hornagy had tracked him this far after all, and asked his boss whether he was supposed to come on home or just have it out with the fool grudge-holder.

The Cherokee breed told him, admiringly, he hadn't been able to follow a quarter of those dots and dashes, even thinking dirty.

Longarm took a thoughtful drag on his cheroot and said, "It's sure to take them the better part of the next hour to get Marshal Vail's reply back to me. Whilst we wait, I may as well send some more, and whilst you're at it, could you dig out any files you have on those made-to-order uniforms you ordered for old Quanah?"

The kid said he could. So Longarm started sending shorter direct messages to other sub-agencies and other main agencies in the Osage, Choctaw, Creek, and Cherokee Nations.

By the time Rogers rejoined him with a file folder, Longarm was able to declare, "Fort Smith says a newspaper-reporting gal I know seems to be on a wild-goose chase. Quanah never went there to visit Parkers he ain't related to. They couldn't tell me just where the gal and old Fred Ryan spent the last few nights."

Rogers blushed like a gal again as he opened the file on the table by Longarm, saying all the business correspondence they'd handled for the busy Quanah Parker was somewhere among all those carbon onionskins.

Longarm was careful with his ashes as he leafed through the pile. The records showed the progressive chief had ordered, received, and paid cash for one gross of police uniforms, cut to the same pattern as those worn by the so-called Sioux Police. That jibed with what the sincerely sober Sergeant Tikano had told him.

Billy Vail had never sent him to look into the business dealings of Chief Quanah Parker himself. But seeing he had the files handy, and recalling what they said about that process of elimination, Longarm nosed around enough to see Quanah didn't have any of his uniformed police collecting fees or even recovery rewards from anyone.

Longarm made sure by asking the B.I.A. clerk what some of the obscure typing meant. Rogers said Quanah naturally reported tribal income to his own agent, Conway, who relayed it on up to Anadarko by way of the wire here in the liaison office. The breed added that the B.I.A. had felt little call to rein Quanah all that tight, seeing he had a rep among red and white folk for honest dealings and gave the B.I.A. a lot fewer problems than old sulks like Pawkigoopy or even Necomi.

Longarm saw by the wired bank statements how Quanah could afford new blue serge and brass buttons. Aside from leasing tribal grass to white neighbors, Quanah bought and sold riding stock on and off the reservation at a handsome profit. For being a product of both cultures, he knew which end of a pony the shit dropped out of. He'd already taught his Comanche wranglers to saddle-break stock to be mounted from the near side so cowhands could get more use out of them.

It got downright spooky when you got to the real-estate deals a man who could pass for Comanche or Texas Parker was capable of pulling off. For thanks to having been accepted by his late mother's kin all over North Texas, he was in a position to put on some pants and make a profit from any proven homestead he could get off some greenhorn cheap.

A mean thought crossed Longarm's mind when he came to that. But he'd have heard about any recent Comanche scares down the other side of the Red River. Meanwhile, two out of three homesteaders went bust with no help from anyone but the grasshoppers and fickle climate out this way. He noticed most of the part-time Indian's cropland deals had been just east of Longitude 100°, where dry farming or dairy herds had more of a chance. He wondered who in thunder had ever taught a Comanche war chief you needed just over ten inches of rain before you dared to bust your sod. Poor Cynthia Ann Parker had only been nine when she'd had to learn more about weaving baskets and tanning hides than agriculture. One suspected that in spite of his long braids, old Quanah had to be another sneak who reads books when his pals weren't watching.

The papers he was reading inspired Longarm to send other questions to the outside world. When he contacted Anadarko again to see if they had anything on Colonel Howard's column yet, they wired back that the cav had stopped for a trail break at the dinky sub-agency at Elgin, meaning Howard was really taking his own good time and that he'd be lucky to make it up to Anadarko by sundown.

Then the main agency wired that they'd been getting other scattered reports, or complaints, after putting out their own wires about those mysterious riders.

Few had been hurt or seriously shaken down, but now that they all thought back, there had been some Indian Police chasing a bunch of Kiowa stock thieves, and as a matter of fact the Indian Police had been given food, fodder, and some travel expenses they said Quanah would repay, in his own good time, as they wandered the big reserve.

A more recent report from an Indian settlement along Beaver Creek, east of Fort Sill, said about a score of riders, dressed more like Saltu cowhands than either police or a warrior society, had skirted to the north a sunset back, despite the wind and rain they'd been riding through with night coming on.

Longarm grinned up at the Cherokee breed as he took the last of that down and said, "They're running for it. They knew the army had caught up with me and thought I knew more than I really do."

Hino-Usdi batted his lashes like an admiring schoolgal and asked what all that really meant.

Longarm replied, "From my very first words with that Sergeant Black Sheep they've been out to clean my plow, as if they suspected I suspected something the moment I laid eyes on them."

The Cherokee breed suggested, "What if that one who speaks such American English could be wanted by the law?

Wouldn't he be afraid you might have recognized him? You did tell him you were a federal lawman, didn't you?"

Longarm nodded thoughtfully and said, "That only works partway. If we'd ever met before, I'd have *really* recognized him. That Ben Day process that allows you to print photographs on paper is too new for *older* wanted posters to enter the equation. And he'd know better than to front for the outfit if he was on any *recent* ones."

Rogers shrugged and said, "You did say they went right to war with you, didn't you?"

To which Longarm could only reply, "Damn it, kid, I just now *said* I didn't know why they were so scared of me. Suffice it to say, they were. They tried more than once to gun me out on the range. When that didn't work they just ran for it. Hold on. I want to wire some other Indian Police I know in Atoka."

As he started to, Rogers said, "That's way off this reserve."

Longarm said, "I know. Ed Vernon picks up his private liquor there. That's the best place for sneaks with Indian features, no offense, to board a railroad train. They'll expect me to wire Spanish Flats, but hardly another Indian agency by a handy railroad."

Rogers marveled, "It's no wonder they were afraid of you! They'll take ever so long to ride all those miles between here and Atoka, and your Choctaw friends will have plenty of time to set up an ambush!"

Longarm said, "Not if I don't wire them sometime today. I might as well get word to Fort Washita, halfways there, whilst I'm at it. Lord knows Colonel Howard wouldn't be able to head 'em off *now*, even if I could tell him which way they seemed to be headed!"

He got to work on the key, the cheroot gripped between his bared teeth as he glared unconsciously at the wall beyond. For no matter how surely he worded his messages, he still had no idea what he'd done to scare them clean off the Kiowa Comanche reserve!

He sent a few more messages to agencies along the 160-mile route of the fugitives, assuming they weren't headed another way entirely.

By the time he'd finished and lit another cheroot, Western

Union was sending Billy Vail's reply to his earlier report. Their telegram delivery boy had made good time.

Vail told him Smiley and Dutch had been down to Trinidad and back with little additional light to shed on old Attila Hornagy's domestic problems. Some neighbors said the pretty young Magda Hornagy had run off with that same tall, dark, and handsome stranger. Vail had a dozen good guesses as to how Hornagy could have learned, or guessed, which way his own chosen home-wrecker had flown. Longarm could think up more, starting with, "Say, did you see my pal Longarm passing through here just the other day?"

Vail agreed Fort Sill wasn't working out so well as a hide-out, and flatly forbade a ride up to Anadarko. Sitting at his Denver desk, the sly old marshal had come to the same conclusions about Hornagy and a buckboard on muddy lonesome roads. He ordered Longarm to give Quanah Parker another day to get back and state just what in thunder he'd had in mind before he wandered clean off the damned reservation. Vail said it sounded as if the army and B.I.A. had as good a grip on those fake police as any one man was likely to manage. So Longarm was to spread the word and do what he could, as long as he was there. Then, about the time Attila Hornagy could possibly hear he'd just missed him yet again, and go tear-assing down to Spanish Flats, Vail wanted Longarm to return those first ponies near the depot, ride a train one stop east, and head for, say, Waco aboard another. Vail said they either had to find Hornagy's runaway wife for him or shoot him. He added he was working on a report about a tall tinhorn and a brassy blonde with a mighty thick accent up around Fort Collins.

Longarm wired back that he'd possibly cut the mystery rider's trail the easy way, and agreed to do the rest of it old Billy's way.

Then he leaned back, heaved a smoky sigh, and said, "That's just about all of your battery zinc I need to use up on you for now. Looks like I'll be staying here at least overnight. So I reckon I ought to start considering where."

The baby-faced breed blushed a dusky rose, but sounded downright bold as he suggested, "I could put you up, if you've no place better to bed down. Our quarters are right out back, and since Agent Ryan won't be staying here tonight . . .''

"Can't use another gent's bed behind his back," said Longarm, getting to his feet with a suddenly uneasy feeling about that flat-chested but mighty girlish young jasper.

Hino-Usdi Rogers insisted, "Uncle Fred won't mind. But if you're bashful, why don't we just go back right now and have a little fun in *my* little bed?"

Longarm found himself backing away from the fluttery but brazen advances of the eager young squirt. He laughed awkwardly, and said, "I hate to be the one who has to tell you this, but I'm incurably queer for women, if that was the fun you had in mind."

The breed licked his pouty lips and purred, "I can do anything for you any woman can. Better! Don't be bashful. Nobody else need ever know, and you can't tell me you've never been even a little weeny bit curious about the joys that dare not speak their names!"

Longarm laughed, too loudly for the way he felt, and confessed, "I've always wondered what the main entrée at a cannibal feast might taste like too. That don't mean I'm ever fixing to *eat* anybody!"

The breed flicked his pink tongue like a snake's, and told him not to refuse a friend just a little taste of his own flesh raw. Longarm had to shove past to get closer to the door. So he did, saying, "I don't hold with hitting other gents just because I don't agree with their, ah, tastes. But don't start no wrestling match if you ain't ready to land flat on your ass, old son."

The breed kid wrapped both arms around Longarm and buried his head in the taller man's tweed vest, sobbing, "Don't humiliate me this way! You said you and Uncle Fred were pals. How was I to know you were one of those blue-lipped Holy Rollers who can't admit their own passions?"

Longarm gently but firmly disengaged himself from the confounded clerk as he observed, "I doubt you've been to many gatherings of the Pentecostal Movement if you don't find them capable of passion. But through no fault of anyone, everyone feels passionate in different ways. I'm sorry I ain't like you and your Uncle Fred. But that's just the way things are and . . . Hold on, am I to understand that Fred Ryan is a, you know . . . ?"

"Queer is the word you were groping for," said Rogers, striking a haughty pose. "We prefer to call ourselves free to love as we please and . . . what's so funny, damn you?"

Longarm sheepishly confessed, "Wasn't laughing at you. Laughing at *me*. I thought old Fred slick-talked a gal away from me the other night. I reckon she did too. But he must have just wanted company on that long ride east, unless he was one of them free thinkers who like *everybody* a heap. You call gents like that *bicycles*, right?"

Rogers laughed despite himself and said, "The only way Uncle Fred would screw a woman would be if she was willing to take him through her back door. Sodomy seems to really make him feel romantic!"

Longarm shrugged and said, "Lucky for you. Most Indians I know are tolerant of your kind, but no more inclined than the rest of us to take you up on your kind offers."

Then he brightened and said, "That's it! I was wondering what old Fred had to offer that newspaper gal that I couldn't match. She *was* one of them adventurous gals who wanted to try everything. But somehow, I don't feel as jealous about the two of 'em now."

Hino-Usdi blanched and demanded, "Are you suggesting Uncle Fred is *cheating* on me, with a *woman*?"

To which Longarm could only reply gently, "Why not? You just now tried to cheat on him with a man."

Then he was out the door, smiling wearily but not sure who might be the biggest fool of them all. Life would surely be less confounding if folks got to screw like flowers, just letting the bees worry about who got to couple with whom.

By this time it was pushing noon and he hadn't had a warm meal in recent memory. So Longarm went over to that officers' mess and treated himself to eighteen cents worth of corned beef and fried spuds. He washed down his raisin pie dessert with two cups of black coffee, and then, feeling human again, he strode on up to the sutler's store to replenish his tobacco supply.

Ed Vernon seemed surprised as well as glad to see him. The sutler said, "We figured you'd ride north with Colonel Howard.

Wasn't you the one sending up them smoke signals yesterday?"

Longarm nodded and said, "Told Lieutenant Standish why too. Never told him those mystery riders were headed north for certain. I reckon they were in too great a hurry to wait for me this morning. I had to carry two ladies home to Comanche Town. I could use another dozen of these same cheroots."

Vernon reached under the counter for them as he said, "Maybe just as well. Quirt McQueen just said he was riding after the column to have some words with you. I don't know if we talked him out of it or not."

As Longarm reached in his jeans to pay for the smokes he muttered, "That makes no sense, if we're talking about that silly kid who rides shotgun for the mail ambulance. There's no way in hell they could have driven all the way to Fort Smith and back by this morning."

Vernon handed over the fistful of cheroots and accepted Longarm's quarter as he casually explained, "Quirt says they fired him at the Mud Creek relay stop. Seems to think you had something to do with it. I told him if he wasn't working for the government no more I couldn't let him wait here on a military post to clean your plow. Last anyone I know seen of Quirt, he was getting liquored up over in Shanty Town, allowing he meant to kill you on sight and asking if anyone would lend him a pony."

The sutler handed Longarm his nickel in change as he added in a cheerful tone, considering, "By now someone's sure to have put him on a pony, if only to get rid of him. Quirt can be obnoxious as all get-out when he's drunk."

Longarm put his tobacco and change away as he thoughtfully said, "He ain't all that pleasant sober. But there's no way I could have wired mean things about him to Mud Creek. I didn't know he was there, and even if I had, I'd have been out on the range with more serious things on my mind at the time."

He lit one of the smokes he'd just bought as he considered all his options. Then he said, "Reckon I'll have to track the kid down, if he's still over yonder, and just *ask* him what this is all about."

The sutler blinked and replied in a worried tone, "You

don't want to meet up with him before he's had time to cool down and sober up a mite, Longarm. Quirt is one mean drunk, and he's sworn he means to slap leather at the sight of you!"

Longarm shrugged and said, "You told me that. Now I'm going to go find the little shit and ask him what makes him so mean."

Chapter 18

Having just sort of growed, like Topsy, the haphazard collection of canvas and frame structures on the far side of Flipper's Impossible Ditch would have been an unsolvable maze if it had been much bigger. But Longarm asked directions, and heard the tinkling piano playing in Spike's Parisian Pavilion. Once he found it, it looked a lot more like an old threadbare army mess tent. It likely was. He shut one eyelid to let his right pupil unwind from the noonday sunlight as he strode for the opening facing the muddy lane out front. So when he stepped inside and slid sideways along a canvas wall, he only had to open his shooting eye to see well enough in the sudden shade.

A third of the big tent, toward the far end, was walled off with painted canvas. The piano stood against that, played by a skinny young squirt in his shirtsleeves and derby. A long bar had been improvised by laying planks across piled shipping crates. The floor was a squishy expanse of trampled muddy sod. Longarm wasn't sure whether the open sale of hard liquor or the painted gals in scandalous satin outfits lounging around the piano and bar would have upset Lemonade Lucy Hayes, the President's lady, the most.

A Philadelphia lawyer could likely make a case for the joint sort of squatting on an Indian or military reservation. You weren't supposed to sell hard liquor on either under current regulations out of Washington. But they were a long way from

Washington, and that was between old Spike, whoever he was, and the nearest provost marshal, whatever he got to look the other way. Longarm didn't ride for the War Department, and was only on loan to the Indian Police, who had no jurisdiction over white business permits.

Longarm was far more interested in the familiar sullen figure at one end of the bar, drinking alone as he tried to attract attention to himself by sort of singing along with the piano. Saloon gals had no call to flirt with saddle tramps who drank alone, and the few male customers at this hour seemed more uneasy than amused.

Nobody seemed to feel any easier when Longarm strode to within spitting range of Quirt McQueen and announced in a tone that could be heard clean through the music, "I understand you've been looking for this child, McQueen."

The piano stopped halfway through a bar, and the professor slid off his stool to join the painted gals in a sort of crawfish stampede around the far end of that canvas partition. Those few customers who didn't simply duck outside moved back as far as they could from the bar as the gent who'd been serving drinks behind it ducked down out of sight.

Quirt McQueen looked as if he was fixing to throw up. He gulped hard and said, "Howdy, Longarm. I heard you was on your way up to Anadarko with that cavalry column!"

Longarm curtly replied, "You said you were aiming to chase after me too. But I don't see you doing it, Squirt."

The kid protested, "They call me Quirt, not Squirt, if you don't mind. Could I buy you a drink, pard?"

Longarm shook his head and snapped, "I don't drink with mean little kids, Squirt. How did you get back from Mud Creek if you don't have a pony to ride, and what's all this shit about me getting you fired?"

Quirt swallowed some more and said, "I never said it was you in the flesh. Your B.I.A. pal and that newspaper lady said something to the jehu, and he must have said something to the station manager at Mud Creek. How was I to know they were your pals? They both sort of laughed at you when we all passed by you on the prairie that time. I told them how you'd refused to fight me over to the fort and—"

"Bullshit! Fill your fist!" Longarm declared.

Then he had to smile as the kid started pissing down one leg of his pants, whimpering, "Jesus H. Christ, can't anybody take a joke out this way? You know I never meant it, pard!"

Longarm said, "I knew it. Let's talk about why your war talk got Fred Ryan and Godiva Weaver so het up. Are you saying they rode on from Mud Creek with nobody at all riding shotgun messenger?"

McQueen shook his head and said, "There was this hard-case Indian Ryan knew, working as a stable hand at Mud Creek. Ryan said he'd feel safer with a more experienced gun waddy seated up front. But I ask you, was that fair?"

Longarm nodded and said, "Sounds fair to me. Fred Ryan has his own odd notions. But he is an experienced Indian agent and, no offense, you don't make a very convincing bad man."

Longarm pointed at the doorway with his thumb as he added, "I can see why Ryan didn't want you guarding him and Miss Weaver all the way to Fort Smith with nothing but your mouth. Squirts like you make *me* a mite nervous too. So now I want you to go find the pony you rode back on and just ride it, anywhere's you like, as long as I don't see you around me no more."

McQueen protested, "What are you talking about? You can't run me out of town! What if I just refuse to go?"

Longarm answered pleasantly enough, "That's your right, under the U.S. Constitution. I know I can't make you go. But I can surely make you sorry as hell you stayed."

He saw the kid was too drunk, or too ignorant, to grasp his full meaning. So he quietly but firmly explained, "Asshole. You've told as many witnesses as I'd ever need that you meant to gun me on sight. So here I stand in full sight, and would any court in this land expect me to hold my fire until you'd killed me?"

McQueen tried, "Aw, shit, I told you I was only joshing."

Longarm shook his head and said, "That ain't what you told Ed Vernon and some others who don't like you any better. You'd best leave now, or make good on your brag, you yellow-livered little shit, because I am fixing to take you up on it within a number of seconds I'd as soon count off silently."

Longarm wasn't really counting under his breath. He'd seen more than one man die counting aloud toward ten and getting shot around seven or eight. But the four-flushing McQueen must have *thought* he was counting. For he was suddenly running for the doorway as if the Hounds of Hell were in hot pursuit.

Longarm leaned over the bar and quietly said, "War's over and I'd like rye with a beer chaser, barkeep."

The ashen-faced barkeep was filling his order when one of the saloon gals came over to tell Longarm that his drink was on the house and that Spike would like a word with him in the back.

So he drained the shot glass, picked up his beer schooner, and followed the drab back behind that canvas wall.

On the far side it smelled even mustier, and he saw they'd divided that part of the big tent into a maze of tiny partitions. He had a fair grasp on what went on in some of them. The drab led him into a sort of canvas-walled office, where an older but prettier gal with funeral-black hair was seated behind a couple of planks laid across two flour barrels. She declared her friends called her Spike. Then she waved him to a stool on his side of the improvised desk. The younger gal with far more face paint ducked out without being ordered to leave. Longarm sipped some beer and waited for the lady to have the first say.

Spike said, "You had us worried. Quirt McQueen had a rep until a minute ago. He was a pest and bad for business as well. So to whom might we owe the honor?"

Longarm introduced himself. She didn't ask to see his badge. She laughed and said, "I'd have left town too. My help told me the kid was talking big about a lawman with a rep. I frankly never expected anyone famous as *you* to show up!"

Longarm modestly replied, "I doubt Quirt McQueen was either. I come across punks like him all the time. It's safer to threaten grown lawmen than some total stranger with a less certain reaction to your brag."

The lady known as Spike chuckled and recalled, "I saw the amusing outcome of such an encounter in Coffeyville, just before they cleaned it up and ran me out. There was this quiet little gent drinking alone at the bar. Looked like a windmill salesman, had anybody paid enough attention to speculate."

She reached in a box in front of her and took out two Havana Claros as she continued. "Anyhow, this big rough mule skinner packing a .45 on one hip comes through the door, already in his cups and doubtless feeling even bigger, to declare it's a Saturday night, that his Indian blood is up, and that he can lick any son of a bitch on the premises."

She handed Longarm one of the cigars and added, "Naturally the little lone drinker just drew and drilled him directly through the heart without a word. He declared as he was leaving that he had never let anyone talk about his dear momma like that."

Longarm broke out some matches to light them both up as he said, "The mule skinner would have been safer daring the town law to fight him. I'm surprised he didn't. Most mean drunks learn how much safer that is by the time they've been beaten up a few times. I've had some professional boxers tell me they have the same trouble. It's a lot safer to challenge someone like John L. Sullivan to a bare-knuckles brawl than some blacksmith or even a bootblack who'd be more likely to take you up on it."

She placed cool manicured fingers against his hand to steady it as he lit her cigar. He wondered whether they were flirting or not. She hadn't said what she really wanted of him yet.

He said, "There's no mystery about Quirt McQueen. He somehow got the notion he could bluff me beyond reason. But now he knows better."

She leaned back, blew a sort of octopus cloud of blue smoke at him, and quietly asked, "Why did they send such a famous lawman here to the Indian Territory, Custis?"

So now he knew what was worrying her. He smiled through the smoke at her and said, "Nobody in Denver or Washington, most likely, has ever heard of Spike's Parisian Pavilion. I'd be lying if I said the War or Interior Departments *approved* of your doubtless well-meant services to lonely troops a long ways from home. On the other hand, a heap of old army men and even Indian agents are more worldly than Queen Victoria or Lemonade Lucy Hayes. They know, or say they know, a soldier blue with some place to let off steam close to his post is less likely to go over the hill or, worse yet, molest some handier Indian gal. I had to chase a cuss clean to Mexico after he'd been charged with the murderous mistreatment of an Indian laundress one time."

Spike blew more smoke at him and quietly asked, "Then why *did* they send you?"

He finished the last of his beer, rested one elbow on her desk as he leaned closer, and just told her.

It naturally took a spell, even when he left out the dirty parts. So Spike rang a bell on her desk when he was halfway back from that Kiowa camp, and another drab came in with a pitcher of beer and two tumblers on a tray.

She set it on the desk and backed out. As Spike poured she said some troopers had told her why they had to ride up to Anadarko. She said it was going to be lousy for business. But she was glad nobody had double-crossed her.

Longarm waved his cigar warningly and said, "Stop right there, ma'am. Any deals you've made with white folks are betwixt you and white folks. Like I told you, I was sent here to give Chief Quanah a hand with his new Indian Police and as things turned out, Quanah ain't here. My orders are to give him another twenty-four hours to get back and explain his fool self. Unless he has something to say that ain't on record, I'm as good as gone. From all the files I've had a look at and all the folks I've questioned, there's nothing all that wrong with the way the Indian Police have been set up in these parts."

She asked, "What about those fake Indian Police, working with a band of fake wild Indians?"

He shrugged and said, "Quanah set up his own police force to deal with such crooks on his own reserve. Him and the B.I.A. have the army to back their play. They don't need one more white lawman all that much, and like I told you, I suspect I've somehow managed to scare the gang back to wherever they came from. I sure wish I knew how."

Spike laughed and said, "That's no mystery. I was watching through the canvas when the piano professor told me Quirt McQueen had met up with that jasper he was fixing to fight. You're *scary* when you're on the prod, Custis. I could see by your gun-muzzle eyes, clear across the saloon, it was time for that boy to slap leather or start running!"

Longarm shrugged modestly and said, "I don't usually start out as annoyed. I never locked eyeballs with that Sergeant

Black Sheep. He just took it upon himself to go to war with me. If I knew what the fuss was about I might know how I *won*!"

She agreed it was a puzzle, and then, since they'd finished the two drinks she'd poured and she wasn't pouring more, Longarm said he had to figure out where he was going to spend the coming night.

He could see why they called her Spike. She had no suggestions to offer. She didn't even walk him out front when he rose to leave. He wondered who she was paying off at the nearby fort, with what. But it wasn't any of his beeswax. An army provost marshal seldom heeded and never appreciated helpful hints from the Justice Department.

As he ambled back to the fort afoot, he laughed at himself for concerning himself with the business dealings and dubious charms of a gal too old for him. He decided it was likely because a nice-looking gal of any age was such an improvement on the offer that Hino-Usdi Rogers had made him. He decided to keep the hard-eyed but decidedly female Miss Spike in mind when he turned in alone at the hostel that night. A man would feel silly as hell having wet dreams about Cherokee breeds who only *thought* they were gals.

Crossing the parade, he noticed the mud was sunbaking back to 'dobe again. 'Dobe was what you called clay soil with lots of lime in it out here whether anyone molded it into bricks or not. Kids in Denver molded it into bitty balls to have 'dobe fights after it set solid as plaster. Those mystery riders wouldn't be leaving hoofprints much longer as they rode across thick sod rooted in drying 'dobe.

Colonel Howard and his column were headed the wrong direction in any case. If the gang was smart enough to split up and drift into the rail stop at Atoka in scattered twos and threes, they might even get by the Choctaw Police, dad blast their sneaky ways!

Longarm went back to the stable to get his saddlebags and Yellowboy from the army tack room. Then he toted them to that hostel to ask for the same room if they had it.

They did. So he put his personal baggage away after shaving and such down the hall, and this time he wedged a match stem under the bottom hinge as he shut and locked his hired door. He was just about sure he'd seen the last of Quirt McQueen, but it could pay to take the routine precautions.

He was standing on the veranda, lighting another smoke while he pondered whether he had enough questions left to pester the signal corps, when a familiar figure on a paint pony reined in a few yards away to hail him.

It was Sergeant Tikano of the Indian Police. The moon-faced Comanche said, "They told me you might be here. Quanah just rode in. He was bringing another beef herd up from Texas when he heard about all the trouble you've been having and rode on ahead. Do you want me to bring him here or will you ride with me?"

Longarm said he was in a hurry to compare notes too. So as the Indian trotted his mount beside the walk, Longarm hurried back to the stable and saddled the bay he'd hired in Spanish Flats, and they loped out together for that Comanche sub-agency just over the horizon.

Along the way, Longarm brought the Indian police sergeant up to date on his early chores with a telegraph key. Tikano agreed the rail stop at Atoka, on the Choctaw reserve, made heaps of sense for the mystery riders, if they were really running for it. He said they'd have ridden smack into Quanah and two dozen real Indians if they'd taken the Cache Creek Trail for the depot at Spanish Flats. Longarm asked how Quanah had found out enough to worry him at all, and Tikano explained, "He's been buying more beef down in Texas all this time. He likes to act more like his Saltu relations when dealing with the Saltu. That is why nobody else knew where he was all this time. He met your friends from the Running X as they were riding home to Texas. The trail boss called Carver told him about those police who were not police and others who might or might not have been Black Leggings. So now Quanah and Agent Conway are drinking much black coffee, trying to figure out what to say when they ask Agent Ryan's clerk to wire the main agency at Anadarko."

Longarm allowed he had to study on that too. As they topped a rise and saw that church steeple ahead, Longarm casually asked the Comanche if he'd ever heard any gossip about young Hino-Usdi.

Tikano replied simply, "We call him Ta Soon Da Hipey.

Every now and then a boy is born who grows up that way. It is wrong to use such a young man as a woman. But it is wrong to hurt him or even mock him as one might mock a real man who missed a shot or fell off his pony. Nobody asks for such boys to happen. Eyototo, the chief of the spirits, must have some reasons for making some people awkward, crippled, crazy, or just different. They are the ones to be pitied. Sometimes, if you give the pitied ones a chance, they turn out all right. One of the greatest war chiefs of the Arapaho did everything with his left hand. But the blue sleeves couldn't kill him at Sand Creek, even though they hit him with many bullets, many. The Cheyenne had a chief called Left Hand too."

Longarm said, "I noticed that the time Dull Knife lit out from Fort Reno just north of here. My point about that Cherokee kid, and the agent he works for, was that few if any Indians would think to blackmail such gents, whilst Spanish-speaking Christians might."

Tikano asked what Mexican outlaws might blackmail Fred Ryan or his clerk into doing for them.

Longarm answered, "Don't know. Maybe nothing. Maybe heaps. I'd best compare notes with Quanah before I send any more wires."

So he did. When they rode in they found Agent Conway and the taller Quanah Parker, dressed like a Texas trail herder with long braids, out on the front porch as if they'd been watching from a window.

Once Longarm had dismounted and shook hands all around, already knowing the stern-faced but agreeable chief to talk to, Longarm wasted no time in bringing everyone up to date, including the little he'd just found out by wire.

Quanah nodded soberly and said, "Our friend Harry Carver told me much of what you just said. When my young men and I got to where you Saltu met those police who were not police, we found nobody there to demand money from me in my name. But we scouted for sign and found where they had planted tipi poles crazy. Some with four main poles, as our women plant, but others based on a three-pole tripod, the way Arapaho put up a lodge. They had no idea at all how a tipi should be facing."

Longarm nodded and replied, "I just said I thought they might be Mex bandits with a mighty unusual approach."

Quanah said, "I had not finished. When we came to where Harry said you and that girl shot it out with Black Leggings, we scouted around those sod walls carefully. The rain that had just fallen gave away a lot of sign they may have thought they'd covered. The reason you and those cowboys never found those dead Indians is that they were buried in a draw a good ride to the west. We might not have found this out if the rainwater hadn't found the softer earth under the replaced sod easier to wash down the draw."

Longarm resisted the impulse to declare he'd never thought those rascals had been treated to any Horse Indian sky burial. It was tough to remember that despite a lot of white manners, Quanah Parker still followed Indian manners when it came to conversation. Indians broke in while others were speaking about as often as white folks belched or farted at such times.

Quanah said, "People do not rot as fast buried in 'dobe. So we knew they were not anyone we knew. They were wearing black leggings, but their war paint was silly. We who paint ourselves don't just daub it on like Saltu children going to a Halloween party. Paint is worn for *puha,* or to warn your enemies what kind of a fighter they face."

The erstwhile war leader wiped two fingers down a hollow bronzed cheek and sneered, "One had yellow lightning bolts running down green cheeks like tears. That *is* the paint of a great warrior lodge, but neither Kiowa nor Comanche. Only the Arapaho Black Hearts, not Kiowa Black Leggings, paint their faces that way."

The experienced war paint enthusiast put his fingers to his hairline as he grinned in a surprisingly boyish manner and said, "Another had a red half-moon down his forehead from his hair, with both cheeks solid red. That looked Kiowa. A Kiowa *woman* paints her face that way when her man rides off to war and she wants him to come back alive."

After they'd all chuckled at the picture, Longarm said, "They must have copied designs from some picture book. We've about agreed no Horse Indian ever called water *agua.*"

Agent Conway cocked a brow and asked, "You sure you don't mean *mauga,* pard?"

Longarm thought back before he decided, "Might have been *mauga* as easily as *agua.* Why do you ask?"

Conway sounded sure as he replied, "*Mauga* means *dead* in Pawnee. I rode with Pawnee Bill and his Pawnee Scouts one summer, during the Sioux wars. Everytime they nailed a Sioux, or vice versa, them Pawnee said the one on the ground was *mauga.*"

Longarm and the two Comanche speakers exchanged glances. Quanah suggested, "They say the Wichita and Caddo are related to Pawnee, but would even a Caddo be dumb enough to paint himself like a Kiowa *girl*?"

Longarm smiled thinly and said, "I know a Cherokee who might. Were any of them mysterious cadavers tattood Wichita-style, Chief?"

Quanah Parker said, "I don't think so. You have to understand the bodies were muddy and starting to turn funny colors under all the mud and war paint. I don't think the younger Wichita have tattood their bodies as much since they rode northeast to join the Pawnee. People laugh at you when you act different on purpose."

Agent Conway suggested they all go inside and have a sit-down over coffee and cake. But Quanah said he had to get back to those cows his boys were herding up the Cache Creek Trail.

Longarm said, "Hold on, Chief. I got places to go as well. So why don't you tell me why you sent for me by name in the first place?"

Quanah grinned like a mean little kid and said, "I think you have already done what I was going to ask you how to do. We were having the same trouble as they've had up around Fort Reno, with some few Arapaho willing to be Indian Police while the Cheyenne call them woman-hearts or worse. I haven't been asking my father's people to put up with this civilization shit because I've forgotten the old ways. They have to learn new ways because the old ways keep getting them killed. I tell them they can all be blown away by field artillery, live as animals in a zoo while they tell themselves they are still proud warriors, or learn how it is that even your twelve-year-old boys can leave home and support themselves with no B.I.A. to feed and clothe them."

Longarm nodded soberly and said, "I expect gents like you to get the vote before most white women or colored men. But I know what you mean about some unreconstructed Horse Indians holding out. I talked to your Kiowa pals about acting more progressive. I doubt I made any impression, though."

Quanah Parker said, "You're wrong. Some of Hawzitah's young men have said they would like to hear more about becoming Indian Police. If we get any Kiowa into those neat blue uniforms, with extra money to spend at the trading posts . . ."

"I get the picture," Longarm said. "If that's all you wanted from me, like I said, I got my own row to hoe. Got to get my ass somewhere's else before that column comes back from Anadarko. You gents know as much as me about those mystery riders, who could be long gone for all I know. So let me ride back to the fort for my saddlebags, and I'll ride down the Cache Creek Trail with you, Chief."

But Quanah said, "If I wait that long there won't be much riding for *me*. By now that herd should be just over the horizon to the south. I want to rejoin my drovers and make sure they have the beef bedded down well east of here before sundown. It makes a mess when I try to distribute beef too close to this settlement. Some people would rather just shoot a cow and cut it up on the spot than drive it home."

Longarm allowed he'd been there when B.I.A. beef on the hoof had been divided up. He squinted up at the sun and added, "No sense in me sleeping along the trail when I don't have to. I've hired a bed under a roof at the fort. Riding alone from an early start I could likely make it to another before nightfall by loping some. Got me a mess of wires back and forth to consider in any case."

So they all shook on it, and Longarm said he'd let them know if he got any helpful answers to some of the questions he'd sent earlier about those mysterious riders.

He loped back to Fort Sill, considered reining in out front of the B.I.A. liaison office, and had a better idea.

He dismounted in front of the army Signal Corps installation, went inside, and asked for the gent in charge.

When the skinny gray sergeant in the front office said that

was him, Longarm introduced himself and explained his problem.

The army man chuckled, said he'd heard that Cherokee clerk just down the walk was a sissy, and agreed to contact anyone Longarm was waiting to hear from, provided he'd write it all down.

Longarm accepted the yellow writing tablet and block-printed each address and query on a separate sheet. He lettered a longer progress report for Billy Vail, but didn't say when he'd be leaving. Vail would know his own travel instructions and nobody else needed to. Asking a total stranger not to show these sheets of foolscap to a Hornagy who might offer money to see them would be stretching one's luck.

He offered to send the considerable dots and dashes himself. But the sergeant said his own telegraphers could use the practice. So Longarm blocked out a few more queries as long as he was at it, and said he'd be back after supper-time to pick up any replies.

He led the spent pony on a shortcut to the stable across the now dry and solid parade. A stable hand who met him just outside to take the reins handed him a small white envelope, saying, "Compliments of the colonel's lady. They told her at the hostel you'd ridden off post, sir."

Longarm took the envelope with a nod of thanks and said, "I ain't no damn officer you have to salute and sir, pard."

He tore open the envelope to discover he'd been invited to supper on officers' row. So, checking the sun against his pocket watch, he saw he just had time to make himself more presentable.

He took a bath at the hostel while he was at it, and showed up at the Howard house before sundown, as he'd been invited, with a clean shirt and shoestring tie, his rumpled tobacco brown tweed suit, and a good splashing of bay rum. He'd picked the prairie primroses out back of the stable. Fortunately, the kind with white blossoms grew later in the summer than the pink evening primrose.

The plump Elvira Howard opened the door to him herself, wearing a paisley print dress a size too skinny for her, along with a heap of jasmine scent and, he suspected, a fresh henna rinse.

She took his hat and the flowers with a happy coo, as if she'd never seen a vacant lot overgrown with prairie primrose, and led him in to the dining room, where two places had been set at their damask-covered table. She cooed some more when he helped her into her seat. Being the colonel's lady, she was likely surprised by good manners. Then she rang a small brass bell as Longarm was sitting his own self down, and a young corporal in a fresh-pressed blue uniform came out of the kitchen and hit a brace as if he expected her to make him recite all twelve general orders.

She told him serve the first course instead.

This turned out to be cold potato and onion soup that she called a "vicious wash." He had to agree that no matter what you called it, it seemed just right for such a warm summer evening.

After the cold soup was cleared away, they had cooled-down roast chicken in a nest of iced salad greens. Then they got down to business with steak and mashed potatoes. Elvira said she hoped he'd forgive her for such a simple meal, but she had this weight problem and the regimental surgeon had suggested she and the colonel cut down.

Longarm gravely replied two servings of spuds seemed enough for one supper, and so she had them served a modest dessert of strawberry shortcake under whipped cream.

After that his hefty hostess suggested they have their demitasses with Napoleon in the drawing room. So that's where they went. Nobody named Napoleon was waiting there to drink with them. They called the fancy brandy that went with the fancy coffee Napoleon.

She told him it was jake with her if he smoked while he was at it. But he allowed the coffee and brandy would do him as he waited for her to get down to brass tacks.

It took her a spell. They had to jaw about her husband and that cavalry column off to the north, and he told her about his conversation with Quanah Parker while the shadows lengthened and nobody came in to light any lamps. He was about to offer to do it when the plump redhead took a deep breath and suddenly blurted out, "What were you doing over there with Spike Wilson's place, Custis?"

He blinked in surprise, then told her honestly enough, "I

went to Shanty Town to have it out with young Quirt McQueen. That's where they told me I'd find him. I did. But he was more willing to fight with me behind my back than face to face. So I just told him to get off this reservation, and I reckon he has by now."

Elvira Howard insisted, "You wound up in Spike's back room with her, for some time."

Longarm shrugged and explained, "She was curious about me too. She said she'd been expecting more of the notorious Quirt McQueen. I never asked her who she paid off over here at the fort. So she never told me, if that's what this is all about."

The plump Elvira paled enough to notice, despite the tricky light, but said, "I don't know what you're talking about. Are you suggesting those white trash on the far side of Flipper's Ditch pay someone here at this post to look the other way?"

Longarm sighed and said, "I ain't suggesting nothing, ma'am. I just told you I never asked Miss Spike about purely War Department beeswax. I was sent here to help the B.I.A. and Quanah Parker set up the Indian Police a tad better. Running into those mystery riders your husband is out hunting was extra cheese on my pie plate. I ain't interested in anything else that might be going on in these parts, and as a matter of fact, I'll be on my way before your husband or any other officer Miss Spike might know could possibly get back. I'm only booked into that hostel down the way for one more night, and thanks to you, I'm ahead of the game at the officers' mess. I'll be riding on just after they serve breakfast in the morning."

She placed a thoughtful hand on his tweed pants and softly asked if he'd like to have breakfast there with her.

Longarm stared at her incredulously in the gathering dusk, gulped, and said, "It ain't nice to treat animals cruelly, Miss Elvira. You've no idea how tempting that offer sounds, but . . ."

"Our enlisted help will be leaving for their barracks any minute," she said, moving her hand up his thigh as she crooned, "Nobody else need ever know, and we have so much to talk about, Custis."

He grabbed her soft wrist, wryly aware how it felt when a

gal stopped him that way, as he protested, "I'd know, ma'am, and as fair of face and form as I find you, I don't hold with adulterating married ladies."

She chuckled and softly sang:

> Some folk say I am a knave.
> Some folk say I can't behave.
> Now I jack off on her grave,
> With my old organ-grinder!

Longarm told her flatly, "I never sang that song to *you* the other night, Miss Elvira."

To which she demurely replied, "I know who you *did* sing it to. She said you were hung like a horse and energetic but gentle. It's been some time since a man like that rode off on me to get shot off his horse in the hills of Tennessee."

Longarm could barely see her now as he quietly replied, "I was at a Tennessee crossroads called Shiloh one time. I'm sorry about your beau getting killed in the war, ma'am. But you did wind up with Colonel Howard, and like I said, I don't mess with married ladies."

She snapped, "Who did you think you were with the other night just after the dance at the club, Little Red Riding Hood? She was the wife of the regimental Romeo who got caught with yet *another* wife just down the hall!"

Longarm had to total the score in his head before he laughed and said, "You mean that was the poor innocent victim you talked the colonel into posting to Fort Douglas with her rogue of a husband?"

Elvira Howard sniffed, "My Morgan runs his regiment. I run everything else around here. But Spike told you all this, didn't she?"

Longarm laughed and insisted, "Honest Injun, she never did. Can't you get it through your pretty head I just don't care about that, ma'am?"

She sniffed, "I know how pretty my head is. There was a time, before boredom and the sands of time weighed me down a bit. Or might it simply be that you can't afford to be compromised by a woman you may have to testify against in federal court? Our mutual friend on her way west to Fort Douglas said you were hardly this prim with *her* the other night!"

Longarm started to explain the obvious as he felt himself getting hard in spite of himself. Anyone with a lick of sense could see what a difference it made when you knew for certain a gal was married up with a gent you knew to howdy. She was likely just out to make sure he'd be in no position to bear witness against her, the wicked old thing.

Then she had her hand on it and marveled, "Oh, my, is all this for little old me?"

So he decided he was damned if he did and damned if he didn't as he reeled her in for a friendly howdy, seeing she was already hauling his raging erection out into the cool shades of evening.

She kissed back with a passion suggesting she might not just be gripping his shaft that tight to prevent his arresting her. When they came up for air and he asked if she was sure they were alone in the house now, she gasped, "I told the boys to leave the dishes in the sink, but I don't care! I want you now. Right there on the rug, the way we used to do it when I was eighteen and we could have eloped if you hadn't ridden off with your damned regiment, darling!"

So they wound up on the rug with half their duds off, screwing the hell out of other folks long ago and far away.

Longarm didn't know who her darling was, once she'd wrapped plump but surprisingly limber legs around his waist. He decided she reminded him of good old Roping Sally, up Montana way, who'd had such a well-rounded rump they'd never needed any padding under it. Although, as this one thrust her twat in time with his thrusts, it felt different. He was glad they *all* seemed to feel a mite different. For if all of them felt exactly as swell, a man would have no call to ride on, and *then* where would he be?

An hour later they were in a small bed in what she described as their guest room. It didn't make him feel as dirty as it might have in a bed she shared with the colonel. He didn't want to hear how many "guests" she'd been this nice to.

Her shorter, plumper body didn't seem at all like Roping Sally's as they came again in the nude on top of the bedding. But he didn't care. Old Elvira had a lot to offer, once a man persuaded himself he was sacrificing himself in the cause of investigation.

Sharing a smoke with her as they cuddled in the dark like old pals, Longarm had little trouble worming the petty details of a familiar arrangement out of the no-longer-worried colonel's lady.

She had the colonel sincerely convinced it was better for their enlisted men to let off steam in Shanty Town than, say, some Indian settlement a short ride further out, where they'd be harder to keep an eye on.

In return for this reasonable attitude, Miss Spike and the other trash whites just outside the gates gave "presents" to a lady with appetites her husband couldn't afford on his army salary. Longarm was paid by the same government. So he had to agree President Hayes seemed mighty tightfisted.

He didn't go into the mostly civilian government officials he'd had to arrest for augmenting their modest civil service salaries with the graft almost built into the system. He didn't want to remind her how Washington gave petty officials almost god-like powers over richer folks and then paid them three-or four-figure salaries to get by on. He'd often thought it was dumb to pay a bank teller barely enough to eat on and then trust him with the combination to the vault too.

Once he'd convinced her they hadn't sent him all this way to see where the troops at Fort Sill got laid, Elvira seemed more interested in the case he was really on.

He snubbed out the cheroot and got his bonier hips between her plump thighs again, to slide it back in sideways half erect, as he repeated there were only a few details to clear up and that he was leaving them to the army and the Indians.

She thrust her own hips languidly as she said, "Oh, yes, this is a nice friendly way if the man's, ah, man enough. But why were those mysterious riders act so mysterious to begin with, dear?"

He shrugged a bare shoulder, thrust a stiffer erection, and told her, "When the cat's away the mice will play, as if I had to tell *you* that. Somebody heard Quanah's Indian Police were resented and not too well understood by the folks around here. Meanwhile, Quanah was away on his own mysterious business, and this gave them the chance to move in and try the

Black Hand flimflam from New Orleans.''

She said, ''I thought you said they were Mexican, or maybe Pawnee. Could you move a little faster, honey?''

He could. He rolled atop her as he explained in the same conversational tone, ''They read about war paint in books. I ain't saying the mastermind is Indian or Mex. He adds up as some sneaky white. But as soon as any of 'em are caught, they'll doubtless talk. So like I said, I can't hang around forever to pull routine police chores.''

She moaned, ''Oh, Lord, don't you dare leave before you make me come again! I'd forgotten how grand it can feel and . . . Jesus, Teddy, why did you have to get yourself killed like a mere human being in that bloody mess at Lookout Mountain?''

He started to tell her a lot of Confederate widows doubtless shared her distaste for that particular battle. But he never did. He knew Elvira was thinner and younger and coming with her Teddy right now. So he just thrust it in and out of her moaning flesh until they'd both gone to Heaven again. Then all hell seemed to be busting loose outside in the night, and he pulled out of her as she gasped, ''My God! We're under attack! That was gunfire just now!''

He sat up, reaching for his duds at the foot of the bed as he said, ''Two six-guns, fired fast as possible but empty by now, with nobody shooting back. Stay here and I'll find out what's going on out yonder.''

She didn't argue, but groped for her own clothes as he quickly got dressed, buckled on his own six-gun, and grabbed his hat on the way out. Nobody was looking his way as they all converged on the post's guest hostel down the parade.

Longarm had time to break out his badge and pin it to the lapel of his frock coat before he got to where he'd booked a room for the night. It was just as well he had. Two military policemen were blocking the front door to the simply curious. They let Longarm through. Inside, four uniformed figures were poking about with confused expressions. One wore the arm brassard of the Officer of the Day. Another had the gilt oak leaves you'd expect on a post provost marshal. Before they could ask Longarm anything, or vice versa, another officer and two enlisted military policemen came down the stairs, confused in their own right.

The shavetail in charge said, ''We found the room clerk upstairs, Major. Shot in the back in one of the rooms. There was nobody else with him. But the bed had been shot up worse! Feathers all over the place!''

Longarm asked if they were talking about the corner room numbered 206. When the shavetail allowed they surely were, Longarm said, ''It was me they were after. I'd booked that room for the night and hung on to the key. The killer or killers came in down here asking for me. The clerk must have thought I was upstairs when he didn't see my key in its pigeonhole. They made him lead them upstairs and open my door with his passkey. Then they just started shooting until they emptied their wheels or noticed I wasn't there. So what are we all standing here for? Whether it was the Quirt McQueen you all know or some other son of a bitch entire, he can't have more than a few minutes lead on you, and it's open prairie all around if he's not holed up in Shanty Town!''

The provost marshal roared, ''You heard the man! I want four squads assembled on the double, fully armed! I want one to sweep this post inside the perimeter, just in case. I want that squatters' settlement turned over like a wet rock, and meanwhile, I want one squad riding north and the other south!''

The O.D. asked what about east and west. The major said, ''*We* are to his west. I don't think anyone but Indians would head for that Indian agency to the east.''

He shot a questioning glance at Longarm, who suggested, ''If Indians passed through your gates this evening, your sentries should have seen 'em, right?''

The major smiled thinly and said, ''They told us you were good. Do you think that was why someone was out to kill you just now?''

Longarm started to say Quirt McQueen hadn't struck him as that deep a thinker. Then he remembered those other more persistent attacks, and contented himself with answering, ''Don't know, Major. I sent me some questions by wire earlier. Reckon I'll head over to the Signal Corps and see if anything came in. Your wire is manned round the clock, ain't it?''

The provost marshal nodded and said it had to be. Longarm elbowed his way out and started across the parade in the tricky light, his mind in a whirl. For no matter how he kept collecting facts around here, he hadn't been able to fit any together worth beans!

He knew he was overloaded with more information than he needed. It had been simple to figure the less tangled motives of, say, Spike Wilson, the colonel's lady, and even that cheating army wife who told tales out of school. He reviewed his simple transactions with all three of them. Old Spike was just selling sin at a price enlisted men could afford. That lady in the dark who'd wound up on her way out to Fort Douglas had just been getting back at her cheating husband, and old Elvira . . . ? She was just getting fat as she pined for the impossible, a young love now dead and buried after falling in the vicious Battle of Chickamauga in the hills of Tennessee.

Longarm took another full step before he gasped, "Jesus H. Christ! That's *it*!" and swerved a tad to bear down on the B.I.A. liaison office instead. There was no light inside at this hour. But Longarm knocked anyway. And it was a good thing he was standing to one side as a whole fusillade of bullets tore through frosted glass and paneling from inside!

Longarm called back, "Give it up, old son! That's *another* time you missed me, and I got it all figured out. After that, you're smack on an army post and they've already called out the guard on you!"

As if to prove his point, that young O.D. and a quartet of his interior guard, with bayoneted rifles, were running his way until he waved his own drawn .44-40 and yelled, "Don't line up with this doorway! We got us a sore loser inside!"

As if to prove the point another shot rang out inside, and then a familiar but unexpected voice called out, "Don't shoot. I *got* him! What's going on around here, for Pete's sake?"

Longarm yelled, "Open up, Ryan."

So Fred Ryan did, wearing no more than his pants, a sleepy-eyed expression, and a smoking Walker Conversion as he said, "I was asleep in the back when I heard young Rogers blazing away out here. When I asked him what was going on and who he'd been shooting at, he turned on me with his two guns and I had to shoot him!"

Longarm mildly asked, "How come? I counted twelve shots just now." Ryan said as calmly, "That's doubtless why I'm still alive. He had the drop on me and I was half asleep when I fired my own gun. Come on in. You can see for yourselves how it was."

As they all filed into the smoke-filled office after him, Ryan turned up a lamp someone had trimmed to a blue flicker earlier. As it flared to display the Cherokee clerk on the floor behind the counter, facedown and bare-ass with a pistol in each dead hand, Longarm followed Ryan through the gap in the counter, observing, "You made good time to Fort Smith and back, Fred. We weren't expecting you this soon."

Ryan said, "I just got in this evening. That's why I went right to bed without making a speech about it. I never went all the way east to Fort Smith. That newspaper gal did, looking to interview Quanah Parker for her readers. I only had to pick up some mail-order stuff of a . . . personal nature at the freight depot in Akota."

Longarm said, "I could keep asking questions and you could keep slithering slimy as an eel all night. But it's over, Fred. I got to arrest you for all sorts of things now, starting with the murder of this Indian ward of the government on the floor."

Longarm hardly expected any sane man to throw down on the law and three armed soldiers blue. But Fred Ryan didn't look too sane as he said dreadful things about Longarm's mother and started to swing the drawn gun in his hand into position.

He never managed it, of course. Longarm sent him spinning across the office with a round of .44-40, and then as Ryan bounced off the far wall, he was hit in the face with a .45-70 rifle ball that *really* messed him up.

The O.D. was fussing at the trooper who'd fired without orders by the time the Indian agent stopped twitching on the blood-slicked floor. So Longarm said, "No harm done, and I'm writing you boys up for an assist in my official report. The son of a bitch we just shot used to work at the Cherokee Agency in Tahlequah, two thirds of the way to Fort Smith. He knew all about ordering police uniforms and such from Saint Lou. He'd done so earlier for the Cherokee Police, and whether he stole some or ordered more after he'd transferred out is a matter we can work out later. Them mystery riders he had pretending to be Comanche Police or Kiowa raiders were Cherokee crooks. The Five Civilized Tribes that were out here earlier have had plenty of time to pick up white habits. They never learned to set up a proper tipi ring or savvy the sign lingo and paint of Horse Indians because the Cherokee were never Horse Indians when they lived in the wooded hills of Tennessee."

The O.D. asked, "Who told you all this, Deputy Long? No offense, but you didn't seem to know that much earlier."

Longarm said, "I'd forgot some things I knew. I jumped to hasty conclusions, trying to fit Mex bandits into a pattern that wouldn't work. I didn't even get it when Agent Conway persuaded me I'd heard an Indian say someone was dead, not that he needed water. Wichita or Pawnee raiders made a tad more sense than Mexicans. But not much, and it only came to me a few minutes ago that Tennessee used to be Cherokee country and that I'd been told, marching through it, how Chickamauga, where we fought that battle, meant Dead River in Cherokee!"

He pointed his warm pistol barrel at the naked Cherokee cadaver as he said, "Cherokee is related to Iroquois and Pawnee the way Comanche is related to Shoshoni, Aztec, and such. A lawman would play hell trying to account for Shoshoni building cities down Mexico way. But at least Pawnee were possible around here."

He pointed at the dead Indian agent to add, "It worked even better as soon as I suspected we were dealing with Cherokee and a white mastermind who literally liked to screw the Cherokee."

One of the troopers said he'd heard young Rogers was like that.

Longarm said, "We might have been able to charge him with crimes against nature on federal property. I doubt he even knew Fred Ryan tried to gun me twice tonight. It looks as if Ryan killed his lover boy for the same reason he gunned that clerk across the way. To shut them both up. So's he could play innocent."

The provost marshal barged in with more troops, demanding answers. Longarm pointed to the O.D. and said, "The lieutenant knows as much as me so far. I got to get up to your Signal Corps installation and see if anyone I wired earlier can tell me anything more."

He pushed his way out as the O.D. started explaining the mess in the B.I.A. office. The provost marshal must not have been satisfied. He caught up with Longarm up the line, just as the tall deputy read the last of the few telegrams waiting there for him.

Waving a penciled transcription at the older army man, Longarm said, "It sure beats all how things fall in place, once you figure the overall pattern of the puzzle. Mud Creek identifies a shotgun messenger who replaced young Quirt McQueen, for no good reason, as a Lester Tenkiller, Tenkiller being a common Cherokee name. Quirt was fired and left to fend for his fool self because Ryan didn't want a witness coming back this way to tell me, in particular, how Ryan had never gone on to Fort Smith with a lady we both knew."

Longarm picked up another message to make sure of his details as he continued. "Ryan was whipping back and forth betwixt here and the railroad stop at Atoka. That seems to have been his home plate. He met his Cherokee pals there, picked up mail-order duds for 'em, and—"

"Atoka's one hell of a ride," the provost marshal said.

Longarm nodded and said, "Handy to the railroad, though. After that, it's a fair-sized settlement where none of his recruits were apt to meet up with either Comanche Police from this reserve or the Cherokee Police from their own. I just wired the *Choctaw* Police to be on the lookout for the Lester Tenkiller who comes through there fairly often. I'm letting the three Indian police forces work out the probable suspects Ryan would have recruited around Tahlequah. It'll be good training for all concerned, and we've accounted for the really bad apple in the bunch. Old Ryan must have figured I'd been sent to catch him personal. He was the only one up to anything crooked, involving any Indian Police. As a liaison man he was naturally privy to all the messages sent back and forth. But he must have been afraid he'd missed something."

Longarm picked up another message and said, "It's too bad he never read this wire from Denver, ordering me home before I'd recalled the meaning of Chickamauga. That enlisted clerk and the Cherokee breed might have still been alive if old Fred had let sleeping dogs lie. I might have missed his petty extortions entirely if he hadn't scared the shit out of me with his wilder-acting Indians. Or burned my ass when he ran off with a wild newspaper gal he was only interested in getting rid of before *she* followed up on some gossip about his operation!"

Chapter 19

A few days later, along about supper-time at the Brewster Dairy outside Trinidad, the pretty young widow was crossing her barnyard toward the main house when she spied a familiar figure on a chestnut gelding.

Longarm had hired it, along with its stock saddle, at a livery near the depot. He could only hope his own saddle and original baggage was still waiting for him at the Union Depot in Denver. He was wearing his suit and tie again, seeing he was calling on a lady.

As he reined in near her front steps, Cora Brewster hurried to greet him there, saying, "I was just thinking of you, Deputy Crawford! I wired you in care of Fort Sill, and they wired back that they'd never heard of you!"

Longarm dismounted and started to tether his hired mount to her hitching rail as he awkwardly replied, "Good help is hard to find these days. I just got back from Fort Sill, after some tedious train transfers. But to tell the truth I spent most of my time with some Indian pals, and I reckon they lost track of me at the fort. You say you were trying to get in touch with me, Miss Cora?"

The young but fully developed brunette in blue calico that matched her eyes dimpled up at him and explained, "That horrid Longarm's back in Trinidad. They said he'd run off with Magda Hornagy, the brute. But he's been sparking another Bohunk girl too young for him by half and the immigrant ladies are all atwitter!''

Longarm nodded gravely and said, ''That accounts for another blond lady who talks funny up Fort Collins way. I've been in touch with my home office by wire, and they just now told me the couple in question produced papers from the Austro-Hungarian Empire when the law paid a call on their rooming house. He used to be some sort of cavalryman they call a Hula Hula Lancer, and his wife had permission to leave as well.''

Cora Brewster said, ''I told you Longarm deserted that *other* blonde somewhere. Why are you tethering your mount to that post? You surely mean to sup and visit with me a while, don't you?''

He allowed he hadn't made any better plans for that evening. So she led the way back across her barnyard, explaining along the way how she'd just given her two hired men and house-girl the payday evening off. Longarm knew enough about cows to assume her dairy stock had been led into their stalls and milked for the last time that day no later than four in the afternoon. She didn't invite him to stable a pony with her cows. The chestnut gelding wound up in the stable with its own kind to gossip with. He noted with approval she fed them all timothy hay and medium-grade oats.

On the way back to the house Cora explained she'd been planning a light, simple supper for herself alone. He said he'd been stuffing his face with peanuts and such aboard many a train for the past few days. She laughed when she thought back to those few hours they'd done the same in that D&RG club car.

She said, ''It seems so long ago, and as if our time together lasted longer. Isn't it funny how well you seem to get to know a stranger on a train, Deputy Crawford?''

He said it sure was, and added, ''This jasper everyone keeps calling Deputy Custis Long, Miss Cora, you've *seen* the skirt-chasing cuss in the flesh your ownself? I mean, you'd know him if he rode in to join us for supper this evening?''

She indicated the way to her back steps as she sniffed and told him, ''That'll be the day! You're so right about him chasing skirts! I swear I think he'd have his wicked way with a snake if he could get some other rogue to hold its head for him! He'd get my broom across his wicked face if ever he darkened my door at supper-time or any other time!''

Longarm naturally opened the back door for her. As she marched through, chin at an indignant angle, she continued. ''That snip of a dishwater blonde he's involved with *now* can't be a day over fifteen, and even a rogue with Longarm's rep ought to know better than to mess with bitty virgin girls!''

As he followed her into her neatly kept kitchen, he smelled fresh-baked bread and something sweeter. He said, ''Leaving the virtue of the maiden to her own conscience, fifteen does seem a tad young. She ain't reached the age of consent under Colorado law. He'd have to get her legal guardian's permission to even come courting.''

Cora took his hat and sat him at a scrubbed pine table near the window as she asked, ''What's poor Bela Nagy supposed to do, challenge a notorious gunfighter with a badge to a duel? That wicked child's poor father is a coal miner who barely speaks English and wouldn't want trouble in any American court in the unlikely event he won!''

Longarm murmured, ''I've noticed ignorant folks can be easy to cow with even a mail-order badge. I just got done exposing some fake lawmen over in the Indian Territory. According to a wire I got just the other day, the real Indian Police have rounded up a bunch of 'em and have 'em singing their little hearts out about home addresses in the Cherokee Nation. It's easy to round up fake lawmen once you notice they're fake.''

She placed a bowl of stew she'd had warming on her stove in front of him, along with a pound of butter and some of that fresh bread he'd been smelling, as she sighed and said, ''I hope you'll forgive me this once for offering so little. I'll make it up to you with a proper dinner tomorrow, if you aim to be in town that long. Why did you just suggest Longarm is a fake lawman, Deputy Crawford? For all the dreadful things they say about his way with the ladies, nobody I know has ever suggested he's not a real federal lawman like you.''

The real Longarm said, ''I'm going to have to catch up with him to be dead certain. But I'm fixing to be surprised as well as chagrined if the bully pestering Bohunk miners' wives and daughters turns out to be the real thing, Miss Cora."

The young widow sat down with her own serving across from him and insisted, "I'm sure Longarm is a real lawman. It was only a few weeks ago we were reading in the *Rocky Mountain News* about the way he'd been in yet another gunfight and won!"

Longarm said, "I read that edition too. Those newspaper reporters go on a heap. I just read a copy of the *New England Sentinel* on the train this afternoon. So I know for a fact that a reporter gal who couldn't have interviewed the one and original Quanah Parker in Fort Smith, Arkansas, just published a long interview with *some* fool Indian. You got to take Miss Weaver's word about him being a big chief."

Cora asked, "Are you suggesting Longarm was never really interviewed by that reporter from the *Rocky Mountain News*? Why aren't you eating your stew? Is it too salty?"

He said, "That reporter interviewed the survivor of that gunfight, ma'am. I was raised with better manners than to slurp my stew without a proper invitation."

She started to ask a dumb question, fluttered her lashes, and dug into her own serving as she confessed, "I'd forgotten what the etiquette books say about the hostess taking the first taste. I guess you think I'm mighty countrified."

He dug into his own grub, saying, "Nobody was ever raised more country than me. I had to read that in a book myself. There ain't no shame in just not knowing. But once you learn there's a right way and a dumb way to act around ladies of quality, it would just be rude not to bone up on 'em."

She blushed becomingly and murmured, "Go on, I'm nowhere near a lady of quality. I'm just a farm girl who's made out all right in butter and eggs."

"By hard work," he insisted. "I got an eye for whitewash and clean sweeping, Miss Cora. Takes a tidy eye and honest sweat to keep a spread this size this neat, even with help, and a lady who'd give her help an evening off before sundown is a lady of quality in my book."

She insisted, "You're making me blush. I swear you're as big a flirt as that dreadful Longarm, albeit I don't feel as frightened as I would if it was *him* across this very table from me!"

The man of whom she was speaking said, "I'm sure going

to have to meet up with this womanizing wonder. You say he can be found in the company of some fifteen-year-old kid from Bohunk Hill?''

Cora said, ''Eva Nagy, and we're not certain she's that old. I doubt you'd find Longarm anywhere near her parents' humble home after dark, though. They say he drives off into the hills in a curtained buggy, with all the greenhorn girls he can get to go with him.''

She got up to fetch the fresh-perked coffee from her stove as she added, ''Accuse me of having a dirty mind, if you like, but I am a widow woman who's not entirely ignorant of human anatomy and that child he's been molesting can't be . . . fully developed yet.''

Longarm could only glance out the window at the lengthening shadows as he murmured, ''Well, they say some gents like their olives green because it make's 'em feel . . . more manly.''

She poured mugs of coffee for both of them as she exclaimed without thinking, ''They say Longarm's hung like a horse, and she's such a *tiny* thing!''

Then she realized what she'd said, blushed beet red, and sat down to cover her face with her apron, sobbing, ''Oh, Lord, I must really be going mad from living alone, the way I read in that book about the lady who lived in a tower in olden times!''

Longarm said, ''That yarn about the Lady of Astolat was only a fairy tale, Miss Cora. Even if it was true, she never went *loco en la cabeza* from living alone up in her tower. She was hankering for Sir Launcelot in particular. Only he never knew it because she couldn't just call out an invitation to come up and stay a spell whenever he rode by in his tin suit. They did things the hard way in those days. Sir Launcelot never knew the Lady of Astolat hankered for him whilst he, in turn, was hankering for King Arthur's wife.''

Cora laughed despite herself and said, ''That sounds a lot like Colorado these days. That adultery at King Arthur's court led to a really nasty brawl in the end, didn't it?''

Longarm nodded soberly and said, ''It often does. The unwritten law calls for blood and slaughter all out of proportion to the fun anyone could have had. Poor old Arthur threw away his kingdom and his life, Attila Hornagy is wandering the world like that Frankenstein monster seeking revenge, and a certain colonel I know has just transferred junior officers to miserable postings because of a few minutes slap and tickle."

He sipped some coffee and wearily added, "Lord knows what *he'll* ever do if he finds out about his *own* lady's views on hospitality. But my point is that there's likely nothing wrong with you, Miss Cora. It's little Eva Nagy, not yourself, up in the hills in that covered buggy as the sun goes down, right?"

She looked away and murmured, "Praise the Lord for small favors. I'd die before I let a brute like Longarm touch me, but I don't know how I'd feel about a buggy ride with somebody nicer."

He said it was too bad he hadn't driven out from town in a hired buggy. She called him a big silly, and got up to serve the peach cobbler dessert from her oven.

He waited until they were on her front veranda, admiring the sunset from her porch swing, before he got out his notebook to ask directions to the cabin of that coal miner with the wayward daughter.

Cora said, "Heavens, I don't know my way around Bohunk Hill! I only know it as a cluster of shacks atop a low hill, man-made or natural, near the mine adits to the west. I've ridden past it, along the Purgatoire Trail. I've never been up in that cinder-paved maze of crooked lanes. I'm only repeating gossip I heard in town."

He put the notebook away, saying, "Reckon I'll just ride on over and ask directions then. If ladies in Trinidad are gossiping about the Nagy gal, folks who live closer ought to know where her folks can be found."

Cora protested, "You'd never make it before total darkness now. There are no street lamps on Bohunk Hill, and they say Longarm can be dangerous in broad daylight. If he should hear that even another lawman is looking for him on a morals charge . . ."

"I got to find the jasper and ask him where Magda Hornagy can be found. What's going on betwixt him and that younger sass is betwixt them and her father. Attila Hornagy is only after him because of his *own* flirty little thing. For all we know for sure, the cuss he's so sure she ran off with could be innocent as me. I know *I* never messed with Magda Hornagy and I'm finding this whole affair mighty tedious."

Cora smiled at him uncertainly in the tricky light and asked what he was talking about. She said, "Surely nobody has ever accused *you* of adultery with that coal miner's wife, Deputy Crawford?"

He smiled sheepishly and said, "Yes they have. Before I go on, are you sure you've seen that cuss they call Longarm down here in these parts?"

She nodded soberly and said, "Plain as day. More than once. He even smiled at me outside the milliner's one day."

Longarm said, "It's agreed he has an eye for pretty ladies. But you Trinidad ladies have his handle wrong. I had a good reason for telling you I was Gus Crawford when we first met. I knew Attila Hornagy was gunning for Deputy Custis Long because I'd just ducked out of a fight with him in the Union Depot. I've yet to lay eyes on this Longarm he's after, but I'd be the only deputy out of our Colorado office that's ever been called Longarm!"

The pretty young widow stared goggled-eyed at him in the fading light. "*You* claim to be Longarm, Deputy Crawford?"

He said, "Deputy Custis Long at your service, ma'am. There ain't no Deputy Crawford riding out of our Denver District Court. I told you I just made that up. I didn't want Hornagy to find out which way I'd lit out. We were hoping to find his woman and calm him down whilst I took care of easier problems around Fort Sill. But as of now she's still missing, her man is still looking to track me down and gun me for running off with her, and so I'd best tidy up around here before I head back to Denver. What are you crying about, Miss Cora?"

She sobbed into the apron she was holding to her face again as he placed a gentle hand on a heaving calico-clad shoulder to repeat the question.

She blurted out, "I feel like such a fool! It was mean of you to trick me into those observations about your anatomy if you were the real Longarm all this time!"

He chuckled and observed, "I just got done teaching some Indian Police how unsupported hearsay and possibly inaccurate mental pictures can lead one astray. The crooks we were dealing with had barely sense to steal with. But we gave them an edge by leaping to conclusions. I hope you've learned your lesson about *me* at least. No matter how I might be hung, I've never messed with either that miner's daughter or Attila Hornagy's wife.''

She laughed like hell and called him a dirty dog. But as she felt him shift his weight to rise, she asked where he thought he was going at this hour.

He settled his weight back in the swing, to be polite, as he told her, ''Looking for the man I owe all this trouble to. I got a pony to ride me anywheres he could take a gal in a buggy. Someone over yonder ought to be able to tell me which way that would be. There's this rise called Cherry Hill, just outside Denver, where heaps of swains park their buggies a spell by moonlight. You can tell, come morning, because of all the . . . sign along the wagon trace.''

She said, ''Don't ride up into the hills after him. Whoever he really is, he has all the other men afraid of him, and coal miners are hardly sissies.''

Longarm said, ''Got to find him before Attila Hornagy does then. Hornagy ain't afraid of him. That gives a man a natural bully might under-rate an edge. It gets even stickier for law and order in these parts if the womanizing bully wins. He'll doubtless know he'll be charged with murder, and once he runs, we may never know what really happened.''

Cora said, ''Well, I, for one, can't really work up much sympathy for *anyone* now that I know even the injured husband has been acting like a drooling idiot!''

Longarm observed the law protected drooling idiots as well as the more refined, but once again she said, ''Don't go. If you have to have it out with that imposter pretending to be you, he's staying at the Dexter Hotel near the Trinidad Depot when he's not out chasing young girls!''

Longarm frowned and muttered, ''You mean this home wrecker has a *home address* and Attila Hornagy was looking for him up in Denver?''

She shrugged and said, ''I don't know how long he's been there, or the name he's registered under. I only heard he took yet another and somewhat older Trinidad woman there in broad daylight, the devil!''

Longarm nodded soberly and said, ''I know the Dexter Hotel near the depot, and I wasn't looking forward to pestering clannish immigrant coal miners after dark. A man with a hotel room who takes an underaged gal for a buggy ride must have more respect for the town law than her immigrant kith and kin. There's a heap of hills for a buggy ride out yonder too. So when do you reckon my alter ego would have had enough . . . buggy riding?''

Cora demurely suggested, ''It would depend on how good a ride he was having, wouldn't it?''

Longarm smiled thinly and said, ''Only way to know would be to find out. I got to find my own place to stay whilst I'm down this way looking for myself. The Dexter ain't a bad hotel, for Trinidad.''

Cora said, ''Don't be silly. We've plenty of room inside, and we can get you started earlier for the mining settlements in the morning!''

He said, ''Don't want to talk to wayward coal miner's daughters just yet. Want to talk to this jasper who's been fooling with all sorts of women in my name. My odds on catching up with him at his hotel in town are better. So that's where I'm headed now, if you'd be kind enough to let me have my hat back.''

She was, but as she led him inside to fetch his hat she heaved a great sigh and said, ''You're right about jumping to conclusions. You're not at all like the Longarm I've heard so much about.''

Chapter 20

Longarm had been on some moonlight buggy rides in his day. So he took his time returning his hired mount and stock saddle to the nearby livery and lugging his Yellowboy and saddlebags over to the Dexter Hotel. He hired a room and tipped generously to have his light baggage carried up the one flight. Then he came back down, wearing just his .44-40 under his frock coat, and offered the room clerk a smoke as he flashed his badge and got down to brass tacks.

The clerk said he was always proud to uphold law and order, and after some explanations he understood why a lawman might feel it best to register under a false name. But then he said they didn't have any other guests signed in as Custis Long, or as any sort of lawman.

Longarm got both their smokes going as he considered this. Then he suggested, "Someone may have added two and two to get five. A jasper who sort of looked like me wouldn't have to say he was me to have at least one feeble mind spread the word around town he was me."

The clerk took a thoughtful drag on the cheroot, shook his head, and said, "I follow your drift. But the only guest we have about your age and build, with a mustache, just won't work. You'd need a feeble mind indeed to confound Mr. Zoltan Kun with an American in any line of work!"

Longarm said flatly, "Zoltan Kun sounds sort of furrin."

The clerk said, "So does Zoltan Kun. Has an accent you

can barely savvy when he's talking slow. He's one of them mining men from the Carpathian Mountains or wherever the Emperor Franz Josef gets his damn coal.''

Longarm said he wouldn't know about that, and said, ''He's a coal miner staying in a hotel this far from the mines?''

The clerk shook his head and explained. ''Mr. Kun don't dig in any mine for coal. I suspect he used to. But now he deals in the stuff. You'd have to ask *him* exactly how he makes out so well these days. Like I said, I can barely follow his English.''

Longarm said, ''I mean to do just that, as soon as he gets in. I see you have one of them tin-titty bells here to page your bellboy. What if you were to ding it three times suddenly the next time this Zoltan Kun comes in?''

The clerk allowed he could manage that. So Longarm went around the corner to a newsstand, picked up the *Rocky Mountain News* and a couple of magazines, and returned to the hotel to camp in a corner under a reading lamp and some potted paper palms.

A long time went by. He finished the paper and as much of the *Scientific American* as he could grasp. Like many self-educated men, Longarm pushed his ever-expanding store of information to the limits by reading stuff by more learned gents.

The third and last magazine was a Street & Smith Adventure pulp, with the stories set in tropical climes Longarm had never been to. He'd found their tales of the American West a mite silly in the past. But for all a man who'd never been there knew, there really *might* be a man-eating plant in Madagascar.

According to the woodcut illustrating the story, the ferocious vegetable looked like a giant artichoke, and had a half-dressed colored gal stuck in it up to her waist. The cannibal folks who lived there in Madagascar had to feed that man-eating plant from time to time, likely to keep it from pulling itself up by the roots and coming after 'em.

The desk bell chimed three times. So Longarm never found out how that gal being eaten alive by the artichoke made out. He tossed the magazine aside and rose to his own considerable height as a tall dark drink of water in an undertaking outfit and pearl Stetson was making for the stairwell.

Longarm called out, "Mr. Kun?" and the stranger stopped to turn and face him. Longarm didn't feel at all flattered as he got a better view of the cuss who'd been mistaken for himself.

There was no resemblance at all. Zoltan Kun was handsome enough, in a hollow-cheeked oily way. His infernal mustache was not only much smaller, but *waxed,* for Pete's sake, the way the young Kaiser and his fancy Prussian officers gussied up.

Longarm said, "I'd be Deputy U.S. Marshal Custis Long, sometimes known as Longarm in the papers. I don't suppose you've ever heard of me?"

The clerk had been right about Kun's accent, but Longarm was able to follow as the Hungarian nodded gravely and replied, "Why don't we go up to my room? We seem to have much to talk about, and I have a bottle of *kognak* you might find amusing."

Longarm allowed he was game. On the way up the stairs the tall Hungarian said, "I don't know who started the rumor I was really an American lawman pretending to be a Magyar labor contractor. I never told anyone I was you. Sometimes I have to agree with the Austrians that my people are a little strange."

As he followed the polite-enough cuss along the hall Longarm said, "Hold on, old son. Are you mixed up in that Knights of Labor outfit, the same as old Attila Hornagy?"

Kun shook his head and said, "I'm afraid the KOL would have me on their black list. I *recruit* greenhorns to work in the mines, as non-union labor. I make no apologies for this. If the miners feel they have the right to organize and demand more pay, the mine owners have the right to recruit greenhorns and pay them less."

He unlocked a door and struck a match. Longarm waited until he'd lit the wall sconce inside before he entered. The room was poshly furnished for these parts. The bed hadn't been slept in recently. Zoltan Kun said easily, "You find me coming in so late because most of this evening was spent with . . . a friend. A gentleman does not say more than that, and I assure you she has no connection to the tiresome Attila Hornagy and his insane wife."

Kun waved Longarm to a seat on the bed. Longarm grabbed

a bentwood chair instead, and turned it around to sit it astride as he asked, "You admit you do know Attila and Magda Hornagy?"

Kun hung his hat on a wall peg, not shy about his baldness, and turned to a brandy decanter and some cut-crystal glasses on his chest-high cabinet as he easily replied, "I know *her* better, if only in the Biblical sense. I know it's wrong to boast of one's conquests, but who conquered whom is debatable, and you are a federal lawman and this is an official investigation, is it not?"

Longarm tipped his Stetson back and accepted the fancy glass of Austrian Kognak as he said, "I reckon. I was hoping you could tell me what I'm investigating. They say you like the gals, and it seems you don't worry yourself too much about what their menfolk might have to say about your, ah, hobby."

The almost handsome Hungarian sat on the bed with his own drink as he nodded and replied, "You would have to be Magyar, I mean Hungarian, to understand. Most of these peasant coal miners were born into a much lower class than mine. Also, as you see, I am not a small man or a poor man."

Longarm sipped some *kognak*—it was good stuff—and said, "In other words you have the Indian sign on your fellow immigrants. I noticed a similar situation over in New Orleans, when I was looking into that Black Hand shit amongst the newly arrived Sicilian folks. There was a white-suited wonder they called their Artichoke King because he got a rake-off on all the fancy vegetables peddled in the produce market by furriners. Plain old Americans, black or white, might not have taken him so serious, without a fight."

Zoltan Kun nodded easily and said, "That's why I never try to push my luck with your kind, or your women. I don't enjoy a fight when the odds might not be in my favor."

Longarm growled, "I said I followed your drift. Can we get back to Attila Hornagy and his safer wife to fool with now?"

The Hungarian looked pained and said, "Magda Hornagy was one of those exceptions that proves a rule. Attila was even crazier to pay her way from the old country with no more than a tintype to tell him what he was getting. *She* got a man old enough to be her father and, according to her, not much of a man to begin with."

He got up to pour another round of strong *kognak* as he continued in a thoughtful tone. "That may not be fair to the poor fool. I like women as much as you say, and the one I just took home had no complaints about our buggy ride. But a night in bed with Magda Hornagy leaves any man squeezed dry, like a lemon. I've never met anyone as mad for a man's juices before or since. I had to break off with her before she ruined my health."

Longarm grimaced, allowed he wasn't there to discuss anyone's health, and demanded, "Are you sure you didn't tell her you were a famous American lawman who could have her and her man deported if she didn't give you a French lesson?"

Kun laughed incredulously and said, "She knew who I was. I never said I was anyone else, and nobody would have to threaten that wild little blonde with anything to get her to suck him off! Magda volunteers to take it all three ways, and yes, I *had* her all three ways, more than once, while her husband was away on union business. But I never told anyone I was you, and I can't tell you how anyone got us confused. I'm well known in the Magyar community over by the coal mines."

Longarm refused a third drink with a silent shake of his head and said, "You ain't as well known here in town. American gossip only has you down as a skirt-chasing simp, no offense. So, assuming old Attila told someone he was going to clean *my* plow for screwing his young wife, and others had seen you with the flashy young sass . . ."

"Why would even a fool like Hornagy say I was you?" the Hungarian demanded.

Longarm said, "He must have been confused. He was out of town and never saw his wife with either one of us. His story is that *she* told him I'd screwed her against her will whilst he'd been out organizing for the eight-hour day. My first notion was that she'd confessed to cover up for you, after he'd heard she fooled around on the side. But you say you busted up with her?"

The Hungarian Romeo shrugged and said, "Not in too bitter a way. She said she understood when I confessed I simply couldn't get it up again without some celibate rest. She might have been trying to protect her husband, you know.''

''By sending him out to fight with *me*?'' Longarm asked without any false modesty.

Kun shrugged and declared, ''I have my own reputation, and I was much closer. Magda might not have expected her fatherly husband to quit his job at the Black Diamond and go all the way up to Denver after a man he'd never met. You would have to be Magyar, but it is not the same if a total stranger seduces your wife or daughter.''

Longarm smiled thinly and said, ''Hill folk where I grew up see it about the same. But Hornagy *did* traipse up to Denver, and right now he's stalking me through the Indian Territory, I hope. I don't want to fight over a gal I've never met. So I'd like to meet her and ask what got into her. I don't have to get her to name you, as long as I can get her to admit she never laid *me,* see?''

Zoltan Kun nodded gravely, but said, ''I can't lead you to her. She's not out there now. I rode out to ask my own questions when I heard crazy gossip about you and me. Her neighbors told me she'd left like a thief in the night with some other man. I say other man because some of the fools thought she'd left in a buggy like mine with *me*!''

Longarm slitted his eyes to picture a curtained buggy winding down a cinder lane on a dark night, and said, ''All right. Let's assume she ran off with yet another lemon she aimed to squeeze. Knowing she wasn't with you, Hornagy would have no call to doubt her confession naming me. I hate to have to tell you this, old son, but it looks as if she wasn't out to protect either of us.''

''The scoundrel was a total stranger to everyone but Magda!'' the Hungarian gasped in an injured tone.

Longarm said, ''I wasn't finished. The cuss she rode off with in that covered buggy *must* have been known on Bohunk Hill. She'd have had no call to say he was me if he was a total stranger, right?''

Kun stared at Longarm with more respect and said, ''You're good at what you do. I'm glad I don't have anything to hide from the law!''

Longarm couldn't resist bringing up an underaged miner's

daughter. The Hungarian shrugged and said, "I understand such a charge would have to be made by the girl's legal guardian, no?"

Longarm grimaced and declared, "That's the way they wrote the state laws. Fortunately for you, I have no jurisdiction unless you screw her on an Indian or military reservation. How does her father feel about them buggy rides, since you brought up your own sterling character?"

Kun shrugged and quietly said he'd had no complaints from any of the greenhorns around Trinidad.

Longarm said, "That Artichoke King in New Orleans had everybody scared skinny too, until some of 'em had had enough and started to whisper to the law. If I was you I'd keep it in mind that little Eva Nagy could cost you some time in the Las Animas County Jail if her dad could get up the balls to press charges."

Zoltan Kun shrugged smugly and said, "He won't. In the old country it was understood that my kind did his kind a great honor by breaking in their maidens for them."

Longarm swore under his breath, and rose to leave before he gave in to temptation. He'd never laid eyes on any of the Bohunk gals this greasy lothario had trifled with. So he knew it might not be fair to pistol-whip the oily asshole without anyone asking. He handed back the sissy cut-crystal glass, saying they had nothing more to cover, and headed for his own lonely room feeling frustrated more ways than one.

Chapter 21

The next morning Longarm hired a different pony and the same saddle to ride out to the scene of his own supposed crimes.

You got to the coal mining country west of Trinidad by following the one narrower trail along the Purgatoire River, named after the Purgatory English speakers didn't want to go to, by the same Spanish-speaking folks from New Mexico who'd spelled Trinity as Trinidad. The orginal wagon trace had been widened and cinder-paved, while a spur line of the Santa Fe ran along the north bank as far as the coal tipples forty miles up the valley. The railroads hauled way more coal than they used. Colorado's coking coal was just right for steelmaking and commanded top prices, which was just as well when anyone considered how tough it was to get it out from under the Rocky Mountains. The Colorado coal seams were skimpy and bent out of shape, next to the coal beds east of the Mississippi. So the coal-mining communities of the West were smaller and more scattered than back East in Penn State or West-by-God-Virginia. Mining for *anything* in the crumpled up bedrock of the Rockies left countless try-holes and played-out mines all along the backbone of the continent, with coal, stone quarries, and such in the foothills and metals from gold to lead at higher elevations, where the bedrock was really from deeper down. The Indians said Real Bear had made the Shining Mountains by ripping the earth's belly all out of shape with his mighty claws. *Something* had surely turned a heap of bedrock inside out up this way.

Longarm found his way to the immigrant settlement known as Bohunk Hill to real Americans of, say, High Dutch or Irish extraction. When he tried to ask some kids poking at a dead cat where the Hornagy house might be, they stuck their tongues out at him and ran away.

He had somewhat better luck with an older woman, dressed sort of like a Gypsy fortune-teller but shelling peas instead of reading tea leaves on her front steps.

She allowed she spoke English, sort of, and knew where the Hornagy house had been. Then she said, "Other peoples live there now. Attila Hornagy quit at Black Diamond to go look for wife, Magda."

The crone made an even uglier face and added, "Magda no good. Her man fool for worrying about she. People moving into house after they gone named Gero. They just get here. No speak English. Never knew Attila Hornagy or crazy Magda."

Longarm dismounted anyway, saying, "I'd best lead this pony up the narrow lanes on foot. I'll take your word there's no sense looking for folks in a house they've both moved away from. I understand Miss Magda ran off with some American cuss in a covered buggy?"

The neighborhood gossip cracked open another pea pod as she shook her head and said, "Nobody knows who she ran away with. Some said it was important Magyar she'd been flirting with. But he is still around, flirting with little girl he should leave alone. Is not right to *bus* children no matter what their fathers say!"

Longarm said, "I was just about to ask the way to the Nagy place, ma'am. If I can't talk to Zoltan Kun's older sweetheart, I might be able to get something out of his *new* gal."

The old woman looked stricken, muttered to herself in Magyar, and said, "You never heard any of those names from me. You can't talk to either of the Nagy women in English. Neither one of them speaks one word of it. Bela Nagy would be over at the Black Diamond at this time of day. He is in charge of the coal-tram crew. You will have to wait until he gets off, after sunset, if you want to talk to him in English.''

Longarm thanked her for the information, led his livery mount in a tight circle, and remounted to ride out of the hill-side cluster.

He circled it, asking more directions from more sensible kids, and it only took him a few minutes to make it to the tipples, shacks, and adit of the Black Diamond Mine.

He dismounted out front of their office shack. A burly gent in a clean blue work shirt came out as he was tethering the pony to an iron-pipe hitching rail. Longarm flashed his badge and identification as he said he was there for just a word with Bela Nagy if it was jake with them.

The shift foreman replied in an American accent, ''I'll send for him. You just come on inside and have a seat, Deputy Long.''

Longarm allowed he'd been down in coal mines before. But the shift foreman shook his gray head and said, ''We've even had our own help get lost in there. We're producing bituminous that bursts into flame if you just ask polite. But some of the damned seams are less than a yard thick and the whole formation's crumpled like tinfoil. Take one wrong turn and you can wind up lost forever.''

He cupped a hand to his mouth and called out to a kid near the tracks leading into the gaping adit. When the kid headed their way, the foreman told him to go down Drift Nine and fetch old Bela Nagy.

As the kid strode away along the tracks, Longarm followed the easygoing foreman inside. They both sat down and before Longarm could even start to offer, the mining man broke open a box of Tampa Coronas. So Longarm had to settle for lighting them both up.

As he did so he asked about Attila Hornagy in a desperately non-caring way. The foreman didn't sound any more excited as he calmly replied, ''Good blaster. Couldn't manage his young wife. We were sorry to see him go. Told him there'd always be a job for him here if he ever got tired of tilting at windmills.''

The American mining man took a drag on his cigar and added, ''Old Attila moved coal like a sculptor carving marble.

You have to know how to set your charges if you aim to shatter the coal face without bringing down the shale ceiling. Hornagy has that rare touch. I swear he could carve his initials with dynamite and dust off the furniture in your parlor without busting a window!''

Longarm quietly asked if their blasting wonder had a rep as a gunfighter.

The foreman looked blank and decided, ''Never heard tell of old Attila fighting anyone with *any* weapon. We don't put up with horseplay around this operation. Digging coal is dangerous enough without the crews acting like assholes. Most trouble I ever heard of poor old Attila having was with his wife. I never met her myself. She was here from the old country just long enough to run off with some other man. But from what some of the younger bucks say, she was wilder than Leadville on payday. You had to ask for it in Bohunk, I heard, but after that you just gave your poor soul to Jesus because your *body* belonged to *her*!''

Longarm blew a thoughtful smoke ring, and said a Hungarian he'd been drinking with had told him much the same story. He grinned wickedly and added, ''Ain't it a pain how you always seem to get there just after all the fun has ended? I mean, I got to Dodge just as the cattle shipping was starting and it looked wild enough to me, until the old-timers told me I should have been there during the buffalo-hide boom.''

The mining man chuckled and said, ''Reminds me of my first gold rush. The last of the gold and the best lay for a hundred miles had just vanished forever. Took me only four more gold rushes to decide my true calling was coal. You ain't after Bela Nagy's bitty daughter, Eva, are you?''

Longarm laughed incredulously and replied, ''Hell, no, I'm a lawman, not a baby-raper. But I see you've heard about *that* wild gal as well?''

The mining man looked relieved and said, ''You can't boss a whole herd of gossiping greenhorns without hearing gossip. I *have* met Eva Nagy, at a company picnic this spring. You're so right in calling her a baby. If she was any kin to me I'd invite that Kun to a showdown. But I know better than to butt into Bohunk beeswax, and they do say that Hunky never busted any cherry there.''

Longarm casually observed, ''I understand Zoltan Kun recruits and rides herd on disorganized labor for your outfit?''

The company man nodded with no trace of shame and said, ''All the coal companies in this valley. We don't put up with any of that Molly Maguire or Knights of Labor shit.''

Longarm blew more smoke and murmured, ''Do tell? I heard old Attila Hornagy was off at some union convention when his wife betrayed him with Lord knows whom. I have to confess I ain't half as sure as her husband seems to be right now.''

The foreman said, ''We don't mind if someone wants to listen to union bullshit on their own time, off company property. Our management takes a progressive attitude towards labor organizers. They can yell and wave their red banners all they want, outside Las Animas County. If they come any closer, well, the county sheriff and his deputies know who pays their wages.''

Longarm agreed that sounded about as progressive as most county establishments dealt with such matters, and asked a few more questions about way they ran this particular mine, seeing so many men he knew of were connected to it.

The American straw boss didn't act as if he had anything to hide. He seemed proud of the way they were winning expensive coking coal with cheap labor.

Longarm had figured they worked the mine around the clock with two twelve-hour shifts. But lots of mines followed the common practice of working their help only half of Saturday and letting them take the Sabbath off. The foreman said greenhorns just got in trouble if you didn't keep them busy. He waved his cigar at the view outside and said, ''Anyone out yonder who can't put in a full day today is free to leave. He just won't have a job here come Monday morning.''

Longarm smiled thinly, and allowed it was mighty progressive to give such undeserving Papists the *Sabbath* off at least.

The straw boss grinned and replied, ''Hell, it's not so much that we give the *greenhorns* the Sabbath off. But us real Americans have to go to church, don't we?''

Before Longarm could answer, a short gnomish man, black with coal dust, came in with his hat in hand, having blown its candle out, of course. Longarm wasn't surprised to learn this was Bela Nagy. He'd figured the kid's dad had to be far smaller than Zoltan Kun.

When Longarm was introduced to him as an American lawman, the wiry little Hungarian protested, "I no press charges! I no make troubles for nobody! My Eva is bad girl, but I spend most of my life in mine and her mother is not strong enough to make her stay in house if she wants to go out!"

Longarm said nothing. Old Bela was doing just fine without any prompting.

A tear ran down through the black grime of the older man's cheek as he stammered, "What you want me to do? In this country everyone is free to tell parents to go *bus* themselves, no? I know Hodiak woman says I should go to the law about my Eva and her buggy rides. But what good will it do us to have child put in reform school? American law will do nothing to big man who thinks our Eva is just right size for him!"

Longarm quietly said, "That may not be true, Mr. Nagy. Fooling with little kids against their parents' wishes is against the law in this state. You could even be in trouble yourselves if you could be shown to be giving your permission to such goings on. Colorado courts can be easy on gents fixing to marry up with a young gal, with the permission of her family. But a father knowingly pimping for a daughter of any age could wind up making little paving stones out of bigger ones."

The gnomish Hungarian blanched under his coal dust and protested, "Who you calling pimp? Pimp is American for lazy no-good who lives off women, no?"

Longarm nodded and said, "You'd best work it out with a lawyer if you can't control your kid. I'm a federal lawman. I have no say on Zoltan Kun's skirt-chasing unless I can prove he's done something a tad more serious. We don't worry about jurisdiction when we stumble across something downright serious, albeit I might have to turn the case over to Las Animas County and the State of Colorado unless I can show someone hauled a body across the nearby state line."

Nagy just looked confounded. The American straw boss asked if they were talking about Magda Hornagy.

Longarm nodded gravely but said, "Don't know. On the face of it I have no evidence she met with more than the good stiff dicking she likely hankered for. But I can't make all I've heard fit a sensible pattern."

He took a drag on the swell cigar and asked Nagy what he'd heard about Magda Hornagy's warm nature.

As if glad to gossip about someone he wasn't related to, the coal-blackened gnome said his wife had told him she was a dedicated slut who was sure to get caught, whether her husband worked the night shift or not. Nagy verified that some of the gossips had said they'd seen her carrying on in town with the feared but handsome Zoltan Kun.

Longarm silenced the little miner with a wave of his cigar and said, "Hold it right there and let's backtrack over a mighty odd pattern. American ladies in town say they'd seen Magda and Zoltan together, sipping soda water and such around his hotel, just before she ran off with someone they also had down as me. I don't look at all like Zoltan Kun, praise the Lord, and he told me he'd broken off with her friendly before she could have confessed to her husband about anybody."

Bela Nagy said, "I didn't see it. After twelve hours in a mine a man needs his sleep. But both Hodiak woman and Ilona Kovaks say they saw Magda leaving forever around midnight, when her man was in mine."

Longarm glanced at the American straw boss as he mused, "A gent in charge of a blasting crew would be missed if he nipped out to murder a wayward wife, wouldn't he?"

The American mining man said he'd just been about to say that.

Longarm said, "I wish he didn't have an alibi. This whole puzzle would have a simple answer. I could say *he* was lying. It just makes no sense for a cheating wife to cover up for a lover who's called her a sex maniac and turned away from her."

The mining man suggested, "She might have been thinking of poor old Attila. Old Zoltan ain't just mean to women. He's got their men scared shitless of him. Ask Bela here."

Bela Nagy whimpered, "Hey, I no afraid to stick up for my Eva. I told you she *wants* to go out with him, and he says maybe, someday, he will make honest woman of our Eva. He say she's still too young for him."

Longarm grimaced and said, "At least he's being truthful about that. He says he's not the man Magda rode off with in that buggy at midnight. Even if he had been, where in thunder might she be now? I know for a fact she ain't staying with him at the Dexter Hotel. Could anyone here tell me whether his labor recruiting takes him a heap of other places?"

The straw boss nodded and said, "He takes the train east from time to time to round up stray greenhorns on the New York waterfront. But now that you mention it, he ain't done that since Madga Hornagy ran off with somebody. Do you remember the exact date, Bela?"

Nagy thought, shook his head, and said, "More than two weeks but less than six. Who looks at calendar when women gossip?"

Longarm said, "Never mind. I can ask at the Santa Fe ticket window in town whether your well-known labor contractor paid one or mayhaps two train fares east in recent memory."

He took a thoughtful drag on his smoke and added, "I doubt he has. Kun struck me as a slick talker. His kind don't tell fibs that are easy as that to check. The picture looks a tad less confounding if we take his word, for now, and buy Magda Hornagy leaving home with some other gent entirely."

The straw boss brightened and suggested, "That's who she might have been trying to protect, instead of Zoltan Kun!"

Longarm shrugged and said, "Sounds a little more sensible. When her man confronted her about gossip he'd heard, it wouldn't have done her much good to name another gent she'd been screwing. Her grasp on English, and Colorado, was skimpy as all get-out. But she could have been slick, and mean enough, to grab the name of a better-known American off the pages of some handy newsprint."

Longarm blew a smoke ring, peered through it at a dusty gob pile outside, and continued. "On the other hand, she might have been out to get a man she hated killed. Everyone agrees she had a spiteful nature, and Hornagy did say she taunted him with the size of a younger man's dick.''

The two other men in the shack exchanged glances. The straw boss agreed, ''She *must* have hated old Attila. That's a cruel thing to say when you know it's true, and you say she just picked out a rival from a newspaper?''

Longarm nodded soberly and said, ''I mean to chide her for that, if ever I catch up with the hard-hearted gal.''

Chapter 22

Longarm didn't want to keep taking his hired mount in and out of the livery. So he tethered it outside his hotel as he went in to see if any telegrams had been delivered there to a Gus Crawford.

None had been. Things seemed to be simmering down over in the Indian Territory. But the room clerk confided, "You had you a caller whilst you was out, Deputy Long. He asked if we had us anyone named Custis Long registered here, and seeing we don't exactly, I felt it best to say no and just ask him how this pal of his could get in touch, should he ever show up."

Longarm handed the helpful clerk a cheroot as he told him he'd always admired a man who could think on his feet. He asked the clerk if he could name or describe the mysterious visitor, and muttered in mighty dirty Spanish when the clerk said it had been Attila Hornagy in that same summer seersucker.

The clerk added, "Said he was staying with friends just outside of town. Said he'd drop by later, after the night train from Amarillo pulls in. Seemed anxious to catch up with you, Deputy Long."

Longarm muttered, "That makes two of us. I've had just about enough of this shit, and by now even a fool greenhorn ought to be able to see I have witnesses on my witnesses if he keeps pushing his luck with me!"

The clerk gulped and said, "I figured he didn't have your continued good health in mind. In this business you get to where you can tell when a couple is really married too. Don't ask me how."

Longarm lit his cheroot for him and observed, "I just now said I thought you were smart. I'll be waiting out front for him when the train from Amarillo rolls in around midnight."

The clerk allowed that might be easier on their potted paper palm trees. Longarm didn't want him going to the local law, so he said, "I doubt it'll come to more than just talk. The Bohunk had me down as somebody else for a spell. I'm sure he's seen the error of his ways after trailing me all around Robin Hood's Barn and doubtless talking to other folks about me."

He glanced at the wall clock and added, "I was wondering how come I felt so empty. It's after noon and I only had ham and eggs with one coffee for breakfast."

He headed for the front entrance, aiming to go round to the cheap restaurant he'd had his breakfast in. But Cora Brewster came through the door breathless, dressed in a riding habit with her dark hair pinned up under a straw boater. The moment the young widow laid eyes on him, she gasped, "Custis! That Attila Hornagy is back in town hunting high and low for you! They just told me at the notions shop! He knows you're somewhere in town!"

Longarm smiled down at her and said, "No, he don't. He was just asking. He thinks I might be coming in at midnight aboard a train from Texas. He must have somehow learned I'd headed there from Fort Sill. I sure wish folks wouldn't gossip when you ask 'em not to."

She said, "Nobody can gossip about you out at my place. I just let my help off for the afternoon and all day tomorrow."

As they walked outside together, Longarm mused, "That's right. This is Saturday afternoon. So my boss wouldn't be in the office to read a progress report if I wired him one, the nosey old cuss."

He saw her paint pony and sidesaddle tethered next to his livery mount out front as she repeated her offer to hide him out.

He asked who was going to milk her dairy herd that afternoon and all day Sunday if she treated her hired help that nice. When she said she was only milking forty head and egging a flock of two hundred, he allowed he could help her that afternoon at any rate.

So they rode out of town together, with Cora trying to talk him out of coming back to have it out with Attila Hornagy at midnight.

He repeated what he'd told the clerk, and added, "The poor simp is likely way more anxious to catch up with his wayward wife, for reasons it wouldn't be delicate to go into. Suffice it to say, I have it on good authority that she's the bee's knees in bed and he'd sent all the way to the old country for her before he could have known that for certain."

She demurely asked if such a loss might not drive a lonely older man to distraction, quietly adding she'd heard being alone, after at least a happy honeymoon, could leave anyone feeling upset.

Longarm replied, "I just said he might have good cause to miss the wayward sass. My point is that he's been chasing me for many a day, and he must have notice by now that I just don't *have* her!"

As they rode on he brought her more completely up to date from the beginning in Denver, not wanting to confuse her with details about other women.

She still wanted to know if he'd messed with that young Indian gal, and he was glad he didn't have to fib. It was funny how easy it was to leap to conclusions when you weren't there watching. When you said newspaper reporter, schoolmarm, or army wife, it didn't sound half as suggestive as a Kiowa half-breed in her teens packing her own gun.

By this time they'd turned into her farm, and they were too busy to worry about Attila Hornagy for a spell as they stabled their mounts, went into the main house, and let her rustle him up the noon dinner he was overdue.

While he put away the steak and fried spuds, she said something about slipping into something more comfortable. But when next she appeared she was wearing a sun bonnet and one of those blue denim smocks artists and farm folks wore when they had messy chores to tend to. He'd forgotten those cows that had to be milked no later than, say, three or four.

She allowed they still had plenty of time as she sat down to have coffee and marble cake with him. He didn't have to say anything about his own tweed suit. She told him one of her hand's fresh-laundered bib overalls would likely fit him and that, seeing they were all alone that afternoon, it wouldn't hurt if he milked cows with no shirt on.

He said that made two folks he'd met that day who could think on their feet. She naturally wanted to know what he meant, and it seemed to upset her when he mentioned old Attila some more.

He assured her he didn't mean to reason with the cuss or shoot him before midnight, and asked to see those overalls.

She led him to her laundry shed out back, and got out the faded but soft clean overalls her tallest hired hand worked in. She left while he stripped naked and slipped the bib overalls on, a denim strap over each bare shoulder. He considered putting his gun rig back on. He decided it looked silly. He unhooked his double derringer from one end of his watch chain and stuck it in the right hip pocket of the overalls. Then, in no more than that and his stovepipe boots, he rejoined Cora in her kitchen.

For some reason her breath caught in her throat at the sight of his muscular bare shoulders. She gulped and said, "My, you *do* seem as manly as described, don't you? The cows haven't started to drift in for their milking yet. But we can gather some eggs if you like."

Nobody *liked* gathering eggs after the first couple of times. But it had to be done and it did beat forking manure. So he toted some of the baskets for her as they crossed the yard to enter her henhouse.

It was easy to forget the full meaning of the old army term "chickenshit," or why so many farm youths ran off to become cowboys, when you hadn't tried breathing in a henhouse for a spell. Longarm was just as glad his strange hand made her leghorns spook when she suggested he just hold the baskets and let her feel for the fool eggs. For two hundred leghorns laid one hell of a lot of eggs, and shit a lot besides.

They both washed up to their elbows with naptha soap at

her yard pump after they'd stored the eggs in the damp cellar under their candling shack. Cora said the good ones would be carted into town by her hired help, come Monday.

Unlike beef cattle, dairy cows were only vicious to human beings when they needed to be freshened by a bull. Cows with full udders and no calves to suckle soon learned to seek out human hands at least twice a day for relief. So as early as three, Cora's cows began to come home to the barn and march into their stalls as if driven by invisible prods. The closest thing to that in the beef industry was the Judas cow that lead young and innocent steers up the slaughterhouse ramp. Cows were a lot like humans when it came to easy assumptions.

Longarm hadn't slaughtered or milked a cow recently, and so it brought back memories, pleasant and not so pleasant, as he helped the young widow woman out by milking close to a score of her cows. Cora milked a few more than he did, the experienced little thing. But she still said he milked pretty good for a lawman.

He only told her some of his reasons for coming West after the war as they poured the buckets into the galvanized coolers and got it on ice for the Sabbath. She said they sold mostly raw milk in town of a Monday, with folks wanting more butter later in the week. She asked him if it still bothered him to think about those neighbor boys killed in the war, and what it felt like to kill boys on the other side.

He wrestled the last of the milk into place in the chill darkness as he shrugged his bare shoulders and said, "It don't feel as bad, or as good, as some would have it. I reckon it would bother me to have a cold-blooded murder on my conscience. But so far, I've never had to gun anyone I could have avoided gunning. The sorry souls who get a thrill out of killing are tougher to fathom. I just don't see what the thrill might be."

She locked the milk away as she quietly said, "We had my husband's body on display in an open casket for two days and this is the first time I've ever told anyone. I didn't feel anything for that stranger in that box. I mean it *looked* like my darling, and I *missed* my darling, but I knew my darling was gone and I just wanted to get rid of that . . . thing before it started to go bad. I think a lot of the others were putting on a big act there too. I don't think any normal person is thrilled or excited by death.''

They headed back to the house as Longarm quietly observed he'd been on some battlefields he'd found more depressing than thrilling. He said, ''The only thing you feel that some might find comforting is how *tall* you seem with all those others spread out flat. Mayhaps the mad-dog killers amongst us kill to feel taller. A cuss growing up with a low opinion of himself might feel he could make a higher place for himself by shooting everyone else down. They're wrong, of course, but sometimes it takes a man with a badge and his own gun to convince 'em.''

She was suddenly all over him, sobbing, ''No, Custis, don't go in to meet that crazy man at midnight! I couldn't stand to see you in a casket like a *thing,* with everyone saying you just looked as if you were asleep.''

He had to hang on to her lest they wind up falling down her back steps together. He gently moved her so her denim-clad rump was braced on the edge of the kitchen table as he said, ''I wasn't aiming to wind up dead at midnight, Miss Cora. There was this younger pest over by Fort Sill, saying he was fixing to shoot it out with me on sight. Only, somehow he never got around to it when I offered. I just told you Attila Hornagy has to know it wasn't me or even Zoltan Kun his wife ran off with, and . . .''

She wasn't listening. She was clinging to him like a limpet from the waist up while she moved everything below her waist with a skill few happily married women or determined whores could have matched. She'd intimated she hadn't had any for a spell, and as she felt him rising to the occasion through the faded denim between their fevered groins, she husked, ''Don't tease me like this, Custis. *Do* it! Do it here and now!''

So he rolled her back across the table, and since he saw when she raised both knees she wore nothing under that loose smock but her natural fuzz, he just shucked out of the shoulder straps to let his bib overalls fall around his booted ankles as he spread her thighs wide with his hands and stepped right up to join her.

She gasped, ''Oh, Kee-rist!'' as he literally walked his

aroused old organ-grinder through the moist part in her black pubic hair.

He paused halfway out to assure her he meant no harm. That was when she locked her own booted ankles in the small of his bare back to haul him in farther than he'd meant to go at first.

She gasped, "Yes! I want you to hit bottom with every stroke, and *please* don't go back to town tonight, darling!"

He just kept thrusting until he'd made her come, she said, for the first time in years. Like most folks, she likely didn't count jerking off. He could tell she'd been keeping that swell plumbing in working order *some* fool way, for just such a time as this.

Chapter 23

It was even nicer, once they'd wound up in her four-poster bed with Cora on top, literally sucking it for him with her warm, wet, love-hungry crotch. He never wanted to stop either, but by sundown they were too spent to do much more than cuddle and smoke as, from time to time, she'd grab his limp dong again and beg him not to get it killed on her.

He promised nothing either way. He knew he had to be there when Attila Hornagy came in out of the dark. But sometimes well-screwed ladies fell sound asleep after going this crazy with a man, and he'd cross that bridge when he got to it.

The crickets were starting up outside now. It sounded nice until they suddenly stopped in mid-chirp, along about nine-thirty.

Cora asked what was wrong as Longarm rolled his bare feet to her bedroom rug and reached for the six-gun he'd brought in from that laundry after their first fun in the kitchen.

He said, "There's something spooking them bugs outside. I wish you had a yard dog, honey. Dogs are more certain about intruders than old crickets."

She sighed and said, "We just lost a good old redbone hound to coyotes. He busted his chain, the poor thing, to go chasing off into the dark after a coyote bitch in heat."

Longarm eased over to the front window, gun in hand, as he nodded and said, "Lots of dogs get killed that way out here. Nobody knows for certain whether it's assassination or a crime of passion. Anything canine will flirt with anything canine of the opposite sex. But any dog that meets up with a pack of coyotes on the prairie is in a whole heap of trouble!''

He could make out moving shapes across the road, thanks to the full moon. But he waited until the moonlight bounced his way from a pair of spooky eyes before he decided, ''Your hound's old sweetheart seems to be looking for him tonight with her big brothers. I make it four, no, five coyotes all told.''

From the bed, Cora said, ''Damn. I told Leroy to make certain he planted that calf deep!''

She went on to explain how they disposed of stillborn calves on a dairy farm. There seemed to be a small bovine graveyard across the way. She sold off her *live* veal, of course, once giving birth had the cow letting down her milk again.

Longarm observed coyotes had been known to dig up dead *folks* from graves dug too shallow. As he came back to bed he said, ''That's how come they say six feet down. Albeit coyotes will seldom dig more than four. Takes a good sniffer to smell dead meat through even a yard of dirt.''

She said she didn't want to think about death, and so he put the gun aside and they got lively as hell for a short sweet spell.

He had her coming dog-style when a distant rumble tingled the air all around them and she murmured, ''Goody! It's fixing to rain again, and you won't find anyone waiting for you on the streets of Trinidad at midnight after all!''

He started to point out that the moon still shone outside from a cloudless sky. He decided it might be smarter to just screw her to sleep. So he did. He almost knocked himself out in the process, but unlike Cora, he knew he had something more important to do before the clock struck twelve.

He had her snoring softly with a contented smile on her moonlit face before eleven. She only murmured another man's name in her sleep as he rolled out of bed, gathered everything up, and got dressed in the kitchen to sneak out across the barnyard.

He might or might not have heard a woman wailing after him on the night winds as he loped into town, anxious to get set up before that Amarillo night train pulled in.

As he rode down the main street of Trinidad, things ahead were lit up as if it was way earlier on Saturday night. Longarm reined in and dismounted on the edge of the big crowd gathered in the street between the livery and his hotel. He saw firemen in leather helmets up on the roof of the Dexter, wading around through considerable smoke. He asked a townsman what was going on. The Trinidad man replied, "Big explosion across the way. Dynamite. Blowed a hotel guest through the roof and set off a fair-sized fire."

As Longarm whistled soundlessly, another townsman volunteered, "They got the crazy Bohunk anarchist who done it. Confessed of his own free will. Said he was after another Bohunk who'd been fornicating his old lady, ain't that a bitch?"

Longarm said it sure was, and elbowed his way through the crowd to break out his badge and pin it on before making his way across the tangle of fire hoses in the muddy street.

A county deputy sporting a pewter badge started to tell Longarm he had to stay back. Then he recognized Longarm's federal shield and they shook on it.

When asked, the Las Animas lawman allowed the victim had been the late Zoltan Kun, now only fit for a closed-casket service. The killer they had over in the county jail, the crazy dynamiting bastard, was one Attila Hornagy, recently a blaster at the Black Diamond Mine.

The county lawman said, "He must have really wanted that other cuss dead. Laid for him upstairs till he got in tonight, and heaved eight sticks of forty-percent Hercules in after him. The coroner's boys say it rolled under the brass bedstead, and still went off with enough force to send what was left of old Zoltan Kun through the roof!"

Longarm said, "He told me he wanted the man who diddled his woman dead. I know Attila Hornagy. You say they're holding him over at your county jail? That'd be ahint your courthouse, right?"

The county man nodded and moved off to shoo some kids. So Longarm got back to his tethered livery pony, mounted up, and circled to the nearby Courthouse Square.

He'd been warning others not to leap to easy conclusions. So he paid his first visit to the county morgue. A cheerful coroner's helper assured him they had Zoltan Kun on ice, but suggested Longarm shouldn't look at him unless he really had to.

Longarm said he had to. So they slid the remains out of their glorified icebox, and the morgue man had been right. A man got torn up considerably when you blew him through a roof.

The morgue man explained, "The blast damaged the rooms below and to either side, even though the roof was built lighter. It was lucky the dynamite went off fairly early on a Saturday night after payday. None of the other guests were in when the lath and plaster went to flying."

Longarm stared down thoughtfully at the naked, shredded cadaver. He finally decided, "That much body hair usually goes with receding hairlines and a bald spot. Hair's the right color too, and you can still see he was bigger than average. You say they're holding the man who did this to him?"

The morgue man nodded and said, "Jail's right across the square. Little Bohunk in a seersucker suit came in before they found this body on the roof. Said he'd blown the cuss up for screwing his wife. Ain't that a bitch?"

They shook on it and Longarm crossed over to the jail behind the courthouse, where another small crowd had gathered out front. Longarm bulled through with the help of his badge.

Inside, he found a portly gray gent with a gilt sheriff's badge jawing with the desk deputy. Longarm identified himself and told the sheriff what he wanted. The older lawman shrugged and said, "Come on back if you want to talk to him. I don't see it as a federal crime, no offense, and I doubt we'll be able to hold him past Monday."

As they moved back toward the patent cells Longarm said, "I just heard he was pleading the unwritten law. But don't damaging property still count?"

The sheriff said, "The hotel can sue him, for all our prosecuting attorney is going to care. It's an election year, some of the Bohunks are commencing to vote, and the late Zoltan Kun was popular as smallpox. I have it on good authority that Magda Hornagy wasn't the only greenhorn gal the bully had his own way with."

They found Attila Hornagy alone in his cell reading the

Good Book. He rose with a sheepish little smile to come over to the bars, saying, "I'm sorry about accusing your fellow deputy Longarm."

Longarm said, "I wish you'd quit shitting me, Hornagy. You never chased me all over the farway Indian Territory without finding out who I was. You tracked me all the way back here. Told a room clerk how you meant to meet my train, and then blew up Zoltan Kun instead. What makes you act so odd, Attila?"

The older man said simply, "I found out I'd been fooled by a false-hearted woman. My Madga told me the man she'd been seen with while I was out of town was a famous American lawman. You know how I felt about that. I'm glad I never killed you before I learned the truth."

Longarm said, "So am I. I know Zoltan Kun screwed your wife. He bragged he had, to me. How did *you* find out?"

Hornagy looked pained and replied, "The same way. I was not fooled by the false name you registered under. I took a room later, meaning to kill you when you got in. I met Zoltan Kun at sunset as he was going out, through the lobby. He recognized me. He asked if I was after him. He laughed when I said I was after the man who stole my Magda. He said he didn't know who she'd run away with, but agreed she'd been a grand *bus*. He said this with neither shame nor worry, as if I was not man enough to do anything about it."

The erstwhile blaster smiled smugly and added, "I did something about it. He came back earlier than I'd expected. I didn't have time to pick his lock and plant my charges as I'd planned to put them in *your* room, Longarm. But as you all see, a bundle of forty-percent Hercules will do the job if it goes off anywhere near a home-wrecking bastard!"

Longarm asked where he'd bought the dynamite. Hornagy said he'd stolen it from the mine and packed it all over creation with him.

The sheriff sighed and said, "He's admitting premeditation. That ain't the problem. Getting a jury of his peers to convict him is the problem. Zoltan Kun had a revolting rep, even amongst our own kind. One of my boys tells me he's been screwing a little twelve-year-old out to Bohunk Hill!"

Longarm grimaced and said, "Fifteen-year-old, but he was

still a shit and nobody can deny this world was well rid of him.''

The two lawmen headed back for the front as the sheriff decided, ''There you go then. There's no sense putting the county to the time and expense of a murder trial when the accused is likely to be acclaimed a public benefactor!''

Longarm nodded soberly and replied, ''That's doubtless why he don't look worried. But have you ever had the feeling someone was trying to bullshit you beyond endurance?''

The sheriff said, ''All the time. It goes with the job. What do you suggest we do about it, pard?''

So Longarm told him. The sheriff grinned like a mean little kid and said, ''Worth a try. I sure admire a lawman who can think crooked as you, Longarm!''

Chapter 24

The Sabbath dawn was breaking over a mine site quiet as a tomb when Longarm dismounted near the empty foreman's shack and tethered a blue roan livery mount. He saw he'd beaten everyone else out to the Black Diamond. So he was sitting on the steps, smoking a cheroot, as a dray pulled into the site, stopped and discharged three county deputies with a half-dozen leashed bloodhounds.

Longarm told his fellow lawmen the suspect's buggy hadn't shown up yet. The dog handler protested, "You should have let me search Hornagy's hotel room like I asked last night. Must have been at least some dirty sock for my dogs to sniff."

Longarm shook his head wearily and said, "I told you then, the suspect *worked* in yonder mine. Bloodhounds would naturally be able to pick out his scent from others after no more than a few weeks. But Hornagy had license to wander all through the diggings, and I was assured that mountain's been riddled like Swiss cheese."

The four of them heard a distant yell. Longarm got to his feet to reach inside his frock coat as a sleepy-eyed but husky-looking cuss with a Greener Ten-Gauge came across the wide dusty expanse to tell them they were on company property, damn their souls.

Longarm got out the search warrant signed by a J.P. in town the night before and said, "We're the law. This here's our hunting permit, and how come it took you so long to notice we might be trespassers?''

The watchman looked sheepish and replied, ''Who'd expect kids or lumber thieves at *this* ungodly hour? It gets mighty calm out here once the last Saturday shift knocks off around sundown. But I heard you messing about over here after a while, didn't I?''

Longarm said, ''You surely did, and if you'd care to help us conduct a murder investigation, I'd be proud to write you up in my official report.''

The watchman said he'd do anything sensible to help them, and asked who'd been murdered.

Before Longarm had to explain, a dusty black buggy drove in behind a span of mules. As the deputy driving it braked to a stop nearby he called out, ''They assured me at the livery that this is the suspect's very own buggy. He had it shipped by flatcar with him from Texas and stored it right off in their carriage house. But there's nothing hidden in it, Longarm. We searched it high and we searched it low for evidence of anything. But Hornagy had all the baggage in the back carried over to that hotel he blew up.''

Longarm nodded, turned to the dog handler, and suggested, ''She'd have wound up on the floor mats up front or in back, whether bleeding or just oozing the way they do.''

The dog handler asked him not to teach his granny to suck eggs. He picked up his bloodhounds in turn to let them slobber and sniff around in the dusty buggy. Then he put them back on the ground and said, ''If they have her scent they have her scent. Where do we try for her trail?''

Longarm pointed at the mine adit with his stubbled jaw, saying, ''All roads lead to Rome. He carried her in through that one rabbit hole if she's in there at all.''

She was. The hounds hesitated at first, confounded by the many scents of both the day and night shifts. Then, when Longarm suggested one side drift, and that didn't work, the dog handler paused near a partly boarded-over opening, posted with a warning to keep out, and the bloodhounds tried to drag him in there on his face.

They didn't, of course. But as he leaned back against the leashes with his heels dug into the black grit, he chortled,

"They're on her trail. Ain't seen 'em *this* sure since a Mex full of mescal and chili busted away from the road gang on us!"

It was more complicated than that. The played-out drift they were following ran a furlong into the mountain to end in a sooty slope of shattered shale. The bloodhounds seemed as confounded by this as the rest of them. Longarm turned to the mine watchman, who'd followed along, to ask if it was possible a longer tunnel had been partly caved in.

The coal-mining man shone his carbide lamp on the rock ceiling and said, "Never caved in. Someone brought it down. See them sort of belly buttons in the shale, there, there, and yonder? That's what you see in the new facing after a blast's been mucked away. Somebody with a star drill stuck just enough dynamite in that ceiling to bring some of it down!"

Once that much had been explained, you didn't have to be a mining engineer to see about how much shale there was to dig through. So they rustled up some loose boards, the mining tools having been put away for the Sabbath, and got to work.

The bloodhounds started going loco before the duller human noses with them noticed. Then one of the deputies working closer gagged and said, "Oh, Lord, something's *died* around here!"

Longarm sniffed and said, "Not something, somebody. Once you've been through a war, you never forget that lovely aroma. I doubt anyone died here in the mine. Neighbors saw a covered buggy leaving Hornagy's house around midnight of a Saturday. He's likely got rid of the snap-on leather covers since. Folks who knew Magda Hornagy's rep naturally never expected her to sneak out in the dead of night with her *husband*. I doubt she'd have gone with him on such a peculiar ride of her own free will. So let's say he knocked her out or killed her right in the house, snuck her out to his parked buggy, and sort of eloped with his own wife in the dark. I keep warning others not to leap to conclusions but I keep doing it myself. So you can't blame the neighborhood gossips all that much."

The same deputy gagged again and said, "We're through. I sure wish we weren't. Kee-rist, that smells awful!"

Longarm borrowed the carbide lamp as he hunkered down

to shine the beam through, saying, ''Bohunks eat all that paprika goulash, and she seems to be laying in a mud puddle, naked as a jay, save for her high-button shoes. Them shoes and that blond hair are all the coroner's jury will have going for 'em now. She's in what the undertakers call a state of full decay. Mostly bones and mush held together by skin as dark and wrinkled as prunes.''

One of the other county lawmen grimaced and observed, ''Going to be a bitch to say how she ever died then. Don't you have to prove someone was murdered to charge even her husband with murdering her?''

Longarm sighed and said, ''Yep, and old Attila is a liar above and beyond the call to duty too. I'd best go have another word with him. If I were you gents, I'd let the coroner worry about how they'll get her out of there and over to the morgue in one piece!''

He didn't have to argue with them to get them out of that fetid drift. As all but the watchman headed back to town, Longarm split off at a cinder path leading up through the warren of Bohunk Hill.

This time he insisted on sensible directions, and seeing it was the Sabbath, he found Bela Nagy and his family at home in their tar-paper shack.

The gnomish Nagy looked more like a white man on his one day off. He introduced Longarm, sort of, to his bigger and fatter wife. She didn't speak English. Longarm had to take her husband's word she was honored, wanted to feed him some grape pie, and knew he hadn't been the American who'd messed with that horrid Magda Hornagy up the way.

Nagy said their daughter, Eva, was in the back, feeling poorly because she'd just heard a friend had died.

Longarm gently but firmly declared, ''I'd like to meet your Eva, Mister Nagy.''

Nagy protested. ''She is not dressed. Even if she was, she no speak English. Why you want to see Magyar girl who can only weep right now?''

Longarm said, ''You can trot her out here or I can come back with a search warrant. It's up to you.''

So Nagy swore in his own lingo, went in the back, and

returned with a willowy young blonde wearing a flannel chemise and a black eye.

Nagy said defiantly, "Here she is. You still think we did something bad to her?"

Longarm smiled thinly and decided, "Nothing she might not have had coming. You all heard about Zoltan Kun, eh?"

Eva Nagy savvied enough English to cover her face with her hands and bawl. He mother smacked her again and chased her into the back.

Longarm smiled thinly and asked, "Did you put your foot down before or after you heard about her balding admirer getting blown through the roof?"

Bela Nagy scowled and said, "Last night I was here, home from mine, when Zoltan come to take out Eva for buggy ride. I tell him what you tell me about father who lets daughter get dirty with older men. He laugh and say he maybe needs night off himself. Zoltan Kun was not a nice man!"

Longarm said he wouldn't argue the contrary, asked Nagy to tell his wife he couldn't stay for grape pie, and left while the womenfolk were still fighting in the back.

He rode on back to town, left the mount at the livery so it could be cared for better as he traipsed around town, and headed over to the county jail to have a more serious talk with Attila Hornagy.

His man wasn't there. The desk deputy agreed it was a ridiculous mix-up, but a county politico looking for the immigrant vote had just bailed old Attila out.

They'd convinced the easygoing J.P. who'd issued that search warrant that a man who'd come forward of his own accord after killing a man in accord with the unwritten law hardly deserved to spend the Sabbath locked up like a common criminal.

Longarm swore, and tore across the square for another word with that same J.P. His Arapaho housegirl said he'd gone visiting. She couldn't or wouldn't say where.

Longarm managed to thank her instead of cuss her. He doubted anyone sneaky as Attila Hornagy would hang around town until the proper county court opened on Monday. Longarm tried to think himself into the older man's boots as he strode back toward the livery near the depot.

He decided he'd be too smart to buy a train ticket or ask for his old buggy back, whether he knew the law had impounded it or not.

A coal-mining man who knew his way around by rail might know a bum could ride for many a mile without a ticket aboard an open coal gondola. They were easier to get into than the average box car. But while Trinidad shipped a heap of coking coal to all points east, it was the Sabbath and no freight would be moving out of the Trinidad yards . . . or would it?

Railroads, shipping lines, telegraph outfits, and such paid way more attention to round-the-clock profits than the Good Book. The freight dispatcher over at the yards would know more about his own timetable. So that was where Longarm headed next.

After a short, interesting conversation Longarm was a quarter-mile up a quiet siding, spooking big butterfly-winged prairie grasshoppers as he eased along what might have passed for a string of gondolas just waiting for Monday, if that dispatcher hadn't said a switcher would be moving them over to the main line in a few minutes.

As any railroad bull could tell you, a man hidden in a car with a gun had the edge, if you went about rousting him wrong.

Longarm moved to the far end of the string, drew his .44-40, and took his time climbing the steel-runged ladder over the coupler, holding on with his left hand.

He peered over the top rim. The gondola was almost filled to the brim with coal. He rolled atop it and worked forward, crunching some in spite of himself.

The next gondola held only coal as Longarm leaped the gap between, crunching the coal much louder. As he tried to ease onward more silently, he heard a not-too-distant puffing, and glanced up to spy locomotive smoke puffing his way. It was that switch engine, coming to pick up the string.

Longarm didn't care. He kept going until, another car forward, he spotted movement and called out, "I see you, Hornagy. Stop right there if you don't want a bullet up the ass!"

The shorter and older Hungarian paused and turned his way atop the coal in the next gondola. He'd gotten rid of his seersucker and had on darker and more practical denim work duds.

Longarm didn't worry about his own tobacco brown tweed pants as he leaped into the same gondola with his man, but they were both staggered when that switch engine banged into the far end and jerked the whole string into motion with a crunch of steel knuckles.

Moving forward again, Longarm told Hornagy, "I see you noticed we found your wife where you'd left her, you poor heartbroken cuss. Would you like me to tell you how the rest of your charade was supposed to read?"

Hornagy must not have wanted him to. He stared wild-eyed, decided not to go for his own hardware after all, and spun around to try for a dash to Lord only knows where on the swaying, crunchy coal.

Longarm bawled, "Don't do that, damn it! There's no place you can run to and you're fixing to fall down betwixt the cars!"

But Hornagy just kept going as Longarm fired a warning shot over him. Then the wily killer vanished from view as Longarm ran forward, stared soberly down at the empty void between cars, and muttered, "I *told* you you'd fall betwixt the cars, you asshole!"

He holstered his six-gun and swung himself down a ladder to leap clear and land running. It felt as if he had to run a mile before he was able to stop, spin about, and run the other way.

He found most of Attila Hornagy between the rails, bleeding all over the cross-ties. Hornagy had lost a right forearm and left foot to the steel wheels. Being dragged across the ballast a good ways hadn't done him a whole lot of good either, but to Longarm's surprise the coal-blasting man was still conscious.

Longarm knelt to whip off his own shoestring tie as the older man croaked, "I should have killed you that first day up in Denver."

Longarm decided the severed ankle was bleeding the most. So he tied that off first, muttering, "You never had the balls to kill anyone wearing pants. You heard your woman was fooling around. You beat the truth out of her right off. But Zoltan Kun was too big a boo for you. He was mean and cocky with good reason. He knew you were scared skinny of him. But the unwritten law called for a man to *do* something about the man his wife had betrayed him with. So you got rid of her before she could say anything different. Then you told everyone a well-known American, not a Bohunk bully, was the man on your shit list."

Longarm heard shouting, and looked up to see a railroad yard bull running across the yards at them with a baseball bat. Longarm called out, "I'm the law and we need us a doctor here! So stop waving that fool club and go get one!"

The yard bull must have thought Longarm meant it. He turned to run the other way. Longarm got out a pocket kerchief and went to work on the stump of the sobbing Hornagy's gun arm as he continued in a conversational tone, "You knew full well that had you demanded satisfaction from Zoltan Kun, he'd have laughed in your face, if you were lucky. Had you taken a swing at him he'd have kicked the shit out of you. Had you even hinted you meant to draw on him, he'd have killed you easy. I know it ain't fair, old son, but in real life bullies who've grown to manhood without getting it slapped out of them are tough sons of bitches."

He knotted the bloody kerchief tight around the unresisting man's stump. It seemed to help, unless the poor bastard had just lost too much blood to spurt worth mentioning.

Longarm said, "You knew everyone in town was waiting to see what you aimed to do about your wayward wife. So after you shut her up forever it was you, not her, who grabbed my name and rep as a fighting man off a newspaper laying around your house and declared it was me, not the Zoltan Kun everyone suspected, who'd been strumming on her old banjo."

He shook the mangled man and demanded, "How did you kill Magda? We know you done it because we found her body where you hid it, you sneaky cuss!"

Hornagy croaked something in his own odd lingo.

Longarm swore and said, "Talk English and let's see if we can get a clearer picture. I figure you killed her at the time or not too long after she confessed to screwing Zoltan Kun whilst you were out of town. He might or might not have had to threaten her. We both know he was a dedicated bastard. But you didn't have the balls to kill both of them. You could have left your dead wife for a day or more behind your locked doors. Few if any of the neighbor women had ever seen the buggy a well-known labor organizer kept in a Trinidad carriage house. There was no place for either you or Zoltan Kun to park atop Bohunk Hill.''

Hornagy could have been confessing or cursing for all her could tell.

Longarm shook him some more and insisted, ''Come on, own up to what you done. You drove up your own house in an unfamiliar buggy that *you* kept in the carriage house, with new curtains snapped to the top. It was after midnight, on an early Sabbath morn with the mine site shut down. Nobody really saw Magda getting in to go for such a mysterious ride. Nobody had to. We all go through life with a literal blind spot in each eye. But we never notice, because our brain fills in the bitty gaps with imaginary blue sky or even wallpaper. When a buggy stops out front and the lady of the house ain't there no more, she naturally drove off in the wee small hours with some buggy driver. How were *they* to know you meant to carry her to a casually guarded coal mine and hide her in an abandoned drift?''

Longarm saw that yard bull was coming back with a whole crowd of other gents. He told Hornagy, ''Hang on and we'll get you to a hospital in time to save your worthless life. You'd have likely been better off dropping all that shale atop the body instead of in front of it. I don't envy the coroner, but there are ways to tell whether a victim was strangled or stabbed. No matter how you killed her, you wanted to distract anyone from looking for her. You made your neighbors think she'd run off with her lover because you knew she wasn't with Zoltan Kun. That gave you the excuse not to challenge *him* about your missing wife. Nobody in Trinidad knew shit about *me*. So when you said she'd run off with me, they had no call to look anywhere else for her.''

A man in the oncoming crowd shouted, ''I'm a doctor. How bad does he seem to be hurt?''

Longarm called back, ''Bad. He's lost a bucket of blood and may have a concussion as well. Fell a good ways betwixt them coal gondolas a mile or so down yonder now.''

As the chunky M.D. in black serge hunkered down on the far side of Hornagy, whistled, and popped open his oilcloth bag, Longarm told the mangled Hungarian, "Your bullshit with me was just razzle-dazzle from the beginning. Like another four-flusher I met up with at Fort Sill, you knew the safest man to challenge to a gunfight would be a paid-up lawman with no call to fight a total asshole. *We* have to *account* for ourselves when we shoot kid shotgun messengers or old coal blasters with no warrants out on 'em. You both hoped your pals would be more impressed by your bravery than a grown man might be. You couldn't have expected my boss, Marshal Vail, to play right into your hands by taking your threat seriously. Billy Vail's been married up a spell, and he'd likely get upset as hell if *his* old wife told him she'd been giving French lessons to some blackmailer. How's he doing, Doc?"

The doctor the yard bull had fetched shook his head and murmured, "You were right about that concussion. Is there any point to all this conversation with him?"

Longarm nodded and said, "There is. If you can save him he'll likely hang for murder. The unwritten law only lets you kill your wife and plead passion if you kill her lover at the same time and don't hide any bodies."

As the doctor put some smelling salts to Hornagy's nostrils, the tall deputy said, "You slickered us all pretty good by chasing me so persistently, demanding I pay for stealing your wife. But you overdid it by pestering me and pestering me, until it occurred to me you couldn't be serious about wanting to fight me."

Hornagy blew some bubbles and groaned, "I told you why I didn't want to kill you after all. I wish I had now."

Longarm grimaced and said, "Yeah, let's talk about that sloppy blasting at the Dexter Hotel. Your foreman assured me you could dust a room with dynamite and never bust a window. Yet Zoltan Kun wound up on the roof and there was structural damage down to the basement. How come you used so much dynamite unscientifically, old son?"

Hornagy didn't answer. The doctor said, "He's gone."

Longarm asked, "What's he trying to say if he's dead then?"

The doctor said, "Nothing. That's called the death rattle because you have to be dead to make that funny sound. It's a change in the acid balance in the throat tissues. It'll stop in a moment.''

Longarm stared down at the dead man's glassy eyes and muttered, ''You sneaky old son of a bitch. You knew I'd never be able to prove my case against you unless I could get you to confess. So you up and croaked on me without confessing!''

Then he smiled ruefully and added, ''What the hell, mayhaps it's just as well this way. It's not as important *how* you murdered your wife, now that you've saved the taxpayers the expense of trying, convicting, and hanging you for it!''

Chapter 25

Some time later, Longarm was washing down some of the fine free lunch served by Denver's Parthenon Saloon when his boss, Billy Vail, grumped in with a manila file folder in hand. Longarm had hoped that might not happen. The file looked thicker today than it had when he'd had young Henry type up his official report.

Vail joined Longarm at the free lunch counter, grabbed a ham-on-rye sandwich with his other hand, and said, "We got to talk. Let's go back to one of the side rooms."

They did. Like most first-class saloons, the Parthenon provided a maze of semi-private chambers, great and small, for the discreet get-togethers of patrons too delicate-natured for the main taproom up front.

Along the way, Longarm caught the eye of a barmaid carrying a tray of beer schooners, and pointed his own half-consumed beer at the doorway they were headed for.

Billy Vail led the way in and plunked his stubby form down on one side of the table, taking up a good part of the space in there. Longarm left the sliding frosted-glass door slightly ajar as he took his own seat across from his boss, placing his beer schooner on the table between them.

Vail said, "You'd best shut that door all the way. This is private."

Longarm said, "Trixie will be coming to take our orders. You'll be glad I was so thoughtful when it sinks in how salty that ham you chose really tastes. What's so infernally delicate about the report I just filed for you, Boss?''

He was bluffing, of course. Billy Vail tracked as good across a report as a Digger Indian across fress snowfall. But Longarm hadn't been dumb enough to write down any lies.

Vail said, ''Most of it's just swell. Considering I was only out to keep you from getting shot as a skirt-chaser, you done us proud in the Indian Territory. The War Department is pleased with you, the Bureau of Indian Affairs is pleased with you, and even the *Indians* are glad you showed up when you did.''

Trixie came in with a flounce of her Dolly Varden skirts to ask what they were drinking back there. Longarm suggested a pitcher of draft and an extra glass. When Vail didn't argue, he asked Trixie if she could throw in some of those devilish eggs and mayhaps some good old pickled pig's feet.

Trixie said she knew how to serve a growing boy, and flounced out. Vail cocked a thoughtful eyebrow and said, ''I'd *ask*, if I thought I'd get a straight answer.''

Longarm shook his head and said, ''Don't talk dumb. I like this place too much to trifle with the hired help. I told you in the very report you're holding how Fred Ryan was augmenting his four-figure salary as a junior Indian agent. Catching him was no big deal.''

Vail said, ''Chief Quanah seems to think it was. Thanks to the prestige the Comanche Police gained at the expense of those crooked Cherokee, your Sergeant Tikano is turning away Kiowa and even Kiowa-Apache volunteers!''

Longarm said that was why he'd let the Indians tidy up the loose ends themselves.

Vail said, ''Let's *talk* about loose ends. Are you sure you really put down everything about them crazy doings around Trinidad at the last, old son?''

Longarm met Vail's thoughtful gaze—it wasn't easy—and managed to reply, ''Like I wrote, me and Las Animas County agreed Attila Hornagy broke no federal laws when he lost his temper with his wife. Coroner in Trinidad says he strangled her. Despite ther condition of her body, there's this small ring of bone wrapped halfway round you windpipe, and when it's busted—''

"You're shitting me," Vail cut in. "I know Hornagy killed his wife when she confessed her affair with Zoltan Kun. I see why the desperate cuss put us through that charade to avoid a showdown with a meaner Bohunk who had the Indian sign on him. But after Hornagy chased you to the Indian Territory and back, I'm supposed to believe he all of a sudden found the nerve to kill his big boo after all, clumsy as hell for any professional dynamite man?"

Longarm smiled sheepishly and said, "I wish you weren't so smart. Are we talking off the record, Billy? I've good reason for asking, and I told you that case wasn't federal."

Vail frowned thoughtfully and decided, "Tell me the whole story and I'll decide whether it was federal or not, damn it!"

Longarm sighed and said, "You got to understand Zoltan Kun was a human wolverine who got what he had coming, Billy."

Vail nodded and said, "You put down how the shitty labor recruiter plucked immigrant gals like flowers from his private garden, whether they were spoken for by lesser men or not. You explained how Hornagy was terrified of him but had to do or say something to *somebody* when his neighbors saw him as a pathetic excuse for a Hungarian husband. Now explain that unprofessional dynamiting at the Dexter!"

Longarm took a deep breath and said, "Hornagy never done it. He never went near Zolton Kun. He'd come back from Trinidad, figuring he'd chased his missing wife and her lover far enough for his honor. He'd learned I was in town and, knowing I'd be leaving on my own in any case, made more war talk so he could say he ran me out of Trinidad."

Longarm took a sip of suds and continued. "Meanwhile, Zoltan Kun had started up with a younger greenborn gal with an even shorter father. His name was Bela Nagy. There was no need for him to appear on paper. So he don't."

Vail softly asked, "You mean *he* was the one who lobbed that sloppy dynamite through Zoltan Kun's door?"

Longarm nodded and said, "He thought he had to. He was smaller than Attila Hornagy. But he put his foot down, locked his wild child in her room, and told Kun she wasn't going on any more buggy rides with him. Kun laughed it off and jeered he'd try again some other time. So Nagy followed Kun home with more than enough dynamite from his mine, and the rest is unofficial history. After Nagy ran off, old Hornagy saw the chance to be the hero he'd never had nerve to be. He came forward to take the blame, and the credit. He'd have almost no doubt been asked to take a bow and run for public office if we hadn't found his wife's body. I never would have searched for it if the lying bastard had left me alone!''

Vail chuckled and said, ''I like your official version better. But there's one question more. All you just said happened over two weeks ago. So where in blue blazes were you after that, old son?''

Longarm explained he'd had to help the county coroner tidy up, and then he'd spent some time consoling a poor local widow.

When Vail protested he saw no widow connected with the case, Longarm shrugged and asked, ''Where in the U.S. Constitution does it say a widow has to be connected with a case to require some consolation?''